THE SOUTH WILL
RISE AGAIN

MEMOIRS
OF
A SON OF THE SOUTH

AS TOLD BY
C.W. ARNOLD

ISBN: 0615763197
ISBN 13: 9780615763194

Thank you to those who gave kind words of support and encouragement especially my Mother and Father, Laura, Lori, Shea, Drew, Shannon, Monica, Mark and my children Austin, Savannah and Connor. I would also like to thank those who still believe in knights, far off lands, and fighting dragons because it was in your words that I found my story.

A little rebellion now and then is a good thing and as necessary in the political world as storms in the physical.

THOMAS JEFFERSON, letter to James Madison, Jan. 30, 1787

"[Our situation] illustrates the American idea that governments rest on the consent of the governed, and that it is the right of the people to alter or abolish them whenever they become destructive of the ends for which they were established."

JEFFERSON DAVIS

PREFACE

I can't tell you why I thought I had some chosen path or grand destiny in this life, but I most certainly did. Despite my efforts to understand this journey, I was on track to certain failure and the notion that I was relegated to a life with no special purpose or deep meaning was quickly taking hold.

Fortunately, life took a turn and one day while helping remodel a large older house in the city where I lived everything fell into place. It was a home that time, neglect and its many occupants had taken their toll causing the structures useful life to be in question. But like many things I looked through the flaws and saw the home as it could be, inspiring me to take particular care in my work.

While painting in the living room a loose board in the closet caught my eye. For some reason I was drawn to it causing me to climb down from the ladder where I had been working. I knelt down and tugged at the board removing it from where it rested. The house it seemed had revealed a secret for me. To my surprise I retrieved four leather bound journals from inside a compartment hidden between the floor joists. It may also have held my purpose too because after reading them I felt a kinsmanship with those who wrote them and an overwhelming desire to put their story together. Mind you what you are about to read is not my tale but theirs.

ONE

CAMPELL – *As I remember it I was sitting behind my desk staring at the thank you card that hung thumb tacked to the temporary wall of my cubical. The card marked my tenth year on the job. Unfortunately, it also noted the fact that I might never realize my dream of becoming a journalist. I had started from the bottom just to get a chance to work near the clanking sounds of giant presses and the smell of drying ink. Back then I thought that this job would lead to much larger endeavors and the realization of that dream.*

Somewhere along the way my passion had changed. I couldn't put my finger on what exactly caused it but it definitely had. Looking around another realization hit home. When this world was new to me the large room where I sat was crowded with people and a hub of activity. Now it somehow seemed lonely, sad and also suffering from a case of lost passion. Over the years many had gone but most hadn't been replaced. This fact made me now one of the last holdouts, part of a dwindling old guard. Those that had been replaced were of new blood made up of the self righteous half wits or flat out liars with not a lick of imagination between either of the two groups. Something was definitely different about them too. Lost in the moment I stared at the card once more thinking, "Ten years, can it really be 1991."

Thankfully, the ring of the phone broke the trance that was quickly moving me toward a state of depression. On the other end was an elderly, southern sounding woman who said her husband found my stories of alien abductions and Elvis sightings interesting reads. She went on to say that he would like to meet me and had a story that I would want to hear. I tried to gather as much information from her as possible to see if the trip would be worthwhile. However, she was resolute and told me that this was his story therefore he needed to be the one to tell it. I looked at the clock debating whether to make the appointment or not. Having no story for the upcoming edition, with the deadline fast approaching, the deliberation was quick. So, I decided to take the chance.

The cab ride over was its usual joyful experience of traffic, foul smells and foul language from a driver who hadn't quite come to grips with the English language. It did give me time to think, and was a pleasant break from an office of people who didn't really seem to grasp the English language either.

Not being from New York still made a difference. I hadn't fully adapted to the lifestyle, the crowds of people or the traffic. It unsettled me and at times it felt as if the entire city was closing in around me. I was in a sea of people and concrete with no visible horizon in view. I missed the open spaces and big sky of my home, Arizona.

I have long known that I am an observer of things. This trait alone led me to my career either by choice or chance but it led me never the less. As we passed by the people on the streets, I would catch a glimpse of certain individuals and wonder about the lives they lived, the people they loved, and what stories lay hidden in each and every one. I began to ponder my own uneventful life and suddenly I became uneasy. A strange sensation coursed through me, and I quickly became overwhelmed. I closed my eyes for a bit and tried my best to close off the rest of the world as the cab shuffled through traffic. Refocusing my thoughts to the open places of my youth and the relative safety of the backseat where I rested.

A few moments later I was in that happy place just before actual sleep takes hold when the vehicle came to a sudden stop. The jolt was a shock to my system. I gathered myself and looked up through squinted eyes. At first all I could make out was the building they called home. I was familiar with this area and knew the inhabitants tended to be older and many had lived there for years. It was a place that smelled of old money and had a personality that clung to a not so distant past.

I walked up the granite stairs and looked for the name of Conner near the doorbell. After a few tries I heard the same southern voice through the intercom that I had heard on the phone. The door buzzed and I entered the building. A few stairs later I saw Mrs. Conner standing in her doorway.

Mrs. Conner was a small framed woman in her seventies with gray hair and piercing blue eyes. For her age she moved about adeptly with a certain grace that reflected her upbringing. She asked me into their home and offered a drink of sweet tea. She briefly told me of her husband's situation. She commented on his age and current physical condition. Then she asked me to be patient, so he would keep his facts straight. As we sat there I noticed she was a lady of manners and conduct. Every movement she made was with purpose and in a calculated order as if all tasks in life were to be completed in a particular fashion. This left me with little doubt that she was a master of the noble and the appropriate.

Perhaps it was her magnetic presence but I just couldn't help myself. My eyes followed her every movement. In awe of her I stood frozen listening to her as she spoke. Just in those first few moments I began to wonder what this lady had been like in her younger years. What those blue eyes had seen and what secrets lay hidden behind them. I thought to myself that she must have been quite something in her day.

We sat and chatted for a few minutes and, as she would say, got acquainted with one another. It was most certainly a character check on her part. I must have made the grade because a short time later she escorted me down a long hall into her husband's bedroom.

When we entered his dimly lit room I stood by the door as she woke him. She opened the blinds to let in the last of the days light and said, "Mr. Conner wanted to be well rested for the meeting." She kissed her husband gently on the forehead and moved his bed to an upright position. Then she fluffed his pillow and smiled. "Is he all that we expected?" Mr. Conner asked.

"I think he'll do." She replied. She winked at me and closed the door behind her.

"Mr. Campbell, please have a seat," Mr. Conner stated happily.

"Sir, would you mind if I stood while we talked? I get caught behind the desk all day."

"Suit yourself," he replied and went on. "Mr. Campbell, do you have any idea why you're here?"

"Your wife said you had a story for me and she was quite protective of it."

Mr. Conner grinned and replied, "My bride is a fine woman, and she always could keep a secret." Then he continued. "Yes, I do have a story son and it is all true. I've been quite entertained by your tales over the years. But the reason you're here instead of someone else is just as important as the story itself. The truth is son I picked you because you have a story to tell, it just hasn't been written yet. I can see it in your words that you want more out of this life than what you have. That you are not living up to your expectations of yourself and truthfully you seem a little lost. In the mean time you'll just have to put your life on hold and be satisfied with hearing mine. We have many things in common, Mr. Campbell; you just don't know it yet."

Probably out of frustration for my bad day I smugly replied, "Was it the stories of aliens posing as city officials or fish men swimming the local rivers that told you all that about me?"

Mr. Conner, although weakened by age and wear, wasn't a man to be trifled with. He let me know it that day too by sternly advising me that it would be in my best interest to sit down, shut up and listen. "This story is very important and not just to me. It's no tale; it's not a myth but pure simple fact. I'm not some old fool neither waiting to die nor losing his marbles, but the truth of the matter is I may not have much time."

Realizing my poor behavior, I did as the man said and took my seat. I quickly found out that there was a quality about him too. Something deep inside that worn body, perhaps a hardened soul that likely willed his body to keep going. From that point on I respectfully gave him my full attention as I sat in the room for over an hour that first night. He told the story with such clarity and detail my pen easily went to work. Mrs. Conner eventually entered the room and told Mr. Conner to call it a night. She looked at me and said, "If you want the whole story, you'll have to let him rest and hear it in pieces." I didn't want to leave, but I could tell he was tiring. I gently tapped him on the foot, and asked him if it would be all right if we met the following day; to which he obliged.

On the way out I took a moment and looked around the room noting the smallest of details within it. The dark wood trim, the fireplace that hadn't been used in ages and the pictures that hung on the wall were just a few. Earlier, I had been so focused on him that I had hardly noticed any of it. The room itself seemed to reflect the man that I had just spoken with. Silently, it told his story revealing who he had once been. The room itself drew me in even further.

Mrs. Conner escorted me down the hall to the front door. Before leaving she patted me on the shoulder, and told me that I had done well today. During the cab ride home my mind was buzzing and still focused on the story as he retold it through my notes. That night I wrote the following entry in his words.

I was born in 1909 and lived in the low lands of South Carolina with my family. It was a place of hard work and little profit as men did their best to scrape a living out in the sandy soil. The land was nestled between the swamps that fed off the Pee Dee River and the more fertile soil further to the west. It was a place where the wind carried the scent of the sea and the night air carried the ghosts of Francis Marion and his men. It was the four of us then both my parents and my younger brother Will. My father worked a piece of ground for extra income, but his job was at the mill. He was young, lean, dark and his hair black as midnight. My mother was a beautiful woman her small frame seemed to disappear in my father's large arms. She had long auburn hair which always had a ribbon or bow in it.

What I remember most was our family seemed full of love and happiness. We had laughter in our home and parents who were deeply in love with one another. A tragedy within our family changed all of that with the death of my younger brother, Will. He fell sick at the age of four and was gone in a matter of weeks. My mother fell into a state of depression. She never knew it, but I could hear her cry at night through the thin walls of our home. My father worked late into the night likely to mourn in his own way. I often pretended to be asleep when she came into our room to sit at the edge of my bed. For long periods of time she would just sit there and stare at Will's empty bed. Before leaving the room she would pat the blankets as if he were still nestled underneath them. By the time she closed our door I was usually in tears trying to quietly choke them back, so she wouldn't know. Even though I was only nine when he passed I knew that's what men did back then and I more than anything wanted to be a man.

Two years passed and I began to think the sun had risen on our little home once again, but that notion wouldn't last. Walking home from school one day down the dirt road I reached the top of the hill that overlooked our home. There I noticed the Sheriff's car parked in front. My pace slowed as I observed what was happening.

From my vantage point on the high hill, I could see the scene on the front porch. My mother, Mr. Fenton, Mrs. Fenton and the Sheriff all gathered together in a circle. I saw my mother put her hands to her face and run to the Sheriff. Then heard her yelling, "No, No." I stopped frozen in my tracks by the last fence post in the row.

I continued to watch as my mother fell into the Sheriff's arms. Mrs. Fenton grabbed her, and led her inside the house. The Sheriff and Mr. Fenton spoke for a moment, and then the Sheriff walked to his car. It was then that Mr. Fenton looked up and saw me standing there. He stopped in his tracks when our eyes met. I steadied myself with my hand on the post. Then he looked to the house and brushed his hat with his hand. He walked toward me with his head down. I almost felt as if I should run, but I tried to lift my feet and they wouldn't budge. Fear it seemed had taken over, and wouldn't allow their movement. Even my small hand was out of my control as it held firmly, and wouldn't release its grip from the post. Finally he lifted his head and I could clearly see the heaviness of his face.

He leaned down to eye level with me and said, "Son it may be best if you come with me." I looked into his eyes for any hint of what had happened. His aged weathered face held all the secrets to what had taken place but revealed nothing. I asked to see my ma and he placed his giant tanned hand on my shoulder and said, "In a while boy, in a while." He led me to his truck and opened the door. I stared out to the now empty front porch looking for signs of my mother or Mrs. Fenton, as his old truck sputtered and pulled onto the road. We traveled a short distance while Mr. Fenton stared blankly trying to find the words to say to me. His one hand wiped his mouth as his other fought the rutted road. He slowed the truck to a stop and looked squarely at me. I looked down at first, but then my eyes moved to his as I was taught.

"Son, I liked your Daddy and I think he would be fine with me telling you about this because of the situation. It pains me to tell you what I'm about to," he paused for a moment. I prepared myself as I knew this news would not be good. I looked into Mr. Fenton's kind face as he spoke.

"There was an accident at the mill. Some machinery went wrong and your father was killed. That's why your ma can't see you just yet. Let her calm down a bit and I'll bring you home later. For now let's just head up to my house for a while."

I said nothing just looked down at the truck's seat.

I had known Mr. Fenton for as long as I could remember. My father worked part of his land and we rented the home that had once been his mothers. His family had owned the land for generations, but they were far from wealthy. They were just getting by like everyone else. I think he and my father had become fast friends in part because they had a son about his age. He had moved away a year before my parents came there. I think he was glad my father had shown an interest in working the ground because Mr. Fenton was getting older and slowing some. This fact of course would never have been shared with Mr. Fenton. My mother too was close to the Fenton's. She would visit with Mrs. Fenton often bringing me along.

I sat quietly grappling with the situation until we arrived at their home. We walked inside, and I sat on a chair in the kitchen. Mr. Fenton poured us a glass of tea, and we sat in silence for a few minutes. I hadn't spoken since he told me the news. He asked if I was all right. I shrugged my shoulders and told him I was fine. Mr. Fenton went on and told me that now more than ever my ma needed me to be strong. He said that I needed to be a man about what had just happened. He stood up and asked me for some help out in the barn. I followed Mr. Fenton and helped as best I could. He likely just wanted to occupy me for a bit until things settled down. Later that day he asked me to stay on at their place for a while. Then he went on alone down to my house to check on things.

Later I overheard that when he arrived he came onto a scene. The Sheriff had returned with some of the men from my father's work, carrying his mangled body in the back of a truck. My mother insisted on seeing my father. Mr. Fenton was driving up just as she pulled back the blanket that covered him. She shrieked at the sight and fell away fainting. She had to be carried back into the house. Mr. Fenton told the men to move the truck around back and place his body in the barn. He met the men in the barn and they started to build my father's coffin.

Mrs. Fenton had one of the men drive her to check on me bringing a plate of food in the process. She had been at my house all day caring for my mother, and cooking for all the men there. She told me that we needed to bury my father tomorrow, because the following day was a Sunday. She went on to say that it was likely for the best, but everyone would have to work into the night for that to happen. She bent down looking squarely into my eyes and pressed her hand against my face asking, "How are you, Jimmy?"

"Fine ma'am," I said.

"No, you're not but you're at least acting like a man about this, all cold and distant. I know different, but it's helping me help your ma. Mr. Fenton will be back soon to stay with you. Let me take you to young Tom's room."

Tom was in his thirties by that time, but the both of them still referred to him as either young Tom or Thomas. His room still had many of the items from his childhood. The room itself seemed as if it awaited his return. She produced a set of night clothes from the dresser and asked me to put them on. She sat at the end of the bed and stroked my hair. I likely reminded her of Thomas in some way. She probably enjoyed that moment as much as I did because it likely took her back in years. I closed my eyes and feigned slumber. When I heard her leave the house, I snuck out of bed and watched them pull away.

Mrs. Fenton checked on my father's condition as any good women would have at that time. Once they had prepared him proper; they laid his body inside its wooden resting place. Two of the men stayed out in the barn with him, just so my father wouldn't be left alone on his last night on this earth.

Mr. Fenton returned home late that night, and found me asleep on a chair in the living room. He carried me into Thomas' bed. I imagine every ounce of his remaining strength had already been sapped, but somehow he managed that little kindness never the less.

TWO

I woke the next morning thinking about the funeral. The notion took me back to my brother Will and his funeral. I tried my best to remember the details to steal myself and be prepared. I knew my mother would be brokenhearted again, and that tears would be flowing from her eyes.

The Fenton's drove me down to my house and my eagerness to see my mother was being replaced by fears of the day that lie ahead. I remember sitting low in the seat next to the Fenton's dressed in their Sunday best.

Mrs. Fenton had the local Preacher and his wife stay with my mother so she could get herself ready. Once the truck stopped I halfheartedly reached for the door. I sat frozen in place with my head down afraid to look up. Mrs. Fenton seeing my situation opened the door, took me by the hand, and led me to my home. Inside the preacher and his wife sat in our small living room. I watched Mrs. Fenton pause at my parent's bedroom door. She knocked before entering and to my relief left me standing in the living room waiting.

Moments later Mrs. Fenton stood in the doorway motioning for me to come in. Slowly, I walked toward my parent's bedroom. On the way, I glanced over my shoulder, and saw that all eyes were on me. Once inside the room I saw that my mother was not fully dressed, and was still lying on her bed. Mrs. Fenton said, "Your boy is here."

"Will? Will's here?" she asked.

"No, it's young Jimmy." replied Mrs. Fenton.

"Jimmy? Come here son,"

As I walked past, Mrs. Fenton whispered in my ear, "Now pay her no mind, the doctor has her full of medicine to calm her nerves."

I ran to her, and hugged her. Tears began to stream down my face as she held on to me tightly, but that lasted only a moment.

Mrs. Fenton said to my mother, "Now we need to get you ready. You have to do this." Then Mrs. Fenton said, "Jimmy you go get your best clothes and get yourself ready." I still in my mother's arms realized she wasn't herself. I could see something was terribly wrong with her, and was afraid to let go. Then Mrs. Fenton put both hands on me. She said, "It will be all right Jimmy. Let go of your ma and let her get ready." I stood up wiping my tears. It was then that I noticed the large bottle of medicine on her dresser with Laudanum on the label. Reluctantly I placed my hand on the door knob. I looked back to see her being helped to her feet and I remember thinking that I had to be strong for her. Outside Mr. Fenton stood waiting to escort me to my room.

Back then young boys didn't have many clothes. Mr. Fenton asked if I needed help. He adjusted my jacket, and made sure I combed my hair. "You're a good looking young man Jimmy," he said. "Your father would be proud of you right now." He put his arm around me and we walked out the door. There more people and a mixture of buggies, wagons and vehicles filled the drive. Mr. Fenton and I headed to the barn; where my father's casket lie atop two large saw horses, and we watched the men load the casket into a wagon that would lead the procession. It was then that he leaned down and said, "I have something of your father's, and I'm sure he would want you to have it." He handed me my father's white handled pocket knife.

He said, "A boy should have a knife and somehow the best blade you'll ever have is the one that was your fathers. You're plenty old enough to take care of it." I opened it and saw an inscription on the blade. I looked up at him and he said," Yes, I saw that too. I think it's Latin and if you ever find out what it means would you tell me?"

I shook my head yes. Then he reached in and produced another item from his pocket and asked, "Jimmy I've never seen anything like this before? Can you tell me about it?" He then handed me a bronze coin. I took it and then looked at the other side. One side had a lady standing tall with seven stars over her head and below her were words I couldn't understand. On the back was a scorpion. I had never seen it before, and shook my head in response.

"It was near your father's body when they found him. Would you mind if I hung on to it for a bit?" he asked. The coin meant little to me at the time compared to my father's knife. I told him no and continued to eye the knife. The procession was about to start, and it was time to pay respects to my pa.

They took my father's body up to Campbell's crossroads where the cemetery stood. The Preacher's wife and Mrs. Fenton helped my mother up the small hill where my father was to be put to rest next to my brother Will. This made me feel a little better because now Will wouldn't have to be alone. The group all gathered around and I stood holding my mother's hand with the Fenton's close by. As the preacher spoke I looked at the people in the crowd. Most eyes were on the preacher, but one man stared at my mother and when our eyes met he smiled at me, and then looked away. I could feel my mother sway with her hand in mine. She seemed to have little grip, but it was the blank stare into the distance that troubled me most. She seemed a thousand miles away; likely holding on tight to some moment that her and my father shared in a past memory.

"Ashes to ashes and dust to dust," the Preacher's words rang in my head. Everyone stood silent, and looked to my mother. There she stood still frozen somewhere far away from the little cemetery on the hill. Mr.

Fenton took the lead by reaching down and grabbing a hand full of the freshly dug soil. He slowly shook it in his hand, and dropped the dirt into the hole where my father lay. Holding his hat he whispered something only those two could hear, and stepped back away from the grave. Each mourner in the group stopped and made their peace while my mother and I stood there. After all had passed, I reached down and grabbed two handfuls of dirt, one for my mother and one for myself, dropping them on my father's coffin. I was the only man in her life now, and I needed to be strong for her. We all walked mother down to the preachers automobile, and I opened the door for her. She sat inside and Mr. Fenton asked me to ride back with him. Along the way he said, "Your mother is in some state of shock. This is really hard on her. The Doctor stopped in yesterday to bring some medicine to help calm her nerves."

"The laudanum?"

"Yes, that's right." He stated. I reached in my pocket to feel for the knife. Doing so gave me some solace in that moment.

After the funeral we went back home. People visited outside briefly and then went on their way. The preacher went to town, leaving his wife to tend to my mother. I went up the hill with Mr. and Mrs. Fenton to their house.

I think Mrs. Fenton was just glad to be home. She sat on a chair in the living room and stared out the front window. The last few days of worry and constant care of my mother had taken a toll on her. But a moment was all she took. She let out a sigh, stood up and went back to work. When she left the room she patted me on the head, "Why don't you change clothes, and lend Mr. Fenton a hand in the barn. I bet you boys have been slacking while I was gone," she said with a smile.

After changing I met Mr. Fenton in the kitchen. Mrs. Fenton was already back at work with a full head of steam when I walked in, she seemed tireless to me. I stood there and looked at her small frame and aged body moving around the kitchen with great purpose. Mr. Fenton walked over and put his hand on Mrs. Fenton's back as she washed the dishes. "Why don't you take a moment and get some rest?"

"I'm fine and things need to be done." She replied. He lovingly kissed her on the cheek and said, "I'm glad you're home. Every time you're away I realize that I have quite a lady in my life." They reminded me of an older version of my parents. He turned and went for the door. Along the way he smiled at me and said, "Jimmy, if you can find one like my bride, you should consider yourself a lucky man."

She smiled and said, "You boys better get to work." We walked out the door and headed for the barn. I enjoyed working with Mr. Fenton. He had a kind patient manner, and I believe that he didn't much mind the company either.

Once dinner was finished Mr. Fenton and I went out on the front porch with Mrs. Fenton following a few paces behind. Mr. Fenton sat in his chair and packed his pipe with some of his home grown tobacco. He took a special pride in the fact that it was grown on his land as he puffed away. Mr. and Mrs. Fenton spoke about the past few days, and planned for the next day as we all sat there peacefully. The sunset and darkness filled the sky while the red glow of the pipe and its sweet aroma added to the moment. To this day I can't smell a pipe without being reminding of Mr. Fenton and it always takes me back to their little place on the flat lands.

Later that night when I was in bed, I could hear the Fenton's talking. I heard Mrs. Fenton say that the preacher had called the doctor from town to have another look at my mother. The doctor felt she needed rest, and he left another bottle of the laudanum. I was old enough to understand that the medicine made her not herself, but hoped it would help her to get better. I laid there certain that she would be better in the morning.

The next morning I walked into the kitchen. Mrs. Fenton already had breakfast on the table. Mr. Fenton came in and could tell I was eager to see my mother. "Hold on boy" he said and smiled. "Let's eat and then we can go down to your place."

I smiled and ate my food as if I hadn't eaten in weeks. Mrs. Fenton looked at me and said "Are you ready to be back home and rid of me?"

"No, ma'am just ready to see my mother." I stated.

"Hold your horses, and let Mr. Fenton eat. He will take you down when he's finished." After she thought about it a moment she said, "You know this may take a few days. So don't get your hopes up about sleeping in your bed tonight. Besides I want to keep you for myself." She passed her hand through my hair making it stand on end in the process.

"Yes, ma'am," I said smiling.

Mr. Fenton stood up and said, "Let's go Jimmy." Mrs. Fenton looked at him replying, "You've barely eaten."

"The boy wants to see his ma." He said with half smile.

"All right then, I'll cover the plate, and you can take it with you."

"I'm telling you Jimmy I have quite a bride, quite a bride indeed." he replied.

Just then a knock pounded on the door, and Mr. Fenton walked over to answer. I followed and stood in the kitchen doorway. I saw the preacher's wife and heard her say, "Come quickly, something's wrong" Mr. and Mrs. Fenton hurried for the door. I ran in Mr. Fenton's footsteps, but he turned and said, "No, Jimmy you need to stay here."

"But......" I said.

"No, Jimmy let us find out what's going on. Stay here, we'll be back to get you."

I knew something disastrous had taken place. The preacher's wife was covered in sweat, and was breathing heavily when I saw her. She had run the entire way up to the Fenton's. I stood helpless on the porch as I watched the three of them drive away toward my house.

About an hour later, the sheriff's vehicle passed with the preacher following not far behind. I couldn't wait any longer and ran down the road on foot. I once again found myself standing next to the fence post observing the scene on my porch. Outside the sheriff, the preacher and Mr. Fenton all stood in a circle. The doctor walked outside and shook his head from side to side. Mr. Fenton turned kicked the ground, and then placed his hands in his pockets. He again looked up and saw me standing there. But this time I was freed from the chains that days before bound me, and I bolted toward the house. He grabbed me as I tried to run by him. I pulled at his arm and the preacher came over to help Mr. Fenton. He looked at me and I asked crying, "What's going on? What's happening to my mother?"

He said, "I don't know but it's already happened son." He put his arms around me, and I held on to him. The preacher said, "Your Ma's with the angels." Mr. Fenton looked at him crossly, "I'll handle this." Shocked the preacher stepped away and I asked, "Is it true?"

"Yes, Jimmy, I'm afraid so." He told me.

"What happened?" I asked.

"We don't know for sure. It looks as if she's taken too much of the laudanum, and by the time the doctor arrived it was already too late. She's gone son, there was nothing anyone could do."

Mrs. Fenton came to the door. She stood there with her hand to her mouth and I could see her crying. She ran toward me, and wrapped her arms around me holding me tightly.

"This is just awful Jimmy." She said between sobs. "But don't you worry you will stay with us; we will take care of you."

I couldn't speak. I just held her and cried. Eventually, I asked to go in and see my mother. Mrs. Fenton had told me to say everything I ever wanted to say to my mother, that she could hear me. Struggling for words I could only choke out a final, "I love you," as I stood there crying.

After a few moments I heard Mrs. Fenton say "Come along Jimmy." I followed her out of the room.

Two days later I was at the cemetery once again and standing in front of yet another grave of my family. I stood there the lone representative of what the Conner family once had been. The preacher's words floated past my ears as I tried to get my mind around the situation. I was surrounded by some familiar faces, but mostly strangers, with no kin to share my grief. During the ceremony I noticed a car driving down the road which slowed momentarily. I saw the face of the man who smiled at me during my father's funeral as he looked toward the people gathered around the grave. However, this time he didn't stop, he just drove on.

When the preacher's words came to an end I reached down and gathered a handful of the freshly dug earth. I felt the cool grains of dirt in my hand as I released them on my mother's coffin. Each person shook my hand or hugged me as they walked past. Many looked at the Fenton's shaking their heads whispering words of concern. Emotionally exhausted, we drove on past my empty house, and for the first time the realization hit me that my future was uncertain.

THREE

*T*he next day I returned to the Conner residence. I wasn't sure where this story would lead, but I was eager to return for another visit, and felt compelled to hear the man out. I walked in and was greeted by Mrs. Conner. She once again sat down with me to share a few words and a sip of tea.

"Have you thought much about the conversation you two gentlemen had last night?" She asked.

"Yes, ma'am," I stated, "But I'm not certain I have anything I can use at this point."

"You will Mr. Campbell, if you finish it to the end, it will be quite valuable to you." She remarked confidently and then escorted me back to Mr. Conner.

"Mr. Campbell, welcome, I'm glad you made it back." He said.

"Of course I made it back, but you were almost put on hold by an alien that was controlling the Congress." I told him.

"Ha," he chuckled, "Seems like it at times doesn't it. Well, let's get to it, shall we?"

I began taking notes once again as Mr. Conner continued on..........

Over the next week we made a few trips down to my house. Mr. and Mrs. Fenton had been nothing, but kind and caring toward me and my situation. She gathered my parent's personal belongings and I mine. I was, for all accounts, moved into the Fenton's home where I resumed a normal existence not too far from what I had always known.

One night I overheard the Fenton's talking as they discussed the night my mother took too much of the laudanum. They couldn't decide if she had taken it on purpose, or if she had just accidentally over medicated herself. The possibility of her intentionally leaving me didn't settle well. I never asked them what they really thought, and the matter was left undecided between them as far as I could tell. I guess it didn't really matter in the end because either way she was gone, and their concern was me.

One morning, a week or so later, I woke up later than usual. I remember this because I had an uneasy feeling that I had let Mr. Fenton down by not helping him with his chores. I quickly dressed, and ate only a few bites of my food carrying the rest with me. When I finally made it outside, Mr. Fenton was already finished and leaning against the fender of his truck.

"Finally, awake Jimmy?" He asked.

"Yes, sir I'm sorry." I replied

"Care for a drive to town?"

"Yes, sir!" I stated enthusiastically.

Going to town was something special for us country folk. My father usually made the trips to town for us on his way home from work and rarely took me or my mother. The nearest town was by no means a city it was just a small rural village. Never the less, it was still exciting for me.

We parked outside of a store and walked in. The floors were long dark wooden planks, smoked meat hung from the ceiling, can goods lined the isles and candy filled a glass case. The owner behind the counter looked at me and asked if I was the Conner boy. Mr. Fenton took him aside out of my ear shot. I didn't mind because I was busy fogging up the glass case that held an assortment of candy with my breath. They came back a few moments later and Mr. Fenton continued to look for his goods. The owner came over and told me to pick anything from the candy jars that I wanted and patted me on the back. I thanked him as I reached up grabbing a piece of liquorish. He then handed me a few more to take along for the ride back home.

Mr. Fenton told me to head out to the truck while he finished his business. I walked out onto the dirt road in front of the building and perched myself on the rear bumper of the truck. There I sat enjoying the treat I had been given and watched the people pass by.

A few moments later a black man pulled up in a wagon. He tied his horse to a post out front. Then he went inside the store. A young boy hopped down with his sister, and the children started talking to me. Everyone I had ever known up to that point was white. It was a strange moment for me, and I couldn't help but stare. Both children eyed my candy as I broke off a piece to share. They thanked me, and we exchanged smiles. Then I climbed inside the truck. Mr. Fenton brought out his goods placing them in the truck's bed. We drove off heading back for home. I never told him about the children I had met. I kept that matter to myself.

That night when we arrived back from town Mrs. Fenton took Mr. Fenton aside to talk. I went outside to look at the stars from the front porch. They both came out, and Mr. Fenton lit his pipe. I sat on the top step looking back at them. Mr. Fenton began to speak saying, "Jimmy a letter came from your grandfather today. We sent one out when your mother passed. From the looks of it he will be coming down and will likely take you with him."

I looked at Mrs. Fenton fearfully and she sat down beside me. I felt as if I was losing them now too. She placed her arm around me and as always had a way of making everything seem better.

"Now, Jimmy it's your grandfather." She said. "Didn't your father ever talk of him?"

"No," I stated.

"Your ma's parents are gone aren't they," she asked.

"Yes," I said.

She looked over to Mr. Fenton then back to me and said, "Well, if he's anything like your father I'm sure he's a good man. We won't let anything happen to you. Let's just see what tomorrow brings."

"Tomorrow!" I exclaimed.

"Yes, his letter stated that he would be here tomorrow." Mr. Fenton said.

My heart sank to the pit of my stomach, but I did my best not to let them see it. I went to bed but slept very little that night. I looked around Tom's room realizing that I had made it mine over the past few days. I made up my mind that if I didn't like it at my grandfather's I would leave, and make my way back to the Fenton's. But, I would give it a try out of respect for them.

I remember waking early in the morning to Mrs. Fenton hanging clothes on the line just outside my window. That comforting moment was brief as I quickly remembered the conversation from the night before and what this day would bring. I stood in Thomas' room, and took a moment realizing that I had just spent my last night there. My belongings were all packed and stacked neatly in the corner, sitting at the ready for my departure. The clothes I was to wear for the trip hung neatly on the back of the door. I dressed, and walked out of the room meeting Mrs. Fenton within my first few steps. She was on her way back to the kitchen where she had breakfast ready. I took in the smell of her cooking one last time as I sat down to eat.

"Good morning Jimmy," She said not turning from her task.

"Morning," I replied. She fixed my plate and placed it on the table. Then she poured my glass while still saying nothing. I started eating my meal as she walked past me into the living room. I heard her footsteps stop directly behind me. I turned to see her bending down to hug me from behind. Her face had tears rolling down her cheeks. I too began to cry.

She said, "You have been so brave, and so good Jimmy. You have brought a little life back in this house. I am sorry for all you have been through, but at the same time grateful for your stay."

"Can't I just stay?" I asked. She squeezed me even tighter.

Just then Mr. Fenton walked in and said, "Now, what's all this about?"

He came over placing his hands on both our shoulders and said, "Jimmy you're a fine boy. You should be proud of yourself. I for one am very proud of you. You've been a wonderful help to me. We would like to know how your getting along. Could you do me a favor and write a few lines to Mrs. Fenton from time to time?" I nodded. "Good Jimmy," he said. "Besides you know how women are!" I smiled back and said, "Promise Mr. Fenton I will."

"Come on," he stated as I followed him outside. He handed me a stick and I pulled out my knife. He pulled out his and we whittled for a bit. I sat there quietly smelling the pipe, listening to him puff. A short time later I noticed a cloud of dust from the road.

The vehicle that pulled in the drive was the Sheriff's. He seemed to never bring me any good news. Mr. Fenton yelled for Mrs. Fenton and she came out wiping her hands with a cloth. She just stood in the door for a moment. Mr. Fenton told me to grab my things, and bring them out. I brushed against Mrs. Fenton with my head held low. Her fingers passed through my hair as I walked by. When I returned I stood on the porch watching the Fenton's walk over to the car. The Sheriff was first to step out and then another man dressed in black. He stood up placing a hat on his head. His figure was heavy and tall.

He looked out into the fields and grimaced. Then he walked over to Mr. and Mrs. Fenton with his hand held out. They all four spoke for a moment, and Mr. Fenton motioned for me to come over. I took a step off the porch. Mrs. Fenton was there before I could finish the other two. She stretched out her hand, and I took it. She led me over to the man and said, "This is your Grandfather James Conner." He stretched out his hand for me to shake it. It was large and soft unlike that of my father or Mr. Fenton's. "Have you ever been on a train?" He asked. I shook my head and said, "No."

"We'll remedy that by the end of the day. I need you to run along and gather your belongings." Moments later, Mrs. Fenton came out with some food for our journey. My grandfather thanked her for her kindness, and the care that they had given me. She bent over and hugged me for the last time. Mr. Fenton walked behind me and placed both hands on my shoulders. Then he told my grandfather that I was a good boy and had been more than well behaved. "Mr. Conner, we have taken a great liking to having him around." He said smiling. "Stay good son, and remember what I asked." Mrs. Fenton walked over giving me one last hug. I don't think she could take much more her eyes were heavy with tears.

I looked at her and said, "Thank you I'll be fine." It was all I could do to choke out those words, but she seemed as upset as I was and I hoped it would make her feel better if I acted strong. My Grandfather asked if we could make a short visit to the cemetery. The Sheriff nodded his approval. I turned around one final time and looked out the window. Through the dust I saw Mrs. Fenton leaning on Mr. Fenton while he had his arm around her. They both waived until I was out of sight.

Mr. Conner pausing for a moment added, "The Fenton's were the most respectable people I have ever known in this life. It's a interesting thing isn't it Campbell, that people we meet for just a brief moment in this life might just cause a connection that a person can carry with him long after they are gone." He then briefly pondered what he had said and continued on.

We passed the only home I had ever known, and my grandfather looked at it with a brief glance then turned his eyes forward only saying, "I'll send for your parent's personal belongings. I gave the furniture and other items to the Fenton's. We won't have a need for them at Shadow Wood."

We arrived at Campbell's crossroads, where we exited the car. We walked up the little hill to the cemetery. He asked if I would show him the location of my father's grave. He paused there a moment, and mumbled something I couldn't make out, then turned to me and said, "We need to get your father and mother a respectable marker." We started to walk off, but then he stopped in his tracks, and asked about Wills grave. I told him about my brother, and how he died. My grandfather had no idea that he had a grandson named Will. He shook his head and said, "We'll get him a more appropriate marker too." We walked away slowly, and he asked me to look back just once more before we left. We stood silently and then he said, "You have to put this behind you son." I looked up at him, "Right here, right now, Jimmy. You can't do anything to help them by spending your life mourning their death." He stepped away leaving me alone. For a moment I stood there to take it all in. Then I walked over opened the door of the waiting car and we drove away.

The sheriff drove us to the nearest town with a train station. My Grandfather shook his hand, and offered to pay him for his time. He declined the offer stating that this was the least he could do.

I had never seen a train up close before. I was amazed by the large machine. My grandfather shook his head in disbelief that I had been so sheltered from the world around me. We boarded the train and I was introduced to a new set of sights, and smells. The whole production excited me, but I kept to myself and quiet about the whole affair. The train made its next stop in Columbia, South Carolina. As we neared the city my nose was glued to the window beside me I had never seen a city so big. I repeatedly refused my grandfather's requests to sit down and remained standing as the train approached the station.

From Columbia we continued on and rode through the night. In the morning we made our final stop in Macon Georgia. There we were met by Henry, who was my Grandfather's driver, butler, grounds keeper and about any other role required at the house he called Shadow Wood. He reached his large black hand out to grab my bag as he smiled at me. I didn't know it then, but he would become as much a part of my family as anyone ever had. He looked down at me strangely and said, "Mr. Conner sir, he does look like his father from head to toe doesn't he."

"Yes, he does." Replied my grandfather, "but I'm afraid he has his mother's demeanor. He's awfully quiet and seems a bit backward."

"Probably, too young to tell Mr. Conner that boy has been through a lot; enough to make a grown man quiet, let alone a young boy."

"Maybe so Henry," he remarked.

I stepped into the large automobile sitting in the back with my grandfather. It was a far cry from the old trucks and vehicles that traveled the dusty roads in front of my home.

"Does Miss Ida have us a plate waiting?" asked my grandfather.

"I'm sure she does Mr. Conner."

We drove through town while Grandfather read the local paper. I was once again glued to a window. I noticed long rows of two story homes, rows of large thick green trees, and children playing on the brick streets. All seemed clean, neat and orderly. I could only think of a few homes this size in the country, but these homes stood one after another and seemed to stretch for blocks. I asked grandfather if everyone in the city was rich. To which he replied, "No, of course not," and then continued to read.

We drove until we came to a large home standing alone on the last block in town. We entered the gate and continued up the drive. Grandfather looked up from his reading and said, "Ah, we are here Jimmy, Shadow Wood your new home." Up to that time I had never seen anything like it. A fountain in the front yard with a man holding a large sphere on his shoulders immediately aroused my attention. The house had two stories; a porch that covered the width of the house and on the right corner was a circular tower with its own round pointed roof. It reminded me of a castle and gave the home a formidable appearance.

Henry grabbed my bags as Grandfather and I walked toward the door. We were greeted by Miss Ida, a large black woman in her late forty's with big arms and a warm smile. She ran over and hugged me before I even entered the door. After a quick once over she asked my grandfather if he had fed me on the way home. He grimaced, quickly retorting that he had.

Miss Ida said, "Jimmy come on inside and get cleaned up. I'll fix you something to eat." She hovered over me with both hands on my shoulders guiding me to the bathroom.

"Campbell, the interesting thing about Miss Ida was I often questioned if she even realized that she was employed by my grandfather. He was a proper and distinguished man, but she often overruled him and got her way. She always made him smile. I think it was her great warmth that made him keep her close by. It was a very odd relationship indeed."

I had little time to look around, but I remember being amazed by the staircase. I quickly finished up in the wash room. When I came back downstairs our food was sitting on the table. Miss Ida had prepared quite a feast for my arrival.

I must have been a sight. Everything seemed giant to me, the room, the table, the food was all on a proportion that was unfamiliar to me. Grandfather and I sat quietly at that first meal. He spoke only to ask me questions about my education, religion, and general upbringing. I kept my answers short and direct often only replying simply, yes or no. He didn't seem one for small talk, and I wasn't going to provide him with any in return. I had some time to explore that day after Miss Ida showed me to my room. She told me it had been my father's, but unlike Tom's room it was void of anything that reflected him or his life here.

I was excited about Shadow Wood although it seemed too big a place to call home. Finally, night fell upon it and Miss Ida came in to turn down my bed. She seemed happy about me being there and asked me all manner of questions to get to know me better. Again I answered only in a direct fashion, but it was much harder to maintain a distance with her, because she made me feel so welcome. I figured I would be fine as long as she was around.

Grandfather on the other hand didn't even come in to tell me good night. I was surprised to find out she knew my father and mother. She asked me many questions about them that night. Before turning out the lights she looked at me one last time and said, "You sure do remind me of your father." It was comforting for me to hear because I was so far from all I knew. That night I stayed up late looking out the window at the surrounding city lights.

The next day Miss Ida took me as my grandfather would say, "to find proper clothing." We went into town, where she seemed happy about getting me situated and fitted for clothes. I had never owned clothes that the city boys wore in those times. Mine had always been suited for a life in the country. I liked the new clothes and felt good wearing them.

That week at Shadow Wood was an experience for me. Grandfather had gone away for business and I felt like a king in a giant castle. I was getting accustomed to my new surroundings. Miss Ida proved to be my primary source of company and care. We bonded quickly because she was quite good to me. I knew she held a genuine concern for my happiness.

My Grandfather arrived one afternoon with some time to focus his attention on me. I was called to his office, where I sat in a small chair opposite him at his large wooden desk. He once again started asking me questions about my upbringing.

"Jimmy, you said that your family didn't attend church regularly. Have you ever been to a service?" He asked.

"No, sir," I told him.

"Have to ever been to a church function?" He asked.

"No, sir,"

He sat there looking frustrated and asked, "Do you know of God?"

"Yes, sir and Jesus,"

"At least they weren't raising a total heathen. Jimmy we're Methodist have you ever heard of that faith?

"No, sir," I stated.

He grimaced and then went on, "I need to know about your education in Mathematics, English, and Science. I suppose you went to a country school?" He asked.

"Yes, sir."

"And for how long did you attend this school?"

"The last three years," I stated.

He then reached up from behind his desk grabbing a book from the shelf. Then he asked that I read a passage as he placed the book in front of me. I began to read stumbling with the some of the words. "Enough," he stated shortly after I had started. He then placed a piece of paper and pencil in front of me. "Jimmy, I want you to write a story. Something made up would be fin but something you've learned from history for instance would be better. I'll leave you alone and you can come out when you're finished. Just leave the paper and pencil on my desk."

He left the room, while I sat there having no idea of what to write. I considered something I had learned from school about South Carolina, but I chose to write a letter to Mrs. Fenton instead. I had promised I would and wanted to tell her about all I had seen.

Once I was finished I came out and Grandfather walked over to the desk. I think he was surprised by the fact I wrote a letter to the Fenton's. Looking back I'm sure any other topic would have been followed by a lecture, but I think this letter struck him, and for a moment his gruff exterior was softened.

"Jimmy, come around here. Let's look at this together." he said. "It's a good thing to write the Fenton's. They are good people, but when we do something, we do it right. We're Conner's, and that's a name that carries with it responsibilities and one of those is to do things in the correct manner." And then he went on making corrections to the page. He asked me to rewrite the letter again to prove the point. Once I finished he handed me an envelope. I put the letter inside to go out in the next day's mail.

Grandfather sat back in his chair and I could see by his expression that he had something to tell me. He went on to say, "Jimmy, I was afraid of this. I would prefer for you to spend time getting to know me, but it seems we have bigger concerns. I must do what's in your best interest. At this moment your best interest is your education. It has been neglected and I need to correct that issue. Tomorrow we leave and I will make arrangements for you to attend a school that I am familiar with. It would be best if you started to pack your belongings."

I felt as if I had been tossed around enough, and now it seemed that my grandfather didn't much care for me because he wanted to send me away. I was just getting use to my surroundings, and now I had to leave again. My orders were simple; pack only one bag for two days worth of travel.

That night I couldn't sleep, so I walked outside to the backyard closing the door quietly behind me. There I saw the glow of a cigarette. It was Henry sitting down enjoying the night sky. I had only spoken to Henry a few times, but never one on one.

"What are you doing up roaming around at this hour," he asked? I stood there and shrugged.

"Can't sleep?" He asked.

"No," I replied.

"Too much floating around in that head of yours I bet. You're starting to look like that Atlas fellow in the fountain." He said smiling.

Henry motioned for me to sit next to him. The night air was cool, and he handed me a coat.

"Here put this on. Being sick doesn't help you sleep much either."

Then he pulled out a knife, and began cutting on a stick. I sat there, watching for moment and pulled out my father's. It was never far away from me.

"Hey, that's a dandy knife. May I see it?" he asked.

"Sure," I replied as I handed it to him. He looked closely at it while commenting, "Looks familiar I think your grandfather has one like it."

"It was my Pa's," I replied.

"Best not let your Grandfather or Miss Ida catch you with it. I'm not too sure they would think much of you having it. He started whittling again, then asked, "Do you have anything on your mind James?"

"No, not really," I stated.

"I don't believe that for one minute, but we don't have to talk about it. We can just sit here a spell and cut on this wood. Sometimes it's the best thing for a mind that's working too hard."

We sat outside for almost an hour then he finally told me to run along inside. That was the thing about Henry he could talk or just be. We didn't have to say much to be together. He knew silence was just as powerful as any advice a person could give. Over the years we spent many nights like that together.

The morning came quickly. Miss Ida wasn't pleased with Grandfather for sending me away. She tossed his breakfast plate down on the table.

He noted the action by saying in a stern voice, "Ida!"

"Don't you Ida me!" She said.

"Don't you make a scene." He replied, "Besides this is the best thing for him."

"Best thing, shipping that poor boy off" She said.

I sat there quietly eating watching the event unfold.

"Ida, he needs a quality education. I am away on business too often to be responsible." He stated.

"It's not responsible sending a small boy off to some school far away."

"It's where his father went and you know it."

My ears began to perk up as I thought maybe this wouldn't be too bad after all.

"And you see how that turned out Mr. Conner don't you?"

"That had nothing to do with Bransford and you know it!" He said sharply, "Enough of this. That's final!"

"You're right, Mr. Conner, that wasn't fair and after all James' mother was alive to help you decide what was best for him." She said.

"Yes, and she acted like you are now, but I promise this is best."

Once again I found myself on a porch being hugged and leaving people that cared for me. It was becoming a common theme in the recent weeks; one I didn't much care for. Henry drove us down to the station where Grandfather and I boarded another train, this one headed for Mississippi.

FOUR

The train stopped on the edge of a small town where the academy was located. As we walked through town, we followed the long tree lined lane leading to the academy. Out front two cannons sat astride a large flag pole. I watched as two academy boys dressed in gray uniforms saluted the flag as they passed in front of it. They walked by in step and then hurried inside the two story brick building.

Grandfather and I walked up the stairs following the two boys. Grandfather asked one of the boys for directions to the superintendent's office. He smartly answered, "Sir, down the hall the second door on the right."

"Thank you, that's where it used to be," Grandfather replied. Inside we were greeted by two more cadets. One boy about my age was a little heavy around the middle sporting only one stripes on his sleeve. The other boy was much older with a large ornate set of stripes on his sleeve leaving me little doubt of who was in charge.

My grandfather said, "We have an appointment with the superintendent." The older boy looked down at a black book on the desk and asked, "Mr. Conner.?"

"Yes," my Grandfather replied. The older boy ordered the younger boy, a Private Wallace, to notify the Colonel that Mr. Conner had arrived.

To which he smartly replied, "Yes, Sergeant Major" then knocked on the Colonel's door.

We entered the office. There my Grandfather and the Colonel shook hands. The Colonel said, "Mr. Conner, it's a pleasure to finally meet you sir. Your reputation precedes you by many years." My Grandfather replied, "Colonel Tucker the same for you, it is actually quite amazing that we have never met before."

"Please, take a seat gentlemen," the Colonel politely stated. Then he continued, "My duties require me to stay here on campus. I have little time to travel or attend to other matters as I would like."

"Colonel, your duty here raising these boys to be men and attending to their souls brings you to a high honor in the community. Nothing could be more important. You are a Presbyterian minister is that correct?"

"Why, yes it is sir," replied the Colonel. "But we have boys of all manner of faiths here at Bransford. What faith is your Grandson?"

Grandfather looked at me and replied, "I am sorry to admit this, but his education is lacking in many areas. Furthermore, concerning religion, well, I'm afraid my son had fallen quite short in fulfilling his obligations. We are by tradition Methodist. My mother was a Presbyterian and her father, like you, was a minister."

"Very well then," said the Colonel. "We shall get down to business and mold this lad into a man of God, and country, and prepare him for higher learning."

The two men continued to discuss my fate as if I wasn't in the room. Colonel Tucker was an older man dressed in black. Sitting on his desk was a gray kepi, a hat worn by the civil war soldiers both North and South, with three stars pinned to the front noting his rank. Opposite the cap was a worn St. James bible that I would later learn was as much part of his wear as anything else, because it was never far from his reach. Hanging high on the wall was a large sword with a golden tassel hanging from its hilt. I looked around the room and saw a painting of a soldier. I didn't know who it was at that time, but I was soon to learn that it was a portrait of General Lee. In the corner of the room an American flag stood at one end and the flag state of South Carolina the other. In the middle was a large Confederate battle flag. I perked up when the Colonel said, "Very well the matter is concluded." The men stood up and the Colonel said to me, "You should be very proud of your grandfather he is a true son of the South."

Then the two men parted with handshakes. The Colonel excused himself, as my grandfather and I exchanged goodbyes. Grandfather looked at me firmly and told me he could leave me in no better care, that this was the first step in my duty. And that I should act in a manner that would make him proud. I would learn more about honor and dignity here than I could be taught elsewhere.

Then the Private entered the room and said, "Mr. Conner sir, the Colonel asked me to take Private Conner to show him the campus and his billets while you register him in with the Cadet Sergeant Major. "Very well then," said my grandfather. He shook my hand and said, "Jimmy you're a private now. Follow orders and do as you're told. Good bye." I stepped back and I thought about what he called me, "Private Conner." Although uneasy about the situation being called Private Conner sounded pretty appealing to me.

You never know how life is going to take a turn. It can all change in an instant. That day the young Private Wallace was in his second year at the academy. Wallace was a little heavy, and didn't fit into the model of the other kids I saw at the school. He introduced me to some of the boys during lunch. The long dining hall had four long rows of tables. One table at the head of the room was for the Colonel, four other adult instructors, and the upper classman of the highest rank. The room was filled with boys, and each stood in his assigned place. When the room was called to attention, a quiet hushed the air as the Colonel took his place behind his chair. A prayer was given followed with a list of announcements. The first was about my arrival and that the boys should welcome me.

I felt very out of place, but Private Wallace did his best to talk to me, and make me feel at home. He told me which the boys would be friendly; which would give me a hard time. Talk around the table was for the most part allowed, but nothing much above a whisper, or the Colonel's gavel would fall making a thunderous crash. There were the usual looks and gestures made in my direction. I knew to keep my eyes straight and not take notice. I finished my meal in short order, and then helped Wallace clean the tables with some of the other boys. It was then that I realized Wallace and I would be friends. It may have been the meandering through the halls, the conversation at the lunch table or just the fact he needed someone as bad as I did. It still amazes me how when you're a child things can come to a quick resolution. You find yourself friends with someone who was only moments before a stranger. It's too bad that quality in people gets tarnished as life goes on.

Wallace took me back to the superintendent's office. We spoke with the Sergeant Major about my uniform. He instructed Wallace to take me to town and get fitted. We left the campus together on foot, walking the same road I came in on. The further we distanced ourselves from campus, the more at ease Wallace became. He knew better than to do anything out of line because the entire town knew the boys at the school and kept a watchful eye on them. We strolled in and met with the tailor who handled all the schools uniforms. He fitted me with different jackets, slacks and shoes. He made some slight alterations to the uniform while we waited. I asked Wallace about the lack of a stripe on my sleeve. He stated that I was a no stripe private, and he was a full stripe private. That he earned his once his demerits had been cleared. He said a good soldier could have his stripe before the end of the semester if he kept his nose clean. Looking down at the jackets empty sleeve I liked the notion of earning a stripe. I thought maybe one day I'd have the sleeve full like the Sergeant Major. The tailor brought me my uniform then they showed me how to properly wear it. I looked at myself in the long mirror from the shiny shoes, to the gray slacks, and the white shirt with a gray coat over it. The hat issued was a gray civil war style kepi. It was similar to the Colonel's, but it had the addition of a white cloth running down the back that when worn would touch my shoulders giving it a dashing appearance and the practicality of shading my neck. I kept looking at myself. I felt a certain amount of pride in the uniform. The tailor gave me a large bag filled with the rest of my issued clothing along with a Saint James bible. I looked at Wallace and he said, "The Colonel believes that the best soldiers fear God more than the enemy."

On our way back to campus Wallace told me what to expect and how to keep out of trouble. We practiced keeping step and by the time we arrived at the school grounds I was getting the hang of it. He told me we had to meet with the Sergeant Major and the Colonel. I stopped Private Wallace on the first step of the building. I thanked him for his help. It was then that I finally asked him his first name. He said, "We don't use those here." But after quickly looking around he whispered, "Virgil."

"Thanks again, Virgil," I whispered back. He had me stand at attention as he adjusted my uniform before we walked upstairs into the office.

The cadet Sergeant Major said the word, "report," to Private Wallace and he quickly stood at attention stating, "Private Wallace reporting as ordered sir," as he saluted the older cadet. The cadet Sergeant Major said, "Good Wallace. That's how it's done Private Conner, now you try."

I stood straight and tall and said, "Private Conner reporting as ordered." I made my best effort at giving a salute and the Sergeant Major moved me into position correcting my poor attempt. He stepped back folded his arms and looked me over. My eyes wondered to Wallace trying to catch a glimpse of his reaction. "Eye's front Conner," snapped the Sergeant Major he then said, "Very good Private Conner. The salute is an old tradition that goes back to the knights. Remember the forefinger touches the outside of the brow. Let's try again."

We practiced a few more times and the Sergeant Major asked Wallace to get Corporeal Tanner. Wallace smiled, ran out the door, and down the hall. Once satisfied with me not embarrassing myself or him the Sergeant Major knocked on the Colonel's door. The Colonel yelled, "Enter," and the Cadet Sergeant Major approached the desk and then smartly saluted the Colonel holding his hand in position until the Colonel returned the salute. The Sergeant Major turned and took three smart steps to the right side of the Colonels desk turned then faced the door. He yelled, "Private Conner reeeeport." My knees started to shake as I approached the desk. Trying to be perfect but failing miserably. I made my best effort as I saluted the Colonel.

The Colonel returned the salute and said, "At ease," and called the corporal into the room. He told Tanner, "You have work to do here, but I bet Private Conner will do his duty, and make us quite proud. Take the Private and get him situated."

"Yes, sir," replied Corporal Tanner. He looked at me and said, "Follow me Private." I did as instructed exiting the office behind Corporal Tanner.

I followed him down the hall at his usual hurried pace. We walked down the west wing corridor and up a flight of stairs. I noticed other cadets walking through the building in an orderly fashion. A small group formed in front of the entry to the sleeping area called a billet. When the Corporal approached, the boys parted as someone yelled, "Make a hole." He barked back at them for being outside of the billeting area in a cluster. The room was large and filled with long rows of bunks. The Corporal showed me to my bunk. There sat my bedding neatly folded with my belongings and footlocker at the end of the bed. He opened my bag dumped out my personal items looking for contraband. After going through them, he told me to store my belongings in the footlocker. It was then that I remembered my father's pocket knife and that it was still safely in the pocket of my pants. Afraid to ask if having it was would get me into trouble; I just kept quiet about it.

He went through each item that was part of my issue. Then I was told where and how to store it in the footlocker. He then told me that if I had any questions just ask one of the other privates. He said, "We help each other out here, that's the way it is. All issued cadets items are to be stored in the same manner. It is a part of the attention to detail that we strive for around here. Always address me as corporal even though my real name is John Tanner." He said smiling.

Tanner then went on, "I know this is all new to you Private Conner, but you have a lot of people watching out for you. Each side of this hall represents a company. Each company has a Cadet Captain in charge. Divide the rows in half and you have a platoon. Each of the platoons is led by a Cadet Lieutenant. Divide the group half again and you have a squad. In a squad, a Sergeant or Corporal like me is in charge. All these boys are responsible for you, like older brothers." He smiled, and then said, "Well that's the way it's supposed to be anyway. You're now my responsibility, and I'm here to help you. Never lie to me, and always try your best and you'll do fine Conner." He patted me on the back, and went about his duties.

Immediately I began to put my belongings in order. Private Wallace walked by and sat on a bunk. "We're in the same platoon Conner!" He stated. I then knew why he was so excited when he ran out of the Colonel's office. Wallace helped me organize the last of my things as the bugle called us out for dinner. We went down, and sat with our company. I recognized some of the boys from lunch, and again helped Wallace with the cleanup.

Some of the boys went off to duties, while the rest cleaned their area, or worked on their studies. Wallace and I talked most of the night. He told me about his family and his six sisters. He was the only boy in the middle of all those girls. This was part of the reason his father sent him to Bransford. He felt that growing up around so many women would be a negative influence. He felt that he needed to be around other boys.

At one point Corporal Tanner stopped by to check on me. We spoke briefly as he checked my footlocker to make sure it was in order and likely to make sure I was in order too. The evening went by quickly, and the bugle again called. I learned yet another new term, Taps, which means lights out and time for bed. The color guard ceremoniously lowered the flags and respectfully put them in a case for the night. I quietly laid there in my cot. The room was quiet as the other boys slept, but I had too much on my mind to fall asleep easily. At one point I saw someone get up and walk toward me. I didn't know what to make of it, so I didn't move. As the figure moved closer I realized it was Corporal Tanner. He checked on me almost every night that first week. He was a good leader even at that age. It was comforting to know that even though I was surrounded by strangers I had someone watching out for me. I just hoped I'd never let him down.

I woke to the sound of reveille that first morning as I would so many mornings to come. The boys hustled to get ready. Wallace had prepared me to get ready quickly, but I still fell behind. The boys all ran out to the front of the building for morning formation. The corporals and sergeants performed a quick inspection. Tanner inspected me while noting that I looked presentable. Wallace gleamed with pride when Tanner told him that he had done a good job helping me get prepared.

When all the boys had formed up the cadet officers called the regiment to attention. The Colonel recited the Morning Prayer along with a list of announcements. Then Colonel Tucker saluted the cadet Sergeant Major, and turned the formation over to him. The cadet officers inspected the troops, and I met my Lieutenant and the Cadet Captain. Each cadet stood at attention while they were inspected.

This is when I notice my Lieutenant's dislike of Wallace. Once the Captain left, Whittington picked Wallace apart piece by piece ridiculing him about his obsessive weight. After the inspection was over Corporal Tanner walked over and picked up the pieces of Wallace's pride. "Lieutenant Whittington just wants you to be the best troop in the company that's all Wallace." I would later come to find out Tanner's true sentiments toward Whittington.

Everything at Bransford was a routine and we survived by its structure. That and of course Corporal Tanner, who was always watching out for us. Nobody messed with his cadets. He took his big brother role seriously by keeping a watchful eye out for us. It was the eighth week of school, and I was pretty much adjusted and into the swing of things. But I was starting to feel a little home sick for a home and family I no longer had. Trying to ignoring the feeling I decided to get lost in one of my books.

Eventually, I looked up and Tanner stood there with the other boys from my squad while they wished me a happy birthday. He handed me a small cake that he had the cook bake. That moment made me feel very accepted for the first time. He looked down and said, "It's the job of a squad leader to know everything about his troops. Hurry up and eat your cake before you get me in trouble." I shared the small cake, each of us having little more than a bite. But that didn't matter because; it wasn't the cake that really mattered to a boy far from home. That night I realized all I really had was a grandfather, who I barely knew, and the boys of Bransford.

This fact motivated me to do well there. It helped me to focus on my schooling instead of what all that I had lost. I did everything I could do to impress Tanner and very much wanted to be like him. His positive leadership left a lasting impression on me and created a bond within the squad.

One morning we had a full pack inspection. A full pack inspection required our gear from the foot lockers, and weapons from the armory. We looked as if we were being sent away to war. The inspection for our company was going like clockwork. The Cadet Sergeant Major, Cadet Captain and Lieutenant Whittington each had a turn at inspecting us. As they moved passed me I noticed Lieutenant Whittington once again for no reason zeroing in on Wallace, who stood four people past me. He began chewing Wallace out for anything he could find wrong.

I could see Tanner out of the corner of my eye looking disapprovingly at the situation. I knew Wallace would soon be in tears which would make the situation that much worse. When I couldn't stand it any longer I did the unthinkable thing for a soldier, and let the rifle drop from my hand. It fell in slow motion finally hitting the hard surface of the ground. The rifles impact made a distinct sound that overshadowed the commotion just a few paces away silencing them all. Then all at once a low groan rumbled through the formation as the cadets envisioned what was heading in my direction.

The Lieutenant couldn't ignore the situation, but temporarily the heat was off Wallace. Unfortunately it was now on me as Tanner, the Lieutenant, and the Captain all came at me. I saved Wallace and now Tanner had to save me. Once the Lieutenant and captain were finished with me Tanner continued the assault until they were out of ear shot. Then he looked at me knowingly; put his hand on my shoulder and said "You're a good friend, and a good troop Conner."

Tanner could only do so much, Wallace and I had extra duty for a week. We even had the honor of polishing the cannons that stood as centennials at the entrance of the academy, but I was with my best friend and that's all that mattered to me. It's an interesting thing isn't it? How that bond between people just seems to grow when you have to struggle together. Maybe that's the whole point of polishing those cannons. They were forged not just from cold iron and extreme heat but through effort, and attention to detail. And maybe by using those very same qualities in their care a bond between boys could also be forged.

At some point early that year I decided to write the Fenton's and a few weeks later I received a letter from them. Mrs. Fenton wrote the reply herself and was thrilled to hear from me. She asked me numerous questions, and I did my best to answer so she wouldn't worry. I was surprised how good it felt just to read a few words from someone who knew me before I was at Bransford. Mr. Fenton added a note and enclosed my coin. He told me that he could find no answers about the coins origins. Only that the inscription on the bottom of Deo Vindice are the Latin words on the seal of the Confederate States of America and that it means God will vindicate. But he could find no more information about the coin. I held that piece in my hand looking at it closely thinking about the scorpion, the woman, and the stars must all have a meaning too, but I had no idea how to find out. I thought it best to hide it for now.

It was in that second semester that something special happened. My name was called out in the morning formation. I had no idea what happened or what possible trouble I could have gotten into. I left the ranks and walked smartly out to the front of the formation and in front of the entire school. The cadet Sergeant Major called the formation to attention and announced that I was to get my first stripe. That was the first time in my life that I had ever been given any recognition for the work I had done. I felt a tremendous sense of pride and I couldn't wait to take it to the tailor to have it sewn on.

At Bransford, I began my education in Southern history. Even with the revival of nationalism due to World War I, our school held firm to its deeply embedded Southern roots. Mr. Morgan, our history teacher, was a rumored nephew of the famed John Hunt Morgan. He spoke with great enthusiasm about the War Between the States and took special interest in

John Hunt Morgan, the Confederate guerrilla leader. John Morgan led Morgan's Raiders on a seven hundred mile cavalry raid across Indiana and Ohio in hopes of rallying copperheads in those states to the side of the Confederacy. Interestingly, Indiana's Congress in general held a sympathetic attitude toward the Southern cause, but at the outbreak of the war sent a large contingent of soldiers to fight for the Union. Mr. Morgan spoke of the geography and landscapes playing key factors in the battles from the Greeks to the recent battles of World War I or the Great War as it was called back then. It was Mr. Morgan who taught me about the proper use of the natural landscape and the importance of terrain giving us examples of Gettysburg, Maryland Heights at Harpers Ferry, and numerous other battles.

At that point I broke into the story: "Mr. Conner, Indiana?" I asked.

"What Campbell, you don't believe that the war was about only about slavery?"

"Sir, the Confederacy didn't even carry Kentucky and Tennessee barley seceded how could they carry Indiana?"

"True Kentucky was a border state and the legislature chose not to secede but think of it this way. Lincoln was born in Kentucky then moved to Indiana then on to Illinois. Many families made a similar journey and the southern halves of those states held close ties to the South. They tended to be old immigrants, from families that lived in the states for generations. The northern half of Indiana and Illinois tended to have blood of new immigrants and those fresh off the boat. Had Lincoln not been from Illinois that state may have turned too who knows. The fact remains that the Indiana legislature was sympathetic to the Southern cause. The governor saved the state for the Union by using private money to fund the state government after the legislature denied the State's authority to levy taxes."

I looked at him questionably as he continued. "Campbell, the strength and role of the federal government is a debate that started with the founders. Jefferson and the others debated this issue for years. Each state chose to be in the Union why couldn't they chose to leave it? Slavery was an issue, an important issue but also remember the institution of slavery was important to both the North and South. Many in the North benefited from the practice just as they did in the South. The days of slavery were numbered. Most of the world had outlawed it. It was an unfortunate tool used by both the North and the South for economic and political reasons. But in the end some rural boy in Maine or Wisconsin fought miles away from his home for his state that supported the Union. Just like some boy from Texas or Mississippi fought for his state in the South that didn't. Even General Ulysses S. Grant said, "If I thought this war was to abolish slavery, I would resign my commission and offer my sword to the other side." Now let us continue."

Religion was a corner stone at Bransford and part of our daily education. The Colonel acted as the schools minister and spiritual leader. He made us each feel as if God would lead our lives in the same military manner that he led us in school. Colonel Tucker's version of the Presbyterian path to god seemed to be one of discipline and strict devotion. It was our duty and he going lead us to heaven whether we liked it or not.

I spent that first summer at Bransford with a few of the other students. I really didn't mind, new friendships were formed and Bransford had become another home to me. At the end of my second year I had big plans for that summer. I was excited about using the time to get a position in the Troop which was the cavalry company. The chance to work with horses had a great appeal to me. Another important attraction was that Tanner had become a sergeant, and was moving to that company. The Troop came with more responsibilities. Because of this fact only the best boys were chosen to participate in it.

Of course we were all schooled in the different tools of the military trade; artillery, infantry, and cavalry. But there was something about having my own horse that appealed to me. It was quite an honor to be associated with the troop. My marks were good but I was in competition with many boys, some who were older. I needed the summer to pull ahead. I was very excited about spending the summer with Wallace and the other boys who stayed. Then I received a letter from my grandfather stating that he would be arriving within the week to pick me up for the summer.

This did not sit well with me. Sending a letter to state my protest wouldn't reach him in time. So, I went to Tanner for help.

He suggested we speak with the Colonel which brightened my day. Tanner presented me to the Colonel and then exited the room. After stating my case, the Colonel sat back in his chair, paused for a moment then said, "Private Conner, I have a few things to say to you. First and foremost is that I am quite proud of you and the way you have adapted to life at this academy. Unfortunately, when you're a soldier you have orders. Your grandfather has given you yours. I would like to make a suggestion concerning this situation, and it's something for you to remember. A soldier in the field doesn't always see the grand scheme of things. Your role has not been relieved to you, but in time it will be. Therefore I suggest you prepare yourself for other duties this summer and likely the summers to come. Now, this matter is concluded. Conduct yourself like a Bransford cadet should. Carry on!"

I walked out of the office with my head low. I felt dejected. I wasn't satisfied with the Colonel's speech on the subject. Tanner knowing I was down, tried to cheer me up by volunteering me to work in the stables with him and the horses for the rest of the week.

When my Grandfather arrived he commented on my appearance. He was impressed with my military attitude and bearing. I asked to speak with him privately, and walked with him outside for a moment. I strategically walked him towards the stable and introduced him to Tanner. Tanner made the impression that I desired. My grandfather listened to my protests but in the end said, "Jimmy in this family we have many duties and I need to prepare you for some myself. Expect your summers to be filled with those duties. Go tell the boys good bye, then meet me out front. You have ten minutes."

"Mr. Conner it seems Bransford had quite a tradition," I stated. "Very proud tradition," he replied. "I'll tell you a quick story that pertains to this one. One day we had a

speaker, a veteran from World War I. It was that day we learned that Bransford was represented on the battlefields of France. Sergeant Dwight Patterson lost his leg fighting in the trenches. He told us the story and all boys looked at him with great respect. He had taken an old guidon that was to be retired from the Bransford troop. Apparently, it had caused the class a lot of heartache because the flags were to be respectfully burned when they were too worn for use. The missing guidon was the big talk around the campus at the time and threats of punishments were given.

Patterson kept quiet about what he had done and walked off the campus knowing he was going to enter the service just days after graduation. He carried the guidon to France with him sewing it inside a hidden pocket in his bedroll. When his spirits were down he would place the flag on the edge of his trench to show the Germans that the Bransford boys had come to fight. Patterson admitted to the deed bringing the flag home and presented it to Colonel Tucker, who gleamed with pride upon hearing the story. It was placed over the main entry of the mess hall inside a glass case and bearing the hole of a German marksman's bullet."

"Campbell, do you even know what a guidon is?" Mr. Conner asked.

"It's a flag right." I replied.

"It's a standard of a company or platoon. Each army, brigade, battalion, company has a flag or banner. For instance the cavalry usually has a red and white guidon for each of its companies. Generals for centuries would watch the colors of their army's banners on the battlefield. They could see their army's progress during the confusion of battle. They would use them to react, and make strategic decisions. When the responsibilities for the unit are passed to a new commander the standard is passed from old to new. Ceremoniously the banner is handed over with great honor and dignity. When you witness the ceremony you realize that many men have stood under that banner, and it represents those men and now you. Men have died carrying those banners and flags proudly dropping their weapons to move that piece of cloth forward, while with each step moving it closer to the enemy's bullets, possibly the flag bearers own death. Those flags are more than pieces of cloth. They are held high for a reason. It's because men have made those markers of their own courage and sacrifice. When you stand there underneath it you become a part of it.

FIVE

We drove back to Shadow Wood manor that day. Disappointed as I was at having to leave Bransford I was happy to see the gate of Shadow Wood.

Henry greeted me at the door, "Welcome back Jimmy," he stated. I replied back in an authoritative voice, "That's Cadet Private Conner can't you see the stripe?" I smiled and Henry said, "That is quite something Private Conner. How could I have missed that? You did bring your knife along didn't you?" I patted my pants pocket, he smiled and said, "We'll find some time to use it and catch up."

"Deal," I replied.

Miss Ida let out a yell as she came in running to give me a hug. Immediately, she ordered me to get cleaned up for dinner. I went up the stairs to my room. She ordered Henry to carry in my bags, as if he wouldn't have just done it anyway. Not much had changed in the time I was gone. I hadn't known them long, but I had missed them. As I passed the kitchen I noticed the smell of Miss Ida's cooking, and it was welcome reminder that I had a home here. I went upstairs and looked in my closet for a change of clothes. To my surprise I had grown because I couldn't find anything that fit. I had little choice but to continue wearing my uniform and headed downstairs. I told Miss Ida about the situation, and she promised to look into it in the morning. In truth it really didn't matter.

I had grown so accustom to wearing my uniform that anything else seemed strange and uncomfortable.

That first night home was filled with laughter and stories. Now, that I was there I didn't mind so much being back at Shadow Wood. A few days later, Grandfather asked if I would like to go with him on business. I eagerly jumped at the opportunity.

That first morning we tended to his business affairs. He had told me to keep close at hand and pay attention because his interests were varied, and I would have to understand how the many pieces of the puzzle came together. I'm not really sure how he kept all of it in order actually. He did much of the note taking and figuring in his head, and never missed a tally.

Later that night we had dinner with a friend of his, a Mr. Bedford, his wife and two children, Lucille and Charlie who were both about my age. Lucille was proper and quite contrite; she put on airs about her importance. She would smile at me, and for the first time I noticed how I overlooked certain flaws, just because of a little attention. Charlie on the other hand didn't share any of her saving graces; he was obnoxious and bragged incessantly. I did my best to bite my tongue as he was a hard boy to like.

The night ended and Mr. Bedford asked if I was going to be introduced at the meeting tomorrow? I had no idea what he was talking about, but I did hear Mr. Bedford say that Charlie would also be there.

As we walked back to the car, I asked my grandfather what Mr. Bedford was talking about. He explained that there was a club of which he was a member. Many fathers would bring their sons, and sometimes three or four generations would all be represented. He asked if I would be interested.

I replied that I was interested, but hoped Charlie wasn't the standard issue member. He said that it would be good for me to meet these business men and their sons. He also mentioned that my father was in the club when he was about my age. This fact alone gave me more interest in the organization, and I told him that I would like to go. He went on and said, "One thing Jimmy, and this is important. Everything you see is a secret. Everything we do in the meetings is a secret. So, if you can't keep a secret, then you can't be in the club."

The following day we drove into town to enter a large warehouse. Inside the building I saw all manner of goods that were stored on the first floor. I walked along the wooden planked floors and noticed the last of the day's sun light being filtered through the windows. Through those rays, I could see the particles of dust floating in the air hovering around the room.

We met Mr. Bedford and Charlie on the main floor then walked over to a cargo elevator. Charlie immediately said, "So, Conner you're a new inductee. My father said I was to show you the ropes. Which I guess puts me in charge of you huh!"

Not exactly thrilled by the proposition I looked at my grandfather disapprovingly. He put his hand my shoulder, as I turned to Charlie and said, "Sure Charlie show me the ropes."

The four of us entered the large elevator, before Mr. Bedford closed the gate. Charlie asked if he could pull the lever which lifted the platform upward. I had never been in a building so large let alone an elevator. When it moved I felt awkward as my body seemed as if it was being pushed toward the floor. "Don't be scared Conner," Charlie commented. I was too busy looking up as the cables were pulled through the spinning pulleys overhead to reply to that remark. As each floor passed by I peered through the gate fence to catch a glimpse of what was stored on each level.

Once we reached the fourth floor, Mr. Bedford opened the gate and Charlie said, "Come on Conner I'll show you something." He ran to the nearest window with me a few short steps behind. From this vantage point we could see most of the town. Then we ran to the opposite end and looked out to the east side of the city where we could see Charlie's house.

As he identified each landmark, he smiled and for a moment I didn't mind him so much. Grandfather hollered for us and we ran back to the two men. We walked over to a closed door where a man stood outside guarding the entry. The man greeted Mr. Bedford and my grandfather with a handshake. They introduced me and told us to go on in.

We walked up a series of stairs to the fifth floor. There were already quite a few people standing in small groups talking to one another. Charlie took me around the room to meet some of the other boys and my grandfather made similar introductions. The men varied in age from very old to the young boys who were gathered together in one corner. A bell rang and all took their seats. Quickly the room full of people became quite hot. The men started to take off their coats and undo their ties for relief. Large electric fans hummed in the corners of the room. On a small stage in the front of the room stood a podium with the flag of South Carolina at one end and the standard of Dixie on the other. I looked around for the American Flag which stood in the far corner alone. I found this strange and began to inquire about it to my grandfather, but a large man walked over to the podium and pounded a gavel before I could ask. He yelled out for the Sergeant at Arms to confirm that the room was secure, and that all men present were Sons of the South. The Sergeant confirmed the question and remarked that all present were in fact members. "Then let us commence with the meeting," the man announced. "The first order of business is the introduction of new candidates." He stated.

My Grandfather stood up to say a few words about me. Then he announced that I would like to become a member of the boy's organization. I was asked to approach the stage. An older boy asked me to place my hand on a bible, and to raise my right hand.

I swore that day to never revel the secrets of the Sons of the South and that no mention of its existence ever be spoken. I swore an allegiance to the South, and to always honor the names of Jefferson Davis and General

Lee, and that the secrets of my brothers were also my secrets and to hold them as if they were my own. That I would always be beholding to my brothers, and to the great state of Georgia. If I broke that trust of the brotherhood I would be banished and befriended. So, help me God.

I was then turned to face the group of men as they all stood and applauded. I felt a strange sensation of acceptance and pride standing there. Then I saw my grandfather looking at me intently clapping. He broke into a smile which made me feel much better because I thought this would make him happy with me. The boys were sent to another part of the building, and one man was put in charge of us. He had two older boys practice handshakes, and show me secret signs. They even gave me a password to remember. This was all very intriguing to me.

The other boys worked on what appeared to be a pamphlet of some sort showing a calendar of events. Two boys operated a press and the others handled the paper. The press was rather loud, but the boys seemed to be having fun. I asked one of the boys what the pamphlets were for. He stated that they were announcements for the club. I wondered what the need was for so many copies because there seemed to be only about sixty people in the meeting. He told me that this club was only one of many in the area and that in all actuality the organization covered most of the South. Once the meeting was over, we all came back into the main hall with the men. The men were standing up shaking hands with one another. I overheard my grandfather speaking with one of the gentlemen about a council meeting the following night. I made inquiries of him on the subject because I liked the new boys I had met. He said tomorrow's meeting is only for select members and since the meetings were only monthly he would help find other ways to keep me involved.

Good to his word my involvement with the club began to increase to a twice week affair. I began to get to know the boys, and they seemed to like me. I unfortunately spent quite a bit of time with Charlie. He was always getting into some sort of trouble and pushing the limits of the rules. I was rather rule oriented by nature and his disregard was hard for me to take.

Over the summer my Grandfather had given me a job spending part of the week helping Mr. Dalton. He was a short man in his thirties and he ran one of my Grandfather's warehouses. The trucks would come into the docks and men loaded goods for shipment.

It was in that summer I began to understand how extensive my Grandfathers business interests really were. They covered not just the local area but some reached into other states. Our bond became stronger over that first summer. I realized he wasn't necessarily being hard on me. He was being disciplined about the work he did, and he expected me to the same.

SIX

The summer ended, and I returned to Bransford. I walked up the stairs in uniform ready to greet the boys, and to hear about their summer adventures. The first person to meet me in the hall was Wallace. He stayed at the school over the summer, and was more than ready for me to be back. He had been stuck with Lieutenant Whittington for the majority of the time with only a short break of relief, when his mother traveled down, and brought him home for a week's visit.

Whittington greeted me, and stood there while I unpacked. I was careless and he saw my knife lying amongst my belongings on the bed. He quickly spotted it and picked it up asking "Conner, how did a flunky like you get a knife like this?"

"It was my fathers," I stated reaching for it. He pulled it away before I could get it.

"Hold on," he said, "I just want to see something." He opened the knife's blade and read the Latin inscription. "Say this is just like my knife but the inscription is different." He pulled a knife from his pocket and opened it up. "This one is my fathers." He said, "I borrowed it. Look yours says Nex Cuspis on the blade and mine says Resurrecto Per Factum, which means renewal through action. Interesting they are identical other than that." He said looking at them.

"Regardless, you shouldn't have this, I better confiscate it." Tanner overheard the conversation, and once again came to my rescue.

"You have one sir." He stated. "If he's in trouble I guess you should be as well." Tanner was standing there next to his best friend Corporal Michael Peabody. Peabody chimed in, "Yes, sir that's pretty much the way it would run over in B Company. Lead by example!" Whittington gave a look and dropped my knife on the cot. Saying not a word, he just walked away.

Peabody, a member of B Company was bigger and stronger than Tanner. Those two were as thick as any two friends could be and would often compete with each other over the smallest of things. But push come to shove they watched each other's backs. If you made the mistake of tangling with one then you might as well figuring on having to handle the other. Tanner informed me that his promotion to Sergeant was going to take effect once the session started. He would be leaving to go live with the cadets in the Troop.

He sat down and said, "There's something else I need to tell you. They picked Private Styles from B Company to fill the other vacant spot. You lost out Conner. I'm sorry but at least he's a good cadet and there is always next year. Keep your grades up, follow orders, and I'm sure you'll be in the saddle before you know it."

I'm sure I looked upset, but I congratulated him and then looked at Whittington. Tanner recognized my concern and said, "Yeah, I know. I'm sorry Jimmy, I wish I could stay but this is a good opportunity for me."

"I know I'll be fine," I replied."

That year was beginning badly and I hoped it would change soon. I was upset that my summer with Grandfather had taken me out of the running for the Troop, and I blamed him. I saw nothing that I learned over the summer as being worth that lost opportunity. The good news was I still had Wallace. My new squad leader, Corporal Stephens, was newly promoted and did everything Whittington told him. Although likeable Stephens was the definition of a yes man, he would never put himself out there to save any of us from Whittington's wrath.

The one saving grace for the year came late in the fall. I was in a deep sleep and awakened by Sergeant Walker. He told me to quietly get ready, and to meet him in the hall. I did so and we walked outside and down past the stables. Once there I met with five other boys, Tanner, Peabody, Whittington, Wilcox and Williams. Not a word was said between us, but I was comforted by the fact that Tanner was with us.

We headed out into the darkness, and walked quietly out of the building and into the woods that stood behind it. It's a strange sensation being out in the woods at night. A sense of wilding happens to a young boy as he explores the darkness. The excitement was compounded by the risk of getting caught. I felt more alive than usual as I quietly took each step with a deliberate purpose making my way down the trail.

We stopped in an area facing a stone cliff about a half mile from the school grounds. A large flat rock rested at the bottom and Peabody took position on the far side of it. He was now clad in deer skin leggings. He had two red streaks of paint below each of his eyes. He then unsheathed his large knife and placed it next to the book on the rock. We all stood there quietly facing him. He nodded for me to step forward. Wilcox nudged me to approach the large rock alter. Peabody asked, "Conner you have taken an oath of secrecy before have you not?" I wasn't sure what to reply but I stated, "Yes." He looked at me then said, "We are all loyal Sons of the South." He moved his hand forward, and we shook hands in the fashion of the club. Peabody read from a book the following passage:

"You are about to take another step in your journey and become a member of the Kirby Smith Club. Stand at attention Private Conner." I quickly snapped to attention.

"Are you prepared for this step," he recited.

"Yes," I replied.

Then Peabody asked, "On what date did the beloved General Lee surrender at Appomattox?"

I smartly replied, "April 9, 1865."

"When was the great president Jefferson Davis captured by those Yankee dogs?"

"May 10, 1865 near Irwinville, Georgia." I replied!

"Very good," Peabody said as he smiled. He then corrected himself and became straight faced for the next statement.

"Five names are to be remembered within this group. The First: Lieutenant General Richard Taylor Commander of East Louisiana, Mississippi, and Alabama. He was the son of President Zachary Taylor and Brother in Law to Jefferson Davis. He surrendered May 4, 1865. The Second: John "Rest in Peace" Ford a Texas Ranger who fought in the last battle in the War for Southern Independence at Palmito Ranch Texas. The Third: Brigadier General Stand Watie a three quarter Cherokee and the last Confederate general officer to surrender on June 23, 1865 in the Choctaw Nations. The fourth: General Edmund Kirby Smith who surrendered the last unit May, 26 1865 and fled to Mexico with 300 men and then to Cuba and didn't swear Allegiance until Nov, 1865. And Finally: The CSS Shenandoah, after learning the war was over in August they still refused to give up the colors of the ship to the Union. They instead surrendered the ship to England Nov 6, 1865."

He continued to read from his book, "The General Kirby Smith Club is a society of brothers who remember that all is not lost until all options are exhausted and that you must dig deep within yourself until you can find no other option but surrender. This is your duty!"

Briefly pausing Tanner looked at me and asked, "Are you a man of duty, principles and honor Private Conner?"

"Sir I am," I replied.

Peabody stood tall, and all the boys came to attention. He then he yelled, "Where was the last battle of the War for Southern Independence fought?" I stood silently but all the boys yelled, "Palmito Ranch Texas" "And who won that battle?" Again all boys yelled, "The South!" The boys let out their best rebel yells and hollers.

"You may continue with us." Peabody stated. We all began talking and Tanner explained from that point on we were not to use ranks. That we are all equal in these woods, but once we were back at the barracks it was business as usual. He told me that many of the parents and grandparents that sent us to the school were associated with the Sons of the South, and that Bransford was part of that tradition.

We continued to walk to an old cabin. Once there I stood before a dilapidated structure that appeared as if it were about to cave in. The woods hadn't swallowed the old building just yet, but it appeared as if it was gaining on it by the moment. To me nothing could have been more perfect as a boys club hide out. The door creaked open and we stepped inside. Then Whittington, the keeper of the flame, quickly went to work starting a fire. He really didn't say much to me, but he did remark to one fact of interest. Standing by the fire he looked of over to me and said, "Nex Cuspis."

"What?" I asked.

"Nex Cuspis, the engraving on your contraband knife, it means deaths point." I looked at him questionably and replied, "Interesting thanks." He grumbled something as was his tendency and walked off.

Peabody pulled up a floor board and produced a box. Inside he placed the book from which he had earlier read.

He sat back down and held his knife as he spoke with one of the other boys. I asked Stevens about Peabody's Indian look. He told me that Peabody's family had a few members that fought for the cause. One was a full blooded Cherokee, who fought in one of the two battalions made up of Indians that sided with the Confederacy.

Stevens went on and said, "That's one of the things you do in the Kirby Smith Club is to find your connections to the past. Do you know of any?"

"Well, I really don't." I replied.

Stevens stood up and said. "Gentlemen I would like to announce that the new inductee Conner has no recollection of ever being told, notified or otherwise that he has a relative that fought for the Southern cause. I say we here by task my new brother to find out!"

"Aye," said the boys.

Tanner said, "Motion approved Stevens."

Wilcox chimed in saying, "Be careful though you might find out you have some Yankee blood running through your veins like I did."

Peabody ran his hands threw Wilcox's hair making it stand on end. Then said, "Ah, brother we just let you in because that relative was a collaborator for the Cause. He wasn't really a Yankee."

All the boys laughed.

I looked at Peabody, and asked him, "Do you know any Indians? I mean. Do you have any family that is Indian that you've met?"

He listened to me stumble over my own words and replied, "No, my grandmother was full blooded, but she died before I was born. She met my grandfather when he worked in the mountains of North Carolina not far from the reservation. They ran off, and she assumed a life as a white when they moved down to southern Georgia. My mother said she spoke to her about her past, but it was kept a family secret. She said that my grandmother's only regret was not seeing her family back home one last time. I think one day, I might do that for her. I mean, you know go see my Injun cousins." He said smiling.

The Kirby Smith Club had a long tradition at Bransford, and the boys brought in new members to balance out the ones that would be leaving soon. We met when we could, but never more than twice a month. No formal announcement just a simple signal was made. It was one everyone would see daily, because in the far corner of the mess hall, encased in a frame, hung Sergeant Patterson's flag, bullet hole and all. A golden lanyard hung from the frame, and a knot would be tied in the lanyard signaling when the meeting was called to order.

One thing was true once we got back to the campus it was business as usual. Whittington gave me no slack; Kirby Smith or not.

"Another event took place that bares some remark in this story." stated Mr. Conner. "In 1917 a monument was started. The construction was delayed because of ration cuts during the First World War, but restarted in 1922 and finally completed 1924. The monument is located in Fairview Kentucky. There, a 351 foot obelisk pays its respects to Jefferson Davis."

"There is a monument to Jefferson Davis? I asked.

"Of course there is he was the president of the Confederate States of America."

"That somehow seems a little odd." I stated.

"There ya go, thinking like a Yankee again Campbell."

"But that was built over fifty five years after the Civil War had ended."I stated.

"It seems that the dream of Southern Independence was still held strong in the hearts of some people even after all those years."

"See it all started with Simon Bolivar Buckner. He proposed the idea at a reunion of the Orphan Brigade."

"The Orphan Brigade?" I asked.

"They were Kentuckians orphaned due to their state legislature's lack of commitment to the cause, and they as individual citizens fought for the Confederacy. The unit was formed and a Major General by the name of John C Breckinridge was named commander. Breckinridge had been a Vice President of the United States under the 14th president James Buchanan. He was the youngest Vice President inaugurated at the age of thirty six. Interestingly enough he ran against Lincoln for the presidency, but once the bells of secession rang he answered by following his calling to South. Another later commander Benjamin Hardin Helm was the brother in law to Abraham Lincoln. The unit served with great distinction, and finally surrendered to Sherman during his march to the sea.

Still puzzled I commented, "I never knew there was a monument to Jefferson Davis."

"If you sit here with me everyday no telling what you may learn Campbell. Richmond, Virginia has a monument that bears his name too. Even a highway that ran from Washington D.C. to California was to be named after him. Did you know that after a short exile he came back to the South? He was to be tried for treason, but he was considered an expert on constitutional law, and many feared his proposed argument for secession might cause more trouble. So, they never brought him to trial. Think about that for a minute Campbell.

While I'm on a roll, General Lee is respected by both sides as a hero of nobility and gentlemanly conduct. Hardly a man has ever walked this earth with more dignity than he. He requested his U.S. citizenship be reinstated after the war. It wasn't until years after his death during Gerald Ford's Presidency that it was given to him. He even had a U.S. submarine named after him in 1963. Did you know that he was asked to take command of the Union army, before the war?"

"I had no idea." I replied.

"Best you stay awhile then and learn a few things."

SEVEN

The semester had ended and once again I came back to Shadow Wood. Even though the Troop remained a primary goal I was actually looking forward to my summer. I now had friends through the club, and working that summer seemed a welcome change from the routines of Bransford.

After a brief stay at Shadow Wood, I was told by Grandfather to pack my belongings. The following morning we traveled north of Savannah and then into the countryside. I wasn't sure exactly what business he had in that part of the country, but he told me I would find out soon enough. We finally stopped at a small run down house in the middle of nowhere with a black woman standing on the porch. My Grandfather stepped outside leaving me sitting alone inside his vehicle.

The woman greeted my Grandfather with a hug and kiss on the cheek. She laughed as they spoke. My curiosity was peaked, and I cracked the window. Their voices were barely audible, but I still strained to hear them anyway, and made out what I could.

"This is getting to be a tradition with you Conner men, now isn't it." She commented.

My grandfather replied, "Well, now Miss Rose it's more than a tradition it's a life altering event in a young man's life. I suspect the lady is intact as agreed."

"Yes, she is and I've had offers much higher than yours. That's all right though Mr. Conner I feel the same as you. The first time is something you should keep for yourself besides it's like I said, a tradition."

"May I see the young lady before I head down the road," My grandfather asked.

"Sally," she yelled. "Come on out here so Mr. Conner can get a good look at you."

A girl walked out on the porch wearing a blue dress. She was light skinned tall and well-shaped. I looked away, and then stared in her direction through the corner of my eye. My Grandfather asked me to step out of the car and come over. I opened the door, and walked toward them.

He said, "Miss Rose this is James Conner my grandson"

"My, what a fine lad this one is." She said as she walked around eyeing me. "He has the look of his father doesn't he? He has that strong Conner chin just like his grandfather. He'll do fine," she said. "Sally, help this boy with his things." I stood there looking at my grandfather.

"You're going to spend some time here with these folks. They are long time friends of the family. I'll be back in a few days. While you're here do as Miss Rose tells you."

I really had no idea what was going on. Sally who had yet to move a muscle stared at me with a look of disapproval about her face. I could hear Miss Rose and my Grandfather continue to talk as my foot reached for the front porch step.

She said, "We'll make a man out of him. Would you like to stay for dinner maybe breakfast Mr. Conner? Like old times." She asked smiling. He just looked at her and smiled back.

"And how come you don't visit like you used to on one of your trips down this way?" Rose asked.

"Miss Rose when a man gets to be my age such foolishness isn't as important as it used to be." He remarked.

She stood there with her hands on her hips and said, "When a man gets to be your age such foolishness is exactly what he needs. That way he can be reminded of what it was like to be young and foolish!" Grandfather walked to his automobile waving good bye.

She passed by me and said, "Come on in boy you better get settled. Have you had dinner yet?"

"Ummmm No, ma'am." I replied.

"What's wrong Jimmy? I figured you'd be a well spoken boy considering your family. A cat got your tongue? Are you a James-a Jimmy? What exactly would you like to be called?"

"Either is fine ma'am," I replied.

"Hmmm, have a seat there at the table I want to get acquainted with you Jimmy, James. What is it that I am to call you?" She again remarked.

I sat down and said," Miss Rose, Jimmy will do."

"Jimmy it is then," said Miss Rose. "A man has to know his mind and his name is his calling card."

"Yes ma'am I'll keep that in mind," I replied.

"Young Jimmy, tell me about yourself. I heard your Pa passed sometime back."

"Yes, ma'am he did"

"And that your Ma did too."

"Yes, ma'am she did."

"Um um umm that is a shame. I met your Pa years back. He was a fine young man, very handsome too. So, now tell me do you go to that school the Conner men attend?"

I was very puzzled this woman seemed to know things about me and my family.

"Yes, ma'am I do.

Sally placed the plates in front of us, and sat at the end of the table quietly.

"Do you make good grades at the school, and learn all kinds of good manners and such?"

"Yes, ma'am," I replied.

"That's one thing I like about military boys. At least they know how to be polite. Even though they don't always act that way, they at least learnt some manners."

Sally sat there not saying a word. Miss Rose looked over at her and said, "Jimmy we've been sitting here all this time, and you haven't once told my niece how pretty she is."

Once again I was taken back, "Yes ma'am."

"Yes, ma'am what? She's pretty or yes, ma'am you didn't say so?"

"Yes, ma'am she is pretty," I stated too embarrassed to look in Sally's direction.

She stood up, walked over to me and placed a hand on the top of my head and the other on the bottom of my chin, turning my head in Sally's direction and said, "Not to me I know how pretty she is. Say it to her, Jimmy. There's a place for polite, and this isn't it."

I looked at Sally and said, "You are very pretty."

"There now Jimmy, first lesson. If you have a chance to tell a pretty lady she's pretty you best do it. Some other boy will come along and say it. Then he'll sweep a young pretty thing right out from underneath you. There is a time to be humble and quiet, and a time to speak your mind. Women like a man who knows what he wants. Not one stuttering around trying to find the words."

Sally just sat there and looked at her food. Miss Rose sat in her chair leaned back and said, "Say it again Jimmy. Say Sally is pretty." She looked at Sally who was looking down and said sharply, "Sally look at that boy when he's talking to you." Sally slowly lifted her head.

"Now say it once more and look into her eyes." Again I said, "You're very pretty." This time the words came out with ease.

"Once more Jimmy. This time tell her she's beautiful. Tell her something nice about herself."

I looked at Sally trying to find the right thing to say to her and said, "Miss Sally you really are very pretty and your eyes, they..... they dance Miss Sally."

Flush with embarrassment I looked down.

Sally looked away and smiled then looked back at me. She spoke for the first time since I was there. "Thank you Jimmy."

Miss Rose paused while looking at me and said, "Very good Jimmy. You Conner men have a way. I knew you had it in ya. Sally your eyes dance. That was very nice Jimmy, very nice indeed." She stood up and walked out of the room smiling.

Sally turned the radio on, and cleared the table. I asked if could help with the dishes, and pumped some water into the basin. We stood shoulder to shoulder while she softly sang the words of the songs on the radio. I didn't say a word as I dried the dishes. That night I gathered my belongings, and asked where I would sleep. The home was small only four rooms in all. One room was for Miss Rose the other for Sally and her older sister, who still hadn't arrived yet.

Sally took me to her room and told me to place my things on the other bed. I protested and asked, "The couch will be fine anyway isn't your sister going to sleep here?"

"Miss Rose's orders are for you to sleep in Ruth's bed and that's that. You're a soldier aren't you? You should know how to follow orders." I stood their still holding my bags and asked, "Sally, why am I here? It doesn't seem right."

"Why because we're colored," she asked?

"Is the white boy too good to be around colored folk?"

"Not at all Sally," I said. "That's not it. It just doesn't make sense to me for me to be stuck way out here."

"Maybe your Grandpa thinks you should spend some time with women folk instead of being around boys everyday. Maybe he's worried you'll start liking boys or something." Then she looked at me and said, "You do like girls don't you Jimmy?"

"Of course!" I quickly replied.

I reluctantly put my belongings on Ruth's bed. She asked me to step out of the room so she could change into her night gown. I changed in the living room. When she was ready Sally yelled for me to come in. I reluctantly entered the room. It was dark all but for one oil lamp dimly flickering in the corner. My bare feet cautiously felt their way across the planked floor through the darkness. Sally had already pulled the covers back making it easy for me to just slide in. She was lying in bed saying her prayers. Once she finished she asked, "Jimmy do you need to sleep with light in the room. Are you afraid of the dark?"

"No." I replied, "Of course not."

"Well, then how come you didn't blow out that light?" She asked.

I started to get up and she said, "Oh, I'll get it Jimmy," and she crawled out of bed and walked toward it. She stood between me and the lamp. I could almost see her naked form through the thin layer of clothing that made up her night gown. She then blew the lamp out. Darkness covered the room, and I couldn't see her any longer. I heard her crawl into bed and she told me, "good night."

The next morning I woke to Ruth standing in the doorway looking at me. As my eyes cleared she said, "A white boy sleeping in my bed and a thin gangly one that." Sally woke up and said, "Jimmy don't mind her she's probably still drunk"

I was trying to gather myself with all this banter going on when Ruth said, "Mighty lanky boy for the first time, if you ask me." Miss Rose walked in and took Ruth by the arm leading her away from the door. "Ruth," she said. "Hush your mouth, and leave those two alone." She led her outside and scolded her. Sally was already up, and walked to the door, just ignoring the situation as if it was a daily ritual. I dressed, and asked Miss Rose what I could do to be helpful. She pointed me in the direction of the shed out back and said, "Check the hens unless you're scared to get your hands dirty."

I retorted, "No, ma'am I was raised with a hen house out back." To which she remarked, "Well, now aren't you a typical Conner man."

Having no idea what she meant by the comment I walked out the door and went out to the shed. The chickens scampered around my feet as I grabbed the eggs, and about the time I was ready, Sally yelled for me to come back up to the house.

She looked at the basket full of eggs and said, "Good job for a rich city boy."

"I'm not a city boy," I remarked.

"You look like and act like a city boy! "

"Well, I'm not. I was raised on a dirt road just like you!"

"My, oh my, you city boys sure do get in a huff don't you?" She said with a smile.

Embarrassed I wondered why being called a city boy bothered me so much; why it bothered me so much more when Sally said it.

We went inside and sat down at the table. I felt very out of place with the three women but more than that I was outnumbered as they continued to razz me about everything under the sun. There was a point when the focus shifted from me to Ruth. I started to laugh, and looked in Sally's direction. In that moment it seemed as if everything was in slow motion as she moved the fork from the plate to her mouth. She seemed so happy sitting at that table smiling and laughing. It was then that I realized that none of the razzing meant anything. These women who were at each other's throats and mine really didn't mean a word of it. It was simply the way they communicated. I expected this from the boys at Bransford but not from a family of women. The notion was foreign to me and took some getting used to.

I helped Sally clear the table. Rose and Ruth were headed into town. They left us on our own which I didn't mind too much. Sally and I walked out in the back to tend the animals. She asked me questions about life at the academy, and I asked her about hers here in the country. I told her about my interest in the troop. She looked at me, and asked me if I could ride.

"Sure I can." I replied.

"Sure you can?" She stated. "I don't believe you. How do expect to be in the cavalry and not be able to ride?"

"Well, I've been on horses," I retorted, "Just not very often. They will show me all I need to know once I get in the Troop."

"Best if you have an idea of what you're doing before you get there don't you think? Come on I'll show you." She stated.

"How do you know about horses?" I asked.

"When I was younger one of Ruth's men friends taught me." She replied.

We went out to the barn where a beautiful bay filly with black socks and mane named Babe stood. I asked her how she came by such a pretty horse. She told me that a man owed Aunt Rose money a few years back. Babe was how he paid her, and that she was to be sold soon.

She handed me the bridle. Then folded her arms and said for me to get Bade ready to ride. I struggled with the bridle finally situating it in place. She climbed on the fence, hopped up on the back of babe and then motioned for me to climb on. I protested and asked, "I'm in back?"

"Yes," she said, "Unless you're afraid." Feeling challenged I climbed on placing my hands on her waist as we rode out of the barn. She took the horse through the paces: the walk, trot, canter explaining the rhythm of each.

I tried to pay attention, but I couldn't help myself because my focus was on her alone, and how she felt in my hands. That day we spent hours in the field behind her house. We came in only briefly to grab food for lunch, and then headed back out. She had me take the reins, and she climbed behind me. I could feel her close to my back with her hands touching my waist.

We rode out to the woods behind her house and then walked the horse in the shallows of a stream to water her. In one motion Sally jumped down from Babe kicking her shoes off in the process. She was barefoot before hitting the ground. She waded in the water while I sat on a rock on the bank. I watched them both as the water flowed over their legs. The light filtered through the trees as they waded in the knee deep water. Somewhere between the light and the shadows they walked in water that shimmered with a sparkling light reflecting below them. It was in that moment that I felt for the first time the sensation of love. That's how it always was for me, no matter who was the focus, there was always this moment that just grabbed me, and in that small fraction of time I just knew.

We followed the stream on horseback and found a field to take a break while we ate. We both fell back in the tall grass, and talked while looking up in the sky. Then Sally asked me if I had ever kissed a girl.

I said, "Sure, plenty of them."

She smiled and said, "So, you know girls like you know horses, Jimmy Conner?" I sat up with my arms on my knees and picked the grass and said, "Okay Sally, I've never kissed a girl." There was a moment of silence. Then she crawled over to me, and put her face close to mine and asked, "Jimmy would you like to kiss me?"

I nodded and kissed her, more of a grazing blow actually, one which brought a smile to her face. I quickly looked down and asked, "What did I do? Did I do it wrong or something?"

"No, Jimmy you kiss nice. I'd like you to do it again." She placed her hand on my check, and gently pulled my head to hers. I could feel the heat of her breath, and then her moist lips touched mine. We held the embrace longer this time. "Much better," she commented. I agreed and we spent an hour or so in that field before we headed back.

When we arrived at home, Miss Rose and Ruth were already there. We walked in and Ruth looked at Sally and said, "Spending the day all alone with that boy. Did you make him a man yet?"

"Be quiet," Sally snapped back.

"Awe, you probably didn't even kiss him yet, did you!"

Miss Rose yanked at Ruth's ear and told her to hush. Ruth looked down and continued to peel the potato that was in her hand.

"I don't know what all the fuss is over this boy and her. Sure didn't have this much fuss with mine," commented Ruth.

"Yours had nothing to do with me only because you wouldn't listen. You gave yours for free to that Lawrence boy in the barn. Cause you loved him and were going to be together forever! Now where is he? I'll tell you, living in Charleston with that Burrows girl." She snapped.

Both Ruth and Sally we're mad and once again fighting with one another. In hopes of changing the subject I asked, "Miss Rose do you need me to do anything?"

They all paused for a moment and Sally spoke up saying, "Jimmy and I are going for a walk." She led me out of the room while we took a break from all the commotion. Unfortunately, the break was too brief, and we reluctantly came back to make dinner. The tone between the two women had changed and a little peace was in the house. After dinner I was asked to leave so the women could all bathe in a tub that I brought into the kitchen.

I sat outside for quite some time on the porch reading a book when Miss Rose yelled for me. I walked in and Sally was in the tub, her front was covered by a towel but her back was naked and bare. I acted as if I wasn't looking when Miss Rose asked me to get something from the top shelf for her. I had no idea why she needed it at that moment. But I was compelled and when I turned I saw Sally standing there with her naked back facing me. Miss Rose started pouring warm water over her. I handed her the box, and walked out of the room to the porch.

A short while later Miss Rose yelled for me to come in the kitchen and she said, "Now it's your turn."

I retorted, "A bath here!"

She said, "Yes, or do you city boys not take baths."

"Yes, ma'am city boys take baths."

Then she said, "Get them clothes off and Sally will bathe you."

I began to protest, "No, ma'am I can bath myself just fine."

"Either me, Ruth or Sally is to give you a proper bath."

"Oh, I'd love to give that skinny white boy a bath," commented Ruth.

I hung my head down in defeat, "Sally would do fine ma'am." Rose and Ruth left smiling as they headed for the porch.

I told Sally to turn around and took off my clothes then stepped into the water. Looking down I saw only a few suds floating on the clear water. Fearing the embarrassment close at hand, I asked for more soap.

"There is plenty of soap Jimmy." She replied.

I positioned the foam as best I could. Sally began to wash my back with a brush that was fit for a horse.

"Sally I need that skin back there are you trying to completely rub it off?" I asked.

"Quit being a baby, city boy." "

"Being a city boy has nothing to do with this. Are you mad at me or what?"

"No, I'm not mad." She said. "You just seem to have quite a bit of dirt on your back. Have you been rolling around in the fields with some pretty girl?"

I laughed and said, "Maybe I have Miss Sally, maybe a very pretty one indeed."

She switched from the brush to a cloth and gently cleaned my neck and behind my ears, and then my hair. She looked down and handed me the cloth and said, "I bet you can do the front on your own now can't you?"

"Yes!" I exclaimed, "Yes, I can, thank you."

"Stand up." She commanded.

"No, Sally I can do this part too"

"Aunt Rose!!!" She yelled.

"Ok ok I'll stand up. No, looking though, hand me a towel."

"You got nothing I wanna see, Jimmy Conner. You can trust me on that." She said.

Miss Rose and Ruth were out on the porch sipping homemade hooch of some sort. While Sally and I were getting ready for bed I grabbed a book and asked, "Sally would you mind if I keep a lamp on." She replied, "Only if you read out loud, Jimmy." I considered that a fair trade. I sat up and began read to her. I would occasionally look over to her direction to check if she had fallen asleep. She laid there facing me. From time to time she would open her eyes and smile. Eventually, I finished the chapter and blew out the light. A short time later I heard Rose and Ruth stumble in. I figured they would be quite a sight. Thankfully, I had blown out the lamp, and they didn't bother us.

Late that night I felt Sally's hand on my shoulder and her warm breath on my ear. She asked me to follow, and we climbed out the window running into the field behind her house. The night air was cool and the grass wet beneath our feet. We ran to a shed, and Sally produced a blanket from behind it. We unrolled it on the ground, and laid there holding hands. I held her close as we looked out into the night sky.

She told me that she would often sneak outside, and lay there alone for hours wondering about all the people who would be looking up at that same sky. She pointed up to a star and said, "That star there is mine!" "Why that one, and who exactly gave you a star?" I asked.

"See those three stars in a row? The one on top is mine and as a matter of fact someone did give it to me. When I was small I asked an old man about those stars. He told me that those were the most important stars in the sky. The bottom one is what was, the middle represents what is, and the top star, that star is most important because it's what could be. If you live following that star then when life gets hard, you just remember what could be and try your best to let it guide you." I asked him, "If I could have it and he gave it to me."

"Oh," I said, "Simple enough may I have a star?"

"Yes, you can Jimmy. I'll give you hmmmm that one." And she pointed to star very near to the other three.

"That's a nice one and why did you pick that particular one?" I asked.

She said, "It's bright like you, it's white like you and it's close to mine. So, when you see yours you'll always think of me being close to you like we are now."

I didn't know what to say so I leaned over and kissed her. I laid back and we didn't say a word we just looked up into the night sky until it was time to go back in.

The following morning I woke up early, before anyone in the house. It was one of those mornings where you're immediately wide awake. I laid there for a moment looking across the room watching Sally. She was sleeping on her back. I could see her stomach move as she breathed. She looked peaceful and pretty just laying there. I decided I'd better get up, and hung my feet over the edge of the bed. I looked down and curled my toes as I reached to touch the floor. I inched along the planked floors, and made my way to the window trying not to make a sound. I looked out over the road and the field in front of the little house. The light of the morning had already peaked over the trees, and I could see the steam rise across the fields.

It came to mind that the rooster hadn't as of yet let out his morning shriek. I slipped back across the room and laid back down. I closed my eyes and tried to go back to sleep. A few minutes later Sally began to stir. I kept my eyes closed, and I could hear her feet hit the floor. She began to walk toward me, and I could feel her presence as she stood next to my bed. She laid her blanket over mine, and lifted the corner of both. I opened my eyes, then slid back toward the wall to let her in. She climbed in and laid there with her back against my chest. She grabbed my arm, and pulled it across her stomach. I laid there with her hair in my face and her body next to mine, unable or just unwilling to move a muscle.

Eventually, we climbed out of bed. It was still early when Sally took me out to the old barn, and we prepared for our morning ride. Now, she put me in the lead with her hands wrapped around me. I began to feel my confidence grow with both the horse and my passenger. We talked about everything in those fields, but mostly our hopes and dreams.

When we arrived back at the house Miss Rose and Ruth were getting ready to leave for town. It was a Thursday night and Ruth had business to attend to. Sally told me that we had the house to ourselves. I helped her with the chores and then we cooked dinner. We listened to music and Sally would sing along. It was strange to sit at a table alone with a young woman, even Sally. We had the entire house to ourselves, and spent most of that night either out on the porch or later out on the blanket looking at the stars.

Sally and I had called it a night. She was lying in my bed when we heard a vehicle pull in front of the house. Ruth opened the door and stepped in. I heard the loud steps of another person, then two of them rustling about the room. Sally put on her robe to find out what was going on. When she left the room I heard Ruth say that Aunt Rose would be home later, and that she needed a place to entertain her friend.

That comment angered Sally and she said, "Not in here and not to-night." Ruth said, "You ain't got that boy yet? Ah, you ain't ever going to get him." I walked over to the door and peaked out through a small crack. Sally's back was to me with Ruth standing there with one hand on her hip the other holding the hand of a large colored man who seemed to be trying to leave.

Sally and Ruth continued to banter back and forth. Finally Sally spun in my direction, then headed back toward our room. I could hear Ruth say to the man, "It's all quiet now come in here to the couch and sit with me for awhile." Sally laid down in her bed with her arms folded all in a huff. A few minutes later I walked over to her, and asked what was wrong. She scooted aside, and I sat next to her. Within moments I could hear moans from the next room. I looked over at Sally, and she looked at me and we both smiled.

She got up and led me to the door. I was afraid to look but curiosity got the best of me as Sally pushed me closer to the door. I could see the lovers on the couch, their nakedness in between the shadows of the dimly lit room. I stood there for a moment then I could feel Sally's hand on my waist pulling me away from the door. We both faced each other and smiled. We crawled into my bed, and whispered to each other.

"Sally they aren't even married!" I said.

"There would be a wedding every week for Ruth if that was the rule."

"It's wrong to do that, and not be married." I remarked.

"It likely is Jimmy, but it must be very enjoyable because men come looking for it all the time." She replied.

"Have you?" I asked.

"No, I haven't Jimmy but I know who I would do it with if I did."

I didn't know what to say. Then she whispered, "Let's go take an-other look before the ruckus is over." I smiled and we both crept toward the door.

It was much later when Miss Rose came home. I heard her make the man sleeping on the couch with Ruth leave. I then heard her crack our door. She looked in on us, and I was afraid she would see Sally in my bed. She didn't say anything, not a word, and to my surprise she just closed the door.

The next morning Sally cooked breakfast for me, and we sat at the table quietly and ate. Ruth only once peaked out over the top of the couch, and asked for Sally to keep the noise down. I laughed, and she retorted, "You're too skinny white boy" as she laid back down. I never did actually see Rose that morning.

I had only been with Sally's family a few days and began to feel a routine, and I liked routines. The mornings consisted of chores, and riding. In the evenings I would read to her and later we would sneak out and stare at the stars. I especially liked waking up with Sally near me. I had expected none of this, but now I wasn't looking forward to my Grandfathers return.

Later that day we rode back out through the fields I began to ask Sally questions. One's that I wasn't sure if I wanted to hear the answers to or not.

"Do you know why I'm here?"

"Why do you think you're here?" She replied gruffly.

"I'm not sure, but I think it has something to do with you?"

"Do you now," she retorted. "And why exactly would that be?" She replied coarsely.

"I don't know," I replied then dropped the subject. Maybe I just didn't want to hear her reply. She didn't say much on the ride home. But as we rode up to the corner of her fields she said, "I have dreams Jimmy. I don't want to be the wife of some sharecropper, and live out my life here. Do you know why I like listening to you read at night?" She asked.

"Well, Miss Sally that's because I'm a wonderful reader." I replied mockingly.

"A wonderful reader? Really now Jimmy, how can you be so wrong?

I just grinned not saying a word, and listened to her speak. "No, Jimmy it's because I hear in those words the places I want to see and the things I want do. I have a cousin who sings. She has made a life for herself in New Orleans and that's where I want to go. I want out of here Jimmy. I'll never be happy here. I'll end up like Ruth."

"And how are you going to get to New Orleans?" I asked. She sat there quietly. "I have a way. It's something Aunt Rose and I worked out."

"A plans a good thing to have Sally," and I left it at that.

We rode back to the barn, unbridled the horse and brushed her down. She said, "Jimmy you're riding real good now. I think you'll make a wonderful cavalry soldier if you keep working at it."

"I hope. That's what I want." I said. "And you'll make a real fine singer one day."

"Let's go up to the house to clean up." She replied.

When we made it back up to the house Miss Rose and Ruth were getting ready to go back into town. Ruth looked as if she was still drunk, but Miss Rose was fit as a fiddle and dressed up for the night. Miss Rose called out a list of chores for both Sally and I to have completed. I didn't mind and strangely Miss Rose leaned over and hugged me before walking out the door and closing it behind her. She then opened the door again, and looked squarely at Sally and said, "Mr. Conner will be coming to-morrow to take Jimmy back."

I sighed deeply even though I knew it was coming. We ate and then together we worked on our list of chores all the while the music played. At one point Sally stopped, bowed and asked if I would dance with her. I had never danced and once again Sally showed me something new. She told me to listen to the beat, and we shuffled around the room laughing at my clumsiness. "I'll need much more time to show you how to dance than I did to teach you how to ride."

She asked me to bring in the tub, and to fill the stove with wood so she could warm some water. While we waited for the water to warm she remarked, "This is our last night. We should go outside and find our stars." We ran outside in the night air looking up at the sky. I should have been sad about leaving, but I was in the moment, and was just glad to be with her.

Once the water was warm enough she filled the tub. She asked me to undressed and step in. I of course was still shy about being naked, and asked her to turn around. Once again she said, "You got nothing I want to see!" and then she turned around crossing her arms in front of her. She reached for the brush, and I cringed when I saw her carry it over. She smiled and said, "I've got to get you clean, but I'll use the wash cloth this time."

She started washing my back. I closed my eyes, and sat there somewhere between embarrassment and thoroughly enjoying the moment. Knowing I was completely calm she poured a cool pitcher of water over my head breaking my peaceful moment. She laughed, and then began to scrub my head with the homemade soap that they used. She handed me a towel, and I dried myself. I was facing the opposite direction as her. When I turned around she was standing there naked, and kissed me on the lips.

I was stunned and she grabbed my hand and led me to the tub as she stepped in and crouched down. "You wash my back now," she asked. I started at the center of her back as she lifted her hair for me. I gently washed her neck and shoulders. Her neck was long and thin. Her dark skin contrasted with the soap in my hands.

"Jimmy please don't get my hair too wet it will take too long to dry on this night."

"No Sally, I won't." I replied.

I could see over her shoulder and looked down at her body. Trying not stare or bring attention to what I was doing I continued to wash and rinse her. All at once she stood up and said, "I'm done now."

I of course looked away and she said, "Jimmy I've seen all of you and wouldn't be fair if you didn't see all of me now turn around." I stood there for a moment and slowly turned in her direction.

"It's moments like that, Campbell, an old man can still picture even after all this time." He said.

Sally then took me by the hand, and led me into her room. We crawled into her bed and she squeezed up close to me. I was honestly terrified but I couldn't keep from looking at her. She said, "Jimmy, no matter what happens or you what you hear or think I want you to know that I'm glad it was you." She then pulled me on top of her and nature took its course.

Afterwards, we laid there for a moment. I was in disbelief at what had just happened. She on the other hand was very sure of herself, and stood up to put on her night clothes.

"You better get dressed so we don't fall asleep all naked." I leaned up and asked, "Sally, are you ok?"

"Yes," and she laughed at me for asking.

I said, "I mean shouldn't we get married or something?"

"Of course not," she replied. "I don't have to go through this again, and tell you about all the husbands Ruth should have then. Do I?"

"Well no, but I think we should do something shouldn't we?" I asked.

"Yes, we should," she said.

"What?" I asked.

"We should go to sleep."

I put my night clothes on and climbed back in bed where Sally was waiting. She placed her head on my chest while I laid there staring up at the ceiling thinking about what all had happened that night. Sally quickly drifted off to sleep, but I couldn't. Instead I laid there caressing her arm just looking at her memorizing her every feature.

The next morning I noticed Sally wasn't in the room with me. I put on some clothes to find her. I found her in the kitchen cooking. I sat at the table thinking about what had happened last night. It came to mind that nothing for me had really changed, as I thought it would. I wasn't taller or hairier. I didn't feel any more like a man than I did the day before. I was puzzled by it all, and then I looked over at Sally, and thought maybe something had changed. Sally seemed more to me than before. I couldn't peg it exactly, but something deeper it seemed. I didn't have much time to ponder it.

A moment later Miss Rose walked in; she tugged at Ruth's feet which were hanging off the end of the couch. "Get up and get some breakfast in you." She bellowed.

Ruth shouted back, "Auntie, no! It can't be morning so soon," as she covered her face.

I sat there not saying a word. Finally, everyone made it to the table. Ruth sat to my right with her face down in one hand while she moved the food on her plate back and forth with the other. She tried to eat only nibbles instead of bites. Rose sat to my left, and she was only in slightly better shape.

She said, "I'm not sure this getting old suits me! But I don't look the worse for wear compared to you Ruth. Can't you keep up with your Aunt Rose?" I looked at Sally across the table. She didn't look at me, she just sat there quietly. Rose leaned back in her chair looking at Sally, then me. I immediately looked down.

"Sally," she said, "I wonder what happened here last night?" Sally looked at her disapprovingly then stood up and stepped back from the table. "Aunt Rose do you want anything to eat?" she asked.

"Uh huh," Rose looked and nodded. Ruth quickly became aware of the situation and looked over at Sally and said, "About time you earned your keep around here Sally." Sally quickly said, "Ruth Hush!"

Ruth looked at me and said, "Jimmy, got to be a man last night." I looked back down and finished my last bite. Then I stood up, and walked away from the table too embarrassed to speak.

Sally snapped, "Hush now Ruth!!"

I walked outside as I heard them argue back and forth. I believe a dish flew or fell off the table because of the commotion. All I knew for sure was that Sally was in the middle of it. When Sally came out she was in a huff. She grabbed my hand, and we both ran for the barn.

I asked Sally what was wrong. She said, "I've had it with Ruth."

"Sally, are you mad at me? Should I not have done that to you last night?" I asked.

"You didn't do anything to me that I wasn't wanting you to do? It's just….. I don't know, Jimmy, I wasn't supposed to feel like this, and now you're leaving."

I hung my head down and said, "I know, I was thinking about that last night."

Miss Rose was just outside the gate and yelled for us both. We walked up together, and she said, "I'm not sure what I'm going to do now. I got word that your grandfather has been delayed, and won't be here for a few more days. Sounds like trouble for me but that's up to him."

She turned away and walked back inside. We both tried to hold back our excitement, and walked back to the barn smiling at one another. As soon as we turned the corner I grabbed Sally and kissed her.

We stood there for a moment and I said, "Sally, I have to tell you that I couldn't have heard any better news than that." She put her head on my chest and said, "Jimmy you have to listen to me and not let either of them know that we're happy about your grandfather being delayed." I looked at her and said, "But they didn't seem to mind about last night."

"If you want more of last night its best you act like you don't like me all that much," she replied.

"Oh, I liked last night. Whatever you think is best," I told her.

The extended days gave Sally and I more time together. Every chance we had we used to the fullest. The days were spent on horseback while nights were filled with the stars and each other. That Monday, Rose caught us kissing in the barn. She said, "Your grandfather better get here soon." She pulled Sally aside dragging her toward the gate. I heard her say, "Don't you go and fall in love with this boy. We had a deal and the road you're on will only lead to hurt." Sally yelled, "Leave us alone," and ran back to the barn. Rose headed up to the house in a huff. The horse was already saddled, and she hopped on and said, "Ride Jimmy, just ride!"

We rode for about an hour, and didn't say a word. She just held me tightly as if she wasn't going to let me go. We stopped in a cool spot where we could water the horse and listen to the creek trickle by. She stood there wading in the ankle deep water.

"Jimmy can you keep a secret?"

"Yes Sally, I'm getting good at keeping secrets." I replied.

"It's not really as secret as much as it's something I need to tell you." She replied. "I wasn't going too, but everything is so different."

Curious I said, "Go ahead Sally. It's all safe with me." She kept her head down, gently sliding her feet back and forth through the water.

"Aunt Rose was raised in the house where we are staying now. When she was old enough she left and told her ma that she was never coming back. She had big dreams, and she was heading up north as soon as she had enough money. She walked up the road to town and started looking for work. It was just after the war, and she said times were very hard here in the South. She walked in front of a large house and saw a lot of men and scantily dressed women standing about. She knew what kind of place it was, and she stood there looking back down the road from where she had just come. She said that first step was hard, but she wasn't going back. And she ran up those stairs with her head held high. She talked to the Madam, and they struck a deal. The Union soldiers were garrisoned just outside of town. There was a lot of money that could be had for a young pretty girl. She was started with the wealthiest men in town. She said they couldn't wait to try her. Some men came from other cities even other states. In time she saved enough to head up north. But when the madam got sick she asked her to buy a share and my aunt had a choice. Follow her dream or stay and make money. She chose to stay and bought into the house becoming a part owner. Before long she had the finest house in the area, and owned the whole thing out right. It was decorated tapestries from foreign countries like India and Pakistan. She even had white girls working for her. My Ma worked there, but got sick and died when I was young. Everything my Aunt had was wrapped up in that place. When she was about to sell out, a fire swept through town and took it all from her. That's how we ended up here. Now, she and Ruth go into town. While Ruth works, Aunt Rose helps to keep things in order for a madam that was once her competition.

"So, let me get this straight," I said. Your Aunt was a madam, your Ma worked there, and Ruth goes to town and works in a brothel."

"Yes," she said.

"I thought something like that, but I wasn't sure."

She said, "You thought something like that?"

"Yes, I thought as much. Ruth it didn't seem if she was out looking for a husband. And me being a city boy, I know a little about the brothels from our town." She looked at me puzzled.

"Sally, I don't care about them. I like them and all but I don't care what they do or did. But I know I care about you."

"Jimmy you don't understand...... Let's just get back home. We can take the long way if you like."

When we got back Rose was sitting at the table and Ruth was standing in the doorway to Sally's room. I noticed my belongings sitting in the corner of the living room.

Rose said, "Now come on in you two. We ate and at some point Rose said, "Jimmy, you can sleep on the couch until your grandfather gets here."

Ruth chimed in "Jimmy I hope you didn't get a liking to my bed." Sally just sat there as if she knew about the scolding that was to take place. "Jimmy your fun with Sally is over. Ruth and I are going to keep close watch on the both of you."

I wasn't about to argue, but I did say, "Ma'am? The horse ridding isn't going to happen anymore?'

"The horse riding, the time alone, the crawling in bed isn't going to happen for neither of you. You're leaving Jimmy, and I have to do what's best for Sally. If you too keep this up one of you will get a terrible hurt."

"I'm not here to break anyone's heart. I didn't ask to be here in the first place." I stood up and said, "I love Sally! Why would I hurt her? "

A moment of silence hit the room as I realized what I said. I looked at Sally who was smiling back at me. I then looked over at Rose who was now leaning back in her chair.

"Oh, you think you're a big man now just cause you bedded down with her." She slammed her hand down hard on the table.

"Sit back down in your chair. Who exactly do you think you're talking too? Telling me about love, and that you love this or you love that. What does some snot nose boy know about love or even what's good for him?" I just sat there. "You going to run off, and take her away? To where? What are you going to do? Did she tell you about me?"

"Yes, ma'am she did."

"Did she? Well, I've seen love come and go out the front door many times. I've seen men promising women and young girls everything under the sun. And even if they make it past the first day those girls come back all hurt and heartbroken. Money makes your dreams happen. It's the silver and gold coins that make life your own, not promises from some boy. Sally told me her dreams, and I'm going to help her make them come true."

She went on and said, "Sally you told Jimmy about me, but did you tell him about our deal?"

"No, Aunt Rose don't!" She said.

"I'm going to put a stop to this here and now."

"Jimmy she's going to New Orleans to stay with family. She going to work there, and when the time is right she's going to try her hand at her dream."

"And what's that got to do with me?" I asked.

By now Rose was yelling and Sally sat with her face in her hands crying. Rose yelled for Ruth to get her out of the room.

"It's got everything to do with you Jimmy," she said. "Your Grandfather and I go way back. He was a gentleman that I entertained years and years ago. He would stop and stay with one of my girls and when I would let him he might even come for a visit with me." I sat there and listened.

"Then it was your Pa's turn, and he came along not much older than you are now. He had him fixed up with one of my girls for his first time. I was about to hold an auction for the first night with Sally, when I got word from your Grandfather. Men used to come from a great distance to get a virgin. Especially, a light skinned one like Sally. That one night could have sent her off to her dream. He wanted someone one special for you and a deal was struck. I thought it would be better than with some old man anyway. But now I'm not so sure. We were paid well for your night Jimmy, but that night's over. Sally will get her share like promised. So, don't be falling in love, and getting her all stirred up by making promises you can't keep."

Deep down I already knew, but I still I didn't want to believe it. I stood up from the table mad at Rose and Sally but mostly disappointed with myself. Feeling like a fool I walked past Ruth and Sally not saying a word. I didn't even look at her as Ruth ushered her back inside. I walked out to the barn and talked with the mare while I stroked her mane.

I had nowhere to go and in a couple of hours I started to walk back to the house. I stopped and looked up, and found her three stars and then saw mine standing all alone. I came inside and crawled on the sofa.

At first light the crow called out much like the bugle. Now, I longed for its sound. I was so ready to get back to the academy that I think I would have even been happy to see Whittington. I stood up and walked outside grabbing a slice of bread along the way. Immediately I headed for the barn not wanting to see any of them. I took the mare out by myself and headed for the fields and eventually the stream. I sat there alone think-ing about Sally. The fun we had, and how close I had gotten to her. But it was the hurt I felt that filled the majority of that day.

By the time I got back, I saw a car in front of the house. I rode up close enough to see Miss Rose and my Grandfather talking. He looked over at me as I closed in on the barn. I took the bridle off and gave her a quick brush, then said my goodbyes and thanked her for being a good horse. She shook and her skin quivered just before she took a roll in the stall.

I walked out of the barn and approached them. Rose still stood by Grandfather and I noticed Ruth standing on the porch but Sally was no-where to be seen.

"I'll go inside and grab my things." half hoping to catch a final glimpse of her. Miss Rose stopped me, and said that my things were al-ready packed and in the car. I turned back to the door looking for Sally and now saddened stepped inside the vehicle. Rose grabbed me, gave me a hug and thanked me for me being helpful as if nothing had transpired between us. My heart sank as I sat in the vehicle. In part aching to see Sally and in part feeling like I missed a chance to show her I didn't care. The mixture of emotions at that moment almost brought me to tears but I didn't dare. We quickly pulled out and I looked back to the house from the mirror. I watched the little house grow smaller and then finally out of sight from the distance and dust.

We drove nearly twenty miles before Grandfather finally broke the silence. "Sorry about the delay, I had no intentions of taking so long.

My business had details that needed immediate attention, and I couldn't get back." I looked at him crossly and asked, "Did you pay her? She deserved every penny."

My Grandfather fired back, "She was paid well most I ever paid for any whore."

I cringed at the comment. And said," She's not a whore!"

"I beg to differ she took money to pleasure a man. Well a boy," he stated.

The fire in my stomach was too much to hold back. "She wasn't one until you and Rose schemed up a way to make her one!"

"She would have been a whore either way. I thought you'd be grateful for the experience, but I guess I was wrong." He stated.

"A whore." The comment sent a chill down my spine and I couldn't hold back but before I could say a word I felt the back of his hand come across my face. He started to pull off the road and his hand pushed my shoulder against the passenger door.

"Look boy, you need to wake you up and get a hold of yourself real quick. I paid for her so you could take a step toward being a man. Rose told me what went on between you two. You best realize the difference between love and lust. If your hearts broken now it's better than later in life and for that lesson alone I got my money's worth. Make no bones about it. This pain you feel can be a lifelong affliction if you let it. If not her then it would be some other woman, and it's best if you never let it come to that." He lowered his hand and put it back on the wheel. I wiped the blood from my nose and he went on.

"Now you know of love and have a taste of hate. Best keep those feelings in check for now though. Keep them close, and don't go wasting them on some colored gal who took money from your pocket!"

He smiled and turned to me and said. "But I do like that fire she woke up in you. Remember it; you'll likely need it one day."

Grandfather and I settled on an uneasy peace for the remainder of the trip. We arrived back at Shadow Wood in the evening a day later. I sat my belongings in the corner, and crawled into bed. I laid there and decided not to ever speak of Sally again. But it didn't take long before I realized, I couldn't help myself. I pictured her wading in the creek. I remembered those days in the fields and the nights looking at the stars under the big sky. The thought of her crawling in bed next to me began to make me really miss her.

Late that night I found myself on the front porch. I sat on the swing for a moment and started to get mad again. Through the darkness I saw the red glow of Henry's cigerette. "Mr. Jimmy can't ya sleep?" He asked. I didn't say anything.

"No, I suspect not or you wouldn't be out here swinging, now would ya?" Then he sat next to me, and snapped his hand down on my knee. "What seems to be ailing ya?" I just looked down and said, "A girl I guess but it doesn't matter."

"Do you want to talk about it?" He said.

"No," I replied.

"Oh, ya think ole Henry doesn't know about women now do ya? Let's take a quick step around the block it's a nice night."

I peeked out under the overhang of the porch, and saw the night sky lit up with stars. "I'd really rather not," I said.

"All right then Mr. Jimmy I bid you good night, but may I suggest that you let these problems go because they'll likely be there in the morning. Just not as bad I would bet."

"Yes, thanks Henry I'll turn in." I walked back inside and eventually fell asleep.

The next morning I woke up still thinking about Sally, but I was glad to be home. I thought to myself that this was actually starting to feel like home as I walked down the stairs.

Breakfast was on the table waiting for me. Miss Ida scampered around the kitchen, and as usual made me feel better. Grandfather remained aloof to me and my situation. He probably thought it best if the matter was dropped. We spent the remainder of the summer going about our business as usual, and avoiding the subject altogether.

EIGHT

I arrived at Bransford a few days before the semester began that year. On my first day, I was called in to meet with the Sergeant Major and the Colonel. I was asked to show a new student around the campus. The new student was Will Howard who was roughly my age. He had many questions about life there, and wasn't happy about being at Bransford. He told me of the tearful moment when he left home, seeing his mother standing on the doorstep waiving her handkerchief as he drove away. It was hard for me to hear, and made me miss my own mother.

Eventually, we made our way to the stables. Once inside, we saw Mr. Downey and Mr. Hillenbrand. Hillenbrand was the instructor of the artillery unit. Downey oversaw the stables and taught horsemanship. Both men wore gray kepis like those of worn by the regular Confederate Army except that Hillenbrand's had a thin red band to denote the artillery branch of service. Neither had served a day in the military but their grandfathers had and the competition between them was fierce. Especially, the question of whose grandfather served in the toughest battle of the Civil War. At times the debates would get quite heated and Downey's face would often turn as red as his hair. Mr. Downey was born a Southerner but his Grandfather had been fresh off the boat just after the Civil War broke out. He remained true to his Irish heritage and somehow the more heated the debate the more pronounced his accent became.

Mr. Downey sat working on a saddle and greeted us in his normal fashion, a quick spit of tobacco, and a grimace on his face. Then he looked at us strangely, wiping his mouth with his sleeve and said, "So, now Conner just exactly who do you think ya are?"

"Excuse me, Sir?" I asked.

"You walked into my stables, and you didn't pay the proper respects." I had no idea what he was talking about.

He said, "Do a left face, and tell me what you see."

I did so and asked, "A statue?"

"Oh, I see. Just a statue! Well, never mind then." Downey said mockingly. Mr. Hillenbrand smiled and said, "This is where I leave," and immediately he walked out of the stable. Downey couldn't help himself he shook his head, then pointed his leather punch at us, and again replied, "Just a statue! Look at the face again Conner. It's a statue of none other than Colonel Jeb Stuart himself." He stood up and walked over placing a hand proudly on top of the statue. "Let me tell you about the good Colonel here. He was only the greatest cavalry commander to ever live!" Pausing briefly, and then he added, "Expect for maybe Genghis Khan. Never the less Colonel Stuart's exploits are legendary. My father served under him ya know."

"Yes, sir but Mr. Downey I've never seen it before. I replied.

"That's because it's never been here before. I saved my pennies and had him ordered. I'll be making a permanent place for him in here amongst those who he would want to be closest to. Good idea don't ya think?"

"It's very nice,'" I commented.

"Nice, it's nice that's all you can say about him, huh Conner. Aren't you wanting to make the Troop?" He asked.

"Yes sir, very much so."

"Well, then don't you two belly dragging cadets think the Colonel deserves the proper respects? How can you make the cut if you don't have enough military courtesy between the two of you too pay the proper respects to a Colonel?"

"What? Mr. Downey?" I asked.

"Don't what me Conner. You salute a Colonel don't you?" He exclaimed.

"Yes, sir you do." I said.

"He's a Colonel isn't he? Get to saluting."

"Salute a statue?" I asked.

"Oh, back to just a statue huh. You salute the Colonel coming and going from this location do ya hear me?" He barked.

"Yes sir, Mr. Downey."

"Conner, who is the lad with you?" he asked.

"Oh, this is Will Howard, he's new."

"Well, carry on then." We both saluted, and turned away with Mr. Downey grumbling about the lack of discipline within the academy, and then something about his Grandfather and Jeb Stuart rolling over in their graves. I looked at Howard who seemed a little shaken up by the whole incident and told him that everything would be all right. It was too early for Mr. Downey's whiskey to have kicked in, and that it would be in his best interest to make sure to salute the Colonel on the next trip to the barn.

Cadet Howard and I walked the grounds, and we met some of the other boys. Wallace was already back, and he took to Howard quite quickly. Wallace had spent that summer with his parents. It was the first time in a few years. He said his father even made him work through summer which he seemed to enjoy. We spent the first few days catching up and instructing Howard on the happenings at Bransford.

I received word early that the proposed candidates for the troop were quite close in total points, and that I was one of the three selected for the final cut. In the spirit of competition there would be a riding contest of sorts for the vacant position. This would be the first such a competition in quite some time. I wanted to ask for Tanner's help, but he was also a judge, and now the Captain of B. Company. Now more than ever, I was thankful for the time I spent with Sally.

That year many changes had taken place as cadets graduated and others advance. Whittington was acting Cadet Sergeant Major, and the right hand of the Colonel for the semester. My new captain was Tanner's best friend Captain Peabody. He and Tanner were in a heated battle for Whittington's position the final semester of the school year.

I went at it alone, and tried my best to remember what Sally had taught me. I spent every chance I had at the stable. One day I walked inside the barn saluted the statue of Colonel Stuart, now out of habit, and then quietly asked him for help if he had the means to provide it.

Mr. Downey always kept a close eye on me, but didn't say much, only the occasional keep your heels down or back straight as I rode by running the horse through its paces. I had only ten days to prepare before the tryout. I never quite felt ready, but I kept working at it.

Those days went by quickly; now my ability as a rider was to be tested. I woke up that morning before reveille and quietly started to get ready. Still tired from a sleepless night I sat on the edge of my bed. Looking down in my locker, I noticed the book that I had read Sally just weeks before. I reached down and picked the book up. For a moment I sat there holding it; wondering what had become of her. Only then did I notice a piece of material protruding above the other pages. I opened the book and out fell a note and a folded piece of blue fabric. The note read:

Dear Jimmy,

I know you won't believe this but I need you to know. I meant everything that happened between us. I wasn't with you because I was made to be but because I wanted to be with you. I truly love you Jimmy. Please believe me;

you just have to believe me Jimmy. I stayed up and made you a book mark. It's from the same material that I made the dress that I was wearing when you first saw me. When you read will you use it and think of me. I will always remember you and your star.

Love Always
Sally

I sat down on my bunk. For a moment, I didn't feel as empty inside as I had in the days before. A sense of relief came from that note. But those thoughts were brief because they were interrupted by Wallace's voice. "Are you nervous about today, Jimmy?"

"Yes, Virgil I am but you know….. I think today is mine." He then looked down in my hand and asked, "What's that?"

"Nothing just a piece of silly old cloth," He patted me on the back and said, "Jimmy, you'll do great today I just know it".

"Thanks Virgil," I said.

He walked back to his bunk, then I looked down at the book mark in my hand and placed the note back in my book. I sighed and said to myself, "No time for this now." I grabbed my belongings, and took a short walk down the lane to get my head right, and met up with the rest of the boys in the formation.

We were released for breakfast. I sat there picking at my food. The talk all seemed to center on the competition and it just made me nervous. I scanned the room for the other two boys, Baker a boy about my age and Tally who was a year younger. I had heard that Tally knew how to ride and I considered him my biggest threat.

I walked to the barn as the sun was still hanging low just behind the trees. By the time I made it to the stable my boots were glistening with the wet dew of the morning. The other two boys walked down together.

No one spoke once they entered the barn. They didn't salute the statue either but I made no mention of it.

The three of us prepared our horses and tack. My mount was a rune gelding with a dark back mane and long black socks named Cisco. I was pleased because we worked well together. When you're dealing with a horse it's a team effort. Both horse and rider have to be at an understanding. If one of you is having a bad day both of you pay the price.

Tanner was last to enter the stable. He wished us all good luck and prepared himself for the event. The entire school stood around the arena. The Colonel, Mr. Downey, Whittington, and the other company commanders were to be the judges.

The three of us followed Tanner to the center of the arena. We faced the judges who were seated just outside the fence. We saluted, and moved to the far corner as Tanner and his mount took to the center of the arena. Tanner addressed the academy explaining the rules of the competition. He then turned to face us and barked out a command. We followed his lead as we rode in a formation. Tally rode to my right and Baker to my left putting the horses through their paces as a unit would be expected too. Cisco worked, following my commands around the ring flawlessly.

Tanner rode once again to the center announcing that he would show us what was expected as individuals of the Troop. His mount proudly pranced around the ring quickly moving between obstacles, over jumps, making turns and precession stops. He put on quite a display of horsemanship.

Baker was the first of the three of us to take to the ring. I had planned on paying attention, but my thoughts took over and I was in my own where all else vanished, but me and my thoughts. Baker rode past me and in a flash I woke from my trance. I took in a breath and the world around me opened up again. I could see the faces of the boys I knew in the crowd as they stared back at me awaiting my next move.

This was my moment of truth. The Colonel gave a salute. I quickly snapped one in return. I paused a moment looking down to regain my focus while feeling the leather reins roll between my gloved fingers. Then I beckoned Cisco to move forward. He responded and I brought my mount from a walk to a trot, then canter, and finally to a gallop. We then moved through the obstacles and over the small jumps. As I dug my heels in Cisco for the final obstacle I felt a sense of relief, because I knew we had performed well.

Dismounting I glanced at Wallace who gave me a smile that made my adrenaline calm. Tally took to the course, and went through the paces also performing well as expected. The judges took a moment and spoke amongst themselves. Again the three of us rode to the center of the arena. The Colonel stood and spoke to the assembly of cadets about the hard work, effort the dedication that was displayed.

He continued on and once again the world began to fade for a moment. I reached my hand in my pocket, and felt for the book mark that Sally had given me. I wished that I could go to her to tell her about this day. She was a part of this moment, and I began to wonder if maybe in some way forever a part of me.

The silence of the Colonel caused my mind to reawaken. The judges handed the Colonel their ballots. He looked down to read the name. "The next cadet to receive the honor of representing the Troop is Private Conner." He stated. The cadets all applauded, and I shook hands with both Tally and Baker. I then saluted the Colonel, and took Cisco back to the stable.

Wallace of course was especially happy for me. In some ways he actually seemed even more excited than I did. We walked back to the barracks together as boys congratulated me along the way. Once inside, we both realized that I wouldn't be sleeping a few bunks down from him, but that I would be living with the troop on the east floor.

He helped me carry my foot locker and other belongings to the troop area. Attention was called on the floor, and all boys stood tall. In walked Captain Tanner, the Colonel, and the rest of the company. They once again shook my hand, and told me I had performed well. Tanner said smiling "And just to make your day even better." He called out, "Attention!" Everyone once again snapped too. "You are now promoted to Corporeal!" He then placed the stripes in my hand.

"You deserve it." Then looking at me sharply he said, "Don't let me down Corporeal Conner." I saluted, and Captain Peabody looked at me and said, "That's right! Don't let him down or there will be hell to pay from me! Good job today." I couldn't imagine a greater feeling than that day. Wallace looked over. We both smiled then unpacked my locker.

I wondered how he felt. I had passed him in rank, and that notion really bothered me. Being the good friend he was, he didn't wince or show any feeling that might dampen the moment. The whole day was likely the best of my young life. Well, the second best. I settled into my bunk and laid there thinking about all that had happened.

The next day I was happy to be informed that Cisco was to be my permanent mount. I went down to see him and once I entered the stables I snapped a salute to Colonel Jeb Stuart. Quietly, I thanked him for any help he may have given the day prior. I then prepared my tack with the other boys, the trooper's life was a ritual, and that day the boy's baptized me with leather soap and polish. The experience meant for a good laugh and the rite of passage was taken in stride.

Later, I stood there with Cisco watching the troopers perform drills. They practiced jumps under the watchful eye of Mr. Downey, so the cadets wouldn't get over zealous. It didn't take me long before I was completing similar jumps and becoming more than just comfortable on the back of Cisco. We became as one in the routines, and he understood them as well as I did. I was now a leader, which meant setting an example to others who depended on me. I tried to set an example like Tanner had taught me. In the process I became very close to the other boys.

Some changes happened for Wallace too. With Whittington off his back he seemed to be much more comfortable with himself. He even made Corporeal a short time after my promotion. Wallace took particular interest in those damn cannon, the one's we polished almost daily under Whittington's regime. Wallace and Mr. Hillenbrand would be on in the parade field daily going over the big guns. I couldn't help but smile, when I thought about Wallace's possible target once he got it down.

One night I met up with Wallace, and we climbed out a window to the top of our building. We sat outside and had a conversation about the changes that year. The November night air surrounded us as we tried to fend off the cold. We hadn't spent much time together that semester, and like most male conversations the topic eventually ended up on the subject of girls.

"Girls? No, just Katie. She's my neighbor. I hadn't seen her in while."

"Really," I asked. "Do you like her?"

"No," stated Wallace. "Well, she's nice and all, and sort of pretty, but she's barely a girl. I don't really like talking to her much."

Then Wallace asked, "What about you? Did you fall in love with some girl over the summer?"

"No," I stated.

"You met one I can tell," he said.

I looked up and found my bearing in the night sky and said, "See those stars Wallace?"

"Yeah, why?" he asked.

"Those three stars belong to a girl I met over the summer, and that one lone star below the others. Well, she gave it to me." Wallace said, "Let me see if I have this straight. That top star belongs to some girl, and that one over there is yours?"

"Yeah, it's kind of silly huh." I said.

"Jimmy, I bet Orion isn't going to like that because those three stars the girl is claiming are hers make up his belt. Now your star is in the constellation of Pleiades." He pointed toward the sky and said, "See, Orion the hunter is chasing the Pleiades, across the night sky."

"You know the stars?" I asked

"Yes, of course, and quite a bit about Greek mythology too," he said confidently. Wallace continued educating me on what all he knew about the night skies and told me spectacular stories relating to the constellations.

"Quite impressive, Virgil," I stated. "I have something I want you to see." We climbed back inside and then to my footlocker. I showed him the coin that Mr. Fenton returned to me. He looked at it and asked, "Where did you get this?"

"Never mind that," I said. "But don't they sometimes put gods and goddesses on the coins?"

"Sometimes," Wallace replied. I pointed to the female figure on one side of the coin and asked, "Any idea who that might be?"

"Maybe Pleione," he commented. "She was Atlas's wife of sorts and the mother of the seven daughters I told you about." He pointed to the circular object behind the female figure and told me that it was a symbol of the universe. Which as the myth goes is what Atlas carried on his shoulders. The fountain at Shadow Wood came to mind.

"You know the star that girl gave you?" Wallace asked.

"Yes," I replied

He pointed to the sky as if actually pointing at something tangible just inches away and said, "Asterop, Taygete, Maia, Celaneo, Acyone, Electra, and Metope the Jimmy star. They are Seven Sisters of Pleiades. Oh and over here are Atlas and Pleione their parents." He stated.

I was shocked and said, "Impressive Virgil, I had no idea."

"You can usually only see six stars of the constellation but there are seven for sure." Then he looked down at the coin and said, "Hmmm, you know there are seven stars on here too."

"Any ideas about the other side?" I asked.

"Just the Latin at the bottom." He said.

"God will vindicate." I replied.

"Paying attention in class?" He asked.

"Yes, but that's not how I know." I said. "Thank you Virgil."

The night ended with me lying in bed very curious about the coin again. I drifted off to sleep with thoughts of my family that seemed miles and miles away in time, and a life that was quite different from the one that I led now.

NINE

One night that same year, the sign of the tied knot on the display flag was given in the mess hall. We crept out and headed for the old cabin to our Kirby Smith Club meeting. It was a bitter cold night for Mississippi, actually snowing as we left the campus.

We began our night with the secret mission of acquiring a sample of Mr. Downey's special Red's blend chewing tobacco. We never really knew exactly why it was called that, but figured it was either from the color of Mr. Downey's Irish red hair or possibly the tint of the chew after it landed on the floor. I suspect he dyed it special for a little flare.

Never the less Whittington was in charge of the procurement of that particular item. Later he met us at the cabin and came in gleaming and bragging almost immediately. Tanner had started a fire and the boys all reached for a pinch of the special chew. Tonight was mans night at the old cabin and Whittington said, "Boys the underneath of Mr. Downey's cot released a special treat for us." We all looked at him our mouths full of chew. Whittington unveiled a jar of clear liquid with a small peach floating in the bottom.

"Tanner, take a whiff," he stated. Tanner grabbed the jar and inhaled deeply.

"Good night that's moonshine." Tanner said whencing in the process.

Whittington replied, "I suspect the valleys best."

"We'll get expelled for this for sure," commented Tanner almost as if it were a dare.

Peabody grabbed the jar and said, "Gentlemen it is my duty to inform you that particular rule only applies if we get caught."

We all laughed as he grabbed the jar and took the first swig. Intently, we watched his next move. His head shook and then he exhaled. The boys all roared, and now Tanner was on the spot. Not to ever be out done Tanner swallowed his share, then passed the jar to Whittington. Stevens had the worst of it, his face began to change shades and he sat there quietly for a moment. I asked if he was all right. He looked at me shaking his head yes then no and he ran outside, as laughter quickly overtook the room.

My head already felt light, and my face warm just from the tobacco. Likely, I would be next right behind Stevens, and the jar hadn't even made it to me.

The jar of liquid fire as it was now being called finally made its way to me. I held it up and inhaled the fumes. Whittington yelled, "You don't smell it ya drink it," as he slapped me on my back. I closed my eyes and took a swig. The name liquid fire was right on the mark. When it ran over my tongue I could feel my mouth get hot. The mixture of the alcohol and tobacco was too much for me. I bolted for the door. Outside, I heard the boys roar with laughter, but I didn't mind and walked back in smiling.

Whittington started in on me. He took the opportunity and wasn't about to let up. The name calling and poking fun of me just didn't sit well at that moment. I'm sure Whittington could see my face redden, but he didn't let up. It was then that I walked up to him. He held the jar and I took it from his grasp. I again took a swig, and defiantly handed back the jar.

Whittington continued his taunting though. He stood there and a crack of a smile crossed his lips followed by a mocking laugh and a story about all the cannon polishing he made Wallace and I do. His words fell on the fact the he didn't much care for my friend Wallace. That he was a fat kid, and shouldn't be here at Bransford. Whittington said, "I'm telling you before this year is out, I'll have that kid crying wishing he would have stayed home with his mommy. How can you stand him Conner he's about worthless?"

I had enough of Whittington. Enough of his arrogance, his contempt, and his plain meanness for the sake of just being mean. At that moment the world closed in, becoming very small, my vision focused tightly until it was only him in my view. Nothing peripheral mattered; at first all around me became blurry then just dark. I stepped up to him squarely with my fist clinched, and drew back a hay maker striking a blow to his nose. A stunned Whittington stood there as I drew back and released another. Whittington fell back, and stumbled to the ground. I stood over him the words just falling past my lips, "Leave Wallace alone you arrogant jerk!" Over and over I hit him. He laid there on the floor curled into a ball covering his head. Tanner grabbed me stopping the assault.

Peabody helped Whittington to his feet. Whittington now realizing what had just happened stood up and started yelling, "I'll get you!" He exclaimed. Peabody held him back telling him to calm down. Whittington made his way for the door wiping the blood from his nose. When he reached for the door the knob began to turn on its own. At that moment the door opened hard slamming against wall. Standing there in the entry were Downey and Hillenbrand.

"Well, boys what do we have here? A group of boys acting like a rabble, all fighting and carrying on as such. Oh, look there Mr. Hillenbrand it appears my jar has wondered off and decided to rest here half empty amongst the boys," remarked Downey. He walked over and took a large swig from the jar. Then he pointed to the floor in the process stating, "Look there on floor it appears to be the remnants of my tobacco! I'm curious did you boys like Red's Blend?" He asked.

Everyone either stood or sat quietly heads down. Hillenbrand yelled out, "Boys do you like Mr. Downey's Tobacco?"

"Yes sir," we murmured.

"At least that's the right answer," touted Downey, "It wasn't too sweet for ya there Tanner was it? What about you Cadet Whittington standing there bleeding everywhere. Was it too tart for ya or maybe a pinch to dry?" Saying nothing, we all just kept our heads down.

"Boys let's get ya home," Downey remarked. "Mr. Hillenbrand and I will deliberate about this fiasco and decide what we're going to do with you in the morning." We all filed through the door and Whittington whispered to me, "I'll get you Conner."

Tanner looked at Whittington and said, "No-No you won't. It stays here, and it ends tonight Whittington!"

Once Whittington was outside Peabody patted me on the back and said, "Tanner won't let anything happen. You've got sand Conner and I like that about you, but especially I like the fact you stand up for your friends."

The walk back was longer than normal. It seemed as if the woods itself sensed that something was amiss. It carried an unusually eerie silence that made our march of a few boys seem like an army crashing through the brush. We quietly whispered amongst each other trying our best to cover all the bases. Only the occasional bark of Hillenbrand to shut it up righted our thoughts.

Once back on the campus we all quietly crawled in bed. It was late and reveille sounded all too soon. It seemed as if my eyes had barley closed and it was already time for me to get dressed. Tanner walked by and said, "Now, it's time to pay the piper Conner! Heck Wallace might even out rank us all after last night." He said it with such an air of confidence, even smiling, that I admired him that much more. Peabody a step behind wasn't any different. He pushed Tanner forward, and said, "Get a move on that dragging butt." Peabody then reached over and smudged Tanner's Captain bars with his thumb and said, "We don't want the new captain getting these looking all pretty." He must have pushed a button with the remark because Tanner gave him a nasty look. Then he motioned for me for to follow saying, "Come on Conner time to stand tall." Once out in the morning formation the names of all the boys involved were called one by one.

We stood in a formation of our own, and were told to meet misters Hillenbrand and Downey at the stables. All other boys went about their day as we marched on toward the stables with Tanner leading the procession. He brought the five man detail to a halt just outside. Hillenbrand and Downey were standing there waiting with a look of disapproval on their faces. Hillenbrand stood arms folded with his kepi cocked to one side. Downey was seated on a barrel, head down, whittling a small stick. Tanner barked, "Detail reporting as requested." Holding his salute and awaiting the return. Downey stood motionless. Looking down he said, "Mr. Hillenbrand what will we do with these boys?" Hillenbrand replied, "Mr. Downey has stalls to clean, and there is plenty of work to be done in the ole stables. Take off your blouses gentlemen let's get to work."

In short order he had us running in every direction. Stalls were cleaned, old tack taken out of the loft, and even the making of a permanent place for the bust of Colonel Jeb Stuart. The entire time I worked side by side with Whittington. Downey wouldn't let us separate. Every project we worked on; we worked on together. In retrospect, that was about Whittington and me learning to work together again. Out of necessity we needed to put last night's events behind us. I was willing to bury the hatchet, but Whittington had other thoughts on the subject.

At one point we were to dig a drainage line away from the stable. Whittington ordered for me to grab the shovels. Over hearing him Downey quickly interjected by saying, "No rank today Cadet Whittington. Fetch your own shovel." Tanner also kept a watchful eye on the situation. The thing was, Whittington may have had rank on Tanner and Peabody, but deep down he knew better than to cross either of them. I was well protected and he knew I knew it. But the fact remained that I had embarrassed him and he would likely seek reprisal.

My only relief from the close quarters with Whittington was when either Downey or Hillenbrand would pull us aside individually and start questioning us. Usually, questions about the group, asking us why we were there or who else was involved. They would ask some calmly and others with more pressure. Peabody took the brunt of the yelling during the questioning. By the end of the day we were all beat. We had done everything that Downey and Hillenbrand had requested, and I was glad the day was over.

The two men asked us to gather around. Mr. Hillenbrand confronted Whittington and asked, "Do you still have a beef with Conner?" Whittington replied, "No, sir." Then it was my turn and he asked the same of me, and I too replied, "No."

"Boys expect no more talk or discipline on the subject, but we need you to understand a few things," commented Hillenbrand.

Downey interrupted, "I'd like to handle young Conner if I may Mr. Hillenbrand." Not Knowing where this would lead I cringed. Downey continued, "Conner, had you ever punched a superior in my Grandfather's cavalry no matter the situation. You would be doing much more than digging a drainage pit, grave more likely."

He walked over to Whittington and stood inches from his face. The hard bill of his kepis bouncing off Whittington's forehead, and he said, "And you Whittington I have to wonder what you could have possibly done to make this boy actually punch you? Was it the booze, the heat of the moment? Do you care to explain Cadet Whittington?" Whittington just stood there not saying a word. "Awe, it doesn't matter any longer. But boy's I will tell you this, when you're a leader you carry that with you every day! And the respect you seek goes both ways. Whittington if you haven't figured that out by now you'll never know it. You're close to graduation and it is my hope that you get it figured out real quick!"

The men began to pace around the group and then Hillenbrand said, "Boys we didn't go to commandant with this. We told him we had a situation that we needed to handle, and he respected our wishes, but there is so much more going on here than just a bunch of boys running through the woods late in the night. We all know what happens back in the old Senator's cabin."

We all looked around at each other. Downey piped up. "Boys do you think your blazing a new path back there? Ever consider it's a beaten down trail? You older boys Peabody, Whittington, Tanner you were brought there by other boys weren't ya? Do ya think we don't know about the knock, the handshake, or the signal?"

All stunned we just stood there as Downey continued, "The senators Cabin is why we have a campus here in the first place. He was the original Son of the South!" It was then that Hillenbrand told us to have a seat. We all listened intently as Hillenbrand continued, "Mr. Barnes had been a senator earlier in his life before the Civil War took place. Once the war broke out he refused to be called Senator any longer, calling it a conflict of his loyalty. He felt that if he hadn't been a Senator for the confederacy then he wasn't a Senator at all. Having no children of his own and on his death bed, Mr. Barnes asked for a school to takes these grounds and for it to be named for his favorite nephew, who gave his life for the cause at Big Bethel by drawing fire from a Yankee gun boat. Lieutenant Bransford, like myself, was an artillery man." He looked over at Downey and smiled.

Downey quickly retorted. "Oh, here we go again the with blessed artillery. Boys best to lie down, and prepare yourself for a story with no romance, guts nor glory to lull you to a sweet slumber!"

"No gentlemen, I won't bore Mr. Downey with the glorious confederate defense on the water ways and tributaries of the Chesapeake Bay nor the Potomac that led to the Yankee capital of Washington. Nor will I spin you tails about neither its importance to the cause, nor to the fact and I do mean fact that artillery was the only way to defend it other than the Navy. No, I wouldn't want Mr. Downey to get his spurs in a snag, not at all but I will tell you this; we are all a lot more intertwined in this than you think. There are many reasons why you boys came here and a proper education is just a part of it. The cadets that graduated before have gone on to universities, the military, and to important positions in their communities. The road they went down leads back to that cabin. You best learn to get along because you will be seeing each other again in this life, and you will have to work as one for a cause much greater than your own personal gain. Prepare yourselves boys that oath you took is binding. It binds you together and to us for we're Sons too. Learn from this day and from here on, because a lot more is at stake than a bloody nose or bruised pride."

I noticed something about Hillenbrand and Downey that I hadn't noticed before, both men wore a ring like my Grandfather's with a red stone. I realized then that there was more to this than just some club. I still couldn't quite grasp what all Hillenbrand and Downey were talking about then, but I knew there was a bigger picture.

Downey stood up and said, "Boys you've done real good keeping quiet about what you were doing in the cabin. If we were hard on ya, especially you Peabody, it was for a reason. It's important for you to remember today. Secrecy is why we're still here. It's what keeps us safe, hidden, and protected. Don't trust anyone with our secrets. There are some boys, who may be Sons in time, but they aren't yet and there are others that won't be. So, keep to yourselves, and keep quiet about the cabin, and for pity sakes do better not to get caught. Use your time well to understand what is all going on here. It's not just a place for you to let your hair down and howl at the moon. The Kirby Smith Club and the cabin are far from the biggest secrets you'll be keeping.

When I think back to the bond that we had at Bransford it makes me wonder about what all went on with the boys at West Point Military Academy just before the start of the Civil War. Those boys had to be just as close as we were and the decision they made to go back to their home state and fight against the Union and their friends had to be incredibly hard. Imagine being a young man having to make that hard choice to fight against a beloved friend or roommate. Interestingly enough, once war seemed eminent it was decided to change the oath at the academy from one where they swore allegiance to their individual states to one swearing allegiance to the Union. It had to make them consider their loyalty. No cadet had ever refused to take the oath until that day.

In all, over three hundred West Pointers went south because of the defection of the Southerners the North considered all West Pointers contemptuous causing officials to hold back the West Point graduates in their careers while the South welcomed their men home possibly leading to the great success the of the South early in the war. Men like Jeb Stuart, Stonewall Jackson, A.P. Hill, and interestingly George Pickett, a Virginian, moved to Illinois and was appointed to West Point by a Congressmen named Abraham Lincoln. All these men provide their steel in battles for the South, but it was the gentleman soldier, Robert E. Lee that most damaged the North.

Lee graduated second in his class at West Point. He proved his worth and loyalty to the Union time and time again even leading a group of Marines to stop John Browns raid. Lee opposed slavery, and was a supporter of the Union. In all he spent over thirty years in service to the Union but when his state seceded he was left with a tumultuous decision. His family's rich legacy from signers of the Declaration of Independence, to Henry light horse Lee, and his wife's connection to George Washington deeply bound him to the very fabric which formed this Union. To make matters even more difficult Abraham Lincoln offered him control over the entire Union Army but in the end it was the call of his beloved Virginia that he answered.

I'm not sure I had the moxie to fight against my friends Wallace, Peabody, or Tanner.

TEN

It was my seventeenth year, and once again I stood on the front porch of Shadow Wood. I saw Charlie and his sister, Lucille, coming toward me. Charlie and I had formed an uneasy friendship over the past few summers. Uneasy I would say for me not so much Charlie, who sought me out whenever he had a chance.

They both came up to the porch. Lucille was comparably quiet at first, and I noticed she had matured even more this past year. Charlie, always curious about Bransford asked, "Jimmy how is that army school you attend? As I told you before, Father wanted me to go too. Thankfully, my mother put her foot down. You guys sure do look silly in those uniforms."

"Oh, stop it Charlie." Lucille stated, "I bet Jimmy looks quite handsome in his uniform with those shiny buttons." She placed her arm under mine, and escorted me toward the swing. "Let's sit a spell and catch up."

"Well, I was just......" and then Miss Ida walked out and said, "Jimmy I'll fix you and your friends a sip of tea if you like."

"No, that won't be necessary Miss Ida, I was just getting ready to leave."

"Now, Jimmy where are your manners we walked all the way here and I'm parched. Could you have your help get us something to drink?" Lucille asked.

Miss Ida frowned at the comment as she mumbled something unrecognizable under her breath as she walked inside.

"Jimmy, what do you do at the school anyway? Do they teach you to march and things like that?" Lucille asked.

"I bet the older boys had fun being mean to you ordering you around. Now, that you'll be a senior you'll get to do the bossing." Charlie commented.

"It's not exactly like that Charlie, I mean some did of course but most of the boys are good friends, and we watch out for each other."

"Jimmy do you have your uniform here?" Charlie asked.

"Yes," I said.

"Show us!" he quickly remarked.

I reluctantly went upstairs as Ida walked past on her way out to the porch. She looked at me as she said, "I don't much care for that Bedford girl, Jimmy. She thinks she's something special!"

"Yes, I know." I replied.

I walked down carrying the uniform, and Charlie immediately laughed out loud and said, "You have to wear that! I wouldn't wear that for nothing."

Lucille interjected and asked, "Jimmy I bet you look very handsome. Let us see you in your uniform."

Charlie said, "Yeah, let's see you in that monkey suit!"

Fearing further ridicule I protested and said, "No, I shouldn't."

Lucille latched onto my arm and said, "Charlie Bedford you hush. Jimmy, for me? Would you please let me see you in your uniform? I'm sure you're the most handsome boy to ever go to that school and I bet you look like a real soldier."

"No, Lucille that's okay. Shall we drink our tea and head to the park for a bit?"

"No," she protested, "I'm not moving one inch until I see how handsome you are." She said then smiled, and batted her eyes. "Please Jimmy just for a moment I promise we won't laugh. I'll think you're handsome, I promise!"

Being a sucker for a pretty girl and a please I went upstairs and changed into my uniform. Walking down the stairs I realized it was the first time I felt a little ashamed of wearing it. Pausing briefly at a mirror near the bottom of the stairs I thought, "Ashamed, Not me! I'm Lieutenant Conner cavalry trooper," and held my head high as I walked out. Charlie was sitting on the rail of the porch to get the first look at me. I opened the door and he fought back a laugh. Seeing his reaction caused me to laugh too. The moment of levity and knowing he was visualizing me with an organ grinder was comical even to me.

Lucille scolded him as she walked in front of me. She stood there as if to inspect me. Out of habit I didn't move, I stood tall eye's forward. She brushed a small piece of lint off my shoulder, tugged at my sleeve, and smiled.

She then said, "Jimmy I do declare you are quite something in your uniform."

She stood on her toes and placed one hand on my shoulder. As her face came close to mine I could smell her perfume. She pressed her moist lips against my cheek and said, "I always wanted to kiss a soldier and now I have." It was at that moment I looked at Lucille a little differently. She had changed since last summer. She seemed somehow older and more womanly.

Lucille asked, "Will you walk us to the park and tell me all about your adventures?"

"I'd prefer to change."

"But I want to show you off to my friends and brag about my handsome soldier."

Ida must have over heard the conversation. Knowing I was in trouble she interjected to save me from myself. "Jimmy you best not be wearing that uniform. I'm ready to mend it and let it out a little." I looked at Ida "Yes, ma'am." Then I commented, "Maybe another time Lucille."

"Only if it's a promise Jimmy,"

"I promise." I reluctantly replied.

After changing, the three of us walked over to the park. It gave me a chance to see some of the kids from the previous summers to get reacquainted with them. Charlie put on a display but he wasn't so bad. He was practically the only friend I had back at home. Lucille seemed to be quite fond of my arm as she walked with me to and from the park holding it tightly. The entire time we were there she was rarely more than a foot away from me. At one point she insisted that I start calling her Lucy instead of Lucille because as she told me formal names were for strangers and we were old and dear acquaintances.

Once the visit to the park was over we left for Shadow Wood. My grandfather, seeing us, offered to drive them home. I rode sitting between them. Once they left the car my Grandfather asked me about Lucille. He said, "That would be a good match between you too. Her father is high in the organization and she knows how to carry herself like a lady. Best too not treat her like that Sally girl though Lucille is the marrying kind." That remark immediately took my mind back to Sally. I didn't dare mention her to my grandfather on my own. Actually the entire encounter between us was something I would rather not discuss. I was uncomfortable the entire ride home, but the comment prodded me, and fearing another opportunity to bring it up would never arise I asked, "Do you think I could I visit Sally and Miss Rose again?"

He smiled and said, "So, you'd like another go at it would you? Best if you sow your oats with another you might get attached if you go back too often. A boy your age needs a little variety, but only if you're with a woman that knows how not to get you into trouble. I'll see if I can arrange something for you." The remark troubled me because that wasn't what I'd had in mind. Grandfather, a typically reserved stately man, had made me very uncomfortable. I'm not sure if he was trying to bond with me on some level, or if he was condoning a boy's will be boy's attitude on my behalf. Never the less I walked inside not wanting to discuss the subject any further.

The rest of the summer was spent learning about the organization and business interests of my grandfather. He began relying on me. Using my skills in arithmetic to read ledgers and keep track of books. He also made sure my work was of a physical nature when possible and loaned me out to the different headmen he had in his hire. He often said the best way to learn how things work is to be a cog in the wheel, not to just watch it spin; a rule which he made me live by. In truth he was right. It helped me to understand the operations as well as the nature of labor involved. Working with people as one of them helped me be a better judge of character. I could quickly discern which men were willing to work and also which boss would be right for a particular job.

When you work with men who are trying to make a better life for their families, and in many cases just put food on the table, your prospective changes from that of the high porch of Shadow Wood to one of basic survival. It made me wonder why my father had chosen a life away from the safety of that porch; going off on his own. Afraid to question grandfather on the subject, I kept my curiosities to myself.

At the end of the day, Miss Ida would always have a meal ready for me on my return. Better yet, she always made sure I had a good meal to take to work. I could trade Miss Ida's food for just about anything at meal time. I might trade a portion of a meal or the whole thing usually making the deal fall in their favor. I already had so much more than those men would ever have. Times were prosperous in the twenty's for some but not for all. I worked with many a man who had little to nothing. There is a line between being charitable and looking foolish though and the trick is to know where that line is drawn. I was always conscience of what the men thought of me, and wouldn't do anything to make myself or my grandfather look foolish. I definitely didn't want to come across as a Charlie Bedford looking conceded, or like a wealthy kid with no concern for others.

I knew I had to prove myself constantly because any slacking would be reported to my grandfather but more importantly I might lose the respect of the men I was working alongside. I felt fortunate to be in a position where I had so much. I was being constantly reminded of the fact by seeing those who had so little. I knew at the end of the day I would walk into a big home and have a nice bed. These men would not have that luxury. In time I could see my approval with my grandfather getting stronger and I liked the feeling.

Lucille and I spent the summer getting to know each other better. She seemed to like me and I liked that fact. Our time together was short and before long I headed back to Bransford as the summer ended. Before leaving she asked me to write and I did on occasion.

I was far from dreading my return to Bransford, but some of the previous year's excitement had passed. My older friends were all gone. Tanner and Peabody enlisted in the military and Whittington had gone on to college. I spent my last couple of years in the Troop with Cisco. Eventually, I became a Captain. I did my best to be a good leader and try to set an example like Tanner taught me.

Wallace too had his time in the sun. Hillenbrand's prodigy quickly became a master of artillery tactics and the Captain of the color guard. He began to shine once Whittington graduated. Wallace's confidence grew after he found his place.

That final year quickly passed and the time came to leave Bransford was upon me. Just a day before graduation I walked down to the stable to say my goodbyes to Mr. Downey, my mount Cisco, and to salute General

Stuart one last time. I stood next to Cisco brushing him and spoke to him as if he understood every word. In many ways it surprised me that I had become so close to him. He was a good horse. He taught me a lot about trust and taking care of something other than myself.

When I was on Cisco's back he seemed to transport me to places other than just down the trail; thoughts of my parents, my home near the Pee Dee River, but mostly to Sally. Having a good memory to hold onto is something that can get a person through the toughest of times. I often clung to thoughts of that one summer lying in the tall grass down by the cool stream with her at my side. I wondered what happened to her. Had she made to New Orleans like she wanted? I cut a few strands of Cisco's mane to keep in a book and I spoke a soft farewell to him. It seemed that I was always saying good bye to the things I cared about.

Downey came into the stable and broke my moment of thought. He walked over and patted Cisco. "Well now Conner, I see you are saying your farewell to ole Cisco."

"Yes, he's a good horse."

"That he is, Conner."

"And you turned into quite a trooper now didn't ya?"

"I hope I didn't let you down Mr. Downey." I replied.

"Let me down?" He questioned. "And where might ya get a notion like that lad?"

"Sir, that day after the cabin, I began to realize that I was the only one of the Sons who competed for a position in the Troop and that's why I got in." Downey chuckled and put his hand on my shoulder, "Now Conner why do you do this? You're a might hard on yourself, you know that? It is true your family has been good to this school and to the Sons, but that had hardly anything to do with you winning. You worked hard to get into the troop. Not just with the horses, but in everything you did; grades and all. Glad you did too lad. You represented it well."

"Thank you Mr. Downey."

"Awe Conner, to be sure the Sons can help you along in life, but it doesn't mean everything you do is handed to ya. I'm quite proud of you and you're on your way to being a fine man. Your father would be proud of you too I'd bet."

We continued to talk as Downey sat down, starting to whittle a small branch. I leaned against the side of a stall with tack on both sides of me and looked around for one last time. The smell of horses, leather, and hay permeated the air. I sat down beside him and asked for a stick of wood then I pulled out my father's knife. Downey noticed it and said, "Let me see that." I handed it over and he looked at it, then me and asked, "How did you come by such a knife?"

I told him that it was my fathers. He then read the inscription letting out a sigh. He lifted his head he looked at me in a serious manner and said, "Lad you need to keep that hidden. It's not for you to use. That knife has a history and meaning all of its own; one not to be taken lightly." I looked at him puzzled. He stood up and went to the adjacent room where he bunked. When he came back he held an identical knife to mine. Again he said, "Lad don't be showing that knife around. I earned mine and it's a reminder of a deed that I had to do. In your circles there are ones who will know it doesn't belong to you. It should have been buried with your father. One day ask your grandfather about it, but not just yet. Wait until you can fully understand and appreciate the meaning of the scorpion. If your grandfather won't explain it to you, then come back and find me, I'll explain it. Until then, it's best if you keep it hidden. Do you understand me lad?"

"Yes, I do."

"Now lend me a hand with a few things before you leave the stable."

I helped Downey saddle up a mount and then he reached over and saddled Cisco. I asked him what he was doing. He replied, "Let's take Cisco down the trail a bit so you can stretch these horse's legs." I looked at him puzzled because I had never seen him ride. I knew the Cavalry was the most important thing him and that he knew everything about horses, but I had never seen him actually ride. I looked and he said, "Come on Conner it's been too long for me. It's time to get a horse under me again and dig in my spurs." I knew better than to ask why. He walked to his room and came out brushing the dust from what appeared to be a cowboy hat. I smartly asked, "Is that a ten gallon hat you got there Mr. Downey?"

"Good god, no boy!" Retorted Downey, "It's a cavalry Stetson you fool. You wear the kepis to work and Stetsons to ride." I climbed on Cisco and we rode away just enjoying the trail for a couple of hours.

At the graduation ceremony I realized my grandfather and Wallace's father knew each other to some degree. The ceremony was small and we quickly parted ways. A few of the boys promised to keep in touch. Wallace and I just knew we would. We shook hands and said our goodbyes but kept the situation light. Deep down I was sorry to have to part with him in our years at school we had become as close as brothers. Riding down the same lane that had taken me to Bransford I had the thought that it was now leading me away to another new uncertainty in my life.

"Mr. Conner may I interrupt you for a moment? You have a wonderful story here and I'm sure you led an exciting and fulfilling life but I'm not so sure this is what my paper is looking for?" I asked.

"So, young love and cadet soldiers don't sell news papers do they?" Stated Mr. Conner holding one eye closed and squinting at me through the other. "What's wrong? Are you afraid I might die before I get to the good part? Or do you really think I brought you all the way down here to tell you I had my first women at fourteen?"

"It is an interesting story but I was hoping there was something more suited to my readers interests." I stated.

"Campbell, it seems I've tested your patience enough. I suspect it's time to get to the heart of the matter," replied Mr. Conner. "If we skip ahead some can you still keep my story inline?"

"Yes, sir I'll get it right." I stated.

After college, my grandfather began to utilize me within his business and within the network associated to the Sons of South. Unbeknownst to me, I was about to take a big step.

The meeting hall was the same as usual. Grandfather and I walked inside to the old warehouse together. I entered the room in the usual fashion by giving the secret knock. I was thinking little of the meeting. I typically enjoyed going because I liked spending time with the men. Many were just boys when we met and over the years friendships were formed. As a young man in my early twenties I had other things on my mind and the notion of a social gathering just wasn't a priority. Grandfather had stressed the importance of social ties to our various interests. He strongly encouraged me to attend. What I mean by strongly encourage is I had little choice in the matter.

When I arrived the room that was normally filled with many people was oddly vacant and dark. All I could see was a long table positioned at the front of the room and a star about four feet in diameter laid out on the floor in front of the table. "Approach the star," a voice called. I closed the door and walked toward the star. I could only see figures behind the table and men wearing masks over there head to conceal their identity. A bright light struck me once I stood on the star.

I could now make out only the figures of eleven men and a large confederate flag behind them. The man directly in front of me asked, "You have been known to keep a secret, is that true?" I stood there at attention of sorts out of habit. "Yes, that is true." I said.

"If you choose not to proceed then all we ask of you is that you keep what you have heard and seen here a secret. Will you keep that vow?"

"Yes, I will." I replied.

The man stood up and said, "This council has decided you are worthy to face the challenges and proceed to the next level of this organization.

Represented here are eleven state flags one for each of the eleven states that chose to move forward and secede from the Union to start a new nation." Left to right each man stood and called out the state he represented. The Great State of South Carolina, The Great State of Mississippi, The Great State of Florida, Alabama, Georgia, Louisiana, Texas, Virginia, North Carolina, Arkansas, and Tennessee." Each state was named in order of secession. The speaker continued, "They chose to break away from the bonds they knew to form a government that was more representative of the one our foundering Fathers had intended; one where the laws that governed a man were in his home state not some central authority to govern them all. You stand here today on the star that represents the states that didn't secede; Kentucky, Missouri, Arkansas and the Oklahoma Territory. From those states our ranks were filled with brothers who took our cause upon themselves individually. Each man alone had to step forward and choose his own destiny and his own fate. You like them will have to take that same step forward and join our cause. Are you willing to take that step?" He asked.

"Yes, sir I am." I told them.

"Now do so," he stated.

I stepped forward, he again went on:

"The smoke from the battles of the war has long since vanished but the cause remains alive. It's engrained in the heart of all noble men of Southern birth. Our honor will forever be tarnished if that dream fades from our souls. Here today it is alive and well in these men you are to call brothers. You have come to our attention because of your commitment to the Sons of the South. James Conner your efforts in promoting the intentions of that organization, your achievements at the Bransford academy, the Kirby Smith club, the university, and the hard work you have been associated with for not just your Grandfather but for us all. I say now bring this man into the Sons of the Southern Cause. What say you brothers?"

One by one, eleven voices rang out, "Aye." Then the speaker continued, "Congratulations son and welcome."

The men each unmasked and shook my hand. I knew some, recognized others, and a few were from other chapters located throughout the South that I had never met. I was moved through stations to learn more about the organization, and a new set of secrets were revealed to me. Of course a new handshake and a set of symbols were also introduced. In this instance a long cross much like on the battle flag was presented. Two stars sat opposite each other on the longest of the four sides. The cross was representative of the confederate flag. The stars represented honor and secrecy. What was revealed that night wasn't limited to organization secrets. Most information was a brief overview concerning specific business dealings that I had no idea we were associated with many involving my grandfather were often intertwined with each of those men. I began to realize the true scope of what I was involved in. To what end I didn't know, but I was certain that the organization was much deeper than I had ever imagined.

One man explained each chapter had an upper level similar to this one, but some chapters only contain a few members of the Sons of the Cause. The networks of chapters were deeply rooted throughout the Southern states. They use their ties with the men of the local chapters and the money and skills of the other chapters to promote the interest of the Sons of the Cause.

Once the meeting was over I had many questions for my Grandfather. He told me to keep my mouth closed about what happened tonight and that this is no longer just an association of Southern business men. This was a place where telling secrets is something that gets you more than just thrown out of the club. That the stakes are now higher, but I would learn more as time went on.

ELEVEN

One of those secrets came later and quite by accident. I had worked hard and was moved to a position in the higher levels of the organization. At that time I was assigned to assist a Mr. Samuel Cloverly, who was holding the treasurer's position. He was a highly respected and admired man, one of the oldest active members.

We worked alone one night finishing final entries for an upcoming meeting of the lead council. We stopped for a moment and he told me, "Jimmy I have grown quite fond of you. You have worked your way up within the organization due to your diligence, loyalty and enthusiasm. To be a young man, and have the knowledge of the inner workings of this organization is quite something."

"Thank you sir," I replied.

"I suspect you to be lead council like your Grandfather at a young age but I haven't figure out why you haven't put it all together yet. It's all laid out before you."

"What?" I asked.

"Mr. Clovery continued, "Jimmy, you see the influence this organization carries; the money that flows through it. It's all for a purpose you know, but you haven't yet asked me to what purpose this organization serves, or how it started. Most of all even question the bigger picture?"

I looked at him and said, "I guess I was too busy with my work to inquire."

"Son that is no way to be in this life, just keeping your head down and working, but not knowing the end result or the why of it all. When you see something the first thing to ask is why! Why is this here? Why are we doing this? Why is it this way and not that way? Why is this person loyal and why is that one not? Why does this woman love me? Why does this person want this?" He clutched his fist and pulled it to his chest.

"All answers in life lay within the why of things! You listen here Conner and you listen sharp. This isn't written down nor is it spoken of but in the closest circles. You are getting it from a man who knows the whys because I was there as he pointed to himself with a smiling snap of pride. Then he went on and told me, "I worked for an honorable man by the name of Cyrus Barnes. He was a wealthy man when I came under his wing. He lived on the ground of that school you attended. Does the name sound familiar?" He asked. I nodded and remarked, "The Kirby Smith Club cabin."

"Good," he said and continued. "Mr. Barnes admired those of loyalty and of good work ethic for which I was fortunate to be graced with both. One night near the end of the Civil War we spoke in the flicker of candle light, and I could tell he was troubled. The war looked bad for the South.

I commented, "It appears as if the cause is lost, sir."

"It does appear so with the fall of Richmond, and the surrender of General Lee it will only be a short time. We must use it to make final preparations," Mr. Barnes said.

"Remember the cause is never lost unless we give up in our hearts and this burden appears to be resting on my shoulders. After a brief pause he called out my name, "Samuel."

"Yes, sir," I replied.

"I know your character and your loyalty to me. I need to ask more of you, if you are willing."

"Whatever needs addressed. I consider working with you an honor."

"Cloverly, what is needed is your mind, your legs and your word. I need you to act in capacities for which I am no longer able. What I am asking may cause harm to your person. The possibly of being shot or hung is likely. But I think you will find the duty just and cause great. Secrecy is of the utmost importance I will make you an aid and privy to all meetings. Will you partake in this journey with us?"

"Yes, sir it has been an honor to be of service to you in the past and now. Whatever you have in store for me I accept."

"Now is the time to call formal council and bring it into session," commanded Barnes. "Kindly send word Mr. Cloverly."

"Consider it done sir. I'll send word immediately."

I sent dispatches to eleven men. Many traveled through Union occupied territory. The South was infiltrated by spies and those with potential to tip their hat to gain favor with the Yankees. Mr. Barnes took not a chance of any connection between the men. Upon arrival each man was to enter the Tipton's general store and ask for a selection of specific items nothing more, nothing less. Mr. Tipton, a trusted friend of Mr. Barnes, was to add one can extra to each of the men's goods. Inside were instructions and direction to a safe house for each.

On the sixth day all but one had arrived. Mr. Barnes decided to make due and continue with the meeting at an old country church. Additional men were sent to the four corners of the church out of earshot to provide guard and secrecy.

The council members one by one entered the church. All men had arrived and the meeting was about to begin, when a horse and rider approached the church. He dismounted the exhausted horse and banged on the large oak doors with a prearranged secret knock. The men inside begin to stir and one pointed out that the knock was correct, but the instructions were specific and stated to forgo the knock, to just enter.

A lantern with a red lens was placed in a widow opposite the door. It signaled the men who were providing security. They came running to the front escorting the man inside. The man seemed ruffled and confused as he stood before the other members of the council. Mr. Pittcock a man of advanced years but still a large imposing man took a step out in front of the others and asked, "Who are you sir? And what is your business here?"

The man replied, "My apologies sir I am Lawrence T. Blakely grandson of Judge Blakely of Austin Texas. I am here in his stead, and have been given the duty to assist you however I can and in whatever endeavor you require!"

Pittcock bellowed out, "Good sir, why is your grandfather not here amongst us?"

Blakely said, "Sir, I regret to inform you my Grandfather has taken ill and is not in a state to travel such a great distance. He has given me his ring and said you are sure to recognize it because at your last meeting you made comment to the stone."

He looked at it nodding his head and said, "It was years ago but that I did Mr. Blakely, that I did. I am sorry to hear that my dear friend has taken ill. I pray a speedy recovery for him."

"Thank you Mr. Pittcock sir," replied Blakely.

"If your Grandfather has tasked you with this commitment then you shall be allowed to stay."

"It is my honor to serve," Blakely replied smartly.

Introductions were made, most men seemed familiar with each other but an additional two were present and stood out as unknown to most. They had all been asked to join this meeting for specific reasons and a special task.

Barnes stood before the men and said, "Gentlemen that which we feared is upon us! We must save the Confederacy if not now then for the future. Our cause took too much faith in our natural borders, the aggressive manner in which we fought, and spirit of our people. Gentlemen it takes more to win a war of this magnitude. A war cannot be won by fortifications, cannon, and gun powder alone gentlemen. It takes financial means, reserve funds, resources, industry, and agreements with other nations, trade goods, railroads, and safe ports. Winford Scott's Anaconda Plan to strangle the South has in the end caused us much hardship and with the fall of New Orleans and the Mississippi we were cut through. We were in effect surrounded by an enemy with the means to keep control of the coils. Through this council and through our influence we must learn from our past mistakes, and provide an opportunity to renew the flame of the Confederacy. I do not know how much longer our beloved South can hold out or what is in store when the Yankees take control but that is inevitable. I have put into motion certain events that will help insure our cause a chance in the future, but more importantly to help provide a life for soldiers when they come home."

All men listened intently as Mr. Barnes continued, "I am here to suggest that we carefully increase our ranks and use our influence to maintain the struggle. We must remain hidden using our secrecy to promote our agenda. We must increase our ranks with patriots of the cause. Only the most loyal of men should be considered. To use more than just signs and knocks that I told you about, but to learn of a man's quality through a series of levels within the society's membership."

One of the men, a Mr. Lawrence stood up and asked, "Mr. Barnes I would first like to say that I am honored that you have called upon me to perform this duty. Sir, I knew in general through our correspondence, as I am sure you all did what this meeting was about but how exactly are we to proceed with such a monumental task? You have given us limited details and it is certain that when this war ends the Yankee's will hang us if even a whisper is heard about this organization. Sir, we have no funds but our own, and for most of us those are greatly depleted. I alone have lost large sums of money during this war just in the devaluation of our government's money. How can I risk my life and that of those that I love at this juncture? Sir, I say this with only the most respectful of intent."

Mr. Barnes once again stood up and said, "Mr. Lawrence I have known you, your father and your family for many years. Your concerns are well founded, and I cannot promise your safety or that of your family. Secrecy is in fact our only shield and must be our highest concern. I have neither a sanction from a king nor a charter from a governor or president. I have no power given by a legislature that will protect us. We have only our wits to provide safety, our honor and duty to each other to protect us. We must be men in the shadows and often hidden right before the very eyes of those we work against. As our numbers increase our veils of secrecy must also increase.

Another of the men rose and stood before Mr. Barnes. A Mr. Allendale, a well known cotton grower from Mississippi addressed the group and said, "But Sir even with the shroud of secrecy Mr. Lawrence's concern of funds is founded. My family has already sacrificed greatly for this war. It has come at a great personnel expense, for which I am not complaining, but I have lost sons in this war. Sons who I needed to maintain all that we had, sons that I was relying on to get back all that we had lost. That was if the good Lord intervened and saved the South. God only knows what life will be like under the control of the Yankees."

Barnes looked to Pittcock who then stood and addressed the group, "Most of the men here have been called upon because you have the knowledge of commerce and keen business minds. Gentlemen the people were led to believe that a great Army with great generals would win this war. God bless our Army and our leadership but it takes more than guts and glory to win a conflict such as this. It is your knowledge and ties that brought great success to your families prior to this conflict. Ties that expanded your families interest's both here in the south and some even abroad. We believe the torrent of punishment that some in the North claim will rain down on us will be short lived. That in time the North will hold us to its bosom, and from there we will be given an opportunity to prosper. It is that possibility that we need to gain our advantage. Men will be coming home to broken and shattered lives. If nothing else then our organization will provide hope to some of those boys in the interim, but the dream of Southern Independence will not fade from our hearts as long as one of us lives, then the possibility of that dream will continue on."

Pittcock called me over and I pulled back a tarp covering many large leather pouches. Barnes stood and said, "Each of you men are to store these in safe keeping and when the time is right you are to act with these funds." Mr. Pittcock reached in one sack and produced a hand full of gold coin. Each of you are to carry back three sacks that should be a good start. We want you to maintain your holdings with this gold, then to properly invest and increase those holdings. When the time is right and upon due notifications give back a portion to further the interests of this group. We can rely on each other to loan or borrow and include each other in our business dealings. Increase not just our personal wealth, but use those bonds to increase the wealth of this organization."

"Where did such an amount of gold come from Sir?" Blakely asked. Pittcock pointed to one of the two men who were seated in the corner. A short and rather thin man with a thin mustache stood up. He held his hat at his waste and addressed the group. "I am Mr. Black I will give no first name and my last matters not because it's not my Christian name. I have acted as a spy for the cause performed many duties for the Confederacy spending much of this war far up north. My duties here will be made clear to all by Mr. Pittcock at some later point as will Mr. Smith's." He says pointing to the other unknown man who sat arms folded with a blank expression on his pock marked face. The men took great notice to these two gentlemen now.

Black continued, "As you know the Confederacy had a limited share of gold. What you may not know is that secret shipments of gold have been sent to aid our endeavor from both English and French financiers. One particular shipment came to us through the southern tip of Texas, and then over land. It was to cross the Mississippi near Vicksburg but was rerouted once the control of the Mississippi was lost. It's now safely hidden in the Oklahoma Territory and in a few caches between here and there."

Blakely asked, "Indians have Confederate gold?"

"Not exactly sir, replied Black but be careful what you say as not to offend our friend here Mr. Smith. His blood is of Chickasaw decent and he has been a trusted patriot of the Confederacy." replied Black. It was in fact Smith who sought Mr. Pittcock as an avenue to best handle this situation. Due to his ties with the government it was Mr. Pittcock's advice on the affair that took the gold to its safe haven."

Mr. Allendale interjected, "That brings to mind a few questions for you gentleman. Why was it not given to the government Mr. Pittcock? Or why did you just not keep it for yourself, for the temptation must have been great."

"To be sure it was Mr. Allendale, I struggled with that notion greatly," Black said in a half laugh. "Unfortunately, my duty is to the Southern Cause and not my own self interest. I was entrusted with this task and by rights I should have delivered it to the Confederate congress but the situation has changed for the cause. If delivered the gold would likely end up in Yankee hands. I contacted Mr. Barnes for his thoughts on the matter. He then told me of his bold plan and noted that financing a lost cause would do the people no good. He too felt it would likely end up in Yankee hands in the end and after much thought on the subject I agreed that this would be a better course of action. It has been reported as lost during an Apache attack. Knowing the details will only bring you trouble. I can say no more on this matter."

Black paused and said, "Smith and I believe in the cause and sacrificed much on its behalf. The gold is not ours, it belongs to the South and we wish it given back in a way that benefits her best. We ask only this in return. In the event of our deaths a small pension be given to our families or that by some miracle we happen to live to a long day we are taken care of in a manner appropriate for soldiers such as us. Our fear is gentlemen that as spies we will have nowhere to go when this conflict is over. We may need your help and safe keeping if the cause fails. We have knowledge and skills that can be helpful to your undertaking and as loyal patriots we offer our service to you."

Allendale once again piped up, "Please elaborate Mr. Black. What skills do you speak of?"

Black replied, "Gentlemen we can be your eyes, ears, and we can also handle matters. Let's just say, matters that you wouldn't want to be associated with; matters that are of a delicate nature.

"To be clear Mr. Black you mean murder." stated Allendale.

"Yes, but I am referring to all manner of work that gentlemen such as yourself should avoid. Sir, I am soldier of a different uniform I think not of it as murder when I kill an enemy no more that a soldier does, but you may call it as you like."

Barnes stood before the group, "Mr. Blakely please come forward and produce that ring once again."

Blakely complied and showed the ring to each man.

"I'd like to suggest that a garnet ring like Blakely's be worn by this council as a reminder of the bloodshed in the name of the cause. Not just the soldiers but the others. Their blood through our vigilance shall not be in vain gentlemen." Most men nod as they looked at the ring.

Pittcock again spoke, "Gentlemen I say it is our solemn duty as patriots of the South to take up this cause and through our actions give her a second chance."

Then each man stood as some clapped while others shook hands. Only the sedate Mr. Smith sat quietly still with arms folded in the chair against the wall. The men stayed in town varying lengths but each man headed home with a list of duties, given by Barnes, and their three bags of gold coin.

In the upcoming days Mr. Barnes used my legs and youth to his fullest advantage. Correspondence between men increased. As news about the war grew bleaker each day concerns grew that the men would be cut off from communication with each other. It was enacted that all correspondence be written in a code of sorts, one which later Black and Smith refined. In that time the name was given to the Sons of the Southern Cause.

That day it was also decided to send a special envoy to South America to gain a foothold in the markets there. Two men were sent and it was decided that Brazil had an appeal. The story goes that Chevez, the President of Brazil, was receptive to the notion that Southern cotton growers might want to immigrate to his country. Brazil was in much need of that type of expertise and he offered his help once they arrived. A man named Norris was chosen to be the leader. He and others would go to set up a colony of sorts; little did anyone suspect that when it was said and done almost nine thousand southerners would make a home there.

The support for this move was well received amongst the membership. It provided many outlets that were not in existence prior to the war. First and foremost, if the colony had success it was a group of people who could speak with possible allies on behalf of the South. It's location near to the ports of the Southern states but out of reach of the Union had strategic appeal. It could possibly provide trade goods in the future that could not be provided during the war. Furthermore, it was also a community that could grow unmolested by the Union because of the fact that they were on foreign soil. If any action were taken against them, then the Brazilian government and possibly other nations might get involved. President Chevez welcomed the Southerners as they came off the ships. By 1867 the colony was established in different locations of Brazil. The possible benefits were endless and the whole affair was strongly supported.

Cloverly went on, "You see Conner this is all for a reason. Now you understand the why. You are reaping a benefit of the seeds sown one night in a little country church by very bold intelligent men."

Mr. Conner looked at me with a crafty grin. I looked at him then looked down at the paper where I took my notes. Apparently so taken by the conversation I had stopped writing half way through.

"Does this story have your interest?" He asked.

"Mr. Conner this can't possibly be true. This story can't have been real." With a subtle knock and the jiggle of the door knob Mrs. Conner stepped into the room.

"How are you gentlemen?" She asked.

"All is well other than the fact our invited guest just called me a liar," grumbled Mr. Conner.

"No, ma'am," I interjected as I stood up. "This can't be true though can it?"

"See, I told you he called me a liar. He just did it again and why are you asking her she wasn't even there?" Mr. Conner said.

"Now James you're getting the man all flustered." She said. "It's a shocking revelation now isn't it Mr. Campbell. Don't you think you gentlemen should call it a night?"

"No ma'am," I said without thinking.

"He didn't like the lovey-dovey stuff–said it wasn't good for the paper. He wanted to leave but give'em blood, guts, gold, and secrets these reporter types start drooling and won't leave the house." I smiled and said, "You're right ma'am I'll be back tomorrow if I may?"

"Please call first and see how he's feeling," she said.

"I'll be fine Campbell; she just likes to treat me like I'm old." Mr. Conner replied.

The next morning Mr. Conner continued his story.

Mr. Cloverly told me once the North declared victory and the battle-fields had grown silent the period known as reconstruction began. It was a time of much hardship for Southerners. A wave of carpetbaggers came in from the North to take advantage of the situation and gained control of what they could in the South.

The Southern boys who survived the war had little to come back too. Their pride may have been damaged but their spirit wasn't broken. It was decided one of the best ways to give these men hope was to keep the Confederate officers in positions of high regard. Unbeknownst to most of them the group had spoken with the leadership of many universities, and suggested that positions be opened for these men to continue in a leader-ship role. It would serve many purposes. As educators they would likely be revered by the community instead of just men from the losing side of a war. They would be in direct influence of future generations of Southern boys holding a deserved status, dignity, and purpose in their lives. This alone would go a long way in keeping the dream alive. As expected many a confederate officer answered the call to teach the next generation.

Reconstruction was also a time of great opportunities and the group was quick to seize them. Having the advantage of capital, which was a rar-ity for a Southerner of the time, the used it to gain influence and in return made large profits. Business connections were at the top of the list for the Sons of the Cause. Those were quickly achieved and used to our benefit. The network worked with each other trading knowledge, information, and monies all to the benefit of the organization. Even the greed of the Yankees was used to gain an edge as huge profits came rolling in.

Mr. Barnes was wise to pick those men. All were noble and loyal, but crafty as a foxes in their business affairs. Mr. Blakely inherited his grand-father's fortune and his exuberance proved useful on more than one oc-casion. He gained special favors with a railroad commissioner and at that time the railroad was a lifeline to all business concerns.

A young man from Georgia became the right hand for Blakely. In time he was sent to work with many men in the organization. He learned skills from each as they passed down their knowledge to this young hopeful until finally he finally ended up on Mr. Barnes doorstep. Barnes had by that time turned over much of his business interests to me. It became my responsibility to further the young man's education and we became quite close. I learned of his qualities, and he quickly earned my respect.

It was decided unanimously to let him in on our secret and fund his endeavors. They sent him back to Georgia where he could use his knowledge best. That man was your Grandfather Jimmy and like we expected he became a valuable asset within the organization. He increased our holdings, furthered our interests, and increased our ranks of membership.

I'm not exactly sure why he told me all this. Maybe he was losing his senses, had I been anyone else I may have been in danger. For that matter, so would he. It helped having a grandfather on the council because I fell under his protection. As long as I kept my secrets to myself, I was safe.

Cloverly confided many details of the organization, most importantly the existence of the Seven. Mr. Conner motioned for me and said, "Grab the coin, Campbell. So, we can speak on it for awhile." He pointed in the direction of its location. I reached up to the top shelf of his book case and handed him the bronze coin.

"Now remember me telling of this coin and what was on each side."

"Yes sir," I replied.

"First you have a figure on the front it is in fact Pleion. She was the mother of Atlas's children. The seven stars represent her daughters and they make the constellation Pleiades; just as young Wallace had said."

I looked at the strange coin as Mr. Conner continued, "A pretty smart boy if I say so myself. Now the seven stars are Maia, Electra, Taygete, Alcyone, Merope, Sterope, Celaneo. Just after secession the Northern papers referred to the first seven states to secede as the Seven Sisters of Pleiades.

I turned the coin and said, "The Latin at the bottom Deo Vindice. Does it mean "God Will Vindicate?"

"Correct you are Mr. Campbell. You've been paying attention."

I turned the coin to the opposite side. "The scorpion; what do you make of that?" Conner asked.

"The scorpion? I really have no idea of the meaning."

Cloverly told me the scorpion is not just a symbol of death, but in ancient times of rebirth. I think the Seven's very nature caused them to be associated with the scorpion or the nature of the scorpion caused it to be associated with the group."

"The Seven?" I asked.

"Hold on! I'm not done telling you about Cloverly. He was quite intrigued by Black and Smith."

Clovery continued on by saying, "I need to lay some back ground on these fellow's Black and Smith. They were the ones that founded what became the Seven. It was their skills that were handed down and laid a firm foundation for the Seven's success. Smith was half French and half Chickasaw. He had come from just outside the Oklahoma territory which was all Indian land back then. He of a shorter stature, quite dark, with a scared face, often dressed in a black suit and a short flat top hat. The necklace he wore was the only hint of his Indian heritage in his dress.

Black was a smoothed faced man, dark thick hair and a well kept mustache. He was always in a suit and usually had a smile that seemed to have a hidden meaning behind it. He is slightly taller than average very thin and considered himself handsome. He likely would have been quite a lady's man if he had time for such endeavors, but he frowned at drawing attention to himself. He would try to look typical for the most part and go unnoticed in most situations.

Black was highly intelligent, cunning, and motivated. Before the war he worked for a short time as a Pinkerton with the Illinois Railroad. Before the war broke out, he migrated south knowing the Confederacy would need a man of his specific talents.

He had a hand in the riots in Delaware, caused descent in New York City, and worked in the shadows on other occasions. He decided his talents weren't being fully utilized to their potential. So he went another route, by lending them instead to the newly established government of the Confederacy. Having friends in the right places that recognized his special skills helped. His early ties in the North and South made him well connected with both rich and poor alike, making his movements between the two sides quite easy. The damage he caused the North could not be assessed in practical terms other than simply stating he was a true Southern asset. It appeared he always had a plan, and knew how to get things done.

I'll tell you something else about that meeting at the church and Mr. Black. I stood by and watched as the gentlemen left one by one. All that was left was Mr. Barnes, Mr. Black, and Smith. Smith finally stood up, put on his hat, and walked over to shake the hand of Mr. Barnes. Before leaving Black said, "It's time for a little retribution for Richmond and thank you for the information on Louis Powell. I wasn't sure what to make of him." Mr. Barnes just shook his hand and said, "Thank you Mr. Black for all that you have done." And the men parted ways.

Mr. Conner asked, "Do you know the name Powell or Payne more likely?" I had no idea and shook my head to that effect.

Mr. Conner went on and said, "Louis Thorton Powell or more commonly known as Lewis Paine was involved with the Confederate secret service and was also associated with a fella named Booth. For that association he was hanged. Now, I'm not saying Black had anything to do with Lincoln's assassination but that always struck me as interesting.

Mr. Conner added, "It has always amazed me hearing stories about Black and Smith right from the first time Cloverly spoke of them. I tried to find out more from others, but most lips were tight. I could always find out a little something here and there but not much with proof behind it.

"Campbell do I still have your interest to keep you around long enough to finish my story or do I need to find someone else?" Conner asked.

"Mr. Conner you have my full attention." I replied.

"I would like to take a break for awhile and continue later if we may." He seemed a little more tired than usual and I replied, "Of course."

"In let's say three hours if that's all right with you?"

"That would be fine sir."

That afternoon I left Mr. Conner's home and took a short walk while I considered the details of what he had told me. To think that I had just about given up on his story and now suddenly it seems that I have been entrusted with the details of a powerful secret organization. I wondered to what end this road would lead me or will his story just leave me with the question, "Has Mr. Conner lost his mind or have I lost mine for believing any of it?"

After our break Mr. Campbell appeared to have rested some and I sat down. Before getting settled he eagerly continued by saying, "Campbell we have gotten a little off track from the way I intended to tell my story. If I may I'd like to get back on course."

TWELVE

After college my life became busy with the interests of my grandfather's and that of the Sons. I had lost contact of most of the boys from Bransford. All but Wallace, we would see each other from time to time. Unfortunately, we were growing increasingly distant as each year passed.

Whittington was also a figure in those years. His grandfather was a member of the council, which caused our paths to cross more often than I would have liked. We both seemed pulled by opposing forces within the organization and he too quickly made his way up through the ranks. On the occasions we were together we were civil, but friction hovered around us like a hazy fog. At Wallace's wedding, where we were on our best behavior, an outsider may have thought we were actually friends. For some reason Whittington had taken Wallace under his wing while in college. They made peace with each other while at the same fraternity. There was just something I didn't trust about him or his new found friendship with Wallace. What bothered me most was I had heard his name in association with a group called the Seven. At that time I had no real idea of what that meant just that Black and Smith created it. Knowing better than to make inquires I just kept quiet about the subject even with my grandfather.

As with most men other interests of mine demanded my attention. Concerns for the welfare of the young, but grown man, Wallace withered.

Miss Lucille Bedford had gone off to school and graduated just a couple of years behind me. I was just getting to know her again before Wallace's wedding.

In time Lucille and I became a steady thing. I wasn't too excited about the proposition of getting married in the near future to anyone, but became engaged to her anyway. Even though our engagement was resoundingly approved by all as a natural step in the process of life, I had a nagging feeling that something wasn't right. I was pushing twenty seven, and she felt that she had put in the time. Under pressure over something I didn't want to face. I did what most men do and buried myself in my work. Never the less, each day the clock ticked and brought me closer to the altar.

I needed out of the marriage gun sights for a bit, so I gladly took reprieve on a business trip. While working in New Orleans I walked the streets and enjoyed the sights and smells of the old city. For some reason I found myself wondering what had become of Sally. If she was here amongst the inhabitants working as an entertainer or some other unsavory profession like her aunt and cousin had. I began looking for her in the face of every woman that walked past. I tried to imagine what she looked like now and wondered if I would feel anything if I happened to come across her.

The more I thought about it, the more I wanted to feel that sensation again. I wanted my heart to stir as it had once before. I was separated from my emotions and yearned for a shared partnership with closeness, depth, and meaning. I began to wonder if it was even a true emotion or something made up in my mind. Possibly just some youthful expression that would fade as wisdom took charge of the more raw emotions in one's heart. Or maybe those feelings never go away they just echo around in the soul and give us a drive and desire for more. Perhaps even to torment us as a reminder of how precious and rare those opportunities really are.

Shaking the notion I considered the other possibilities. Maybe any of the lady's that walked the streets could provide a similar feeling. One thing was for sure I wanted to know before I made the move to be married.

I took a break from the heat for a moment and sat under a covered awning at a street side cafe. I leaned back not saying anything and watched the races of people intermingled in the streets. I took notice of the things that would only happen in a port city. Interactions that would seem out of place anywhere else. The common people and the highbrow alike just steps away from each other talking and exchanging pleasantries while conducting daily business.

I saw a light skinned colored woman pass through my view. She was wearing clothes of a fashionable design and walked proudly down the street. In her I saw something reminiscent of the ghost from my past. It was likely that my ghost was amongst the people meandering the streets of the entire city, but it wasn't likely she would be anywhere near where I now sat. I leaned back thinking Sally was like a dream to me, one that would whisper to me late at night. Then you wake up and for a brief moment you're happy and content only to realize that it wasn't real at all. The whole thing was made up in your head. My mind shifted gears and I said to myself, "But it was real."

I sipped my tea and continued to watch the young woman. A mixture of vehicles and the occasional horse passed through my view. The girl turned and I couldn't quite make out her features. Unable to resist I stood and moved a step closer. "This is ridiculous," I remember thinking but I still moved another step closer. The girl not knowing she was being watched walked in my direction. I began to make out her face more clearly, and she seemed so similar to Sally. Unfortunately, it was in those similarities that I began to notice the differences in the two. With each step closer my confirmation became clear. She passed by my side and must have noticed my look of disappointment saying, "Good morning sir," as she passed by. I was too deep in thought to respond. I just stood there with my hands in my pockets. Just the notion of seeing her gave rise to feelings. I shuttered at the possibility that Sally would remain a ghost, one that I carried around deep inside and continued to think about almost daily. "This will be a long life of regret if I you're not careful my friend." I whispered to myself.

A couple of weeks later I arrived back at Shadow Wood, my grandfather called me outside to look at a new arrival. I hadn't seen him since my return, and we walked out to the large garage where Henry was standing. I walked with Grandfather while he told me about a favor that was returned to him in the form of a new car.

"She's Italian, a couple of years old a 1932 model." He said.

"You have an Italian car?" I asked.

"I saw a picture of one just like it and commented to an old friend that it was a beautiful machine, and she was shipped this direction shortly afterwards."

"I know we have connections abroad but in Italy?" I asked.

"None in Italy that I know of, but we do have shipping interests that trade there." He stated.

I approached the front of the garage and there she stood. "A red Alfa Romeo?"

"An Alfa Romeo 2300 eight cylinder spider," he said.

"Can I just call her the spider? "

"No, you cannot," he said.

"I don't want to call her Alfa. I'll come up with something." Grandfather grunted with disapproval.

"She is a beautiful machine." I stated. "Shall we put the top down and take her for a spin?"

Grandfather quickly interrupted, "Henry needs to service her. Besides we have some matters that need to be tended too."

We left the garage and walked inside to the den. There we sat for a few moments and smoked cigars that I had picked up on my travels. I looked around the book filled room as we discussed the meetings and what I had seen during while I was away. The topic soon changed to my future and the life ahead of me. I could see he had a point to make and he stated it was time for a change. He asked if Lucille and I had decided where we would like to live. Apparently, he and the Bedford's had been looking into homes in the area for us. He impressed upon me that it was important that I take on Lucille and provide her a good life style; one in which she could entertain and socially connect us even further.

He seemed proud of the proposition as things were going according to his plan. I paused a moment and looked at him. Then I asked, "What if I'm not in love with her?"

"Oh nonsense," he stated. "Of course you're in love with her you've been with her for years, far too long if I might add. Honestly, I'm surprised you kept her at bay this long. Had the times not been so hard then this matter might have already been resolved. All of your friends have taken the leap; it's time you do the same." I stood my ground and said. "But I'm not in love with Lucille."

He quickly leaned forward and asked, "Are you trying to say that you're in love with someone else? My God this will be a disgrace."

"No, there is no one else."

"Thank God." He said leaning back in his chair then took another puff off the cigar. "Then its just cold feet I would say. It was the same for me when I married your Grandmother but we married much younger. She was a good woman your grandmother. She was kind and gentle. It's a shame I can't share these years with her now."

"I'm certain that I'm not just having cold feet about this. I just can't imagine getting married to someone I'm not in love with."

"Nonsense," he stated. "Love has very little to do with marriage in the first place. I had this same conversation with your father. For me the whole thing was worked out by your grandmother's father. I worked for him and she knew I worked hard and had a future. I knew she had a name and a good solid family. It made sense for the both of us."

"I'm to get married to Lucy because it makes sense?"

"Yes, you're to marry Lucille because it makes sense but if that doesn't suit you then because you've been with her. Haven't you? You can't bring that kind of shame into someone's life."

I looked down and sighed, "Yes, I have but how will that shame ….." Interrupting me he said, "Son these times may be different but you can't do that to the poor girl. You're lucky that you don't have her in a family way already. I was hoping in some way that might happen to get you moving along but it never did." I again said, "It's not going to shame her."

He slammed his hand down on the desk and once said, "It will!!! And you can't shame her! In the end you'll shame yourself and all of us with her. She will be devastated. Do the right thing and marry the girl and all will be fine."

Not wanting to continue the conversation I stood up slowly, and walked toward the door. What started off as a discussion quickly turned into an argument. I left feeling like I was now enclosed in a cage and Grandfather and the Bedford's had the key.

I went for a drive that night to cool down. I drove around contemplating the life that no longer seemed to be in my control. I wondered if it ever was.

The next morning Lucille met me at the door and sweetly kissed me on the check. She could be quite nice at times which gave me hope.

"Morning love," She said.

"Morning Lucy," I replied.

"Are you leaving again?" She asked.

"No, I'm not," I replied.

"Good then I can have you all to myself; hopefully for the whole day." She said smiling.

Ida came in the room and asked," Miss Lucille would you like some breakfast."

"No, Ida I'm fine but I may need someone to help me drag Jimmy out of the house for the day."

"Jimmy, I'll make you two a bite to eat and you can drive Lucille up to the lake. It would be a fine day for a drive."

"Sounds good," I replied.

I was ready and in no time and we started the drive to the lake with Miss Ida's food nestled in a basket in the back. Lucille sat close to me for the moment quiet and then finally spoke breaking the silence, "Jimmy when we get our house I think the maid should call you Mr. Conner. You're of an age now where you should be addressed properly and that would be more appropriate."

"Now Lucy, Miss Ida has been like a mother to me for most of my life, her calling me Jimmy is not an issue."

"It's just not right or proper and she's not your mother, she's colored! "

"Lucy she's been wonderful to me. She's a part of my family."

"If you ask me Jimmy, that's nonsense, she's a long way from being a Conner." She said. Fearing a day of bickering, I conceded but only not to discuss it further.

Once we arrived at the lake we wasted little time and ate the meal that Ida had prepared for us. Later, I watched the water on the lake while lying with my head in Lucy's lap. She seemed content pampering me by ran her fingers through my hair and said, "I can't believe it Jimmy, soon you'll be carrying me across the threshold of our big new house, and we can make love every night instead of always sneaking around. I want to have babies Jimmy. I'd like to try right away." I didn't say anything I just laid there looking at the sky. She continued, "We could have waited some but this long engagement has cost us time."

"Lucy, something about this last trip made me think. Do you love me?" I asked.

"Of course I do silly." She said.

"No, Lucy what I mean is, are you in love with me, or is it all the rest?"

"Jimmy, now why do you asked such things of me. I'll make you a wonderful wife. I wouldn't be here if I didn't think you'd be a wonderful husband. It all just makes sense."

"Makes sense huh. Are you in love with me or the lifestyle?"

"James Conner, it's you! You worry too much about things. We will be the talk of the town." She leaned over and kissed me. I rolled over on my back and she said, "Jimmy I do love you." She kissed me again and unfastened my belt.

"Make love to me now Jimmy," she whispered. For the time being at least, I guess she settled me down.

THIRTEEN

The situation with Wallace was bothering me. We hadn't spoken in quite some time, even though I had made attempts by calling, he never returned them. Soon I was away again on business, and this time my destination brought a smile to my face. Being so close I decided it was time to pay a visit to Bransford Academy. It was much like the first time I laid eyes on the school. I noticed everything, the cadets walking the campus, the academy, and of course the two cannon being diligently polished by a small group of cadets. I had to laugh remembering how many times Wallace and I had done the same. I walked past the boys and told them to keep up the good work.

Inside I caught myself looking around as if I would see a familiar face amongst the cadets. In the trophy case I saw a picture of our class in full uniform with class of 1927 noted in the corner. It had been years since my last visit. I was sure that the Colonel was gone but I decided I would make an appearance anyway. I introduced myself to the cadet Sergeant Major and he told me he told me Colonel Stiles was the new superintendent. I walked in the door and met with a much younger version of the Colonel I had known. We shook hands and made introductions. He knew my family name from the donations we'd made. I asked if he was by chance related to a Charlie Stiles, a cadet that I had gone to school with.

He told me that he was in fact his uncle. I also made note of the gentleman's ring, and that he too was a part of the Sons. He shut the door and sat across from me.

Stiles told me, in confidence of course, that Whittington had contacted him recently and that I needed to be aware of the fact. He said, "I cannot speak much more of the conversation but be warned Mr. Conner do not trust that man." Colonel Stiles was younger, but carried himself with the same dignity and sense of honor that his predecessor had. "Actually, Mr. Conner it's a time to be careful with who you trust at all." Then he began to scribble a list of names that I was unfamiliar with. He assured me they would hold the Sons above personal gain, and I assured him that he need not worry, that everything seemed under control from where I stood. He looked at me as if he didn't believe me and then asked, "Is your visit to possibly see Mr. Downey?"

"Yes, as a matter of fact it is."

"I think that would be of great benefit to you if you did." Stiles commented.

I thanked him and began walking down to the stable. Unsure of what to think about the meeting I realized that I was once again treading in unfamiliar territory and that it was becoming a common theme for me.

The stables were in good condition with fresh paint making me wonder if possibly there had been another late night meeting interrupted by the Downy and Hillenbrand duo.

A boy walked out of the barn and snapped a salute to a familiar corner. That moment brought back many memories for me. Entering the stable I immediately saw Downey with his back to me cleaning the hoof of a horse. As I walked past the statue I heard Downy's Irish voice say, "So, now that you have became a civilian you're all aloof and you can't even pay your respect to the good Colonel. Now can ya?"

"Mr. Downey how are you?"

"I'm in good repair Mr. Conner, but the Colonel over there is still waiting for your salute."

"Very well sir." I stated then turned and whipped a salute to the Colonel. I knew better than to buck Mr. Downey even as an adult.

"There ya go lad." He said.

"You never quit being a cavalry man ya know. It's in your blood now."

"I hope so Mr. Downey. Tell me how have you been? I said as I stuck out my hand.

"Very good to see ya Conner, very good indeed,"

"Is Mr. Hillenbrand around?" I asked.

"No, Lad he moved on to live with family in Richmond he has a sick sister. It's a shame I'm sure he would have appreciated seeing you."

"Me too, if you hear from him let him know that I asked about him or maybe I could visit him sometime. Richmond isn't far from one of my usual stops."

"Well, lad you look fit and quite polished in that suit. I hear good things about you and the organization." He said. "Let's take a short walk over to the pasture shall we."

"Love too Mr. Downey." We chatted for a few moments, and then walked to the gate. Downy let out a whistle and the mounts came running.

"Ya recognize that one Conner?" He asked.

"Why, yes I do." I stated. Standing on the bottom rung of the fence I beckoned Cisco to come closer.

"Great to see you Cisco!" I said as I patting the dust from his back. "Mr. Downey I didn't expect I would feel this way the first time I walked up the path to Bransford, but this place really means a lot to me."

Downey said, "You spent seven years here. You learned things that you'll carry through life, and you had many friends. Do you hear from them?"

"Not really. I've been busy." I replied.

"What about Wallace? You and he were thick as thieves."

"Yes, sir we were but he's married now and strangely sticking awful close to Whittington."

"Hmmm" Downey scowled. "Neither Whittington nor his family are to be trusted. I'm sure you didn't stop in just to visit, Conner. You have some questions for me don't ya? I can see that something is troubling you."

"Yes, sir I do."

"Meet me at the stables after dark, and we can visit a little more. Do you have the time?" Downey asked.

"Well, sir I have questions that need to be answered, so I guess I'll have to make it." I said grinning.

Later that night I returned to continue my conversation with Mr. Downey. On my way down to the stables I nodded as I passed a group of cadets. The light was on inside the stable, and a swarm of moths hovered over it. Downey was out front sitting on a chair whittling. I walked up and we exchanged greetings.

"Do you have an extra knife Mr. Downey it appears I have left mine back at the house?"

"Of course," he replied. We sat there and visited for a few moments and again talked of old times. I had forgotten how calming something mundane like whittling a piece of wood could be. I think a man should just do nothing for a bit each day to unwind.

Downey piped up and asked, "So, Conner care for another try at Red's Blend?"

"Not to insult you Mr. Downey, but I am afraid that would have a similar effect as the last time I tried it."

Downey laughed and said, "You give up on the whiskey too?"

"To the contrary sir, I have grown accustom to that particular vice." I replied.

He went inside once again and produced a bottle and two tin cups. This is only way to drink whiskey. I'm sure you have drank from some very fine glasses, but something in the tin makes this Kentucky whiskey go down a little smoother. It's not Irish whiskey of course but I seem to be a little short of that particular drink. So, Kentucky's finest will have to do." He filled the tin half full and I took Downey for his word and drank a handsome swig. Then shook my head and let out a breath, "Yes.... smooth." I choked out. "There is definitely something to that tin."

"I have some moonshine inside if you like."

"No, No Mr. Downey."

"Well, then Mr. Conner let us sit and deliberate on the issue at hand,"

"And how would you know the particular issue I came here to discuss." I replied.

"Nothing much gets past me Conner. Now, let me see where ya are in your leaning." We exchanged some hand gestures, shakes and signs.

"Very good," he retorted. "They are moving you along at quite a pace. They must have big plans for you. Do you know this one?" Using his knife he then drew in the sand a sign that represented a scorpion.

"Yes, of course..... it's a lot like scorpion on the coin."

"That's exactly right. Conner, I'm stepping out of line and not following orders here but there are things going on that you need to pay attention too. If anyone knew I had told you, it could be the death of me."

"Very well, you have my word."

Downey continued, "The scorpion I made here is missing a leg. It's often drawn in this manner but not always. If you count the two claws and five of the six legs as I have shown the number equals seven. Also, notice that one claw is bigger, that represents the Sons organization. The other claw represents another group, a smaller but powerful group called the Seven. And they, let's say keep things in order. Maybe even make matters move in the direction the Sons desire. Do you remember that knife you showed me?"

"Yes, I do."

"It was your father's is that correct?"

"Yes," I replied.

"Well, you don't just get a knife like that. You have to earn it like I did mine. The knife is symbol of a job well done. It's a rite of passages let's say.......although for me it's something quite different. I keep it to remember."

"Mr. Downey does the Seven have a connection with Black and Smith?" I asked.

"Very good Conner you've been keeping your ears open. As you have likely figured out there are only supposed to be seven members in the Seven at one time but they have access to past members if the situation calls for it. They have tremendous enthusiasm for the cause and a deep loyalty to each other."

"So, you're saying that my father did something to earn that knife?" I asked.

"You can only get the knife one way son and that's to kill for the cause."

"My father was a murderer?"

"They don't think of killing as murder. They prefer to think of it more as a soldier would."

"And you have earned a knife too."

"Yes, of that I'm afraid so." He read the inscription, "Intus Cheles Capisso it means within the claws grasp. Each knife has a Latin name."

"But why would we cause someone's death."

"For the greater good lad at least that's what I tell myself. Truthfully Conner, when I was younger I was a different man and eager to move along. I didn't have the family money like you do. If I participated in the Seven I would be given a position, status, and a career of some note. Because of my association I would be able to provide for my family."

"Were you married Mr. Downey?" I asked.

"Yes, lad I was married and had a little girl but in my situation the grasp of the claw had too much grasp on me. The Seven took me away from my family often, and I began to change inside as well. I have earned this knife many times over. I was a little too good at killing for my own well being. The Seven is supposed to use great discretion, to only take the lives of those asked by a higher authority, but Whittington's father was the lead man within the group. He was a power hungry evil man. He used us for his own personal gain. I was a good soldier and did as I was told but in the end I lost my wife to another and my child went with her. All I had worked for was gone, and I lost heart for the matter."

"How did you end up here?" I asked.

"I was offered much more but I asked to be here and left alone. One night something I'd rather not speak of went wrong, and it was time for me to pay my penance."

"Do you think the Whittington's are making another play for power?" I asked.

"Of course they are lad, I'm certain of it."

"I know of Whittington's Grandfather, but not his father. What happened to him?"

"He's in exile of sorts but don't count of that. It's best to remember that young Whittington is cut from the same block as his grandfather and father. They have the loyalty of many through the seven."

"The council," I asked. "What's its role exactly?"

"Again I'm speaking out of turn. Too much whiskey for this Irishman, the council decides the course of the organization."

"I'm not sure what you mean." I said.

"Lad, I asked ya back tonight for a reason. That's why I'm risking this. You must be careful who you speak too. Watch your friends and your enemies."

"I have no enemies to speak of," I said.

"Conner, we all have enemies when power and money are involved, especially great sums like the Sons have at their finger tips. Friends a penny may part, let alone the wealth that is involved here."

I listened intently as Downey continued, "Most importantly there is a rift for power within the organization. Men will without a doubt pick sides. The Seven is small, but they have a deep loyalty to each other and I'm certain the Whittington's are behind this. I am only telling you this so you protect yourself and the organization. The Sons must live on, lad. Many have given their life for it and some are innocent. I wouldn't want all of this to be in vain."

"I'm beginning to wonder why my father lived way out on the flatlands of South Carolina away from the organization and grandfather."

"I can't answer that lad maybe he chose his family over the organization or maybe he had his own penance to pay. Your grandfather will have to help with those questions. Let us end these matters for the night and enjoy the evening."

We spent the rest of the night talking on subjects of no particular importance. The call of the bugle woke me when reveille sounded. I struggled to get out of Mr. Downey's chair. Downey was already awake and outside. He laughed and said, "Conner you better stay here with me. I never completed your education on drinking and doing your duty the next day. You should stay another week. I'll enroll you in the school of whiskey and rye."

Wiping my eyes I said, "No thank you Mr. Downey but it's been good to see you just the same. Thank you for watching my back."

"Not just your back Conner but that of the Sons too," as we shook hands he pulled me in close.

"I'm warning you Conner take what I've told you seriously. It's not to be taken lightly. The scorpion has more than a stinger, it has claws! You better beware!"

"Yes, sir I'll remember," I replied.

"Next time you're here lad I'll get Cisco saddled for you. The ride will do you good!" Downey said.

"I look forward to it Mr. Downey."

We said our goodbyes, and I drove off. As glad as I was to see Bransford, I left with a heavy burden on my mind. I had business to attend to, but when I got back Wallace was going to be the primary concern.

FOURTEEN

A week later I arrived back at Shadow Wood. However, my stay was brief. I reported the needed information on the holdings to my grandfather but hesitated to ask him about my father and the Seven. He seemed to sense something was wrong, but he never asked and the matter was not discussed.

I left in the morning and finally arrived in Wallace's hometown many hours later. Wallace lived in the northern part of Georgia and I had little trouble in finding his new home in such a small town. I pulled in front of the house, and paused for a moment trying to determine what to say to him. In the mean time I noticed the neighborhood of similar two story brick homes on the street all looking very much the same, but his had an iron fence and large maple in the front yard. I stepped from the car into to the darkness even though it was still fairly early in the night. This was the first night I noticed that the days were getting shorter as the fall drew ever nearer. I loved the fall and the changing of the leaves but the shortened hours of day light were something I loathed.

Finally, I opened the gate and walked to the front door then spun the door bell with a twist of my wrist. His wife Katie answered the ring, "Jimmy Conner, what a surprise. It's wonderful to see you."

"You too Katie," I replied. "Is Virgil home by chance?"

"Yes, he is. What brings you up this way?" she asked.

And then she called out "Virgil, Jimmy Conner is here." Virgil walked downstairs and greeted me hesitantly. He put on his best face but Virgil was a terrible poker player. I knew him far too well not to read his expression. As most men mature they learn to disguise their lack of confidence, through deed or anger. They disguise their lies with smiles or diversions of conversation. They disguise their fears by standing ground on points that just don't matter. But Wallace was different, much different from most men. Wallace had a big heart and at his core he was just plain good. He wore his feelings on his shoulder and I could usually see what was going on in his head. I never considered that a fault though. It's just that his kind nature made it hard for him to be deceitful. It was actually what I liked about him most.

The apparent change in behavior and our friendship is why I came. Something was wrong. I didn't know what exactly but after speaking with Mr. Downey I was afraid George would get him into something serious without regard for his welfare. We walked through the house playing the coy game of two men with something important on their mind, but neither knowing how to say it. Wallace asked, "Would you like to meet the new addition to the family?"

"Sure Virgil, a boy or girl I never heard?"

"A boy," he replied.

"Nice home you and Katie have here." I said.

"Yes, we just moved up here to Birch Street, but it's nothing compared to Shadow Wood Jimmy."

"Shadow Wood is something, but that's Grandpa's home. I guess I don't really have a need for one without a family."

"You have no concern one day it will all be yours Jimmy." Wallace stated with a tone of jealousy. We walked over and I looked down at his four month old son.

"Nice looking boy. What's his name?

"Clarence, after my father."

"How is your father?" I asked.

"He's fine, Jimmy, he is pushing me as always."

"Virgil, I just wanted to talk to you for a few minutes. Can we speak somewhere alone?"

"No, I'm going to have to be leaving soon." Wallace replied. Katie walked in and said, "This is such a surprise Jimmy and with George stopping by it will be a regular Bransford reunion."

"George Whittington?" I asked.

"Yes, he should be here shortly," replied Katie.

Wallace stood up uncomfortably and said, "He's not staying and I'm sorry but we have to leave."

"Oh," I replied. "What's ole George got planned for you two this late at night?" I asked.

"Just a meeting," Wallace shrugged.

"A Sons meeting? I wouldn't mind attending."

"No, just a meeting," and then George knocked on the door. Virgil opened it and I heard Wallace say, "Let's scat, Virgil."

I then approached the door and walked up to George. "Conner? Well, I'm surprised to see you here." Then he looked over to Wallace who immediately looked down to the floor. I walked past them both and reached for my coat.

"You boys have a good night, my business seems to be done for now." I said. "Goodnight Katie." She came in the hall with a large plate of freshly cut snacks. "Leaving so soon?" she said looking disappointed.

"I am sorry Katie. I have to head back."

"George, are you staying?" she asked.

"I'm afraid not, Katie, we need to get going."

"Oh, well then this will all just go to waste." and she walked back in the kitchen.

As I put my hat on I looked squarely at Whittington and said, "Good bye, Virgil."

"Good bye," he replied.

I walked down the stairs of the porch with my back to them and I heard Whittington say, "Yeah, good bye Jim." I didn't turn around but could see Whittington's reflection on the car door as he stood defiantly on the porch. Making no acknowledgement of the comment I just drove off.

For an hour or so I rode around trying to decide whether to leave or not. I ended up at a roadside diner just on the edge of town. I ordered a coffee and a bite of food. I sat there deliberating my next move. Two men entered each wearing the red stone rings of the Sons. I had never met them, but wasn't too surprised. There were so many men in the organization at the first level.

I was tempted to flash my ring but something deep inside told me not too. The smaller of the two men took off his hat and coat. I heard one speak to the other and noticed their accents were thick with the sound of the North. Something in my gut told me to just sit and wait. The two men sat in the booth two tables in front me and began to talk. I asked the waitress for a local paper and she brought one to my table. I could hear the men as they made little effort to keep their voices down.

"Kid seems skittish" said the larger of the men.

"Ya," replied the other. "I figure he won't go through with it."

"He'll do it. That boy thinks his father will disown him if he don't. Plus, that George has him wrapped like a package," replied the large man.

The other said, "Nice job by the way setting it up for the kid to get picked."

The large man commented by saying, "You like that? An old magic trick my dad taught me when I was a kid." And he lifted a coin near his face and said, "Now ya see it. Now ya don't." Then he laughed rather loudly. The other man put his hand on the large mans hands and said, "Put that away. It's supposed to mean something down here."

"AHHHH," said the large man. "Nobody knows nothing," He was about to put the coin in his front pocket, when he looked at me and yelled, "Hey Mac, you know anything?" I calmly looked over my paper and pointed to myself.

"Yeah, you! You know magic?" he asked. Once again he lifted the coin so I could see it. I plainly saw the coin and made out the scorpion image.

"Now ya see it now ya don't."

I laughed and said, "Good one you got anymore?"

"Nah, first ones for free gotta pay for the rest," then he laughed. I laughed too then went back to my reading. The smaller man said, "Best take these off too and they removed their rings. "You were supposed to give the coin back."

"Yeah, but I like it," replied the large man.

"Careless" I thought. It was rare but possible for a Yankee with the right connections to be in the organization but for the most part they never made it past the gentleman's club. It was an avenue to solidify business ties. Even making it appear that much more of a social network. Those two men weren't the type though. Nor could I believe that an associate of theirs was part of the larger network. Unless maybe they had been displaced or moved for the interest of the Sons. Or possibly if a family member were in the hierarchy. But it just didn't seem likely that those two men would have reason or a chance to have access to the organizations true intent. Let alone be associated with the Seven. I walked outside and took notice of the vehicle and its Illinois plates.

None of it made sense to me. Starting my car I drove off in the direction of home. A nagging feeling set in, and I turned the vehicle around heading back to Wallace's. Parking just a few blocks from his house and traveling the rest of the way on foot. I waited hidden around the corner of his home.

A short time later Whittington's vehicle drove up and stopped as I stood there quietly and strained to overhear the conversation between Wallace and Whittington. All I really heard was Wallace telling Whittington good-bye and Whittington replying, "Make us all proud, Virgil."

"I'll do just that, George."

Whittington turned the corner and I approached Wallace as he was unlocking the door with his key. "Virgil, wait," I said. Virgil looked at me unlocked the door and stepped inside. I followed him inside closing the door behind me. "Conner what are you doing here?" Virgil asked as he walked to the window and looked outside; presumably to see if Whittington had left.

"Virgil, what's going on here? What's Whittington got you into?" I asked.

"Nothing, just some business," he replied.

"Business? The Seven's business or George's business?" I asked coldly.

"Seriously, Jimmy you have to go." He stated.

"Virgil, I'm not leaving till I get some answers." Virgil turned his back to me as he hung his coat on the wall.

"Virgil we're friends and you're not being yourself. What is going on between you two?" I asked.

Virgil then looked at me mad as I have ever seen him. "I can keep secrets too Jim and this is one I gotta keep! Is this some test you're putting me through?" He questioned.

"No," I stated, "I'm not playing the game were just two friends talking."

"Jimmy I hear it all time. Looks like the Conner boy is moving up. What are you doing to keep pace?"

"You're Father," I asked.

"Who else?" Virgil replied.

"Virgil you're doing great. Look around at this home, Katie, and now Clarence."

"Jim, Whittington set this up. He is the reason I have this. He's fast tracking me through and placed me in the Seven."

"The Seven?" I asked. "Why would Whittington want you in the Seven? He hates you."

"Not anymore Jim," he said. "We're friends now. He helped me move up and his grandfather is helping me too. They watch my back and I watch theirs."

"What does your father think about this Virgil?

"He's fine with it. He wants me to move up in the organization he...." Then Wallace looked at me curiously and said, "Why, are you jealous Jimmy? Are you worried that I'll catch up with you? Maybe get in the council one day? I don't have people just moving me up like you. It's different for me I have to earn it."

"Listen to yourself," I said. "I'm not competing for anything here. I'm just doing my job, learning the businesses and the organization. Whittington can't do what he's promising. Think about it Virgil, the Seven isn't running things."

"Maybe not now, but things are about to change." he said.

This put me over the edge, and I grabbed Virgil's by his shirt and pinned him against the wall near the hanging coats.

"Listen up Virgil I'm not sure what's going on here but something's not right, and they have you mixed up in middle of it." Virgil tried to push me back, and when he did his coat hit the floor. From the pocket a coin rolled to a stop near my foot. We both looked down and I asked, "What's this?" I reached down and picked it up.

I recognized it as a coin like the one found near my father.

"How'd you get this Virgil I asked?"

"It's nothing Jimmy, give it back."

"You know the meaning of this coin don't you!" He looked down the ground and now seemed ashamed.

"Yes, when I first saw it I remembered Jimmy."

"What does the coin mean?" I asked.

"I can't say Jimmy don't try and make me I can't."

"Virgil, one was found just like it near my dead father. Tonight I've seen two, what does it mean?" Virgil paused and said, "It's a coin of the Seven. We sometimes use them to pick a member to do a task for the Seven."

"What?" I asked.

"When a task is assigned, we draw lots. When the Sons determine a task, the Seven's Chancellor decides how many men are needed to complete it. They put that number of coins into a bag. The other coins are blanks. Each man picks from the bag and the ones with the coin go into a separate room. In that room they are told the assignment. That way the others have no way to implicate the chosen men."

"You were just picked weren't you, Virgil?"

"Yes," he said.

"How many were on this task one maybe two?" I asked. Virgil nodded.

"Let me guess George is the other isn't he."

"I can't say Jimmy"

"Damn it! You were set up Virgil. I don't even think that you met with men in the Seven."

"How would you know Jimmy?"

"I heard something at a diner. There were two men talking and there story seems connected to yours. What are you supposed to do Virgil? What? And when?"

"I'm not telling you that Conner. You won't find out!" He said emphatically. "I'm in, Jimmy, and you can't change that." Virgil began to get defiant as he looked at me. "Makes me wonder why a coin like that was near our father's dead body. Why would he have a coin so close to him?"

"I'm not sure Virgil." I reached in my pocket, and produced my father's knife. "Do you know how my father got this? You have to be in the Seven to get one of these; more than that you have to kill someone to get a knife like this. Now, if my father was in the Seven, and had that knife why would they come and kill him? And why would you think the Seven is going to protect you if they did that to him? Virgil you better be thinking, now more than ever. You have too much to lose to let Whittington play you for a fool. Whittington is neither acting on behalf of the Sons nor the Seven. He's up to something else. Probably his own family's damn greed! Think about Katie Virgil, think about your son!" A moment later I could hear Katie walking down the stairs.

"What's wrong?" she asked.

I looked at Katie and said, "Keep your husband home. Keep him from being a fool and Whittington's lackey." and I walked out.

I headed for Shadow Wood thinking I could fix this, and keep him out of harm's way. All I could hope for now was that he would listen. At least until I could talk with my grandfather. Hopefully, Whittington didn't have anything planned immediately. I drove through the night, and pulled in the drive early the next morning. I walked in asking Henry if my Grandfather was on the grounds. He didn't say anything, just pointed toward the den.

I opened the door to the den, and walked up to my Grandfather who was seated behind his desk. "I need to speak with you sir." I said.

In a rare attempt at humor he said, "Sir, what have I done this early in the morning to be addressed as sir?"

"It's Important," I replied. Then I went into detail explaining to him what all I had seen and heard the night before. He gave a look of concern and said, "Seems strange to me Jimmy. I have not heard of such things in the making. I'll look into the matter directly, but I cannot tell the other council members how I have came by this knowledge. You have spoken to me of things that you shouldn't know yet." I was satisfied for now and thanked him.

"While I'm already treading water that I shouldn't I have questions and want answers." I held up the coin and laid it on his desk then said, "I know what this represents and how you get one." Then I held up the knife. He looked at it rather pained and said, "This was your father's wasn't it?"

"Yes," I replied. He paused and asked, "Were did you get this?"

"The Sheriff found it near my father's body and Mr. Fenton gave it to me. Since then it seems everyone associated with the Sons is trying to take it from me. So, I hid it because it was all I had of his."

"Most men consider the presentation of the Knife of the Scorpion quite an honor, but it seemed to trouble your father." Grandfather stated. "I figured it wouldn't be far from him when he died."

"I know he killed someone to get it; didn't he?" I asked.

Grandfather took a deep breath and said, "Yes, he did Jimmy, and it was all my fault. I pushed him into the Seven. I thought it would harden him, and help him realize that to be a leader sometimes you have to do things you don't want to. Sometimes you have to see through to the greater good even if the road isn't always clearly black and white. And for him being in the Seven solidified his roll in the Sons. He couldn't just ride in on my coattail. I also thought that it might get him away from your mother."

I looked at him not knowing why he wouldn't want my parents together. I sat there and listened as he continued, "We fought about their involvement often. It's not that I didn't like her, she was a fine women James. She just wasn't a woman of standing. She couldn't help your father professionally, and had no family connection within the Sons. I saw it coming, and I knew they loved each other, but it just wasn't enough for me. That part was my fault. Love is a tricky thing James it can make a man do things he ought not do.

It's the same thing for a parent when they love their child. It can make them do things they shouldn't do either." He leaned back in the large leather chair and held the knife. Then he looked to the coin on the desk. He was very quiet, thinking I suspect, pondering deep into the issue. After a few moments, he finally spoke.

"You're father was about your age. He had been in the Seven for a few months. Mostly, he was gathering information on assigned people. I made certain he didn't get into anything too dangerous or over his head. Well, at least I thought I was certain. This time he was tasked with gathering information from a young attorney moving up in his firm. Your father and another man, one I trusted, broke into the attorney's office to find out details of a railroad contract that his firm had been charged with setting in place. The Sons needed the railroad redirected to a hub closer to Birmingham, and we needed information on the proposed route. On this particular issue our man on the inside had failed in persuading the railroad to change their mind and move the route. Our plan was simply to use the pull of our politicians and money to buy out a few key positions on the planned route to make it next to impossible for the railroad to use the proposed plans.

We thought that if nothing else we could delay the railroad and they would just redirect like we needed. The Seven's involvement was just to gather information. Your father liked this type of work. He thought it was exciting, challenging and daring. After some negotiation he convinced his partner that he was ready to go it alone. He provided cover and your father went in by himself. To his surprise the young attorney drove up and he entered the building. The partner gave the signal and your father either didn't see or neglected to take action. There sat his partner waiting as protocol dictated, time slowly ticking by. There was little he could possibly do to create a diversion, but even if he did that might lead to more complications. So, he reluctantly waited. Then he saw a flash of light and heard a gunshot follow. He ran inside the building not knowing what he might find. He ran up the stairs, and saw the door half open. He slowly opened the door seeing your father standing in the center of the room. Blood dripped down from his shoulder, and he held a blood covered knife in one hand. Looking down the partner saw the young attorney lying near his feet bleeding from his chest, making a gurgling noise. He grabbed your father and helped him out from the room. Then he closed the door behind him, as your father walked down the stairs, the attorney went silent.

Immediately I was told of the situation. I fearfully covered his tracks. He was kept safely at a distance from where the incident occurred. When no witnesses surfaced to say different, I called for his return but he never came back. When I went looking for him, all that was found was a note from your mother to her parents. I heard nothing for weeks until one day I received a letter from your father saying only that he wanted out. He wanted to be done with it all, the Sons, the companies, and me. It wasn't what I wanted, but I respected his wishes, and thought that in time he would come back. I had no idea of his whereabouts until I received word about his death. I had no idea about you or your brother either. I never forgave Downey for not keeping him safe."

"Downey?" I asked.

"Yes, Downey, he is a loyal man, and a good man to have at your side, but I trusted him with my son and he failed me."

"Mr. Downey from Bransford?"

"The same," he stated. "He lost interest in the Seven after that night too. He knew with the blood on his hands that we couldn't just let him go. He was too involved and knew too many of our secrets. At his request it was decided that he would be allowed to live out his years at Bransford where he could be kept safely under the Sons watchful eye."

"What do you make of the coin and my father?"

"James he was my son, they wouldn't dare cross that line. Nevertheless the killing of another is only approved through the council, unless of course it's an accident like with that attorney."

"Accident!" I said. "That wasn't an accident an innocent person died, and it was likely set up by the Whittington's!"

"I know there is blood on my hands, but it's for The Cause." Grandfather said.

"The Cause! That can't be the excuse we use for everything that goes wrong. These are people's lives."

"This isn't some game James; it's treason for God sakes. The stakes are high!" Grandfather stated. "I can't change that man's death, but I may be able to help Wallace. I'm just not sure what the Seven and Wallace are involved in. I can't answer that James. I don't even know who is in the Seven that's secret. I do of course have some idea, but I have to be careful."

"What about Whittington what's his involvement?" I asked.

"I'm sure he is a member. His grandfather was."

"And I know his father made a grab for power, didn't he?" I stated

"Yes, but that was controlled and his family has fallen in line since." replied Grandfather.

"I don't believe it. Whittington's don't seem to fall in line behind anyone. I just don't believe they would just give up. They are up to something." Grandfather paused and then asked, "How do you know that the Whittington's made a grab for power James? How do you know what you know?"

"I just do." I replied. "I need you to keep Wallace safe."

"James, I need you to keep safe. My protection can do only so much. Don't go snooping around the members won't like it. You're different then your father Jimmy. You have what it takes to lead this organization. The other members see it in you, just as do I."

"Grandfather, you tell me to hold back, watch out for myself. Then you speak of honor and dignity and the Sons, but there is no honor in watching out for just myself. The honor is in watching out for my friend who is in trouble." With that thought I walked out of the room.

I left my Grandfather's den certain that Wallace was in trouble. Unfortunately, I had little time to address the situation right now. My wedding was fast approaching, just two weeks away and the final details and preparations needed to be made. Especially with the gala event Mrs. Bedford, Lucille and my grandfather had in mind.

For the next few days I wanted to find out more details concerning Wallace, but I had to wait patiently. In the mean time I needed a little relief from all the activities. So, I took Lucy out for dinner at the club. She seemed to glow, and all she could do was talk about how her friends were so excited for the wedding day to finally come. My mind was muddled with issues and not thinking I asked, "Lucy are you sure this is what you want to do? "

"The big wedding?" she asked.

"Yes, of course," I replied half afraid to share what was really on my mind.

"This will be the biggest event in the county! We're down to the final few days, and you ask me this now! Men!" she said. "Now, Jimmy you can hang in there for these few last days. I'll ask your grandfather for some time off for you. He's putty in my hands right now." She said smiling.

"That's not it Lucy and it's not the big wedding either."

"All of our friends will be there Jimmy, all of them. Is this just too much excitement for you?" She asked.

"No," I replied. "I mean this whole thing do you think we are going to be good as a couple?"

She planted her hand on each side of her plate and said, "Jimmy Conner you're not getting cold feet are you? You men get cold feet all the time. You had to practically carry Virgil to the altar."

"That was more about the night before than the wedding." I replied.

"Katie will never forgive you guys for doing that to him."

"What we did! He did it to himself," I said.

"I'm so tired of the talk Jimmy. Do you love me, Jimmy?" She asked.

"Well, yes of course." I said. "I'm sure I do."

"Then Jimmy" and she placed her hand on mine, "That's all I need from you. Just work, and I'll take care of the home, and we will have a happy life. You worry far too much about things. My parents, your grandfather, and everyone thinks we will be a splendid couple. I do wish you mother was alive. I would have made her a wonderful daughter-in-law."

Just then a friend of hers walked over to the table to congratulate us. They continued to talk as I excused myself to grab a breath of fresh air on the back patio. Lucille and her friend didn't seem to mind as I walked away. I stood alone looking out over the green valley below, while I considered my situation. I reached into the pocket of my jacket for a cigar. The flame glowed red as I puffed on the other end. I stood there savoring the flavor enjoying the momentary break. A man approached me and asked for a light.

I said, "Friend you might like one of these better as I pulled out another cigar."

He looked at me and said, "Thank you but no, I'm fine with these." I lit the match as he bent down to put his cigarette near the flame. When he covered the flame with one hand I noticed his red stoned ring. I greeted him as customary, and began to say my name. He interrupted me and said, "It's Conner, I know of you." Thinking little of it, I continued and said, "Then you have me at a disadvantage.

"It's best for all if you only know me as a friend. You have many friends Mr. Conner. Many people are watching out for you."

I looked at him puzzled as he continued, "Do you know this Mr. Conner." and he showed me the sign of the scorpion. Somewhat afraid to answer I replied, "The Seven."

"You do then." When a couple walked out to the patio he gently grabbed my elbow and escorted me to the far end of the patio.

"You have friends there too. Now one of yours is in trouble."

"Wallace?" I asked. He nodded and continued, "He's into something that he shouldn't be. Whittington isn't acting on the Seven's behalf, and Wallace is in danger. You have to get him away from Whittington."

My mind raced with questions, but he stopped me from saying anything then replied, "I don't have all the answers, but its best if you stop him as soon as possible. Wallace is in over his head. I'm sorry, Mr. Conner, but that's all I can say for now."

He turned and walked around the corner and into the darkness. Lucy approached only moments later asking who I was talking to. I replied, "No one in particular."

"You shouldn't be talking to strangers in the dark now should you?" She smiled and grabbed my arm.

"You may be right." I replied.

We went back inside, and finished our dinner. The meeting with the mysterious man kept my mind occupied throughout the rest of the evening. I wasn't sure how I was going to break this to her but I had little choice. Delaying the conversation for as long as possible I waited until we arrived out in front of her home then said, "Lucy, I have something that I need to do."

"What?" she asked. I sighed and said, "Just something that needs to be done."

"Well, then take care of it," she said as she shrugged. Then she opened the door of the car and stood outside.

"No, Lucy I must be gone for a few days." She sat back down closed the door then said, "Jimmy Conner! What do you mean a few days! What could possibly be more important than our wedding? It's just days away and there is so much to do."

"I know," I replied. Then she asked, "Did your grandfather send you away on business this close to our wedding? I'll have my father speak with him. He will make him understand. No need to fret."

"No, Lucy it's not Grandfather, I just can't say why."

"Jimmy you're getting cold feet aren't you. Enough of this foolishness, I have waited my share Jimmy. Don't you embarrass me. Don't you do something that's going to make me look a fool." She said.

"Lucy you have to understand this is vital," she slammed the door and quickly walked away holding her hands to her face crying.

"Oh brother, I've done it now." I said to myself starting the ignition.

I felt bad on my drive back to Shadow Wood, but saving Wallace was more important than hurting Lucy's feelings. I walked inside with a purpose immediately heading up the stairs to pack. Before I could make it half way, I heard Grandfather's voice echo from the foyer. "James, come down here." My first thought was that Mr. Bedford must have called and the phone must have been ringing before I even walked in the door. I reluctantly replied, "Yes, Grandfather I'll be down in moment."

"I need you now."

My immediate thought was that this marriage would mean the additional influence of the Bedford's having a say my daily life. I gritted my teeth at the notion and said, "Just what I need more people telling me what I need to do." Remembering Wallace, I shook my head to regain focus grabbing the final necessary belongings from my drawer. I only paused to deliberate briefly for the case that held a .32 revolver. Then I placed the weapon in my bag.

I went downstairs, laying my belongings in the corner. Grandfather stood waiting with a pained looked on his face. "Come into the den, James, we must talk," he said.

"I know what this is about, and it's not what you think Grandfather." He closed the pocket doors behind me.

"Have a seat James."

"Grandfather, I don't have much time. Let me explain….."

He interrupted, "James, have a seat." Frustrated, I sat down and said, "I don't have time for this. You don't understand."

"No, James it's you that doesn't understand. Now give me a moment. I need to tell you something." He poured some brandy into a glass and slid it in my direction. "I received a call from…." I then stopped him mid sentence and said, "I know the Bedford's. If you'll just let me….."

"James, this is hard enough without your interruptions. The call wasn't from the Bedford's. The call was from Katie Wallace." I leaned back in the chair.

"It appears as if some accident has happened to Virgil." I eyed him quietly as he handed the brandy to me.

"Your friend Virgil is dead, James! He has been in an automobile accident." I swallowed the drink whole, and stood up slamming my hand against the desks oaken trim.

"Damn it, Whittington!"

"Now, don't do that James. Don't go around making accusations of people, half cocked. All we know is Virgil was in an accident." The liquor still burned hot in my breath.

"I'll get George. He's involved. I just know he's is."

"James, sit down!" he said, "You sit down right now! You better get a hold of yourself real quick, James. This isn't a game you're playing and definitely not one to go into without thinking. If Whittington is involved you best be able to prove it."

"Nobody will go out on that limb and accuse the Whittington's and you know it Grandfather. The Whittington's will hide under layer after layer of this organization. They'll use the oaths promises and their people to protect the truth. They know this organization just as well as we do. Wallace is insignificant here. Nobody will go to bat for him. This whole thing stinks. The whole thing the Sons, the Seven all of it is a bunch of lies and hidden truths. The South won't rise again, this about money, power and greed!"

"No, James it's not! It's about the rights of men to govern themselves, and not have others decide their fate. "

"Tell that to Virgil."

I walked out of the den and out of Shadow Wood.

I drove for some time that night. Having no idea really where I wanted to go, I just drove. Everything in my life was a mess. Lucy was mad, Grandfather was mad, and Wallace was gone. I too was upset, half mad at myself, for getting distracted with my marriage, and half mad that Virgil didn't listen. It must have been an hour later, driving the backroads to nowhere that I saw a beacon off in the distance. As I drove closer I saw people walking into a shack of sorts with loud music playing from inside. I parked out front, and watched the colored people pass through the front door. I was drawn to the little shack wondering what could be inside. Everyone coming and going seemed happy, and I needed a little of that sort of distraction. I hesitantly walked up to the door and opened it. Two very large colored men stood there. They gave me a look and let me know that I wasn't exactly welcome. I lifted my hand and said, "I mean no trouble. May I just have a seat in the corner, and have something to drink?" The female bartender nodded and she asked what I would like. I replied, "Whatever is the easiest." Moments later another woman brought me a drink. It was cheap straight whiskey with a bad taste and a bite.

The music played loudly as people laughed and enjoyed themselves. I quietly choked down my drink. I had never been any place like this. This tattered shack was a juke joint. "It's good that these people have a place of their own." I thought. I looked over at the large man at the door and said, "Thank you, it was a little lonely out on the road." He said, "Just sit tight, and I'll watch over you Mr. Conner." I was taken back that he knew me by name. Before I could inquire further everyone jumped up and started to dance, clap, and sing. I couldn't help but take it all in.

The lady brought me another drink and again another. Eventually, my vision and thoughts began to get distorted and out of my control. That's what I wanted, so I just let it happen.

A young woman took to the center of the room. She began to sing and out from her mouth came a beautiful sound that hushed the crowded room. Her words of love and pain glided amongst the rafters of the old shack. I began to imagine her voice floating through the planks of the building and out into the woods behind it. I wondered if she hushed the crickets around the pond as well. And what that sound would be like against the stillness of the cool night air as it echoed through the woods.

Her words alone took me back to the place I longed for in my heart. She reminded me of the Sally I had known. Her form, color and mannerisms were so like the ghost in my memory. It wasn't the drink that made it so. It was the moment, and the way she confidently moved about the room that reminded me of her. I then realized what I had been searching for. I wanted to feel that deep sense of love again. I wanted to be with someone that made my heart move. Someone that shook my soul and made me yearn to be with them. I wondered how a girl from so long ago could still move me in such away. She was miles away, and years away in life. I began to wonder if I would ever know that again. My head began to get heavy and slowly it lowered until finally it rested on the table. I closed my eyes with that beautiful girl in my view thinking of the ghost that roamed in my head and then all went dark.

I woke up some time later in the back seat of my grandfather's vehicle. I looked up to see a large black man driving me into the gate of Shadow Wood. Still drunk, but somewhat alert, I heard him say, "Just stay calm Mr. Conner. I'm taking you home."

"How do you know where I live?" I asked.

"Henry is my uncle." He answered.

"Henry? I do have people watching out for me." I commented.

"Mr. Conner?" he asked.

"Oh, nothing," I replied. The car stopped.

"Thank you that was very kind of you to bring me all the way back into town." I said.

"No need to thank me. The Conner's take good care of my Uncle and Miss Ida."

"Truth be told they take good care of us." I replied. "And thank you again." The man said good night, and walked to the vehicle that followed us home.

As I crawled up the stairs I saw Miss Ida who was already awake and looking at me crossly.

"Miss Ida, please don't lecture me.

"The sun is about to come up and here you are being dragged home."

"I wasn't dragged anywhere Miss Ida. I slept most of the way and walked the final few steps."

"Get to bed Jimmy. Sleep the rest of this off."

I woke sometime around ten with Miss Ida opening the curtains.

"I thought you were going to let me sleep?" She answered, "I changed my mind. I fixed you something to eat."

"My god is the sun sitting in our front yard today!" I replied squinting to keep from going blind.

"Get up and get some food in ya," she said.

The thought of it sounded horrible, but I knew she wouldn't let up.

"Why on earth do I need a wife when I have you Miss Ida."

She looked at me and said, "That's what I'm afraid of the most. That I'll be taking care of you until the moment I die. And by then you'll be so rotten no one will want ya."

"It stands to reason then that you should just leave me lay and let me die in peace." I replied.

"And carry your nasty corpse down all those stairs? Not me, and poor Henry is getting too old for that nonsense. At least be man enough to die at the foot of the stairs. Then we can just push you out in the drive, and let the crows eat you."

"I better just get up. Grandfather wouldn't stand for a dead body in his doorway." I replied.

Henry came in and said, "Too old for what?"

"Carrying Mr. Conner's dead body down the stairs,"

"Why you going to do that Miss Ida the boy ain't dead yet?" he questioned then asked, "You were at the juke joint south of town?"

"I'm afraid so." I replied.

"Mr. Conner that ain't a place for you to be going and they won't carry you anywhere either. They'll just drag you to the pond for the catfish to eat."

"I know, but everyone was quite good to me."

"Land sakes Mr. Conner glad my nephew recognized you." "I'm glad too or I'd be sleeping on the table still." I replied

"The bottom of the lake more likely," he said.

"That wouldn't have been all bad Henry. At least I'd have an angel to listen to as I sank to the bottom. There was a girl there that sung into my soul."

Henry looked at me and commented, "I could arrange for her to sing for Mr. Wallace's funeral if you like." I paused and my heart got heavy again.

"I'm sure he would like that Henry but I'd have to check with Katie."

"Let me know if I can help," Henry said.

"Thank your nephew for me, will you?"

"Gladly Mr. Conner."

Once I choked down my meal I did feel better, but not up to par.

"Miss Ida,"

"Yes, Mr. Conner," she replied.

"Mr. Conner this and Mr. Conner that; what's going on today?"

"Miss Bedford informed me that it wasn't proper to call you Jimmy or James any longer and that we should be more respectful of you." She replied.

"Oh, God! I'm sorry Miss Ida, that's nonsense. Lucy's ain't running my home."

"Maybe not just yet," she remarked.

"She keeps this nonsense up, not ever"

"And when did, "ain't" become a proper way to speak?" Miss Ida asked.

"Never! Too much time working in the mills I suspect; besides it makes me sound much more serious when I'm upset."

"Lucy ain't going to care for it." Ida replied.

"Well, Lucy ain't here to hear me!"

"Spoken like a man all rough and tough until his mama or his wife is around."

"She's not my wife just yet." Speaking of wives and mothers I'm going to visit with Katie, and find out what happened to Virgil. In the mean time you, Grandfather, and Henry are all I have. If there was one thing I found at the bottom of that bottle last night it was that little bit of knowledge. You of all people can call me whatever you like." As I walked by I hugged her. "You're like a mother to me the only one I have left. Better not forget it either."

FIFTEEN

Lucy and I arrived at Wallace's home hours later. A relative answered the door. Many people had already filled the house. Her kitchen was filled with food from supportive friends and neighbors. Virgil's son was being carried by a ten year old cousin with long braided ponytail.

Some of the people who roamed the house were familiar but most I didn't recognize. The presence of the Sons was noted with the numerous gold rings worn by those that filled the house. I recognized a couple of faces from the Bransford Academy days, and of course Virgil's Father who was standing in the corner of the living room next to Virgil's Mother. She wiped her tears with a handkerchief as she greeted people in the room.

Lucy and Mrs. Wallace while I spoke with his father. He wasn't a tall man but large around the middle. He wore suspenders and had a balding head. He was usually distant and guarded like many men of that time who tended to show little emotion. He was a man who always seemed like his mind was working on something, and usually smiled as a first reaction. It was hard to place his thoughts most times, but something seemed different about him this day.

Virgil's Mother was another story her emotions were apparent by the look on her face. She was unguarded, and she didn't mind the fact. I saw so much of her in Virgil. They both knew how close Virgil and I were and I think especially Mrs. Wallace clung close because of our relationship. She even reached out to touch my shoulder, or at times, she grabbed a hold of my arm. I stayed close to them mostly because Mrs. Wallace seemed to need the security of me near her.

Lucy excused herself to find Katie. At one point Mrs. Wallace guided me over to a window to point out the many vehicles that lined the street for her son. She turned and quickly took note to see if anyone was close to us. She looked blankly out the window and said, "Jimmy this was no accident I can just feel it." I wasn't sure what to say or what she knew. I just replied, "Yes, ma'am." And I put my hand over hers that held my arm. We walked back over to Mr. Wallace. Standing next to him was George. The two men stood side by side, and George looked squarely at me and said, "It's a shame isn't it?" Mr. Wallace looked closely at us both, and gauged my reaction. I did my best not to show my hand in any way. Replying, "Yes, George it is."

Then I stated "Gentlemen, if you will excuse me, I need to find Katie I have not spoken with her as yet."

When I entered the room I saw Katie. She just sat there with Virgil's sisters close by while Lucy brought her a glass of water. Lucy looked over at me with concern, as she walked toward Katie.

"Oh, Jimmy," she said, "I am so glad you came. I was worried that you wouldn't because of the fight you two had."

"Just words Katie. That's all, just words." She reached up and hugged me.

"Jimmy what will I do without him? What will little Clarence do without a father?"

Lucy came over and said, "Don't you worry about all that." as she sat down beside her. Katie continued, "I'm too young to be a widow.....aren't I?" Virgil's sister held her hand and added, "Katie it will be fine."

I was handling everything pretty well until then, but seeing Katie in her condition deeply affected me. I excused myself and went to the porch.

A few other men stood outside talking in groups amongst themselves. I spoke with one of the men asking the details of the accident. He told me that Virgil's car was found outside of a small town about twenty-five miles from here. That he had a terrible head injury, and there was no way he survived for even a moment after the impact. I asked why he was up that way. No one seemed to really know. I put my hands in my pockets wanting to find out more, but this wasn't the time or place. I said little on the subject, but listened to all I could for the smallest of details.

Once back inside the house, I stood alone at the edge of the living room for a moment. In walked my Grandfather, and a few paces behind him, another man also entered the room. The man looked in my direction and tipped the brow of his hat before taking it off. I quickly recognized him as the man on the patio at the club the night before. I noticed that neither my grandfather nor the gentleman made acknowledgement of each other as they shook hands with the people inside. I watched the man briefly speak to Katie giving her his condolences, and it appeared that she really didn't know him either. I went about my business and spoke with Mr. Wallace and my grandfather. The two men had known of each other for years, but only as acquaintances really. It was the friendship between Virgil and I that caused them to have more direct dealings with each other. They quickly became friendly even though they were too very different types of men.

I watched the man make his rounds through the house. Eventually he passed me on his way to the porch. I waited a few moments and walked out too. We spoke briefly, and then he pulled a newspaper from his coat. The paper was folded so the headline read, "Fire at Willis Brothers Building." The first line of the article stated that two unidentified bodies were found. The newspaper was from a small city fifty miles from here. I quickly put the paper under my arm, and continued the small talk with him. We parted ways, and I told Lucy that it was time for our goodbyes. We told Katie that we would be back in the morning for the funeral.

We spent the night in the local hotel; all three rooms were adjacent Grandfather's, mine, and Lucy's. Henry and his niece accompanied my Grandfather, but they stayed at a friend's home in town. The next morning I asked Lucy to ride with Grandfather, because I wanted to be there early before the funeral. Virgil's body was at his home now enclosed in a casket in the living room. Katie of course was still in a bad state. A man from the Sons of the South arrived. He was a chaplain from the organization and was present for official business. Within the order there is a protocol for burial like that of many organizations. Some place bibles in the casket or have the dead covered with an embossed symbol of the organization, or some other gesture is preformed. Our organization was no different. The chaplain ensured the deceased's red stoned ring is placed on his finger, a confederate flag pin was to be placed on the lapel, and any affiliate recognition was to be placed in a small pouch near his right hand. If he were in the Seven, a knife was to be placed in his pocket because he has made his sacrifice. That little tidbit of information was another of Clovery's loosely held secrets. The ceremony relating to the dead intrigued me, but at the time I never thought that Cloverly's former post of Chaplin would hold any information of value.

The Sons chaplain requested permission to have a private moment with the deceased. Katie questioningly looked over to me. I told her that was this was customary, and that is what Virgil would want as I nodded my approval. He asked for the room to be cleared, and preformed his obligation. A few moments later he walked out of the room. I wasn't sure why but I needed confirmation, and there was only one way I could do that. I asked Katie if she minded if I looked at Virgil one last time. She started to cry again and said, "No, Jimmy I can't even do that. I have been told not too. He wouldn't want you to remember him that way." I didn't want to upset her any further and said, "I understand Katie, but I would like just a moment alone, that is if you don't mind." She reluctantly let me have my moment.

Once alone in the room I touched the door of the casket and said, "Virgil I hope I'm wrong, but I have my suspensions. And if I'm right, I'm sorry I didn't figure this out sooner. I'm sorry I didn't get there to help you." I took a deep breath to prepare myself, and opened the casket door. She was right, he was a mess, but I tried not to focus on that. I felt his pocket, and no knife could be located inside. I then reached across his body to check the other set of pockets. I reached down and grabbed the small pouch and looked inside it. "Just some normal affiliate pins." I thought. I looked over his body once more, and saw nothing that would show he was associated with the Seven. This of course wasn't definitive proof but went a long way in confirming my suspicions. I closed the lid, and said good bye to my best friend one last time.

The procession continued down the street. Some drove, others walked the few blocks to the cemetery on the edge of town. We all gathered around the coffin and the grave. Once everyone finally arrived the minister began the service. He spoke of Virgil's life, Katie, his son, his parents, sisters, and all he left behind. The moment made me think about my parents and how small a circle of people I really had. I looked at Katie as she cried holding the young child that was Virgil's. Then to Wallace's parents wrought with grief over their child who was gone before his time.

Scanning the faces of the crowd my eyes came to rest on George Whittington. My mind churned as I looked at him for any sign in his expression that he was involved. I saw nothing but a blank stare as he looked and listened to the pastor. Henry's niece began to sing, and for a moment my eyes focused on her. Then they lowered his walnut casket into the ground. In the brief moment before the crowd broke off I looked up, and Whittington's eyes connected with mine. A half smile broke out on his face, and he turned away. In that moment, he told me all I needed to know. I squeezed Lucy's fingers and took a step forward to pursue him. A voice from behind said the words, "rock steady!" A common phrase used from the Bransford days while standing in formation. I was about to turn my head, and the voice again spoke. "Not just yet." I stood firm and watched Whittington step from view, and the final remnants of the crowd disperse.

I slowly turned to see the face behind the voice. The man stood, head held slightly down with the brim of his hat covering his features. He began to look up, and fully exposed the face of Tanner. Before I could say a word he said, "Shhhhh, lets walk to my vehicle." He slid between Lucy and I with an arm around each of us. Lucy was abuzz with questions. She even seemed a little scared. I reassured her by telling her he was a friend from school. We walked to the side of his vehicle, and waited for the last of the people to leave the cemetery. I was about to introduce Tanner to Lucy when he interrupted me and said, "Nice to meet you, I'm James Stuart." I was taken back and almost laughed, but I kept my composure, and asked Lucy if she would mind going back to the Wallace's on her own. She started to protest but with typical Tanner charm he said, "Miss Bedford if you would be so kind I would truly appreciate it. I must leave from here, and I have only a few minutes to visit with my friend." She nodded, and drove back with Grandfather to meet with Katie.

We both sat in the car for a moment when I asked Tanner, "So, how long have you been posing as a dead confederate General? He looked at me and stated, "Quite some time actually."

"J.E.B. Stuart," I laughed and said, "Think a lot of yourself huh!" he started the vehicle and began to drive.

"Listen Jimmy I don't have a lot of time. It's dangerous for me here and I needed just a few moments to speak to you. I need you to lay off Whittington, I'm sure you could kill him right now, but I need you to stay back. Some things have to fall in place, and Whittington can't feel your heat. I repeat do not do anything brave or stupid I'll keep you informed when I can."

"Tanner it's great to see you after all this time. And I appreciate you looking out for me, but I can handle Whittington."

"I know you can, but there is a bigger picture to this," He stated.

"There always is isn't there." I remarked.

"What?" He asked.

I looked out the front windshield and said, "The bigger picture. The Sons is full of bigger pictures."

"Okay, Jimmy what if I told you the bigger picture could get me hurt. Would that help you to sort out what you need to do?"

"What do you mean?" I asked.

"It's best for now if you do not know, Jimmy. Can you leave it be for awhile, get out of town. Just lay low?" Tanner asked.

"No, Grandfather or Lucy for that matter would never allow it. I'm a trapped rat. Hey, did you hear? I'm marrying Lucy next week."

"Great!" he said.

"No, not so great," I quickly replied.

"Oh," he said, "Damn, I wish I had more time to talk. I'm sorry."

"Seriously Tanner, how can me going after Whittington get you hurt?"

"I'm sure I have to give you a good reason don't I?" he asked.

"Yes, I'm certain of it." I said.

"Well, then I was asked to take a job, and be an inside man for the Sons."

"Inside what?" I asked.

"The Treasury Department," he replied.

"Jesus," I said, "You must really want that knife."

"More than that Jimmy, the Treasury Department has me working on case, and I have to infiltrate a mafia group based out of Chicago."

"Wonderful news, I'll bury you next to Wallace." I stated.

"Then it gets sticky," he added.

I looked at him and said "You're right I shouldn't have asked."

"Too late now," he replied. "They are working with Whittington's Grandfather, and I don't know why just yet but I intend to find out."

"Why did you give in and tell me all this? You really should have been more persuasive before you started babbling. Don't they teach you about being persuasive in the Treasury Department?" I asked.

"Here do you mind if we stop at this diner? He asked.

"My partner is waiting on me."

"Oh, I get to meet your partner?"

"Afraid not Jimmy,"

"I have to walk back to Wallace's?" I asked.

"I'm afraid so. Besides it will good for you too cool down a little." He said.

"Who is this partner then anyway?" I asked, "General Lee? A.P. Hill maybe?" I stepped out and looked in the passenger side window and said, "I'll back, Tanner but keep me in the know."

"I promise," he said. "Good to see you Jimmy." As we shook hands, I prodded him again by asking, "General Grant isn't likely is it?" I smiled and stepped back from the window then faced the door of the diner. A man stepped out and looked at me. We passed each other as he walked towards Tanner's car. I quickly recognized him, and tipped my hat. He returned the gesture. We made no other acknowledgment of each other as we passed. A few paces later I thought, "The man from the club patio. I would have bet on Grant before him."

The walk to Wallace's was probably what I needed to put things in prospective. Grandfather met me at the door. Before I could even take a step inside he asked in a low voice, "You didn't go looking for Whittington did you?"

"No," I replied rolling my eyes.

"I was never quite sure when he was watching out for my best interest or that of the Sons."

"Good," he said. "Leave him alone for now, and let me handle this." I walked into the room and hugged Katie, "I'm sorry I have to leave. If there is anything we can do let me know Katie."

"Thank you, Jimmy." She said. Lucy hugged her, and we both walked away.

"See you back at Shadow Wood Grandfather." I said as we walked out the door.

Lucy and I loaded up the car to head for home, not saying much to one another. Once I started the vehicle my mind went to Tanner. With Wallace's death fresh on my mind I realized how much I missed having him around. I thought back about how long it had been since I last saw him. Both Tanner and Peabody had enlisted in the service shortly after graduation from Bransford.

Although both capable students, they chose not to continue their education, instead opting for a life of adventure by joining the infantry. Tanner of course was a horse man, but Peabody wasn't, and they wanted to stay together. The last time I had heard from him was in letter a few years back. It told me how Peabody had suffered a serious injury during training, and would likely walk with a limp for the rest of his life. And that Tanner, through a stroke of luck and horsemanship, did in fact get back in the saddle for the remainder of his enlistment. He liked the service, but chose not to stay. I hadn't heard anything more about either of them.

Lucy reached over to hold my hand and said, "I know you have been through a lot by losing Wallace. It was so sad for me to see Katie that way. It will be hard for her at first, and with the baby she will have a very hard time finding someone else."

The comment struck me wrong and I said, "Why does she have to find anyone? The dirt isn't packed on Virgil's grave yet for pity sakes."

Correcting herself she said, "I didn't mean to be harsh. It just made me think, Katie said she wanted to come down our wedding next week, but was worried she wouldn't be in any condition to make the trip."

"You didn't pressure her did you?" I asked.

"No, not at all. She asked about it Jimmy. What has gotten in to you?" Lucy asked.

"Nothing, just a lot on my mind," I said.

"And I don't have a lot on my mind? With the wedding and all that has to happen?" She retorted. I sat silently and kept driving for quite some time. She turned away, not a word was spoken between us. We arrived in town late that night, and I woke her just before arriving at her parents. She just looked at me still upset not even saying good night. Usually this would have sparked a reaction from me, but tonight I just didn't have the energy for it.

The next morning she arrived and asked for me to step out on the porch for a moment. Still exhausted I went to the porch and leaned against the column. She said, "Jimmy I didn't much care for your tone last night." I listened quietly arms folded as she continued. "Our wedding is the most important day in our lives and I want it to be special. I want it to be memorable. You're not ruining this for me. I have been patient, and I have waited long enough. I just want you to fight for me a little bit, Jimmy." Hearing her say that one particular line, "I just want you to fight for me." The comment turned my attitude from angry to one that was softer more calculating. I paused and looked down then said, "Lucy I do love you but I think you're right. I think you should have someone who will fight for you, and that man is not me! I didn't realize it until the words came out of your mouth. I've been trying to put my finger on it. But I'm not in love with you."

"What?" she questioned. Of course she was taken back.

"That's the problem Lucy, sure I could marry you and we could get along. Maybe, we could be the toast of the town like you said. Have children and go about our business. Those are all nice things. I just want more. There is something more out there for me, for the both of us. I want to be in love with the person I marry. I want to miss her when she's gone. I want my heart to beat faster when I see her. I want to be like those couples you can tell a mile away that they are in love. I want to need the person I'm with, and I want them to need me back. Do you understand that?"

She stood their speechless as I continued. "Those feelings I just described are the feelings I want! I want to have all those feelings like my parents had when I was a kid. I could just see it in their eyes when they were together I had no doubt that they loved each other. All the rest is crap Lucy, it's all horseshit. None of things you talk about; the big house, cars, friends in nice clothes matter. Those are the things you talk of, but that's not me. That's not at all important to me, look around at all those people out there doing without those things. Just because we are fortunate doesn't make us better! And in truth I do you no justice in marrying you while I question my feelings. You deserve more than I will ever be able to give you when it comes to my heart."

She stood back, letting out a sound that I can't really describe then stepped forward, and slapped me across the face. "More… More!" she said, "You don't deserve me!" She stormed away knocking a plant off the porch in the process. I watched her drive out of sight and thought, "Well, that should stir the pot."

It didn't take long for it boil over either. I was out in the garage with Henry when Grandfather walked out.

"James, Lucille Bedford's father called." I could tell by his tone that he wasn't pleased.

"I'm quite sure he did." I said.

"James she's beside herself. Do you care to explain?" He asked.

"I think I already have; at least to the only person that I need to explain anything too regarding my marriage."

"Confound you James this is no time to be toying with her."

"Toying with her?" I'm not toying with her." I said. "That's a ridiculous statement."

"I'm not in love with the girl." I stated.

"Damn it James. I realize you have been through a lot lately but this is not the answer."

"And getting married to someone I'm not in love with is? Grandfather I tried to tell you how I felt before Wallace died. That hasn't changed."

"The Bedford's and I have gone to great lengths to give you a wedding deserving of our families. Now is not the time for cold feet."

"This isn't about cold feet. I appreciate all you have done, but I'm not getting married because everyone wants us too." I stated.

"You'll never be able to save face within the organization if you do this. This will be a matter of honor for the Bedford's."

"Grandfather, I've had enough of all of this. If they don't accept me because I didn't marry Lucy then they just don't accept me."

"You'll be an embarrassment. Where is your dignity? Where is your honor? Then grandfather became angry like I had never seen him before. "I'll cut you off."

"Cut me off?" I asked.

"From the Sons, the money, Shadow Wood, all of it." He replied.

Henry had sat quietly up until now, but then spoke up, "Mr. Conner you don't mean to say such things."

"No, Henry" I said, "He does. And if I had lost my dignity and honor I think I just found it."

I walked in and hastily packed throwing all I could into a trunk and walked back out to the garage. By then Grandfather had made his way to the back of the property, but I was still in his view. Henry said, "Now hold on Jimmy don't do anything you will regret."

"No, Henry I see things quite clearly at this moment. If I do anything other than leave it all behind then what kind of man would I be?" I threw my belongings in the Romeo.

"What are you doing?" Henry asked.

"I've paid my dues." I replied. Then I got behind the wheel and started the vehicle.

"Good bye Henry, tell Miss Ida good bye for me too." I said.

"Now hold on James." He said.

"Henry, this is my life, and I have things I need to find out." I put my hand out, and he reluctantly shook my hand.

Then I drove away in the car sputtering up the drive. As I looked back, I could see my Grandfather seated and looking down. I shook my head and drove the shortest route out of town.

The red Alfa Romeo's eight cylinders roared down the road. Her sputtering hum brought a sense of calm to my wandering mind, and just turned it off for a few hours. My troubles seemed more distant with each passing mile and I felt a since of peace as she continued down the road.

A roadside diner named Ben's appeared in view, and the billboard special was tempting enough for me to stop in for a bite to eat. There I sat looking at a large map of the country on the wall. I needed a place to hide, and had no plan or direction to go. The timing wasn't good. Opportunities were limited by the country's financial situation in the 1930's. I knew I wasn't alone in my plight. During my travels I ran across many a half starved displaced American with all their possessions packed on the four wheels of their vehicles.

California seemed promising with its sun, beautiful women, even Hollywood. I jokingly thought now was my chance to be a movie star. I reconsidered the option, and I thought that I'd done enough acting in this life. Looking back at the map New York came into view; commerce, opportunities, excitement, and a place big enough to hide.

My decision became finalized while sipping my coffee. I paid Ben for his fine meal, and once again saddled myself in the Romeo. I took the winding roads heading north through small towns and large cities alike.

My arrival in New York was less than eventful as I drove past the nice large homes that lined the streets, as I neared the heart of the city. I had just left that lifestyle and wanted to be cleansed from what money had done to my life. I wanted to be judged not by what I had, or what I could do for someone, but by who I was as a person. I needed to be back around those who held every penny as a precious something, a penny that was earned as a reward for hard work and effort.

Quickly, I made my mind up to find housing appropriate for that lifestyle change. I parked the Romeo and walked a few blocks. By the 1930's the tenements of the prior century were being torn down, and replaced by newer more suitable housing. But, somehow, I managed to find a place like I had in mind. I wanted a starting point from near the bottom. A place to purge myself of my past, and to start my rise back to the new person I wanted to become.

The manager was more than accommodating once I placed six months' rent in his grubby hands. The last tenant leaving only hours before was not acquainted with the benefits of a clean lifestyle. Although filthy and in need of paint I planted myself in my new roost on the sixth floor of the building. The view was of the building across the street and not much else.

The second order of business was finding a safe refuge for the prized Romeo. I drove about seven miles away to the homes I had passed earlier hoping I could find suitable housing for her. I was in luck and made a deal with a shop owner who had a garage and paid him to keep the vehicle safe until I would need it again. Although suspicious that it might get him into trouble, he agreed to the proposition.

I made the seven mile trek back to my home. Although late and very tired I stayed up and cleaned what I could. I spent the night in a clean corner on the floor refusing to sleep on a bed that reeked of booze and sweat. It took a couple of days to get the place in order and a new mattress and sheeting was first on the list. Eventually, I had cleaned and painted my way to a proper place to live.

Once my personal affairs were in order I began to seek out employ-ment of some sort. The problem was, in that area, and in those times, little work was to be found. Daily, I would go down to an alley with other men of similar circumstance. We would stand there sometimes for hours as men in trucks would show up and gather laborers to do needed work around the city for low cost. The day would start by us jockeying for a good position within the crowd that could lead us to get picked first. Some days I worked, and some days I didn't. Many a good man stood by my side dejected as we walked home without hope for a day's pay. I could see the burden and strain in their eyes and the hollowness in their spirit. These men were beaten but not broken as they held on to the fact that tomorrow gave rise to hope for a new day and another chance.

When the opportunity came, the hard work was good for me. My body made the adjustment well, and I quickly became used to physical labor again. Something about a day's sweat makes a man feel like a man, and it moves something deep down inside his soul. I had worked alone for so long that I had grown accustomed to the isolation. I also had forgot-ten something about myself. I liked the communion of men working to-gether. It binds them, and no matter what personal differences they have, no matter how hard the work, or how much they hurt, it was something at the end of the day that they shared. And at least for a little while you didn't feel quite so alone.

The closer I became to the men around me; the more I began to take pity on them. I came to the realization that I was poor only by choice.

Those men were in a daily fight for scraps to feed their children, wives, and themselves. They had little choice in the matter, and I on the other hand did.

Those thoughts started to become consuming. I began to see the men's children in their stories and hear the desperation in their voices. Often I would see it in their faces as I drove off watching them standing there waiting for another chance. More than once, I would let another take my spot on the dock. It came to a head one day when a man I knew was hiding an injured hand. He didn't get picked and I knew he had a family to feed. I yelled for him to climb on the truck and then I jumped off so he could take my place.

I walked the streets of the city that day. There I saw the poorest of people. Many once had employment and hope in their hearts. They now stared blankly out from the dark alleys. They no longer sought the light, but instead hid in the shadows. Eventually, the guilt from that sight made me realize how unfair it was for me to take jobs from the poorest of the poor. These men were just trying to fill basic needs to survive. So, I no longer went with the other men. But I had to do something. I once again was with neither direction nor a means to my purpose. I was left with the lingering question of what to do next?

They say all answers come in time, but the answer to that question came rather quickly, in the form of Saint Joseph's Catholic Church. There a soup kitchen was provided for the poor and hungry. My intention was to work, mend, and cleanse my thoughts. I was not seeking a cleansing of the soul. Looking back, my life as always just seems to take a course of its own. Something predetermined would just grab hold no matter how well thought out my plan and change the course. It was there that I met father Timothy McIver who had a familiar accent and charm; like that of Mr. Downey. He was twenty five years my senior. A kind, disciplined, orderly man and at times he demanded a certain amount of respect that only I seemed to understand how to give.

I often worked the soup lines where I looked directly into the eyes of the children and parents of the displaced and needy. Usually, I just worked for the food I ate which was minimal at best. I choked back my complaints, because I had made choices that these people didn't.

Come to find out, I was actually quite a handy man. It didn't take long for Father McIver to take me in his graces by offering me various jobs around the parish. He would often persist in my conversion to the faith and smile at my protests. It became a game to us and we would banter back and forth on the subject. All that he asked was for me to attend Mass and to tell anyone who asked that I was a convert.

Father McIver had a knack, and could do more with very little, better than anyone I had ever known. Often bartering for needed goods, he traded a little hope of salvation to a man with a heavy conscience. At times he would even barter some skills I possessed.

I attended Mass like Father asked. Sitting in the back as the Catholic faithful entered and knelt before the alter of Christ. I noted the many differences of this church compared the one I was accustomed too, but it was in the similarities that I saw the common link between the faiths. Mostly, in that fact that these people were seeking Gods refuge just like those in my church back home.

My time at Saint Joseph's was short, only lasting four months. I was offered a steady position working in a warehouse near the docks, and jumped at the opportunity to be back on familiar ground. When I spoke with McIver he said, "I hate to see you go, James."

"I feel the same Father, but it's a good opportunity."

"Going to Mass brought about good things for you. Just imagine what converting to the faith might bring." He said smiling.

"Father I'll check in on you from time to time."

"That would be appreciated James, and by checking you mean attending Mass don't you?" He asked.

"That's exactly what I meant Father."

"Good I couldn't have people thinking I lost my convert now could I? I have little something for you before you go."

I watched him as he took a medallion from around his neck, "It's a Saint Michael Medallion. He is an archangel and the patron Saint of chivalry. He's God's own warrior ya know."

I was puzzled by the gift and asked, "The warrior? I'm not a soldier." I stated. "With all those Saints isn't there one little more fitting for me?"

"No, something tells me the fit is exactly right for you. There are many types of battles in a man's life. Not just the ones with bullets whizzing by," he stated then he placed the necklace over my head.

"Besides it's much more fitting for you than a priest. Talk to Michael from time to time. With God and Michael hearing, he may just be compelled to watch out for you, if you're true to your path."

"I'm not so sure I believe in all that, Father."

"As Catholics we hold dear the connection between the living and the dead, James. We believe those that pass on before us are still with us. That they look down on us, and watch over us. Your parents still care about your life James, even though they have moved on."

I thought about it for a moment, and decided it couldn't hurt. Then he placed the medallion over my head. We said our goodbyes, and I started down yet another new path.

My labor near the dock was steady and the work was hard. It was familiar to me as it reminded me of summers as a kid working for my grandfather. One thing that I didn't care for though was the fact that one of the Sons businesses was right next door. It served as a constant reminder of the giant shadow that I lived under.

I was new and once again had to prove myself. I had to be careful not to show my hand, because I knew more about this business than many men supervising me. It was a fine line to walk, because for some reason the people above you like to feel like they know more than their subordinates. Instead of considering you an asset, you're marked, and quickly considered a threat. I wanted the work, so I had to learn to bite my tongue, and just do what was asked and little else.

The men I worked with were from various backgrounds and heritages. The groups tended to stick to themselves even around the warehouse. They would live and work within the circles they were familiar. Not functioning together, but as independent groups working in unison. Even in the North the racial, ethnic lines were drawn. So, I tended to keep to myself only occasionally having an issue with one of the other workers. Respect is a hard thing to get, and sometimes just working hard isn't enough. The people around me seemed to always be testing me, and putting me in a corner. I knew that sometimes you just have to make a stand, but I wasn't quite ready yet. I just wanted to do my job and live the way I wanted. I had been tested enough as far as I was concerned.

SIXTEEN

One day I was sitting in my apartment, and decided to see the city in a different light. I went out and bought a new suit and hat. Then came back and cleaned myself up. Feeling good I left my apartment for a night out on the town. I walked down the stairs to the lobby and smiled at the remarks and propositions of the women downstairs as I passed by.

The road led me to the Romeo and her sleek lines. She started with just a little coaxing as her pistons purred back to life once again. I drove on, finding myself in parts of town not yet explored. Once night fell, Harlem began to bustle with activity. People of all walks of life and color would go there for drink and entertainment.

I looked on the marquee and saw both names familiar and unknown to me. I noticed people in all manner of dress from suits to tuxedos. The lights and activity drew me in. I parked and went on foot to get a sense of the heartbeat of this unexplored area. As I walked I could hear the music of the juke joints from the South. Different sounds and rhythms to fit many tastes, but in those days, Jazz was king. This night I was drawn inside one place in particular.

It was Maxine's a long narrow building that opened to a wider more spacious area facing the stage. Here black and white intermingled, and in some cases sat together in the smoke filled room. I sat alone at a small table and watched the people inside. Everyone seemed happy as they listened, danced and interacted. It was very different from the places I had spent my days and nights. I wondered if they were just ignoring the plight of the people outside, or if they just wanted to hide from it for awhile.

After the second drink, I was about to leave when the stage went dark. A beam of light struck the dark center of the stage. A hush went through the room as the crowd sat and waited for what was to happen next. The only movement in the whole room was the smoke from the many cigarettes and cigars rising into the beam of light coming from the spot light.

A female voice coming from a dark corner began to bellow against the silence. The beam moved around the stage but only found darkness. Then it too went dark leaving the stage black as she continued to sing. Suddenly, the light came back on, and I found her at the center of the stage. I sat back down as my attention became focused on her. I was almost paralyzed by the spectacle. The song continued, and she lifted her head. Something familiar caused me to rise. I took the first step forward then another for a closer view. I moved along the wall, not willingly, but drawn toward her as if I had no control over myself.

She was now in full view standing there before me. From her head to her feet I was certain that I was witness to the ghost of my dreams in this woman that now stood before me. The song ended, and the applause snapped me out of my trance. Another quickly started as I regained control of myself and made my way back to my table. I sat there just watching her every action, feature, and mannerism. She had come to form from a young girl to a woman. Now she had a style of her own and learned the grace of fluid movement, but through it all I knew it was her. This was the same person who stood in the tall grass all those years back. The one etched in my memory.

The waitress brought me a drink and I asked her the name of the performer. She said, "That's Miss Maxine."

"Is this her place?" I asked.

"Yes, it is," she replied.

"I liked to meet her." I stated.

"She comes out after her performance, and you should be able to then." The waitress replied.

Once finished she walked out to a table of people she apparently knew. I approached from behind, and she turned almost into my arms.

"Oh my," she said. "I always like falling into a handsome mans arms." Then she laughed and patted me on the chest, and started to walk away.

"Miss Maxine?" I asked.

"Why yes," she said as she turned.

I put my hand out for an introduction and she placed hers in mine. I kissed her gloved hand. She turned and giggled at the table behind her and said, "See ladies Southern gentlemen just have a way about them."

"Do you not recognize me Miss Maxine, or should I call you Sally?"

"Sally?" she said looking at me closely then commenting, "I haven't been Sally for years." I could see that she couldn't place me.

"Jimmy Conner." I said.

Her expression softened as a smile formed on her lips, "My boy Jimmy?"

"The one and only," I replied. Something deep within me was moved as I looked into her eyes.

Then she looked at me strangely and asked, "What brings you all the way up her Jimmy?" She turned and ordered a drink. Then she looked over my shoulder and around me as if I wasn't important enough to carry on a conversation with her. I was momentarily hurt, but quickly regained my composure. I'm not sure what I expected from her but her reaction wasn't what I had prepared myself for. Not knowing what to say, I said the first thing that came to mind.

"Business,"

"Are you enjoying the city?" She asked.

Feeling the need to say something to make a connection I quickly replied, "You'll be glad to know that a horse named Cisco, and I made it into that Troop I wanted so badly. Remember the one at school?"

She laughed and said, "Yes, I remember. That old horse of mine got sold not long after you left." She turned away and looked toward other tables and said, "I'm sorry Jimmy it was nice to reminisce, but I have a bar to run." She walked away after excusing herself.

I stood there for a moment and watched her move from table to table. She didn't look back and it appeared she didn't intend to come over to my table again. I set my half full glass on the bar, and walked out of the building.

The next morning I looked out my only small window into the alley behind my building. The clothes lines hung between the buildings were sagging with the weight of clothing. They swung in the wind tattered, void of color. Mostly grays and blacks the colors of workers. Colors of the poor, resembling their lives just as bland as the clothing they wore. I watched the women as they went about their routine of taking care of their homes, and tending to their children.

The alley was cluttered with trash and debris. Men stood in circles, conversing with one another while the children played among the debris. The adults paid little attention as they dodged and weaved between it all. I looked over at the new suit hanging on the wall, and realized how far I was from Shadow Wood. How far I was from the life I once had on the flat lands of the Carolina's, and that little house where I was raised.

Today was a day I just wasn't sure about myself and my decisions. So, I went walking to clear my mind. It didn't take long before I made it to the markets. The vendors had their food out on display, keeping close watch on me as I looked at the various types of bread. After finally making my choice, I carried the long loaf of pumpernickel under my arm tearing off pieces as I walked down the street. I made my way through the city looking at the tall buildings and the vehicles as they rode by.

After awhile I stopped and handed the remaining portion of my loaf to a couple of men standing on the street looking quite hungry. I eventually made my way to Saint Joseph's. I guess I was looking for a friendly face in this sea of strangers. Father McIver was a welcome sight. We sat on a bench near a dogwood and talked for awhile.

Eventually he asked me, "I'm glad you stopped in to see me, but I see trouble in your eyes."

"I've given it a lot of thought. When I left I thought I was doing what was right, but then something happened last night. This person I've been holding on to appeared out of nowhere. When I met her again, she acted like I meant nothing to her. I just don't know anymore. "I'm not sure what to believe."

"Are you praying for guidance?" he asked.

"No, Father."

"Have ya at least been wearing the medallion?"

"Yes, Father always."

"That's a good thing. It's just a little something to remind you to speak with God on a daily basis." He seemed to be looking right through me and then asked. "This is a question of love isn't it?"

"Yes, Father I guess it is."

"Love is hard ya know. It can make a man do all manner of craziness, but that's the wonderful thing about it now isn't it?"

I looked at him in a questioning manner.

"I wasn't always a priest you know. I've felt the sweetness and the bite of love."

Surprised I looked at him and said, "It does hurt, doesn't it?"

"It does, but it's in the hurt that we learn the most about ourselves. In that hurt we can, if we look for it, find out who we are inside. That's the part that scares us most ya know. If you run and hide from it without looking into yourself, then you'll never understand your true feelings or yourself. God gave us love. It makes us human. It moves our soul to create, to step outside of a one's normal boundaries and take a risk on another. The love that people share is a testament to the Lord. It's the one thing that makes me realize that there is a God and it's just as unexplainable now isn't it? Some things just are the way they are and we have to accept them as such."

I sat there trying to grapple with all that he said.

"Listen James all I can tell you is that in time you may find your answer."

"In time?" I asked questioningly.

"I'm not saying he will provide you with the answer. But I am saying, that when we pray for an answer, it's a start for listening for one? Sometimes when we try and think life through we're not listening for God's instructions."

"God's instructions?" I asked.

"I'm a priest James. I believe in a calling. I believe that I was drawn to this life. I believe we are all on paths in our lives. Priests don't have exclusive rights to being chosen for a calling in life. I would think that all men have a calling of sorts. You just have to listen for it."

"Exactly what should I be listening for? Listen for God to talk to me?" I asked.

"James, listen to what's going on around you. It seems to me that when we don't follow our path in life that God speaks the loudest. The heart is the only avenue that we have to judge the will of God for ourselves. Logic can get us in just as much trouble as love. At least with love we stand a chance at the possibility of a richer fuller life. So, my advice can only be this James. Don't think so much. Don't try so hard to make it happen or figure it all out. Just listen and in time God will help you find your way."

I simply nodded, and then he asked, "Does that help?"

"Well, I was hoping for a more definitive answer."

"We don't all have a mountain and a burning bush to guide us." He said smiling.

He stood up shook my hand and said, "That's why they call it faith, James. There is plenty of strength in a man's heart when it's full of faith and hope. Now, I have to share a little of that hope with the stomachs of the poor."

Then Mr. Conner pulled the worn silver Saint Michael medallion out from underneath his shirt and said, "I've worn it ever since he gave it to me." He paused then looked at the medallion and said, "I think it's time to pass it along. I'd like you to have it." I was taken back. He asked me, "Are you worried I wore it out? You're probably thinking I've upset Michael in some way, and he's looking for me. He likely is you know." Then he said, "Son my time is short here I have grown quite fond of you over the past few days and I have no one to pass it down too. I would like you to have it. It will help you to remember me and one day when I pass you'll remember that connection between the living and the dead Father McIver spoke of. I put it over my neck and thanked Mr. Conner.

On the way out I told Mrs. Conner of the incident and insisted she take it back. She smiled and said, "Now, Mr. Campbell, that man in there has worn it for many years and if he wants you two connected in some way then that is his wish and should be respected by the both of us." She briefly looked at it in her hand and placed it back around my neck and said, "Besides it belongs with someone who has more life ahead of him then behind." I rode home and eyed that piece more than once. It was very worn and tattered having many scratches, nicks, and a lifetime of history. I don't think I'll ever take it off. Days later Mr. Conner continued the story.

I began to walk and thought about what Father McIver had said, but just letting things fall into place or out of place wasn't a strong suit of mine. I made my way back down the streets to my apartment. I walked up the last few stairs pausing to catch my breath. I felt in my pocket for the key and noticed a note tacked to my wooden door. I opened the note and it read...... 9:00 San Pietro's...... On back in different hand writing the words, "Best to wear yesterday's clothes. Thank me later signed, Little G."

Time was short but I could make it. I dressed as instructed and walked downstairs to hail a cab. When we drove up I noticed that it looked swanky and the people going in were dressed upscale. I stepped to curb and under my breath said, "I'll thank you now Little G whoever the hell you are."

I walked in and said, "Conner." The maitre de replied, "We've been expecting you. You have a table waiting." I ordered a drink as I waited. I took notice of the surroundings, ivy grew along the walls, and plants hung from the ceiling. The tables circled the room around a formal dance floor that was tiled with small octagons of black and white arranged in designs. It was a very upscale joint.

I tried not to look at my watch but couldn't help myself. It was 9:15 and I had no idea who I was waiting for. To my surprise I saw Sally walk in. I stood beside the table as she neared. I lifted my hands and she placed hers in them. She turned a cheek for me to kiss. I pulled her chair back, and she sat with a smile on her face. I quickly sat down and waived for the waiter to bring her a drink. "Do you like Italian food Mr. Conner," she asked?

"Italian? San Pietro's is Italian food?" I asked.

"San Pietro is a small city on the island of Sardinia," So, of course it's Italian food." She stated.

"Sardinia?" I responded.

"It's part of Italy. You know Italy don't you Mr. Conner?" she said smartly. "It's that country in the shape of a boot."

"Well, now haven't we come a long way from the back roads of the country?"

"Yes, we have." She said smiling. We are in New York now aren't we? And I thought you Southern boys melted or something if you cross the Mason Dixon line."

"No not true at all," I stated smugly and sipped from my glass. Then said, "Quite the opposite actually. We tend to freeze." She smiled and again hid behind her menu.

"How is it that you know so much about Italy? Have you been there?" I asked.

"I'm sorry to say I have not been there." she stated. "But I do know the owner and he's from San Pietro. So, anything you might want to know he would be more than glad to tell you."

"Ah," I said.

"Mr. Conner did you ever once think about me?" she asked. I looked over my menu and caught her eyes on me.

"Yes, of course I did. Did you ever think about me?" I asked.

"No, not really." she said. "But there was this one time when I saw a boy fall off a horse, and it did remind me of you a little.

"I'm sure it did." I stated. The waiter asked for our order, and then took our menus leaving us with nothing to hide behind. I couldn't help but stare as I noticed every detail about her. I reached out and touched her arm. Under my fingers I felt the warmth of her skin. Something just felt familiar or right to me even after all this time. She placed her hand in mine as we spoke and laughed. I could hardly believe that it was her once again sitting there in front of me.

My ghost was real once again. It's hard to describe what was going on in my head and in my heart, but I knew a joy then that I hadn't felt in what seemed like a lifetime. Although quite crowded the room itself seemed empty with only the two of us occupying the space. We were in some strange magical moment in time, in a world with just us two in it. I had never felt a sensation quite like it before, and never again would I after that night. In that moment I felt complete. I did my best to contain my emotions. I didn't understand them myself let alone want her to know that I was already lost to her. The time came for us to leave and we did so arm in arm.

The driver of the cab didn't seem too happy about driving a mixed couple. I told him to take us to Maxine's. We sat closely, and she kissed me on the cheek. I kissed her on her lips feeling their softness. My eyes wondered to the mirror and met the cab drivers. I didn't care what he thought. Then she whispered in my ear, "Let's go to your place." I whispered back, "Never."

"Is there some place else we can go?" I asked. She told the cabbie an address, and he mumbled something I couldn't make out. Then he reluctantly drove us there. I quickly paid for a room and took her inside.

I awoke later that night, and just laid there beside her. She slept on her stomach, her back exposed and bare, and the sheets lying just below her waist. The room was lit only by the light coming from the streets outside. I couldn't help myself but I just laid there staring at her, running my hand slowly up and down her back memorizing her contours with my fingers. I noted every small detail of her body and soft skin I thought to myself all that time wasted. But now I have my chance to make it all right. My heart was finally full again and that was all that I cared about.

I must have eventually settled into some state of sleep, because when she stepped out of bed I was awakened and watched her cross the room. She asked, "Jimmy, What time is it?" I looked at my watch and said, "8:30." She said, "I can never sleep late in these places."

I wondered if she was just going to get up and leave or stay for the morning with me. I sat there and weighed her every move looking for a hint. Moments later she came over putting her head on my chest. With her hand on my stomach she asked, "Jimmy can we lay here just a little longer?"

"As long as you like." I replied. "I'm not minding this at all." She laid there for a few moments and asked, "Was it like you remembered?" She grinned as she looked up at me.

"Certainly, except there's no grass that I have to dig out of my pants," I replied.

"Jimmy do you have a wife?"

"A wife?" I exclaimed. Laughing at my reaction she said, "I didn't want to ask last night because I didn't want to ruin anything."

"No! No wife, No girl back home either."

"How did Grandpa Conner let you get by with that? You're supposed to be a gentleman with children and a wife who just adores you."

"He almost had his way," I said. "And so did the girl but I escaped. In manner of speaking I did anyway."

"Did you love her?" She asked. Not waiting for my answer she stood up to put on my shirt and walked to a mirror. My eye's focused on every movement she made. She began fixing her hair. I couldn't help myself but to just watch her. Why did that make me feel so good?

Then she said, "You must not have loved her if you had to escape."

I sighed and said, "I thought a lot about that question. Yes, I guess I did love her, but not like I should have. I don't regret leaving her if that's what you mean."

"Good," she said. "I don't want you lying in bed with me thinking about someone else." She walked back over to the bed and climbed in next to me. She sat there looking at me with her hands under her chin. "But you've probably had a lot of girls wanting your affections didn't you Jimmy Conner." She said smiling.

"Nah, don't have much time for women."

"So, all that money your Grandpa paid to teach you a thing or two went for nothing? What a shame! I would have thought being with me would have changed your life for good." I grabbed her wrist and gently drug her up close to me. Kissing her I said, "It did but you still have a lot of work to do."

We spent the remainder of the day together in the room. Eventually, she needed to check on Maxine's, and left just before nightfall. I opened the door to her cab as I took her hand to help her in. Not wanting to let go of her hand, I dared to ask if I would see her again. She replied, "Yes but I am very busy. I'll let you know." She pulled the door shut and the cab started to drive off. I stood there puzzled. Then the cab stopped and she looked out through the window, and yelled back in my direction, "Saturday night." Then the cab sped off, leaving me standing there with my hands in my pockets.

For me the clock moved ever slower as Saturday drew closer. We both had some time to reflect on what had happened between us. I realized nothing had changed for me. My heart was still with her, now more than ever.

I walked into Maxine's once again not certain of what to expect. A rather large black man approached me and asked "Mr. Conner?" I nodded and he said, "Maxine has a table waiting for you." He showed me to a seat much closer to the stage than I was before. I thanked him and he said, "If you need anything just ask them to get Little."

"Little G? I asked. "You put the note on my door?"

"Yes, Maxine had me follow you."

"Thank you for the advice about the clothes, you saved me from certain embarrassment."

"You're welcome," he replied.

"And another thing, I think you're nickname doesn't do you justice."

"My father's name is George and so is mine. I didn't want to be George Junior and Little G just stuck."

"Ah," I said. I have the same problem in my family. We just all answer to James. I think I like your plan better." He laughed and said, "Enjoy the show."

Sally or rather Maxine took the stage, and I watched her perform. I looked around and thinking that she must have saved every penny. She had worked very hard for all of this. I then realized it all might be more complicated than I first thought.

After her set I watched her work the room. She confidently moved from table to table speaking with the guests with not a moment of hesitation. She eventually made it over to my table. We spoke briefly and seemed as if she had something on her mind, but I couldn't quite read her yet.

Eventually she came over and said, "I need a moment off my feet. Did you enjoy?"

"Of course," I said then asked her, "Sally, how did you end up here? We never discussed it." She smiled and said, "I better order a couple of drinks. Do you want one?"

"Yes, I'll have another."

"Let me see where do I start? It wasn't long after you left that my Aunt sold the horse. Between that and the money I earned from your Grandfather, which was at a bargain price I might add, she had enough money to send me away."

"When I left Aunt Rose said, "That's the last man you'll have to have over you unless of course you want him there. It's time to live out your dream baby." Then she put me on a train to New Orleans."

"It's a marvelous city. Have you been there Jimmy?" Not waiting for an answer, she went on and asked, "I never asked you, is Jimmy what you want to be called? Or are you all manly now and go by James? Or do I call you Mr. Conner in mixed company?"

"Stop it." I said.

"I could have called you anything the other night couldn't I?"

"Yes, you could have. I answer to them all. And yes, I've been to Orleans a few times. We have, well, had business interests there."

"Are you sure you want to walk away from all that, Jimmy?" she asked looking at me questioningly.

"I was listening to your story. Not telling mine. Now finish," I said.

"Hmm now finish? Is that how it is?"

"Please, finish your story" I said.

"Since you asked me nicely" She replied. "Now, where was I?.......Oh, I was in New Orleans staying with family. It didn't take long for me to realize that they had other intentions for me than furthering my dream. My family has been in the business too long, and they seem to know only one way to make money. I could have followed their lead, but I had a problem. It appears Jimmy that you got under my skin, and it was enough of an excuse to keep me from following that path. I worked different jobs around the city cleaning homes and such; not going anywhere.

I began to feel hopeless, but then I met Reverend Blackwell. He asked me to attend his services. They were something special. He seemed to have to the whole church riveted to every word he spoke. I attended regularly, and before long I was in the choir.

My nights were mine and I would walk along and listen to music of the honky-tonks. I would sing along while I sat outside. Time went on and I grew a little older and more womanly. The boys would call, but I had my church and I held on to it tight. I've seen too many men ruin a woman's dreams by keeping her at home. Reverend Blackwell wanted our choir to make an album, one he could play through the week at his summer tent revivals. He rented the studio and we sang our hearts out.

I just happened to leave my gloves at the studio, and had to go back to get them later that day. The man who ran it introduced himself. He asked if I would like to sing a solo sometime in the studio. I told him no, because I had to get back to finish cleaning a home, but in truth, the idea made me nervous. I was upset with myself for not trying, but thought nothing would come of it. One Sunday I stayed late after church. Reverend Blackwell spoke with me, asking if I would help him with his tent revival on Wednesday. Excited about the prospect of leaving the city, for even just the day, I quickly accepted the offer. On the way to the revival the Reverend, another gentlemen, and myself all rode together. The revival went as planned and I helped in every way I could and enjoyed it.

On the way back the other man stayed in the town, leaving me with Reverend Blackwell alone for the ride back. I trusted him and didn't think much of it. Reverend was very complementary about what all I had done. We started to talk about going to other revivals with him around the area. We drove a short distance and Reverend Blackwell pulled off the main road and then down a lane next to field. He got the idea that I needed a little of his personal salvation. I left him standing next to the truck pulling up his pants and in pain. I started walking back to the city, and was picked up just a couple of miles or so down the road. I was safely brought home by a very kind couple.

That walk gave me time to think. I realized as a woman, I'd always have to be on the lookout for those who just wanted to take from me. I'd never be judged for what I could do until I had enough money to prove to everyone that I could make it without them. I could see the world was like my Auntie said. And I didn't want to have nobody on top of me that I didn't want! Until I made something of myself, I'd always be in a position where I would have to rely on a man, and that put me in a position that I didn't want to be in. The very next morning I woke up and went down to that recording studio. I pulled out the money I had saved, and paid some men to play. He assumed that I wanted to sing gospel music. I shook my head no, put my foot down, and confidentially said not today mister. That day I sang the music I learned sitting outside of those honky-tonks.

I left grinning not a penny in my pocket and ten records in my hand. It was the happiest day I'd had in a long time. I went around with my records during the day, and left them for the tavern owners. That's how I got my start. Eventually, I had enough money and worked my way north. It took a few years and a lot of work before I found myself here. When the time was right I bought into a partnership. The next thing you know I owned it all. So, here I am, Miss Maxine!"

I clapped my hands and smiled, "Yes, you are Miss Maxine. Very good! That is something to be proud of Sally. You've done well!"

We sat for a moment listening to the next act. She looked out to the stage not making eye contact, and said in a very serious tone, "Jimmy, where will this lead?"

I sat there not saying a word. When she turned, she put her hands over mine and said, "Can't this be just for fun?" Still not saying anything I looked into her eyes. She smiled and asked, "Why are you just looking at me?"

"Sally, I found this the other day."

I placed the bookmark that she made all those years ago on the table. She sat back and smiled then said, "I stayed up all night making this for you." Then she paused, "You did think about me didn't you." Then asked, "The note did you read the note I wrote?"

"Yes, I found it and still have it."

"That's a very sweet sentiment that you hung on to it all this time."

"Sally, I'm not going to take you away from anything. I'm not here to take anything from you. I just know that there is something about us and I want to find out what it is and why it is. I have hung on to you for some reason all this time. There are so many things that I don't have figured out in this life but there is one that I feel very certain about, and it's that I don't want to be with someone for the right reasons. I want to be with someone because my heart tells me too. I can't explain why, but I am drawn to you. "

"There is something about us isn't there." She said as she eyed her creation.

"Just being near you again is enough for me to know that I want to find out more, and for now that's all I need." I said.

She breathed in deeply and said, "All right, Mr. James Conner I'm game. What do you want to find out later tonight?"

A smile cracked on my face, "Well, Miss Sally-Maxine everything I can. Everything I can....." and I kissed her hand.

So, began the next phase of our relationship. We tried to go slow but just couldn't help ourselves. It wasn't long before we moved into a small place of our own. The apartment was on the fringe of both the white and black parts of the neighborhood. A place where there was more daily intermingling of the colors than other parts. It was just a small place of safety from the judgmental eyes of those times.

Sally's work consumed her time, and Sally consumed mine. I spent a lot of time at Maxine's. She asked me to take part in the business, but I was leery of such a move. Maxine's was hers and a job can be defining for a person, especially, for a woman who did it on her own.

Eventually, I would have to find employment, but no longer would I be battling it out on the streets. Something more suited to my experience, but one not likely to draw any attention from the eyes of those that might be looking for me. I thought a lot about that subject and it came to mind that must have been why my father chose such a secluded place in the Carolinas. It was place for him and mother to call home. A place where he carried no status or station but what he made for himself. I was more like my father than my grandfather expected. I would suspect that he was more following his heart than running from something that he may have done. I think he must have found some peace because he loved my Mother and that little place he called home. Maybe that's why I'm chasing Sally. Maybe I saw something in them that I wanted for me.

I finally found work keeping records for a phone company. The position was low pay, but did carry a more professional social standing with it. Most importantly though it held an element of privacy that I required. I wasn't ashamed, mind you, but it just wasn't an acceptable practice to intermix even up north. I wanted to protect myself and Sally from any uncomfortable situations. I liked our little world, and wanted to protect it as much as possible.

Campbell, have you ever heard of the "Cult of the lost cause?"

"No, sir I haven't," I said.

"It's not actually a formal group or anything of the sort it's a name associated with any intellectual or literary group that promoted the Southern cause as a noble chivalrous endeavor. A gentle nudge caused writers to speak out on behalf of the Southern Cause after the war was over. And it was surprising how much momentum that gentle nudge carried. As long as it's talked about the dream remains alive."

"The Sons have writers?" I asked.

"Conner, have you not been listening? This organization has had its hands in everything from politics to bumper stickers ever since the War Between the States ended. Now where were we?" He continued.....

Everything seemed fine for months, she was strained of course from her work and trying to keep things going in our little world but I was never so in love, nor was she. Everything seemed to be working out between us. I decided to make a big move to give us a little something to expand our world beyond our normal zone of safety. She had no idea what I had planned when we left to our destination in the lightly populated regions of New Jersey.

"Do you like the Romeo?" I asked Sally.

"Yes, I do." She said.

"She purrs doesn't she?" I said grinning.

"I'm not so sure a purr is the right term, James."

"Purrs Sally, she purrs."

"Hmmm..... More like clanks"

"Easy girl," I said patting the dash board.

"We're about ten miles from our destination. Please don't upset the Romeo, Sally." I said mockingly. "Close your eyes." I told her. We pulled into a large farm with long rows of white fences. Beautiful horses stood in the fields behind them. "Now open them!"

Sally was excited at the idea of going riding again, but protested that she didn't have anything to wear. I looked at her and said, "I took care of that I too."

"What did you buy, James?" She asked.

"You'll see. We can change in the cottage."

"They have cottages?" She asked.

"Yes, I saw an advertisement and knew this would be perfect."

"Jimmy I...,"

"Don't you worry about a thing; I've made all the arrangements. You go on over and pick out a horse, and I'll get everything finalized."

I followed the sign down the brick walk way and entered the home which doubled as the office. On the desk was a bell which I rang. An older lady walked out from behind a curtain and said, "Hello, may I help you?"

"Yes, ma'am I'm James Conner I called about a cottage."

"Yes, Mr. Conner I have you down for a room for two."

"You have a lovely place here."

"Thank you," She said. "We take a lot of pride in our little farm. You and Mrs. Conner I presume."

"Well, to be truthful….." I stopped myself and then asked, "Ma'am, may I please have your name?"

"Mrs. Willis but you may call me Ethel."

"Well, Ethel Mrs. Conner isn't exactly a, "Mrs." yet but it is my intention for her to be before the weekend is out." And I showed her a ring that I was carrying in my pocket.

"Oh, my lands," she said as she looked at the ring.

"Clarence come on out." She yelled. Clarence staggered to the door.

"Clarence I would like you to meet Mr. Conner." Ethel said.

"How do you do sir?" We shook hands as I continued, "As I was telling Mrs. Willis, sorry I mean Ethel, that I was going to propose and get married this weekend."

"Congratulations," he said.

"Where is the bride to be?" He asked.

"You didn't leave the poor girl in the car did you?" Ethel asked.

"She's stretching her legs, and picking out a horse for tomorrow's ride. She hasn't said yes but I'm sure she will once I actually propose. Please don't say anything to spoil the surprise."

Ethel, smiling walked over to the far window as I continued, "Speaking of which I wanted to do something special for the big moment. We have a long history and a horse sort of brought us together. Neither of us have ridden in years." I stated. "Ethel, do you have any thoughts where we could ride? Preferably, a romantic spot where I could pop the question. No answer came from the window where Ethel stood.

"Mrs. Willis?" I asked again. She continued to look out the window.

Finally, Mr. Willis said, "I know a perfect spot down by the river." Ethel turned from the window and said, "Clarence may I have a word with you please?" She walked by me and out of the room.

"As I was saying a small bluff looks down on a valley with the river below, it would be a perfect setting." I heard Ethel's voice come from the other room, "Clarence!"

"Just a moment, Mr. Conner," I stood there quietly waiting their return. Clarence walked back in with a pained looked on his face and said, "I'm sorry Mr. Conner but we appear to have over booked the cottages."

"What?" I asked. "How can that be? You were just about to hand me the key?"

"I am sorry for your trouble Mr. Conner but that's just the way it is." Ethel appeared in the door way with a tight lipped defiant look on her face.

"Oh, I see. By saying you're over booked is a way of saying we're not welcome." Ethel stood resolute and Clarence half ashamed. I stepped toward the door and turned and said, "This was supposed to be the biggest weekend of our lives. I have plans with the pastor of the Presbyterian church up the road for us to be wed this weekend."

"I'll let him know you won't be making it," commented Ethel defiantly.

"You'll do no such thing," stated Clarence. "I am sorry for your troubles Mr. Conner. Good luck to you."

Not replying I opened the door and walked out. I was so furious and could barely contain myself. I walked toward the car. Sally, saw me and could tell by my pace that something was wrong. Sally came over and opened her door.

"What's wrong Jimmy?"

"They're booked," I replied.

"Oh," she said and sat down. The Romeo roared as I sped out onto the road. Sally, put her hand on mine and softly said, "Okay, take it easy James. Just calm down and slow down."

"I know, but I'm just furious." I said.

"They weren't really full where they?" She asked. My silence on the subject was answer enough for her. And she said, "Been living it for a long time, James. It does make a person mad, but what are you going to do, drive this car fast and make them change their mind?" She said smiling.

Feeling foolish I sighed and slowed down as I continued down the road.

"James, it's something we're going to have to face wherever we go."

"I know I just like the safety of our apartment." I stated

"But we can't always be in that apartment. That's something we have to consider. Just because we're fine with us doesn't make everyone fine with us; black or white." She said.

"Sally, you just don't know how big this weekend was for us. I had wonderful plans."

"It's all right, let's not let other people spoil our time." She said.

We continued on, driving for the coast. Eventually, we found a road side motel to stay for the night, one that didn't mind our business. The next morning things were fresh for me in my mind and my mood was more pleasant. We drove for an hour taking the Romeo off the main road and onto the sandy roads that headed for the ocean. Once at the dunes we sat down for awhile, just enjoying the sun. I said, "You know across the Atlantic there are many places we could go and see. Place where people who wouldn't care about our color."

"Tell me about them Jimmy."

"France for one, In Paris we could get lost in a sea of people. And even if they said something mean to us, it would still sound beautiful."

She laughed and said, "French is a beautiful language I heard people speak it in New Orleans."

"You could drive those French chiefs crazy learning how to cook a decent meal for me."

"Hey, now!" she said.

"It's just something to think about Sally. It could be easier for us to just be there. It's pretty simple for us to be happy together. All the other stuff just seems to get in our way."

"It is something to think about James. You always want to try and figure out everything. Let's just wiggle the sand between our toes, and enjoy the sun for a spell."

I have always been amazed at how well we could just get along with no one else around. For that matter we didn't even have to say a thing. We could just be quiet together with our thoughts mingling someplace else communicating on their own.

We moved under a clump of trees that paralleled the beach and stayed late into the day. Sally sat feeling the breeze on her face watching the waves roll onto the beach, and I just enjoyed the quiet. The sun began its journey over the horizon like a giant ball floating above the sea. The sky was bright with reddish orange tints that glowed against the backdrop of the sky. Sally sat quietly wrapped up in the moment, her thoughts perhaps on a journey all her own.

My toes curled in the sand feeling the coolness between them. The sea's breeze floated over me as I laid there looking at her. Oh, how I could just sit and stare at her.

"Sally," I said.

"Yes, James," she replied still staring off into the distance.

"I had a plan this weekend."

"I know you did James."

"Not that plan, Sally. I had another one."

"Really, those people didn't mess it up did they?" She asked.

"Sort of Sally."

"Yes, they sort of messed up your plan?"

"Not necessarily, you know I love you."

She looked at me chin down with a half smile emerging on her face said, "I love you too James."

"Good, I'd hate to be in this alone," I said. "Sally, I want this. I want a life of moments like this one. I want someone to wake up with that I look forward to being with; I'm not settling. I just won't. There just can't be much sweeter than waking up next to you. When I feel your hand, touch your arm, or kiss your lips, I just know that you love me. It's something I don't have to question, and because of that I want to marry you, Sally." She looked out toward the sea still smiling and said, "You do." I leaned up, and took a step toward her. Then crouched back down and kissed her. She looked into my eyes and I said, "My life has had plenty of things I have to do for this reason or that, but my hearts mine. It's mine alone. This is something I want because deep in my heart I know its right. I have to be with you, and I won't be happy any other way."

I took the ring from my pocket and placed it on her finger. As she looked down at it she said, "It's beautiful Jimmy. I love you so Jimmy. I will marry you. I will be your wife."

I told her of my plan with the preacher how badly that I wanted to be her husband. She comforted me by saying, "It's all right we can wait a little while I want to enjoy being engaged for a bit anyway." She always had a way of making things positive. She continued, "Then we can be newlyweds for awhile, and you know start to get to know each other, like married people do."

"I think we got a little ahead of ourselves there," I commented.

"Don't tell anyone. I run a respectable business."

"I wouldn't dare Sally, I won't tell a soul."

We stayed out on the beach that night listening to the waves roll in.

The next day we headed back to the city early more in love than when we left for the weekend. That evening Sally left the apartment to see if Maxine's was still standing after leaving Little G in charge. I was getting unpacked and cleaned up. I dreaded work after a weekend away. A knock wrapped at my door. I opened it, and their stood Charlie Bedford. "Charlie," I said. I looked at him for a moment questioningly. He stood there looking angry, "Would you like to come in?" I asked. He stepped inside and reached into his pocket. Unsure of what he would pull out, I took a half step back.

"Here," he said holding a note in his hand. "It's from Lucy."

"Charlie what is this about?" I asked.

"I don't know. She just asked me to find you. I can't believe you, Conner, shacking up with a negro gal. I can't believe you did my sister wrong like that. I wasn't even going to give this to you but she insisted. It's probably her begging you to come back. And now that you've done this she won't want ya. I don't want your stain on the Bedford Family name. I'm telling them all about you. I'm telling them all!" I lifted my hands up and said, "Charlie, I didn't leave Lucy for Sally. Truthfully, I don't care if you tell the world! I'm ashamed of nothing."

"You say that now Conner but your Grandpa will disown you."

"Maybe so Charlie that's his choice." He opened the door and stepped out. I could hear him say, "You'll be sorry. I swear it!" as he walked away.

A few hours later Sally walked in. "Still there in one piece?" I asked.

"Yes, it is." She looked a little weary.

"What's wrong?" I asked. She didn't say anything. I assumed it was just that she was tired.

"Long day huh?" I asked. "Why don't you take a bath. I'll run your water, and when you get done I'll have the bed warm for you."

"Sounds nice James, but I don't think I have the energy for all that."

"I'll get it started." She came in a few minutes later and sat in the tub. When I came back she was laying there soaking with a wash cloth on her eyes.

"Charlie Bedford stopped by."

"Charlie Bedford?" she asked. "Who's that?"

"Oh, just Lucy's brother."

"What?" she asked. Placing the wash cloth back over her eyes, "Whatever did he want?"

"I'm not sure what exactly put him up to finding me, but he said Lucy wanted to get word to me. Never the less, he tried to give me a letter, and then strangely didn't. But he did seem quite intent on telling me a few things about my character, and then stomped off."

"Hmmm that is strange. Well, if we have any more surprises tonight I'll go ask those people if I can clean their cottages or maybe even stalls for them." I sat down on the edge of the tub.

"You'll do no such thing. I'd rather buy them out for pennies on the dollar, and then make them work for you! That's how the Conner's do things." She laughed and said, "I like your plan better."

"James, hand me a cigarette."

"Oh, that kind of evening," I handed her one and lit it.

"Not exactly, Little G wants to buy me out."

"Little G?" I remarked. "Does Little G have big money?" I asked.

"Not by himself, but he has an interested partner."

"That's an interesting twist in the weekend Lucy, any thoughts?"

"Truthfully, I don't want to think." She said. "Hand me a towel." I brought one to her and wrapped her in it. She dried off. Put on her robe and said, "James, I'm going out for a minute and have another cigarette."

"Another?" I asked. She rarely smoked more than one unless alcohol or a night out was involved.

"Yes, my stomach hurts, and I need some air to clear my head."

"Mind if I join you?" I asked.

"James, can I just have a moment alone?"

"Certainly," I said. A few moments and more than just one cigarette later she came back in. I had the bed warm as promised. She lay down beside me. Not saying much in the process and I just left it alone for the night.

Morning came and she was already up early. She didn't appear to be feeling well but I went to work anyway. On my ride back home I began to consider a few things. And when I arrived at our place I rushed in and yelled, "Sally." She was still in bed and not feeling well. I sat on the edge and said, "Sally, I've been thinking. I have something I'm concerned about."

"Must be exciting go ahead James." She said.

"I told you about my parents. About how they died, but I never did tell you what I suspected. I wouldn't tell you this, but I am a little concerned with Charlie showing up on my door step."

"Go on," she said. Not wanting her to know anything more than the minimum for her own safety I told her, "Sally, my father's business dealings led him into a circle that may have led to his death."

"May?" she asked.

"I'm not certain, but it's very likely. I'm in that circle Sally or was."

"Can you or your Grandfather fix it?"

"Easily if I go back, but I'm not going. I'm not sure how it all appears to them. That's not all I was thinking about our weekend and sitting on the beach looking out over the sea. We'll never get a fair shake here. If we ever have children, they won't either. And now with Little wanting your business. Maybe it's our time. Let's just leave; leave it all, and start someplace fresh. Like we talked about maybe going to Paris? We'll be more accepted there, and if not, then we won't know that their saying bad stuff about us anyway." Half cracking a smile she laughed and said, "Oh, we will know, trust me."

"I do know, but you can sing there and be the toast of Paris. I still have money, and have access to more overseas. I'm not taking anything that's not mine. We can have a good start."

She looked at me and said, "James you're giving up so much for us."

"I'm not doing it for just you." I stated.

"I'm doing it because I love you. Love is something I need. I don't want to be without you in this life."

"Now, I'm scared something might happen to you and I couldn't bear the thought of that, James."

"Let's leave together. Then you won't have to worry. I know I'm asking a lot of you Sally. I know Maxine's is yours, that it's a part of who you are. But can't you be Madam Mouselle Maxine?"

"I don't know! When do you want to leave?" She asked.

"I'm not sure but a ship bound for Europe leaves every Thursday. What about next week?"

"What?" She said.

"I know next week seems soon, but this may be our opportunity. How soon can Little make his arrangements?"

"I'm not sure Jimmy." I could see her wheels turning in her head as she thought. Then she repeated herself, "I'm just not sure."

"We don't have to rush it, but it would be for the best if we left soon."

The next few nights Sally stayed at work later than usual, I didn't bring attention to the fact for fear of pressuring her on the subject. Even with that in mind I could feel her growing increasingly distant. Eventually, the time came, and I had to ask her if Europe was still an option. I decided it would be best if I sprung the question over dinner.

"Sally, how about a nice meal out on the town?" I asked.

"No, James I just want to be home tonight."

"Are you tired?" I asked.

"No, tonight's our last night here in New York, and I want to remember this home."

"Sally, are you serious!" She smiled and asked, "Can you get our things together tomorrow?"

"Honey, I'm easy. A couple of bags, and I'm ready. It's you that I'm concerned about."

"What I have here I'll put in my memories. The items that have some sentimental value, I'll box tonight."

"What about your things at Maxine's?"

"I've packed what I wanted already. The rest Little G bought. Everything is in place, James. I get paid for Maxine's tomorrow. I'll meet you at the docks after Little and I settle up. You can get everything ready here, and we can board together."

"I promise you won't regret this Sally. I swear it." I said happily.

We quickly sorted through our little place, and packed what we wanted. She only packed a large trunk and a bag. Later that night we went outside for a moment and stood looking at the lights of the city and what stars we could see.

"Do they have the same stars in France?" She asked.

"Yes, In France it's the same sky as New York."

"So, I can still see our stars?" She asked

"Yes, our stars will be there too."

"Will you always remember that night under the stars James? Back when you were a cadet named Jimmy Conner, and I was a young Sally living in the middle of nowhere."

"Yes, I promised I would. I'll make you another promise.

"Oh, what?" she asked.

"That I'll remember tonight too," I said.

"I know Jimmy. We're going to make it."

"Yes, we will Sally."

Before going inside for the night I looked up to the sky once more and saw the Pleiades constellation watching down on me from its lofty perch in the sky and thought, "I won't be able to get away from her even in France."

As planned Little showed up early and carried Sally's belongings to the car. I told her to be at the boat by noon. She reassured me and said, "I'll see you soon, Jimmy."

Before reaching Little's car she turned and ran back to me. She hugged me tightly. I could feel her tears on my neck.

"It will be all right Sally." I said.

"I love you so much Jimmy."

"I know or you wouldn't be doing this for me." I replied.

She smiled and walked away. One last time I said, "Before noon!"

She opened the door and drove off looking back toward our place crying. I looked up too and thought, "We did have wonderful times here."

I gathered the last of my things, looking one last time at the place that made me so happy, so at peace. "You were a good home for us thank you." I said. Then closed the door, and patted the exterior wall as I walked away. I made my rounds getting cash from a safety deposit box that I had in the city, and headed to the docks. I bought our boarding passes as my biggest fear had subsided. I waited with a clear view to see Sally and Little G in the direction they would approach. I pulled out the gift I had bought Sally for the voyage. It was a small heart shaped jewelry box with a note inside. I opened the box and read the note once again.

Sally,
Today we start a new adventure together!
You have always and will forever have my heart.

I began to check off my list in my head over and over. But I had a nagging feeling that something was missing and finally realized what I had forgotten. I thought, "Damn, the Romeo! I forgot the Romeo! I'll just have to send word to Grandfather to tell him where it is when I get to France." That offense alone would make him hunt me down.

I was comforted by the fact that I had remembered the Romeo but time grew nearer to noon, and Sally hadn't yet arrived. As I waited I began to wonder if something had gone wrong. Time past and noon was long gone. I sat there and watched the ramparts from the ship being pulled away as the tug boats steamed closer. The horn blew and the ropes were unlashed from the docks that secured the ship. There I sat watching the ship steam out of the harbor and off into the distance.

A mixture of emotions crossed my mind from worry to anger. I finally succumbed to the fact that she wasn't going to show. So, I walked in the direction of the street to find a cab.

Maxine's was the first stop. I entered and saw Little G standing near the bar.

"Where's Sally?" I said questioned.

"Take it easy Mr. Conner Maxine's safe."

"Where is she? What happened? I waited for almost three hours!"

"This letter will explain it."

"No, Little I want you to tell me where Sally is."

"Miss Maxine told me to give these to you." And he handed me two letters. The first was from Sally which read.

James,

I must first tell you that I love you. Please don't take my actions today as I sign that I don't but that's just not enough for me. When I went out on the porch the other night and saw the note that Lucy had written you. Her brother must have dropped it after talking with you. Jimmy in this world love just isn't all there is. You have been blessed with great responsibilities and wealth. Why would you give that up for someone like me? I'm just a colored girl from nowhere who can sing a little. It doesn't make since and I just can't ask you to leave it all for me. In truth I promised myself a long time ago that I would live out my dreams and living in France just wasn't part of that dream.

If you leave now and go back you'll have it all again. You can have a respectable life with a white wife and children. You can live a very good life with people that respect you and in be a position that you were born for. Not just some fool at the bottom of the heap trying to work his way up in these times. I can't steal that from you James and that's exactly what I would be doing. And I can't be responsible for taking that life from you just because I love you and you'll be taking a part of me away too.

It will never work for us. This is for the best.

I will always love you.
Sally

Not sure what to think. I opened Lucy's letter. If nothing else to see what she could have possibly written that would make Sally leave me.

James,

I'm sorry for what I said to you on the porch that day. I have regretted it and missed you since the day you left. I have spoken with your grandfather often and he seems quite lost without you. Let this foolish romantic notion of love go. In time you and I can learn to be in love just as my parents did. I'm sure you will love me like you want in the end. I think it's time we talked; it's obvious to everyone that we should be together.

Yours always
Lucy

Fuming after reading the letters I asked, "Little, where is Sally?"

"She's gone Mr. Conner."

"Where?" I asked.

"Didn't say, she just jumped in a cab once we signed papers and told me to give you those letters."

"Damn it Little you know. Where is she?"

"Mr. Conner if you keep this up I'll have to ask you to leave."

"Leave! I will not leave until I have Sally!"

"Yes, you will leave Mr. Conner. This is my place now as he held up a bill of sale and said, "Now, Mr. Conner!"

"Little I swear if you don't tell me where she is....." And then it happened. I lost control and it was in that moment that I grabbed the wall of a human that was Little G.

He caught my hand as it was coming down and turned my arm behind my back. I'm sure it pained him to do it but he carried me to the door and said, "Mr. Conner don't make me hurt you." He pushed me outside where I sat ruffled on the street for a minute gathering myself. He stepped near me and said, "Mr. Conner she told me to give you this too." He handed me the ring that I gave her. I held it for a moment and said, "Little." He kept walking for the door. "Little," I again said. He stopped and turned.

"You'll see her again; give it to her for me." He walked back over to me and crouched down and said, "Mr. Conner you are a good man but she just doesn't want you anymore. She told me to give it to you, and I do as Miss Maxine says."

I walked away with no idea what to do. Eventually, I ended up back at our place. That night I was alone in every way imaginable. In the past when I felt this way I held on to the thought that she possibly was out there waiting. But now, I didn't even have that to hold onto.

The first few days I felt in a fog with a hurt deep inside my gut. The kind of hurt that could leave a person bent over in pain. Not eating, not sleeping, just agonizing hurt. I felt that if I could just find her, just talk with her, she would see that I was right. She would see that we shouldn't live this life apart; that we had to be together. But in time that thought began to fade. I became frustrated by the fact that I so close to the brass ring of happiness. That I had it at my finger tips; almost within my grasp to only have it elude me. In the end that frustration changed my mood and mental state. Anger began to take hold, I was mad at her and the world.

SEVENTEEN

Fed up with feeling helpless and out of I control. I rummaged through my things, and put on an old set of clothes. I had a cab drop me off near where I once waited with men looking for work. Something about the pain of those struggling for daily sustenance, and my own pain, gave me a commonality that I needed.

But, instead of the goodness that I sought before, this time it was hurt and anger that drove me. There is strength in those motivations too, and I was tired of feeling weak. The problem with drawing from the worst side of yourself is that in the end you tend to do more harm than good. I stumbled across a group of men. An argument broke out between two of them. First in words, then in fists, men scattered forming a circle. Money began to come out of their pockets as bets were placed. I stood there thinking that I was too hurt to feel pain myself. Then I stepped up, and put myself up for a fight.

My opponent was a man about my age, but larger. Judging from the broken nose and scar above his right eye it appeared that this type of side income was a common event for him. As the fight began men clamored and yelled around us. We stepped closer to each other testing each other moving within the circle. I threw a jab to the body, and then he swung missing his mark. This provided an opening and I landed a few quick punches to his midsection. Then a left to the jaw and somehow I had the advantage but only briefly. The man's large hand caught my right, and with a kick to the side of the leg, I was on my knees. He stood over me still holding my hand. There was little I could do. His size and strength now gave him the edge. Looking up I could see the fist of his right hand coming down on my jaw and momentarily I thought, "He can't hurt me anymore than I already am." That notion was fact because in an instant world went black. The larger man had taken the day and I was out cold. I laid there on the ground covered in blood and dirt. No one bothered to help me. The crowd just parted, and formed another circle for next two opponents to fight.

After a short while I felt a hand lightly slapping my face, and a voice saying, "Conner, CONNER wake up." I tried my best to make out the persons features through the fog of my blurred vision. Slowly it became clearer that this man was my old friend.

"Peabody?" I asked.

"None other"

"God you look like hell, Peabody."

"I look like Hell? Wait till I get you to a mirror."

"I feel fine," I mumbled.

"Conner your sand got you in a pickle this time didn't it."

"Lucky punch," I mumbled.

He helped me to my feet raising me off the ground. "Can anyone just find me whenever they please? I'm supposed to be hiding up here."

"You certainly stink at it," he replied.

We both started to walk out through the alley. Between my wounds, his alcohol, and bum leg he either half carried me or I half carried him I'm not exactly certain. I didn't ask him about the noticeable limp in his gate, but I was concerned about his general condition. The place he called home was a pathetic structure barely suitable to live in. And yet, inside were children wearing the filth and grime of the city as they ran about. We made our way up the stairs and into his apartment, nothing more than a room really. I sat on a wooden chair as he went over to the faucet that let out a moan and a thumping noise as it released its water. I watched him and wondered what had become of that strong invincible boy I once knew. What happened to him on his journey that threw him off course? He was lean washed out and dirty. His face unshaven and eyes darkened from lack of sleep and hard drinking; he was in poor condition. He wet a cloth and walked over to me and said, "Take this and clean yourself up." I put the cloth to my eye and as it passed by my face I noticed a wicked smell.

"God this stinks, Peabody, is it the rag?"

"Could be or the water I wouldn't drink it, something about the tide and this part of town."

"Don't worry I won't drink it." I took another whiff, "It has to be the rag." I said.

"Don't put that in your mouth either." He replied. "So, you're hell bent on getting yourself hurt."

"No, just wanting to make some money," I said.

"Money? Did the Conner's go broke?" He asked.

"No, of course not," I said.

He sat down across from me. He then handed me a drink looking at me with brows raised and asked, "What's this about Conner? Why is a man with your smarts going out there getting his face punched in?"

I replied, "What's a man like you doing wasting away in this hell hole and crawling in a bottle? I think your pride is in the same deep dark well that my smarts are." He stood up and limped a few steps toward the counter. I cringed because of the remark I had just made and said, "I shouldn't have said that Peabody." He kept walking and turned with a fresh bottle of whiskey and said, "Think nothing of it. Maybe we can both find our answers at the bottom of this bottle."

"If not this one maybe the next," I replied

"That's the spirit Conner." He said.

He sat down across from me, and I reached for the bottle. He grabbed my hand with the firm grip of the Peabody I remembered. Then he looked at me with a serious expression and said, "But if we don't find the answer in these bottles tonight. Then maybe we should find somewhere else to look."

"I suggest scotch I haven't looked for anything in the bottom of a scotch bottle in awhile."

"I'm serious Conner! Tomorrow I have business, and we both need clear heads. Deal?" I looked at him hesitantly realizing he was asking for help on some level and replied, "Yeah, Michael it's a deal."

"Then tonight we drink!" He stated.

He poured another glass with no concern about spilling the whiskey on the table. We drank and laughed about old times. We likely toasted everyone who ever went to Bransford Academy. At one point that night I asked him about the knife he had at school, and if he still had it. He just pointed to the ceiling with hundreds of slit marks left behind from the blade sticking in it. He was still quite proud of the knife, and could throw it around the room with a high degree of accuracy even after sharing two bottles of cheap whiskey. I finally broke, and asked him what had happened to his leg.

He told me that he and Tanner enlisted in the service. The fact they joined the infantry was his idea. Tanner being the friend he was didn't protest, even though deep down he wanted to be in the cavalry. Then he went on and described the incident that changed his life forever. It happened at a practice range while a group of men were all standing together. A large wagon carrying ordinance was sitting on a hill above them. It began to roll in their direction. A voice yelled out, and the group began to scatter. Peabody stopped to help one soldier to his feet then pushed him to safety. But he wasn't so lucky and the wagon caught him under a wheel shredding the muscles in his calve. A short time later they discharged him from service separating the two best friends. After the story we continued to drink late into night.

The next morning we woke early. He made a quick recovery gaining his wits much sooner than I could even imagine. He refused to take a shower even though I pleaded with him to. Then he went on to argue with me about me being too clean. He pointed out that it be easier to move about the city if we looked like something thrown out instead of something new. Never the less, I cleaned myself up anyway. The next battle of the morning was my refusal to drink the last swig of whiskey as he requested. I put on yesterdays clothes covered with my blood and the dirt of the yard. Then he messed up my combed hair and said, "Much better."

He quickly made assessment of his room. He then grabbed his knife, a few other small items and a change of clothes in the process. He placed them in a bag that he carried over his shoulder. He eyed the empty bottles of whiskey and said, "Business," and we walked out. After traveling a few blocks we sat on a bench. Then he said, "A few months ago Tanner sent me this." and he handed me a letter.

"How did he know how to find you?" I asked.

"Tanner always finds me!" He replied

The letter read:

Michael,

Things are going well for me. I recently completed my enlistment and now have a job with the Government. My parents are fine and my sister was married last month. Sorry, but I refused to let her marry someone who wasn't at least moderately handsome. Your bad luck I guess. I just wanted to know if you were well and find out how the leg was coming along. Please, be *a little more forthcoming about your whereabouts and situation. Your family is also wondering the same. All for now I have to catch the 4:13 train.*

Tanner

I handed him back the letter and said, "Tanner seems a little worried."

"He's fine. Look closer, notice anything?" I looked and didn't see anything out of order.

"No." I stated.

"Within this letter is another note. We mark certain letters and that makes a key for a cipher. Are you familiar with a cipher?" He asked.

"No," I replied.

"I have to teach you everything."

"Tanner and I used to communicate all the time this way. It was a game to us. We memorized four ciphers in our time at Bransford. Do you remember the Bible we were issued at Bransford?"

"Yes, of course."

"Tanner and I weren't diligently studying the scriptures we were working on ciphers and using the bible and a key."

"A key?" I asked.

"Look again at the note. First line reads, "Now have a job." Then the line reads, "4:13 train." Let's read JOB 4:13. He usually isn't this obvious. We worked out other ways of telling each other which passage to use. That should be where I start the cipher. He probably thought I might be too drunk to figure out anything more complicated."

From his bag he pulled out his worn Bransford issue bible and opened it to JOB 4:13. Then he opened the letter and poked a hole through each marked letter. Then placed the letter over the passage and letters were revealed; the message read, "Bund find name of guest."

"I'm still not certain I understand." I said.

"And that's why we didn't teach you the cipher years ago." He retorted.

"What's does the message mean?" I asked.

"I'm not a hundred percent sure but I have an idea where to start."

We stood up and started walking. I knew better than to ask a lot of questions. Besides I didn't exactly have anything better to do. So, I followed Peabody through town.

"Why would Tanner worry that anyone would read your mail?" I asked.

"He's just overly cautious. Then again doing what he does he has to be."

I nodded in agreement.

"Now Conner, tell me about this hell bent on destruction thing you have going on. Is it over that gal I saw you with?"

I paused and replied, "You saw me with Sally?"

"Yes," said Peabody. "I've been watching you off and on since I saw you at the soup line serving the poor folk like me. You apparently didn't recognize me when I walked by."

"Why didn't you say anything?" I asked.

"At first I didn't know what to say. I just watched you for awhile and then would check in on you from time to time.

I lost you for a short time and found you by chance when I saw that nice car you had stashed out in front of a place called Maxine's. Eventually, I found out why you were going there. I guess I figured you were running from something, and maybe just didn't want to be found. So, I never made any contact."

"Yeah, I guess I was." I replied.

"The way I see it when a man's running, likely its best if you just let him run awhile or you might spook him. Eventually, he'll slow down. Plus you looked pretty happy with that gal."

"I was," I replied.

"What happened?"

"I don't really understand it all honestly."

"There is a lot of that in this life," replied Peabody.

"It just seemed right in my gut. I've never been happier. I thought she was my fate."

"You got the gut part right Conner. I always follow my gut but that's not the way with everyone. Some people think too much and that changes everything. It's all in the gumballs Conner."

"Gumballs?" I asked.

"I think people's lives are full of choices. I also think that there is a fate tied to them. I believe certain things are supposed to happen. They have time and an order in which they happen. The way I see it the whole thing is like a bubble gum machine. The penny goes in and the gum rolls out, now it's tied to that person. But now comes, the rub. We have a choice we can keep it or throw it out to get another one. That decision changes everything for not just for the first person buying the gumball but for the next one as well. And I think when we throw it out sometimes someone else gets our fate or we get someone else's. Have you ever noticed that when things are good then people say, "Its destiny!" and then a short time later when things aren't so good the destiny chatter quickly fades away? Some fates have to be bad wouldn't ya think? Most people just don't follow through to find out the end result.

I mean are we so selfish that we think that all things must be good in our life? That we are key players in the design? How come it can't be someone around us who gets the big prize, and that we are just there to provide a gentle nudge. Or at times, to take a hit maybe even be the one who gets the white gumball. So, the rightful owner gets the blue one and everything falls into to proper order? These fates as we call them are just things that have to happen. It's up to us to accept them or not. And it's not logic that guides you in these choices it's your gut. Logic just muddies the water."

"Were you drinking when you came up with this?" I asked.

"Of course! Nobody with reasoning capabilities could have come up with something so simple. I just sat there watching the people go over to the machine and turn the knob; first a yellow then a green. Some people would turn up their nose others would walk happily away. Seriously, think about it Conner. The gum was in her hand and she threw it out. That single move changed everything for the both of you. All those things that could have been won't be. Well,... they may be just for other people. Never the less all has forever changed. Conner it was my choice to live like this and to drop out from all I knew. That was a fate that I chose, and now someone else might be living the life that was meant for me. Only I can make it right. Only I can follow my own will, my own instincts. But if I am to do something special that's tied to a fate, and I choose to deny it. Then it must be done by someone else. Someone else could be living my life right now. Someone has to fill your spot in the Sons. Someone like Whittington, maybe?"

"Michael, this does nothing to make me feel better." I replied.

"How about this scenario; right now someone could be with your girl Sally, living the life you should have, but choices were made and your out!"

"Please stop, you're making me sick to my stomach."

"Conner, this is the point. It's the fates that matter; not the people. People can't be trusted to make the right choices. The fates happen regardless of who actually carries them out. The choices people make changes the players and who is attached to the fate.

Changing the subject I asked, "Were you following me the day of the fight?"

"No, that was just by chance. Seems like things run in circles. When they cross like they did at the fight, it's best to find out why. Plus, you looked a little like you needed to be found."

"Nope that was fate. We both must be on our path." I quickly replied.

"Maybe," he said.

"I still hurt from that by the way."

"You will for a few days. Let's get a bite to eat; my treat."

"I've got money Peabody."

"It's your money either way Conner. I bet against you."

"You bet against me?" I asked.

"Sure I did! Did you see how big the other guy was? I've seen him fight before. He is very good."

"Of course I saw him, and his rather large fist." I said.

"The other thing was I saw you before the fight, all mad and distracted. I sort of figured you wanted to hurt someone or be hurt yourself."

"Either way is bad isn't it?" I asked.

"Yes, very bad. Either way your heads not in the right place. Men just have this tendency when they are hurting to find a way to hurt themselves' even more. I can't quite figure that one out but it seems to be the case."

I looked at him and said, "They never seem to find that answer in the bottom of the bottle either."

"No, trust me I gave it my best effort and looked for it hard." He stated

We walked in the diner and sat down. The waitress looked at our poor condition and said, "Pay up front boys."

"Well, that's no way to get a tip!" Peabody retorted.

"I'm not sure I want a tip from you two rag a muffins."

"What exactly is a rag a muffin anyway?" Peabody asked.

"It can't be good if she doesn't want money from one." I replied.

We ordered our meal and Peabody handed her some money. She looked at him and said, "Wonders never cease to amaze me."

"I am pretty amazing." He said.

"Amazing isn't the word I was looking for to describe the likes of you? She paused and replied, "How about smelly, dirty, mouthy....should I continue?"

"You could give me a bath." He said.

"I'd have to throw the tub out." She replied.

"I'd do that for you after I put a smile back on your face."

"I'll smile when you leave." She said.

"Deal!" he said. "You give me a bath, I'll try and make you smile, and then I'll leave."

"No deal! Now eat and scat you're scaring the other customers."

She walked away as Peabody laughed. Then he asked, "How long have you been away from the elite class?"

"Maybe I like to wear dirty clothes." I replied.

"That's all right when you have money to fall back on, but I wouldn't advise throwing it all away just yet!"

"I pretty much did."

He looked at me and said. "Let's talk a minute," changing the subject. "By now you surely know the meaning of this." And he drew the cross of the Sons of the South.

"Yes, I know it." I replied.

"Do you know of the scorpion?" He asked.

"Yes, I know the sign of the Seven."

"But you're not a member of the Seven is that correct?"

"No," I said.

"Then how do you know of the Seven's secrets? You don't even know what a cipher is?"

"I just know. That's all I can say." I replied.

"Doesn't matter anyway, let's talk about a few basics before we continue. We're going to a place that's secretive. It's not associated with the Seven as of yet, but I think there is somehow a connection."

"Like what?" I asked.

"I'm just not sure, but I think we're about to find out."

"How do you know about the scorpion? The Sons? You didn't you come to New York after the Army?" I asked.

"No, I went home for a while. I spent a lot of time with my Uncle who has been active for years. Let's just say I became deeply involved but home just wasn't the right place for me. Everyone kept feeling sorry for me and I couldn't have that. So, I came here to get away."

We left the diner and started walking. We went to parts of the city that I had not yet explored. The city always intrigued me; its people, languages, architecture and smells. I thought back to what I learned about Black and Smith and wondered how much different the city must have been in those times. Many immigrants came right off the boats and joined the ranks of the Union. The riots in the city during that period came to mind and how men like Black, Smith and other Southern sympathizers cause the sparks that ignited them. How tied people in the North and South were even back then. The economies were intertwined then as now, and with this economic disaster it was clearly evident.

We made our way through the city slowly walking past a tavern. Peabody made no glance in that direction, but I knew he wanted to stop. I had seen his hand shake from the lack of the alcohol his body now needed. A block or so later sweat began to bead on his brow. I could tell he needed water, and likely medicine to beat this, but he did his best to fend off his demon. The best thing now was for us to just to keep moving.

He stopped at a corner, and he motioned for me to follow him. I walked past the front glass window of the National Socialist Workers Party headquarters. In that time communist, socialist and many other organizations had a foothold in American politics. Finally he stopped in the adjacent alley and said, "This is it."

"The Alley?" I asked.

"Yes, the alley." He replied as he kept walking.

"Why the alley?"

"That's where the trash is!" he replied.

"What are we looking for in the trash?" I asked.

"Not sure," he said and then started to sift through various boxes of paperwork.

I was becoming frustrated and again asked, "Can you at least give me a hint what to look for?"

"All the secrets of the world end up in the trash tucked away in an alley somewhere. We're likely looking for a name of an important person who is coming here. Look for notes, handwritten letters and anything that looks official."

We sifted through the trash piece by piece. We found scraps of paper with propaganda about socialist reform. He found a few pieces of hand written notes and letters written in German. Those he put it in his pocket. Others looked as if they were official documents with notes written in the margins. He picked up a piece and said, "This could be a find." Then he continued digging. A short time later we left. We walked down the street a few blocks, and reviewed what we found.

"This could be what Tanner needed," he said. He began giving me details of a past information gathering assignment of Tanner's.

"Ever heard of Camp Nordlund?"

"No," I replied.

"It's a youth Camp in New Jersey. The Germans are involved in this Socialist movement here in the U.S."

"The Germans?" I asked.

"The Bund mentioned in the letter is short for the German American Bund. It's another name of the National Socialist Workers Party, headed by a fellow named Heinz Spanknobel. Tanner must know something and have a reason for asking us to do this."

"Glad to know I wasn't digging through filth for no reason at all." I said.

"I've been meaning to ask you something Conner. Why did you leave home in the first place?" Peabody asked.

"I told you most of it." I said.

"So, you left because of a girl you hadn't seen in years and had no idea where she was?" He asked.

"Maybe part of it was the fact that I was leading a duel life and didn't like it."

"And you weren't leading a duel life when you met Sally?"

"Maybe so but at least I was true to myself with her." I stated.

"True but she's gone now, are you going to live as someone you're not?" He asked.

"I'm not sure what I'm going to do to tell you the truth."

"Conner you are a good man. You were brought to Bransford as a kid with no parents by a Grandfather you barely knew. A school created to turn young boys into men and teach values and skills important to the Southern cause. You worked your way through the school and made a good name for yourself there. You worked your way into an elite organization that few even know exist. I am afraid you are either what you were or what you have been made. Either way you're a Son of the South just like me. You can ignore that or embrace it. That part is up to you, but I think this organization means more to you than you like to believe. It's in our blood. It's a big part of who we are."

"I'm not sure what to think Peabody. You may be right."

"I usually am Conner. In that case what are a couple of Sons of the South doing up here with all these Yankees?"

"Hiding from what we are I'd say."

"Maybe Conner, but I'm going to do something about it."

Peabody hailed a passing cab. "A cab?" I thought but didn't ask. He gave him an address which I knew, but didn't say a word. The cab took us to my apartment. Peabody said, "Choice is yours Conner, but I'm done hiding. We can shake hands and part ways now or you can go in grab your things, and we can move on to our next step in this life."

It didn't take but a moment to decide. I walked in and quickly gathered my belongings. I never really unpacked from when I was leaving with Sally. In just minutes I was ready. On the counter I saw the heart shaped box the held Sally's ring inside. I wasn't sure what to do with it. I stood there and thought for a moment. Then I walked out back grabbing a shovel along the way and found a small patch of earth where I began to dig. Inside the freshly dug hole I placed the box, and it was there that I buried my heart. No place could be more fitting. Because it was there that I had shared more love than I had ever known before. This is where it belonged; out behind the place that was home to me. In a moment of smugness I thought I don't care what she says. It was real. It could have been great and I know it.

Peabody stood waiting smoking a cigarette with the cab driver. I jumped in back while Michael gave instructions to him about our next stop. After a short drive we stepped out at the location where I kept the Romeo. We both stood there, and he looked at me and said, "Let's go home." I turned looking to the city and replied, "I think it's time." I settled with Romeo's caretaker and walked inside the garage. There I found Peabody already sitting behind the wheel. He looked up at me and said, "Fine machine you got here."

I considered driving myself, but I saw in his face an expression of happiness. It reminded me of when he was a kid.

"You drive," I commanded and then I asked. "You do know how to drive don't you?"

"Let's find out Conner."

I climbed in the passenger side as he turned the ignition. The Romeo painfully purred back to life. Momentarily he sat there listening as he slowly caressed the steering wheel and remarked, "Splendid."

Nodding I remarked, "She purrs doesn't she?"

"Purrs?? He stated as he looked at me and then said, "Have it your way."

"And that is why we're friends Michael!" I stated.

When we drove out of the city, I couldn't help myself and looked back at the skyline. The Empire State Building stood tall against it, a new marvel of the times; I kept looking back as it faded from view. "One day I'll be back," I thought to myself somewhat saddened by the end of that adventure. But now was a time to look forward to the road ahead. I became excited to see my home Shadow Wood again. I looked over at Peabody who was totally in thoughts of his own as he sped past vehicles. I figured this was the best thing for him to keep his mind off the booze that his body was yearning for.

We traveled through the day spending the night near Gettysburg Pennsylvania. That night Peabody thankfully took a long bath cleaning the filth of the city from his body.

The next morning we found a store where we bought Peabody a suit and hat. Something more suitable than the rags he had been wearing. Looking more like men who would be driving the Romeo, we headed for the battle grounds. We toured the site where monuments stood in testament to the men that fought here. Walking out along the path of Pickets Charge we neared the stone wall that marked the point where the Confederacy was turned back, and the tide changed for her. We both envisioned the lines of the Union high on the hill as the Confederate boys were marched to their deaths taking fire from the Union Cannon for nearly a mile. You could almost see the ground littered with men groaning and dying as red blood mixed with the green grass of the field. Yet the men kept moving forward protected from the hail of shrapnel and lead only by their spirit and faith in the cause; ever vigilant, ever hopeful of breaking the Union line.

We walked up a path and sat at Little Round Top. The view from there was impressive looking down at large rocks and boulders. We imagined how hard it would have been to take these locations from a fortified enemy. Peabody and I spoke of tactics and of other battles we had learned about at Bransford. Sitting there made me wonder how different it all would have been if the Union lines had broken on that hot day July 3, 1863, and how would that have changed my path in this life.

We left before dark and found a room for the night on the edge of town. Peabody and I talked late into the evening. He made a remark that I remember. He said, "When you lose something. You have to find something. Not to replace it exactly, but as something to hang on too; a new starting point to grow from."

"What do you mean Michael?" I asked.

"Like you losing that girl you loved. You lost a lot when she left, but you can take a lot from that experience. It's easier to get to the top of the mountain if you are already part of the way there. If you go back to the bottom and start over then you have to walk the whole trail again.

"You're saying that I need to find another girl and move on from where I am now?" I asked.

"Not at all," Peabody replied.

"Then what do you mean?" I asked.

"You likely won't be able to see all the good you took from being with her for a while. But if you spend all your time being mad at her you never will. Take the good if you can find any, and move forward from there. It's like me with my leg being all banged up. I gotta find something that I would have never done. Something that I would have never considered, had this not happened to me, and I've got to do that!"

"What do you have in mind?"

"To find my new starting place…. Somewhere or something to clean me on the inside, so to speak." Then he looked at me and said, "You have to do the same. Remember learning about the knights in the medieval times. They gave up everything, all their worldly possessions in hopes of gaining something bigger than they already had. Something deep inside moved them in that direction and drove them to make that choice. You did that yourself. Think about all you experienced in that short period of time. But now it's time for you to change directions, and seek out the next step in your life."

"What's your plan? Why are we heading for the hills? Are you going from city boy to mountain man?" I asked.

"Thought crossed my mind." He replied, "I'm going to do something for my ma."

"Like what?" I asked.

"Find something. You'll see soon enough Conner. Let's call it a night."

The next day we drove south through West Virginia and on to North Carolina then deep into her Mountains. Once again the talk turned to battles with Peabody taking note that this was part of the geography that we learned about in school. They served as the South's protective mountain defense. These mountains went north into Virginia up to Maine and south into Georgia. Peabody went on and said, "It's a hard thing to do. Move an Army across mountains into enemy territory. They can become isolated, unsupportable and surrounded. Tennessee's Chattanooga was a key to a Union victory. The Southern boys spent months up in the hills sleeping on rocks just to make sure a Union force wouldn't slip through undetected. Imagine how harsh that must have been for them."

The mountains looked formidable from the winding road. Eventually we came to Cherokee North Carolina. A small tourist town likely hit hard by the economy. We stopped alongside a store, and Peabody stepped out of the car. He looked up at the mountains around us and then down at me and said, "I'm going to see if any of my ma's family is left in these hills. Hopefully, I can find some of her people."

"You turning Injun?" I asked.

"I'm just looking for a missing piece of me. Maybe I'll get lucky and find some relative or maybe not. It's the journey that counts." I handed him some money which he refused to take it at first. Then I insisted saying, "Take it you might need it."

"Thanks Conner."

"What about the information for Tanner?" I asked.

"You take it and mail it to him for me."

"What if he needs to find you?"

"He'll find me even in these mountains. He has a knack for such things you know. "

"It seems as if everyone has that knack but me." I replied. We shook hands, and Peabody turned away and walked down the street. I started the car and pulled up beside him speaking over its motor.

"Peabody thank you," I said. He looked at me questioningly.

"My only brother died long ago. As I've gone on in life, I realize that you, Tanner and Wallace are my brothers too. You and Tanner are all I have left. So, take care of yourself, Michael."

"I feel the same Conner."

"Keep up the fight. Don't ever give up like Kirby taught us!"

"You too Conner I'd guess your battles are coming up." We again shook hands as I replied, "Likely so."

I drove off. Once again alone, nothing but my thoughts and the purr of the Romeo to provide me with company. A few miles later, and still in the mountains I pulled over on a side road and parked her. I walked along a trail that led me to a large stone ledge overlooking the valley below. I sat there for a long while as the bright sun beat down on the valley causing shimmering shades of green to be reflected back toward me. I stood alone on this mountain the soul witness to the majestic spectacle within my view.

Even after thoughts of thirst and hunger crossed my mind, I refused to leave my perch near the precipice of that mountain. From there I had the same view as the hawk that soared just above me. I watched it being carried by the winds created by some mysterious force within the valley. As the hawk glided along in his life, I noticed he rarely fought the winds that provided a direction and natural course for him to follow. He flew only making the slightest of adjustments. Those same winds took the hawk to his food, shelter and a mate. "Can it be that a man has the same winds to carry him in his life." I wondered? "Could it be the great efforts we take in fighting the guiding wind could cause us to go off course, and take us away from what would have been provided?" As always such thoughts led me to thinking of Sally. On my way back to the Romeo, I couldn't help but think how she would have enjoyed all I had seen on this day.

EIGHTEEN

A couple of days later I pulled up to the gate of Shadow Wood and sat there for a moment as the Romeo idled. I looked at the magnificent house. This place always made me feel good, and was a safe harbor for me.

Miss Ida was the first to greet me and the first to berate me by saying, "Get upstairs, clean up, and shave that mess off your face. I'll cook something warm for you before you die of starvation"

My room looked untouched since I had last left. I took off my clothes noticing that I had lost quite a bit of weight. Also, I thankfully noticed that my wounds had totally healed from the fight a few days back. It felt good to get the grit and dust off of me from my travels. Ida told me that Grandfather was once again gone, but would likely be home in the afternoon the following day.

I was relieved because it gave me a little time to get myself prepared for the meeting. Ida cooked me a meal that only she could cook, and I savored every bite. "Miss Ida I'm not home until I taste your food." I remarked, and that brought a smile to her face. "You know Miss Ida you are all I have for a mother. I am glad that I have you. You have taken care of me for a very long time. I just want you to know that I appreciate all you have done."

"Jimmy Conner, that might be the nicest thing anyone has ever said to me. Don't tell me all that big city living took the meanness out of you."

"No, ma'am not a chance," I said.

"Did you learn anything of use while you were away?" She asked.

"I did learn a little about love."

"You run off and get your heart broke by a city gal?" She asked.

"No, ma'am she's a poor girl from the dirt roads and sandy soil of the South."

"Oh," she stated, "No belle, I take it."

"Not at all. Only to me but she has my heart so I'm a little biased." I said.

"I'm sorry Jimmy." She said.

"Don't worry Miss Ida. I've got plenty of heart to keep this boy going."

"I would say likely so. Are you going out to see the town?" She asked.

"No ma'am, I'm getting a book, putting my feet up on Grandpa's desk, and being the lord of the kingdom until he gets back."

She laughed, "Best to keep your feet off his desk."

"Ah, the life of a loyal subject. Very well my lady. I shall retire to my reading, and refrain from doing anything that will get this handsome melon separated from the perch on which it rests.

"Have been drinking?" She asked.

"No, just been deep in my own thoughts a little too long. I'll get my book, and get into someone else's mind for a while."

I didn't bother with the study. I went straight up to my room and grabbed a book from the shelf careful not to fall into a trap of a romance or anything too boring. It was good to be back at Shadow Wood. And good to be sitting there reading a book. I looked out my window and watched the lights of the town. Momentarily, I wondered about the lights of Paris but quickly shook off the notion, and went to bed. I must have slept long and hard, because getting out of bed was somewhat of a chore. I was well rested but it actually hurt to stand up as I stumbled across the room.

When I went outside Henry was waiting for me.

"Morning Henry!" I said.

"Morning Mr. Conner." He looked at me and said, "We've got work to do. "

"We do?" I asked.

"Follow me," he said. We walked to the side of the house where the Romeo sat covered in dirt and tar from the road. The car looked in pitiful condition.

"Yeah, Grandpa will kill me."

"Likely," replied Henry. "I thought he was going to shoot you when took off with it."

"Not me. A tire maybe." I replied.

"Cheaper to patch you up then to buy a new tire." He said.

"Good point!" I replied. "Henry sometimes I just get lucky I guess."

"And sometimes you don't." Henry stated as my Grandfather pulled in the driveway. He stepped out of the car, looking in my direction. He shook hands with the other gentleman in the vehicle before it drove off, then walked toward us. "You better get that car cleaned." Saying nothing else he walked inside. I stood there and looked at Henry and said, "I swear it happens every time. All the enjoyment has been taken out of cleaning it. Now, it's something I have to do."

"Don't much care for those hasta's do ya?" asked Henry.

"No, I don't." I said. I looked at him and remarked "hasta?" He said laughing, "I call em hasta's; Henry you hasta to do this or Henry you hasta to do that.

"You're right it's easy do something you don't hasta do." I replied.

Once we finished cleaning the Romeo I came in and saw Grandfather in his den. "The Romeo is clean and ready for inspection." I stated knowing he would cringe at the abbreviation. I continued upstairs to get cleaned up myself. He walked out to the foyer and said, "You mean the Alfa

Romeo Spider C6?" Then he lit a cigar and said, "Come on down here." I sighed deeply, knowing it was time for the alter call. Somehow the feeling of being eleven years old and in trouble slowly crept over me. I quickly shook it off, and walked down the stairs.

"Yes sir," I stated.

"Shut the door and have a seat James." I did as instructed and sat there as he walked over to the window staring outside.

"James, I'm glad you're back. You've lost some weight I see."

"Some sir," I replied.

"You are all I have left on this good earth." He then turned to me, and sternly said, "I presume these foolish notions are now out of your head, and you've come to your senses."

I sat there quietly for just a moment and said, "I don't want to fight with you Grandfather. Frankly, I can't believe this conversation is being brought up again, but to answer your question. No, sir they aren't. And they weren't and aren't foolish. I came back to set some things right, but my hearts mine. I'll marry who I wish."

"Very well James, let me ask you this. Your way, how did that work out for you? Did this woman give you what you needed? How come you're not with her now? Where is she James? I don't see her by your side." I sat quietly gritting my teeth not answering any of the questions.

"James, I blame myself. I should have never left you with Miss Rose so long. It can happen with a man's first; it's an infatuation, one that will fade with time. It's the other things commitment, trust, and shared ideals that keep a marriage together." He said.

"How did you know about Sally? Charles maybe?" I asked. Grandfather just stood looking out the window calmly. Then I said, "That twerp never could keep his mouth shut. Shared ideals? Am I to make a business merger when I get married? I know, Grandfather, why don't we line up every available woman in the South. We'll do a balance sheet of sorts, with items like net worth, father's position in the Sons, and future business ties being at the top. Then we'll assign a value to each of the women and the one with best portfolio will be my wife. How does that sound?"

"Most valuable is it? You think highly of yourself James. In truth your stock has gone down since you've been away and because of your actions so has mine! You have no idea what damage you have done."

"I haven't done anything to anyone." I said as I stood up. "No one is going to tell me who and how much I am going to love. Do you understand that?" I said pointing my finger at him. "It's my love. Mine alone. If that's taken from a man then what is he? I won't be one of the hopeless souls that I met in the city. I looked into their faces and saw deeply into their eyes. I won't be like that."

"Then damn it, be responsible!" He said pounding his hand on the desk. "Do the right thing. Men like those depend on us. We bring food to their tables and give them hope. It's our responsibility to keep things going the best we can, so those men don't have to go home, and face their wives and children to tell them they can't eat today. There is a crisis going on out in the world, and you are telling me about love. You selfish child! You are in a position to make a better life for these people. You, me, and the Sons share that responsibility. Not just with the dream of Southern independence but peoples hopes are in our hands just the same. Your decisions can make men's lives or break them! Those people need you now more than ever. You know what it is to lead. What it is to be responsible for others and you are a leader in this organization. Now, act like it."

I stood up and was about to walk out, but deep inside I knew there was some element of truth to what he said. Before I could reach the door he spoke again saying, "You were right about one thing, James. Within the Sons you spoke of a rift. It was true the Seven has been acting on its own. Namely the Whittington's, they are moving in their own direction. They are making a play for power. Contracting deals not associated with the interest of the Sons. They were using the power of the Seven to manipulate politics, business transactions, and other affairs for their own needs."

"Can we prove Whittington was involved in Wallace's death, and reveal them for who they are?" I asked.

"I'll make no such move just yet," he replied. "Charlie Bedford has been getting close with young Whittington. I can't see how this will unfold just yet, and you have cost yourself and me a great deal of creditability. Let me ask you this James, how are you going to get it back so we can save this organization?" He turned to me awaiting an answer. I sat silent, because I had none. And then he said, "That is your focus for now James."

I let out a huff and said, "I'm not marrying Lucille."

"I'm not saying you have to marry her. Do you have any idea what Lucille has been doing while you were away? Do you? She has been sitting around worrying about you, James. She had been loyally waiting on you until Charles told her about this fiasco with that colored woman."

"Why is it so important to you that Lucille and I marry?" I asked.

"I won't be around forever James. Your marriage to her would provide a family bond that strengthens your position and our families. It would be an alliance that solidifies our station within the Sons for generations."

"Grandfather, you speak of this as if we are kings. This is America there no kings are here."

"No crowns James but there are kings, family alliances, serfs and servants. They all just have different names. Alliances have been made in such a manner for centuries. They strengthen families, provide station and wealth for generations. Do you really think things have evolved so much? Seriously, I doubt that you having to marry Lucille will be an issue. She'll likely not have you James. But I would like for you to at least make amends with her."

I sat there for a moment and thought, "Damn it I hate when he does that." He was skillful in the debate. It was like playing chess with a master.

Patiently he knocks your pieces off the board one by one and finally trades a piece to gain that needed advantage. Before you know it you look down, and he has you a move away from checkmate!

I needed air and walked outside around the corner looking for the Romeo. I stopped mid stride when I saw her in pieces. Henry crouched down near the ground hands covered in grease. "Mr. Conner, are you all right?" Henry asked.

"What's going on?" I asked.

"Your Grandfather told me to properly service the Alfa Romeo. That it was likely in a sad state due to your neglectful tendencies."

I let out a growl mumbling something illegible and thought, "The checkmate just keeps getting worse." Then Henry said, "The Cadillac is in tip top shape Mr. Conner." I felt like a trapped rat but the notion of me sitting in the front driver's compartment as I drove through town was ridiculous. Even Henry commented on the subject, "You can wear my hat if you like Mr. Conner." Then he laughed and said, "You'd look fine wearing it but my head's bigger than yours so maybe not."

"I'm glad you got your laugh for the day Henry. I'll walk, thank you very much." I stated.

"Oh, I did Mr. Conner, thank you. You can still borrow my hat for your walk if want." He said grinning.

I started off a little angry, but with each passing step I felt a little better. Once I calmed down a little I began to think about the long walks I would take in the city. That reminded me of the package that was to be sent to Tanner. I looked down at my watch realizing I needed to quickly get to the post office. When I turned, I could hear the hum from a motor pull up beside me and a female voice say, "James Conner walking the streets."

"Lucy, I'm sorry I can't talk now I have to get back to Shadow Wood."

"Well, silly hop in, if you're in a hurry." She said.

"I'd rather not." I said.

"Suit yourself," she said and started to pull away. Reluctantly, I waived and yelled, "Lucy, I am in a desperate hurry. Could I please just have a ride?"

"Sure," she said. "What's the rush?" She asked.

"I have to mail a package that needs to get sent off today."

"I can take you in to the post office too," She replied.

"Thank you." I stated as we pulled into the gate. I stepped from the car and heard her yell, "Good morning Henry."

"Morning Miss Bedford," he replied.

I ran inside, and quickly grabbing what I needed. On my way back outside, I heard my Grandfather say, "Well, that didn't take long at all. I'm glad you see things my way. Good job, James!" I looked at him shaking my head not answering and ran back outside. Lucy sat ready at the wheel and took off once I was inside.

"My Jimmy you have lost weight."

"Seems to be the consensus," I replied. We didn't say much for a few blocks.

"I spoke with Katie Wallace." She said breaking the silence.

"How is she?" I asked.

"She seems to be holding up good. Her son is getting big."

"Their son," I answered.

"What?" she asked.

"He's still Virgil's son even if he's gone." I remarked.

"All right Jimmy, their son," She replied somewhat ruffled.

"Just stop here," I told her. I ran inside and mailed the package. Relieved, and my mind clear for a moment, I stood inside the lobby looking at the black and white tiled floor. Then I looked at Lucille in the car.

"Chess," I said out loud. Once the postman was finished, I walked outside mad, but rather than fight I just walked past her car.

"Jimmy! Jimmy!" she said. I didn't speak. She started her car, pulled up beside me, and said, "I'll give you a ride back to Shadow Wood."

"I'd rather not." I stated.

"Jimmy, what did I do now?" she asked. I increased my gait and replied, "You know."

Bewildered she asked again, "I know what?"

"This is all a set up. Isn't it?"

"What?" She asked.

"You just happened to be driving down the same road that I was walking because grandfather had the Romeo in pieces."

"Henry had it in pieces," she said. "Jimmy I have no idea what you are talking about. I was just glad to see you, and I thought I'd say hello. Then you asked me to take you to the post office to mail a package."

Pausing, I thought for a moment. Then I realized that Grandfather had no idea about the package. Ashamed at my reaction I stopped, took a deep breath, and then said, "I'm sorry Lucille You've done nothing wrong."

When I stepped into her car she asked, "What has gotten into you?" I sat there quietly. We drove on and the gate to Shadow Wood neared, and I asked, "Can we take a drive?"

"Depends, are you going to yell at me anymore?"

"No, I won't yell at you anymore."

She continued driving the back roads to the country. I saw a long fence row with a large sycamore at the end and said, "Pull in there."

Moments later we both stood alongside her car in the shade of the tree and she asked, "Jimmy, why are we here?"

"I can't answer that Lucille. Maybe it's that I feel like the world's closing in around me again. This whole thing was upside down right from the moment I got back here. Truthfully, it's been that way for a while. I thought I'd have more control of the things that happen in my life."

She stood beside me, her arms folded, as I tossed a small rock into the trees.

"Jimmy, I'm not so sure we have control over much in this life......Why are you telling me this? I thought you hated me."

"I'm not sure why I'm confiding in you, but one thing is for sure, and it's that I don't hate you. Hell right now, at this moment, you're the only friend I have." She smiled then replied, "Lucky fella."

"I'm not feeling very lucky." I said. "That's not saying anything against you Lucy it's just.......It's just those damn gumballs. They just keep coming out, and I don't know which to keep or just throw away."

"Gumballs? Jimmy Conner, whatever are you talking about?"

"Nothing just something Peabody said. It sort of made since at the time."

Lucy just stood there and smiled and went on to say, "Jimmy, I don't know much about the things you worry about, but I do know that I have a place in this world, and I have certain responsibilities. I'm trying to find my place just like you. I don't really know if we have control over them, or if things are just decided for us. Actually, I don't know anything different, then things being decided for me. It's just the way it has always been for me. Maybe that's why I want certain things the way I want. Because, there is so little else I have control over. Maybe that's why I wanted you so much, Jimmy. You were just someone I could see myself with. Someone I wanted to be with."

"I'm sorry I let you down Lucy. It was never my intention to hurt you." I said.

"Jimmy you loved that girl didn't you? You know the one Charlie told me about." She asked.

I didn't say anything. I just picked up another rock tossing it into the bushes. She went on and said, "Jimmy I know I'm spoiled, and I like things my way, but what's so bad about me?"

"Nothing is bad about you Lucille. I just remembered the way my parents looked at each other, and wanted something like that."

"Jimmy this colored girl. I mean, men get infatuated with girls like her all the time. They're different, different clothes, way of speaking, and moving. I heard she was quite pretty too. Men like different for a while. Jimmy, I'd forgive you for being with her, because I think you thought you were in love with her."

"It wasn't infatuation Lucille. It was love," I stated. "And her name was Sally."

"Really Jimmy? Love, the kind of love that makes them feel whole? The kind of love you want to grab a hold of and never let go. Love, where nothing else matters!"

Feeling challenged I looked at her angrily and said, "Yes, Lucille that kind."

"Why did she let you go then? Why Jimmy? If she felt that strongly, that much love for you, then why did she just throw you out?"

I couldn't answer. She huffed, and walked over to the driver's side of her vehicle and said, "Jimmy Conner, I would have never let you go." She started the car, and we rode back to Shadow Wood; not saying a word. I walked into the house as Lucille drove away. For the first time, I actually think I respected her. She was deeper than I had suspected.

Months had passed and Grandfather and I settled into an uneasy peace. A few things had changed since I had left. My reception with the members of the Sons was cool to say the least. It appeared as if I had fence mending to do which I started immediately. Charlie Bedford still considered me an enemy for jilting his sister. In those times some old traditions still carried weight. Mr. Bedford wasn't much better which was a little more understandable, because he had gone to considerable expense in preparations for the wedding. And, I'm sure he spent many days with a crying daughter. I knew I had penance of sorts to be paid.

What they didn't know was Lucille and I had been secretly meeting. What was surprising to me was the loyalty Lucy had shown me, it swayed me on some level. I still wouldn't call it love. More of a devotion to her had developed even though I likely used her to hide from my own pain. I tried to be open to the situation, even though I had a nagging feeling that I just couldn't shake.

The Sons took precedence in all matters in my life. Some new government policies were about to take place, and they could affect some of our holdings. We had decisions to make on what strings to pull, and how to swing the pendulum in our favor. The economy was still at a crisis level, and our holdings were taking a beating. We also had an interest in the new social groups that were gaining power within the States at the time. The reformers for both communism and socialism where slowly gaining popularity. The Sons had to carefully plot its move.

NINETEEN

One afternoon I came home to Miss Ida yelling that I had a received a letter. I opened it and inside was a note from Tanner. In the top corner was a set of numbers like Peabody had described. I guess he assumed Peabody would let me in on the secret. I quickly placed the letter back in the envelope and dug through my things trying to find the Bible that was issued to us from Bransford academy. I read the passage in Daniel 2:13 it read, "And the decree went forth that the wise men should be slain; and they sought Daniel and his fellows to be slain." I thought this letter is either about the Sons or Wallace, and quickly made a key like I had been shown.

The key revealed the hidden message which translated to: Wallace slain, meeting with Seven, Bund, and Chicago. He didn't name Whittington but he did the Seven. Days went by and I waited patiently, but eventually began to get anxious about what was happening.

As hard as it was I had to learn my own game of chess. It wasn't often that I had to work beside Whittington, or even be around him, but when it did happen he played his game rather well. He tried to make a fool of me when possible. On one such night the hot air of the South filled the rafters of the meeting hall. And the ceiling fans hummed loudly as they struggled to move the humid air. The men sat in a large half circle debating the positioning of political candidates in an upcoming election.

We would work in teams for important elections. Each picking a side, and when possible greasing both to get needed results. The first order of business was finding candidates willing to be influenced. It usually wasn't hard. But, at times they could prove difficult, if they already had a strong enough base. If necessary we would simply put one of our own men in the running keeping them pumped with Southern pride as well as Southern cash.

The night ended with most issues in order. The one outstanding problem was that a Chicago based partner wanted a social reform group addressed. As it happened, that reform group was gaining momentum within the South too. The mafia used unions to bust businesses, and we traded favorable negotiations for money. These groups could come into conflict with our common goal. The mafia and the Sons kept their distance from each other. They considered us nothing more than affiliates in a business syndicate that shared the common goal of power and money. They never understood our true nature or design, and as far as we were concerned they weren't going too. The consensus was that our ties be closed door. Limited to a few members, because we knew the Federal Government would be watching their every move. Too much involvement could lead to investigations within our organization, and that was something we didn't want. The men sat around and debated the issue of possibly expanding our ties to the Chicago partner. At the time we were desperate for resources and everything was on the table for consideration.

Grandfather made a speech about his concerns and said, "Gentlemen the mafia is an organization with deep roots and ties abroad. They have an honor all their own, not like ours. Controlling the mafia is like controlling a snake. You can hold it by the tail but have to watch the teeth. They have a mind of their own. This snake is in the garden of the Federal government. They must be handled with great delicacy. Once we cross a new line with them, we cannot go back. The deeper our involvement the deeper the wound if they are compromised. If they fall, our honor falls with them."

Mr. Whittington stood up boldly, thanking everyone in attendance. His oratory began, "In this time of great despair, we must continue our fight by all means necessary. We are lucky to have the benefits of a global operation, but it appears as if the economy is on course to affect most of the world for a long time to come. We see the effects of this with our shipping, manufacturing, and trade companies. We must protect our interests at home first and by all means necessary. The legitimate business concerns of the mafia are safe from prying eyes. We are already tied to them. Thus it is in our interest to contract with them further. These ties can benefit us both in these hard times. Our honor is only compromised through defeat, and with limited funds, defeat is all but certain." The crowd rumbled in approval.

Mr. Whittington continued and said, "I welcome more debate on the subject. Let us hear from our youth within the Sons. Maybe they can provide some insight on these issues. Young Conner, stand up and tell us your thoughts on this subject."

Totally unprepared for such a debate, I rose to my feet. "Thank you Mr. Whittington." I replied. He sat smugly holding a cane between his knees while resting his hands on top of it. He was paying attention to every word I uttered as I continued to speak, "Gentlemen, This economy is in desperate times, and this too affects each of our personal interests as well as that of the Sons. But it is a time of great caution, not extreme risk. There is desperation in the eyes of the people. I have seen it working the soup lines. I just feel that if to error, then it should be on the side of caution. We need to protect the interests we already have." A grumble lightly rumbled through the room.

Mr. Whittington again spoke, "George do you have anything to say on the subject."

George Whittington rose and spoke to the audience, "Gentlemen I have not worked a soup line. I have not stared into the eyes of the hungry or the poor in hope of answers." He stepped out in the center of the room.

"I am a man of my word gentlemen. What I have seen is companies fold, rich men become poor, and the fortunes of men be turned by inaction. These gentlemen in Chicago are our natural allies. They turn their nose up at a government that we don't recognize, and make money to gain footholds in opportunities that we never dream. They have dealt with us fairly asking for only reasonable money in return, and votes in legislature that we too would support. Now, they ask for us to move money for them; to hide it within our legitimate businesses and give us a cut in return. They have proved their loyalty to us. There is new blood in their future too. I say it is time to strengthen our ties. Not run like cowards! What say the Sons to this future!" The first man to rise and clap was Charlie Bedford. His father, Mr. Bedford stood up just a step behind, and a large portion of the room stood in approval.

Grandfather and I rode back in the car together. I sat silently. Disgusted, he didn't speak until half way home, "Soup lines! Soup lines, poor people's eyes, good God James. This was momentous."

"I know. I know I was set up Grandfather." I said.

"Good time to figure that out. An hour after the meeting. Son you have to be on top of it. This is too important. There is more to this than what the Whittington's shared, you know that."

"Yes, sir you're right."

"Hell yes, I'm right! We are involved in a game that we have to win. Did you see the Bedford's leading the charge to rally behind Whittington?" He asked.

"Yes sir," I stated.

"Credibility James, and how exactly are you going to get it back? How?" He asked.

I sat there saying little the rest of the ride home.

That night Lucille crept up to my room. She crawled in bed with me like she had for the last few months. I laid there on my back her head resting on my chest. "Jimmy how was your night?"

"Awful, Whittington ate me alive."

"That's bad news." She said.

"Your brother just jumped on the bandwagon, and immediately sided with George and his Grandfather."

"George and Charlie are friends. They do everything together." She said.

"Does your father still hate me?"

"No, he doesn't hate you. Anyway it doesn't matter what they think of you." She replied.

"It mattered tonight," I said.

"Let's just run away from all this, James. Let's elope."

"Elope? What are you talking about?" I asked.

"We have been back together for some time now. I think you realize we can get along and grow together. I think we have both matured and it's time."

"Lucille I have to admit you are changed, but this is a big commitment. I told you how I felt about being sure."

"James I have waited, forgiven, and I came back. It's time."

"Not just now Lucy, everything is a mess. Everything is out of control." I said

Lucy sat up and said, "James I'm pregnant."

"What? Are you sure?" I asked. "You just blurted that out. Couldn't you have prepared me? "

"Yes, James I'm sure. I have an appointment with the Doc Anderson next week. Women know these things."

I stepped out of bed and said, "Oh God! Your family is going to shoot me. I'm a dead man."

"Not if you do the right thing. Come here James. It's not the end of the world. We made a baby, that's all."

"That's all," I said.

"It will be fine. This happened because it was suppose to happen. We can be happy together, I just know it." She said.

I had enough for one night. I refused to make her leave, but I considered it for myself. I thought about the situation, "Grandfather will either kill me or be thrilled. However, I'm certain either Charlie or his father will kill me. I hope Henry and Miss Ida put some flowers on my grave from time to time." Everything became a haze of gray, and I wasn't sure what to do. I was tired of fighting the current, and I just gave in. Once confirmation of my fatherhood was established by Doc Anderson the announcement was made of our engagement.

The wheels spun fast, and it didn't take for long for the plans to be made. She settled for a small wedding with just a few friends and family. What started as weeks quickly turned into days. I made no protest this time. I felt that I had put her through enough. She had shown me one thing Sally didn't. That was loyalty. For me loyalty goes along way. Loyalty is what Tanner, Peabody and Wallace had always given me. Sally wasn't loyal to either me or to us. She ran when Lucy stuck. Maybe Lucy was the better girl for me.

The night before the wedding I saw how happy Lucy was about the coming events. She radiated with joy and I was happy for her. At that point I had to succumb to the fact that this would likely be a crossroad in my life, one that I had come to before and choose another path. And now I was back at almost exactly the same place. It seemed as if I had little choice but to take the path laid out in front of me. My own personal declaration of independence had proven to be just as elusive as that of the South's. And the proposition of Lucille as a wife didn't seem as bad as it once had. She had changed over time, and she seemed to be handling everything well.

I kept telling myself that this would make everyone happy; Lucille, Grandfather, her parents, the Sons and with a child on the way it just made sense. That night I parked in a field that overlooked a small river as it passed through our town. I watched the moon light dance off the small ripples of water and could make out the trees on the far side of the bank opposite from where I stood. Those trees stood firm and tall. The only view that changed for them in hundreds of years is that of the passing water. The water on the other hand is always moving always getting a different view. Sometimes it passes slowly other times moving quite fast but consistently it moved to the next bend and the unknown.

I sat on the back of the Romeo while I watched the water roll by. I came to a couple of conclusions. One, the arithmetic between Lucy and I was right. The sum of the total of all the parts equaled a good outcome for us. The other conclusion I came too was that I really hated arithmetic. In truth it had no place in the poetry of love, but then again maybe arithmetic made since in life. I kicked back another swig of Grandfather's favorite bourbon enjoying my final night of being alone. Trying to remain positive, I considered the fact that now I would be part of someone else, and wouldn't ever be alone again.

I wished my friends were able to be here. Tanner was nowhere to be found. Peabody was likely living in a tree high in the mountains, and of course Wallace was on his own journey. All I really I knew was the hum of the Romeo's six cylinders provided me with at least some relief from my own thoughts. I turned the ignition and fired up my one friend. She was metal, rubber, and wood but she spoke to me never the less and quieted my thoughts.

When I awoke the next morning, Miss Ida placed my meal on the table. Grandfather sat at the opposite end and announced, "The groom has arrived! Let's talk a moment James."

"Yes sir," I replied.

"I have been thinking that we should buy a house for you and Lucille."

"Shadow Wood should be fine at least for awhile." I replied.

"No, James. You and Lucy should have some time alone all to yourselves." Lucy and I had of course talked about this, but the notion didn't set well. I loved Shadow Wood. It was my home.

"We can talk about that later. We should get Lucy's input too." I stated. Grandfather looked at me and said, "Lucy and I have spoken about the issue, and she is in agreement. This would be the best thing for a husband, wife and baby" he stated.

"All right," I said. I could feel the heaviness in my chest start to take hold. "I'll be back," I stated as I walked outside for a moment. Henry was working in the yard and said, "Hello Mr. Conner, big day for ya."

"Yes, it is Henry." I said. Then I stood there moving my bare foot gently across the grass.

"Henry, you once told me you knew plenty about love."

"Oh, Mr. Conner I've been in love before sure enough, but that was years and years ago."

"Do you think you can learn to love someone?" I asked.

He looked at me and said, "I guess you can learn to love things about someone. But I don't think you can learn to be in love with them. No, now that I think about it Mr. Conner I don't believe you can learn to be in love at all. Why would you want too? It's the same magic that a man's dreams are made of!" He stood up and breathed in and said, "You aren't talking about Miss Lucille now are ya?"

"No, I was just wondering what you thought about such things."

"She's in the family way now isn't she?" He asked.

"Yes, she is." I said. "How did you know? It's supposed to be secret of sorts."

"When you've been around as long as I have, you just tend to know things." He said.

"Did Miss Ida tell you?" I asked.

He laughed and said, "You caught me. Yes, she did."

Smiling I replied, "I didn't even try to get past her on that issue. She knows about things like that before they even happen."

"Yes, she does." Henry stated.

"Nice talking to you Henry."

"You too Mr. Conner," He replied.

I went up to my room and dressed in my tuxedo for the occasion. Grandfather escorted me personally to the church. Along the way he told me that he was proud of me. I was actually quite calm about everything and settled into the compromise that was of my fate. The church was decorated, and a few guests had already arrived. They greeted me and grandfather as we walked up the stairs. Mr. Bedford looked at me questionably but seemed glad that I made it. Charlie didn't speak at all. I walked inside taking my station in the office of the pastor.

I sat there alone calmly trying not to think about what was going to happen. I began to read the Pastor's newspaper and then he came in to tell me that the ceremony would start in a few minutes. I looked out the window and watched the last of the people arrive as Mr. Bedford and Grandfather greeted them. I began to get anxious as the clock's seconds ticked by.

I heard a tapping sound and looked toward the door but saw nothing. Again, I heard the sound, and realized that it was coming from the window. I looked outside and there stood Tanner. I ran to the window and opened it. "What are you doing?" I asked.

"Conner, don't you look spiffy!" He replied.

"Glad you could make it, but you should use the front door."

"Not a good idea." he said. "Come on let's get you out of here."

"What?" I asked.

"No time to explain, come on!"

"No, I'm not leaving. I'm getting married!"

He shook his head and said, "No, you're not." The music started and a knock wrapped on the door.

"There is no time," he said. I ran over locked the door and said, "Yes, there is." The knocking grew louder.

"Here damn it." he said as he handed me a file. "It's from Doc Anderson's office. I had my partner get it last night."

The file had Lucille Bedford's name across the top as I opened it he said, "She's not pregnant Jimmy."

"What?" I said. "This can't be true. I mean she wouldn't do that to me." The door knob jiggled. Grandfather's voice came through the door, "Jimmy it's time."

"Damn it Jimmy, Lucy and Doc Anderson set you up! I don't know if it was her, her father, or your grandfather, but that's irrelevant. The girl's not having your baby!" Just as he said those words I looked down and saw the negative results myself.

"Come on," he said motioning me to come with him. I set the file on the desk opened it to the results, and jumped from the window into the bushes. Tanner and I ran across the lawn of the church to the Romeo. He tossed me the key, and we both jumped in not taking the time to even open the doors.

"How did you get your hands on the Romeo?" I asked, as we drove off.

"I told Henry that you wanted it, and that I was to drive it to the church for you." Tanner said.

"He knew something was up, didn't he?"

"I suspect so," replied Tanner.

We must have driven twenty miles out of town before I eased off the gas.

"I can't believe this," I said. Tanner looked at me saying, "I hate it for you. Deep down you didn't want to get married. So, I made up the whole thing about the negative test results."

"What!" I said about to turn the car around.

"I'm joking. It's unfortunately true. She set you up. I heard about the situation, and was worried about you. I thought it best if I checked into it."

"How did you know?" I asked. He cocked his head and gave me a sly look as if he was thinking how could I ask that question.

"Forget it," and then I asked, "Where we heading?"

"Birmingham."

"Alabama?" I asked.

"For now," he replied.

I knew better than to ask too many questions. He seemed to provide information when he was ready and not a moment sooner. We drove a few more miles, and my mind started to drift to someplace else. Tanner looked my way and he said, "Get you head in the real game. Here's what's important, and he held up a file. These men are the ones that killed Wallace." He showed me a photo. I recognized the men from the cafe. Then he held up another file and said, "Here are all the details about those two."

He began to read the file, "They work for a mobster names De Angelo. He and Whittington have been getting cozy in their dealings. From what I can tell, Whittington is working outside the Sons, and conducting business on his own in the name of the Seven." I listened intently as he went on, "There's more, ever hear of a gentleman by the name of Arthur Zimmerman?"

"No, should I have?"

"Not necessarily, he was the German Ambassador to Mexico," stated Tanner.

"I don't typically follow which German officials hold that particular post." I replied.

"In World War I Arthur Zimmerman tried to get Mexico to attack the United States. If they had Germany would have helped them regain control of the land they lost in the 1800's." He said.

"From Texas to California," I remarked.

"Yes, fortunately British intelligence caught wind of the situation, and the plan was averted. But that and a few other factors led to the U.S. involvement in World War I." He said.

"So, what does that have to do with Whittington?" I asked

"I'm not sure. But serious changes are happening in Germany and the radicals are filtering over to the US. This economy has the world on the fringe. There have never been more socialist or communist organizations here than right now."

"This sound's big and dangerous are you sure I wouldn't have been better off just getting married?" I said.

"Maybe but this is more fun," he said smiling. I know about an eight o'clock meeting at the Red Mountain mine. Whittington, De Angelo, and others will be there. We need to break up that meeting, but first you need to find out what this meeting is about."

The thought crossed my mind that Lucy was in the church likely crying right now. I felt bad about that for some reason, but she shouldn't have tried to dupe me into marriage. What bothered me most was my Grandfather could have been involved. I was glad Tanner showed up even though I seemed to be driving to a more hazardous situation. We drove to the next town, and he told me to take him to the train station. He bought his tickets and said, "Meet me in town at the park nearest the train station at 1 p.m. in two days."

"Where are you going?" I asked.

"To get some help" was all he said.

Walking back to the Romeo I thought, "What in the hell am I going to do now? If I go back to town they will kill me." I will simply choose to just avoid it all. I was sure once they read the file they would figure it out. I rented a room, and laid in bed rolling the Saint Michael medallion around between my fingers and commented out loud, "Thank you Michael if you had anything to do with it all. Thank you." I laid back as I enjoyed the quiet of the room for a couple of days.

Looking at Mr. Conner I asked, "Did Germany really consider backing Mexico in WW1?"

"Just on paper really but you have to keep in mind that the world was imperialistic in those days up until World War II. America was just as guilty and the general population fluctuated somewhere in between, staying isolationist and expanding its influence. It would have been interesting if the Kaiser knew of the Sons."

"They wouldn't have backed Germany would they?" I asked.

"Not likely. America was full of new immigrants back then and many were of German heritage. In World War II you see some heading back to the fatherland.

"But wouldn't that mean a possible war in the states again?"

"If the possibility of war reached our shores in those days, with the scars of re-construction still felt, who knows where the road would have led. Many Southerner's might have called for another go at secession if the government's position on the conflict caused it."

"And the Sons could have made that look possible?" I asked.

"You're catching on." He said. "But don't get me wrong, the idea behind the first conflict was a peaceful resolution. It was the North that advanced on Southern positions."

"After Ft. Sumter," I stated.

"Ft. Sumter was being held by federal troops illegally. It was the property of South Carolina. On her soil, and should have been turned over upon request."

"How can you say that?"

"*Campbell you need to read your history. Each state has sovereignty and the power of the federal government is what was in question. Apparently, if you don't do what the federal government wants then they come down and invade you. Each state joined to form a more perfect union, but when that union no longer reflects the people's wishes, shouldn't that same state be able to separate itself from that Union it joined?*"

"*So, you're saying it's a question of individual liberty?*" I asked.

"*Wasn't that what the founders signed on for? That's the notion behind the Southern spirit. The spirit of the Southern cause is considered to be a continuation of the ideals of the founders. George Washington in fact is the center piece on the Seal of the Confederate States. Those were the very principles that the Southern states were embracing. So deeply felt were those ideals embedded in Southern society, that they became a source of inspirational pride. Take Vicksburg for example. Vicksburg was the last hold out along the Mississippi. Union control of that waterway couldn't be had until that city fell.*

The Union called Vicksburg the Gibraltar of the West, because of the nearly impregnable position it held on a sharp turn in the Mississippi and the high bluffs where it was located. After the Union's many attempts at assaulting the city they finally brought up two hundred heavy artillery pieces and siege mortars to blast the city. The siege which started on May 18th caused the population to dig caves. Starving, they lived off dogs, mules and horses. Lee's defeat at Gettysburg was on July 3, 1863. The following day the Mississippi came under Union control with the fall of Vicksburg. Because of that defeat the citizens of Vicksburg refused to celebrate Independence Day for the next eighty one years."

"*Now where were we?*"

I woke early because I was supposed to meet Tanner later. I fumbled about my room, and walked down to the diner to grab a bite to eat. Waiting patiently wasn't my strong suit but I did my best. Finally one o'clock grew near and I drove down to the park and waited. An hour later I began to wonder if he would show. I finally left just after four o'clock, and drove back to the diner and parked the Romeo out front. I sat in the back of the diner like Peabody taught me. From that vantage point, I saw someone I knew as he entered the door. He walked toward my table and stood there obviously angry and red faced. I sat there shaking my head listening to Charlie Bedford once again berate about the situation between his sister and I. He had his fist clinched and with every word his voice raised. I asked him to step outside, so he could vent without drawing attention to us. We exited the diner through a long hallway and out back into the alley.

"You have twice embarrassed my sister and my family," he said. "If you ever come around my sister again I will kill you James. I swear it." I looked at him and said, "Charlie I am sorry I have you upset, but I was cornered into this under false pretenses! And to tell you the truth Charlie, I liked your sister and would have gone through with it. Notwithstanding the fact that she, possibly my grandfather, and her doctor concocted a story about a pregnancy. Even though deep down, I know that I'm not in love with her! Don't you want your sister happy? Wouldn't you be happier if she was with someone who loved her?" I asked.

"My sister didn't lie to you Conner." He stated. "And that just tells me you have no honor Conner. You have been with her, and won't own up to it. Just like George said."

"George?" I questioned.

"He said you had no honor, no integrity and you would end up hurting my sister. He said that if it was his sister, he would kill you for what you did."

"He did. Did he?" I retorted and grabbed his collar and threw him on the ground of the alley. I stood over him at his feet. "First, you keep listening to that bastard Whittington, and it's only going to get you killed Charlie. He'll kill you just like he did my friend Wallace. Secondly, I didn't seduce your sister! Let's get that fact straight here and now. I never took anything from her that she didn't want taken and if it's a question of honor. Then where is the honor in her trying to trap me? I like you and your sister. We have been friends for years but she is far too manipulative for me to handle. I already have my Grandfather, and that's more than enough! I like her and care about her, but I will never be in love with her. There are plenty of things to not like about me Charlie. But this cause is the wrong one." I looked at the clock and it was past six. "As a matter of fact you're coming with me. I'm saving your ass today."

"What? I'm not going anywhere with you." He said.

"Have I ever lied to you?" He said nothing and I again said, "Charlie have I ever lied to you?" He shook his head no. "I'll show you someone to hate. Someone, who deserves it." I picked him up off the ground, leading him all the way around the building by his collar to the waiting Romeo.

Along the way, and once Charlie calmed down I began to ask Charlie some questions.

"What brings you to Alabama, Charlie?" I asked.

"Father sent me here to check on a mill?" He replied.

"And you found me in the diner?"

"Lucky I guess. There aren't exactly a lot of red Alfa Romeo's around." He replied.

I sat there and began to wonder if Charlie wasn't supposed to meet Whittington here. He looked at me and asked, "Why?"

I began to realize that bringing Charlie may have been a big mistake. But now I had little choice in the matter, and had to trust him. He sat there quietly the rest of the way to the mine.

We drove up close to the entrance of the mine, and parked the Romeo in a nearby wooded area. Charlie began to protest. So, I threatened to lock him in the trunk but he didn't take the threat seriously even laughing because he would never fit inside. That moment of levity reminded me of better times between us.

We walked the last quarter mile following the railroad tracks that paralleled the road entering the mine. I could see the old wooden mine office as we slowly approached the compound. Five cars were parked in front of the building. Two men stood outside the door on the porch. One man held a Tommy Gun the other, a larger man, had a shotgun within arm's reach resting against the front of the office. We slowly crawled along the far side of the tracks out of sight, but eventually we would have to make our way across a small patch of open ground to get near to the shack. When they weren't looking we crept to the side of the building, and made our way behind it. I stayed low to avoid detection, and sat beneath a window where I could hear the voices of the men inside. I peered through the window and saw George Whittington, and six other men I didn't recognize. Charlie peaked in and he recognized only two. He told me that he had seen them with Whittington. One was a man named Mr. De Angelo. The other was a member of the Seven. I could tell by his expression that he was just as interested as I was about what was going on.

The men began to talk and I could hear Whittington say, "Yes, we can sustain financial support for quite some time."

"How do you plan on managing such a thing for months possibly years?" A man with a German accent asked.

"Gentlemen with a little help of course." He said confidently and then went on, "Mostly in the areas of subversive activity and military guidance we will be able to sustain our cause. We have a strong will here in the South and hopefully it won't come to an armed conflict, but if it does we will ask for your support in that situation too. The wounds have not yet healed, and many want vindication. But it's still important that we make it look as if the North is aggressive against us."

"That's not what the man asked. He asked about financial means," replied De Angelo.

"How about gold? Tons and tons of gold." Whittington replied smugly.

"Gold? And you have it all available?" De Angelo asked.

"Yes," replied Whittington. "The organization has been stockpiling gold since before the Civil War ended. First of course to help build fortunes, but every year the organization takes a portion of its earnings and buys large sums of gold. The organization even owns a mining operation along with other minerals of value. The gold is kept at various secret locations. It was always felt that gold was the common denominator in recognition of a country's strength. True independence can't be had unless the world takes us seriously. And gold gentlemen, is taken seriously. Only a small circle knows any of the locations and no one man knows the whereabouts of all the caches. I have knowledge of three and in time all will be released once my grandfather takes his rightful place as the lead council."

"Where are they?" the German man asked.

"We are standing over one. They used a closed portion of this mine to hide it."

"How much?" De Angelo asked.

"Not sure exactly, but when time comes I'll know."

"Surely there must be some estimate. Give me an idea so I know what I'm getting into here," inquired DeAngelo.

"What I know of equals just over five percent of the gold that's reportedly held at Fort Knox, but there is more, much more. What I need from you Mr. DeAngelo is simple. I need a base, a place of safety for my men to work in the North. If we do this correctly, we could be a sovereign nation in a fairly short time. The plan is to once again show the political oppression of the North. This economic crisis proves that they are sapping the South to save the Federal government and the North. It's our time. The time is right for the Southern states to rise up, and break free from the control of this oppressive federal government. Gentleman, I can get my people on board. With only a little help, independence will be ours and you Herr Kemp will have an ally. So, gentlemen can I prepare my people to start The Rise of Pleiades?" replied Whittington. A few comments were made back and forth with Whittington finally preparing to close the meeting and making one significant final remark, "Very good gentlemen, Deo Vindice."

Bedford looked at me and said. "God what's he doing?"

"Sounds like he's pulling allies together for another a Ft. Sumter."

"The Rise of Pleiades?" asked Charlie.

"That's a very old code word amongst the Sons for the start of the resurrection of the cause. The Northern papers had one time called the first seven states to secede the Seven Sisters of Pleiades. It was meant to mock them, but the Sons embraced it, and it's become a badge of honor for our members."

At that moment Mr. Conner flipped me a coin, and I looked at it again. He said, "Deo Vindice. God will Vindicate." I eyed the coin and saw the connections come into play.

"What are we going to do," Charlie Asked.

"You need to get back and tell your Father to assemble the council. I have to stop him before he shares all of our secrets." With those words Charlie crawled back to the tree line.

Not considering any options, I rushed to the back door stood up and kicked it in. The men in the room stood there stunned while the man from Chicago just sat there puffing his cigar. I walked in and said, "Whittington this will never work!"

Whittington stood calmly and said, "Gentlemen this is James Conner."

"Whittington they will never go for this. The Sons won't go to war. The council will never approve of it." I said.

"Not the current council but there are about to be some changes." He confidently replied.

"A coup? You're planning a coup within the Sons?" I asked.

"Maybe it's already started Conner. And thanks for your help by the way. You would be my best friend if I didn't hate you." He said laughing.

"What are you planning?"

"Conner you should be able to figure it all out but I'll be glad to explain. With our help, De Angelo over there is going to take power within his organization. He will be a great ally already placed in the major cities of the North. And with a little help from our German friends, a supply of armaments and advisors. But most importantly, recognition from a powerful foreign sovereign, that we will be a new independent nation. Pretty simple actually."

"Whittington you go too far." I stated. You'll bring war to our soil, but it's not the way to bring about Southern independence. War is the last resort Whittington."

"Why wait Jimmy? Now is our time. Now is the time for the cause to be reborn," said Whittington.

"I'll put a stop to it. You know I will." I replied.

"No, you won't Jimmy because you'll be dead." He said as he pulled a gun from his jacket pocket.

"You're just going to kill me?" I asked.

"Not me and not yet; my friend here will take care of you later. Let me introduce you to some members of the Seven. Did you have any idea how much we increased the ranks of that organization?" He stated. "Almost five hundred members; meet the Captains of the new Republic of the Confederacy." He stated.

Then two men came to my side each grabbing an arm.

"You'll never get away with this." I yelled.

"Jimmy you just keep making it easier and easier for me." Whittington said smugly.

While the men were leading me to the front door, I took a moment to notice the two men on the porch, and looked at them closely. The one I recognized immediately as the man who showed me the coin trick at the diner. The other was, of course, his partner. They both watched as I was dragged to a parked vehicle out in front of the office. Then in an instant a single beam of light shined in our direction and grew brighter as it sped toward us. For no apparent reason it skidded to a stop about fifty feet from my location and just sat there as it's motor thumped breaking the silence of the night. One of the two men holding me shielded his eyes with a gloved hand and yelled, "Get out of here." A flash from the wood line dropped the smaller man on the porch holding the Tommy Gun. That same moment, I saw a flash come from behind the single light and a warm splatter of blood hit my face. I could feel the man to my right loosen his grip. Then he fell face first in the dirt. The large man with the shot gun jumped down the far side of the porch. I struggled to pull away from the other man holding me as he waived his gun about trying to find a clear target to shoot at. The sound of another round being fired echoed in the air and he was dropped to his knees. I rolled to the ground and ran for the trees.

A motor roared and from the single light a motorcycle was revealed as it sped toward the rear of the building. A lone man from the woods rushed the porch and fired shots at the large man with the shot gun. Through the darkness I realize that it was Tanner rushing the porch firing the melee' in the large man's direction. Tanner stepped on the porch and then ran inside the shack. I regained my composure, and dashed for the weapon nearest me. Running for the door, I followed Tanner inside. Along the way, I caught a glimpse of the large man riddled with bullet holes laying face down. I yelled to Tanner to let him know I was coming in behind him. I then heard more shots being fired.

Once inside I saw Tanner standing in the back doorway. As I walked closer I could make out Peabody astride the motorcycle. He was looking down at the corpse of DeAngelo, who lay at his feet and another of Whittington's Seven just paces away. I heard Peabody say, "Three men got away and Whittington's one of them for certain."

"Who else was inside Conner?" Tanner asked.

"A German and a couple of men from the Seven that Whittington had recruited; rogues, not likely members of the Sons," I replied.

"Why in the hell didn't you wait?"

"I did, but you were hours late, and I didn't want miss this."

"How do did you get caught?

"I walked in the backdoor, and over to the desk where Whittington stood."

"Well played." He replied standing there shaking his head. We walked back inside and began to search the office.

"They left in a hurry," said Tanner.

"Incredible" I stated.

"What?" asked Tanner.

"It's a journal. An old one at that." I opened the book and read the first line, then said "Jesus, it's Black's."

"Who?" asked Tanner.

"Randall Black as he was called then. He and another fellow called Smith, started what became the Seven." I replied.

"Never heard of them," he said.

"Didn't they teach you anything?" I replied smartly.

"The Whittington's must have been using this as a guide for their plans. These men were brilliant at espionage."

I flipped through the many worn and tattered pages. One single loose page fell and hit the floor. I picked it up and began to read it. On the page was a list of twenty three names; all with a line through them. I read the list one by one and let out a gasp then said, "James Conner."

"What are you reading?" asked Tanner.

"A hit list," I replied, "One with my father's name on it."

"Why do you say that?" he asked.

"He's the only James that's, dead and the names are all crossed out." I replied.

"Why is there a star behind his name?" He asked.

"Could be because he was in the Seven," but I looked closer and barely legible were the initials of my mother.

"They made it look like an accident. Both of them." I commented.

"Whittington's father did it, and he got a bonus star."

"I'm sorry. How do you know it was George's father?"

"At the top of the list are the words Resurrectio Per Factum. It's the same Latin phrase that was inscribed on George's knife. The one he had at Bransford that belonged to his father."

"What's the phrase mean?" Tanner asked.

"Roughly, renewal through action," I said.

"Jesus, Jimmy I am sorry."

"No Tanner," I stated, "It's a good for me to know this. I thought mother killed herself. I thought she left me on purpose."

Peabody still on the motorcycle kept watch as we continued to sift through what was left behind.

"We have to get these out of here Jimmy they can compromise us all." commented Tanner. He then came across a briefcase. He opened it and said, "Good God! It's filled with money!"

"Bribe money?" I asked.

"Likely. Once again, what you overheard was that De Angelo guy was going to make a bid for control over his organization, and the German was promising to provide supplies and support."

"Sounded just about like that Zimmerman fella's plan you told me about." I stated.

"I'll have to find that German. He knows too much about the Sons." Tanner stated. "Peabody and I will try and find them, you cut out of here."

"How, Charlie Bedford took my car. I sent him to warn his father and call a meeting of the council."

"Hell, Jimmy just take your pick. None of those out front will be going anywhere tonight. Just make sure you ditch it and for God's sake don't take it Shadow Wood."

"Fair enough, I'm right behind you," I said. They sped off Tanner in his vehicle, and Peabody on the motorcycle.

"That couldn't have worked could it?" I asked.

"In time who knows what Whittington could worked out. Besides you only have a vague idea of the inner workings of the Sons."

"But Mr. Conner that is a large scale action he was talking about." I replied.

"Campbell you have to remember that America had a very small army in the thirties, and there were many unhappy people in that time. America sat in isolation until Pearl Harbor and popular sentiment dictated a hands off policy on the wars in Europe and the Pacific. America was divided across the table on many issues. Organizations for social reform crossed the country in waves and people jumped on and off just as fast. Like I said, you only have a small piece of the picture from what I've told you. I think you're not considering the possibilities."

"The possibilities?"

"How far the arms of the Sons actually reach. No matter how often I hint at it, you seem to still be in the fog concerning the matter. Let me shed some light on the subject. Like I said after the war many confederate Generals ended up in Universities. Many of them promoted the cause for generations just by their presence. The promotion of the dream lives on in books, monuments, politics, and representations on the state flags. Campbell even the Army bases in the South, Forts: Lee, Hood, Polk, Stuart, Eustis, Jackson, Bragg don't they sound familiar?"

"All are named after Southern Civil war generals." I said.

"Exactly, do you not think that if the people of individual states rose up again that many wouldn't flock to that old banner hiding in the closet?"

"The Sons has a hand in all that?"

"And more. Much more," he stated. We're coming to the end Campbell let me continue."

I once again opened the book that Black had taken notes in, and for a long moment became caught up with his words. I heard a vehicle outside start, and I ran to the porch as the car sped off. I fired three shots but none found its target. I looked around and took count of the dead men out front. The large man still lay in his blood. The bodies of the two men from Rogue Seven lay motionless. To my left I saw a pool of blood and then a light trail leading to where the car was parked. One of Wallace's killers had gotten away. Out loud I exclaimed, "Damn, Sorry Virgil." Then went back inside grabbing all I needed.

I picked a vehicle and luckily the key was still in the ignition. "The gold!" I thought. I turned around and began walking behind the back of the shack and followed a road that led to the entry of the mine. Piles of coal stood outside and a rail track led deep inside. I looked to a small building near the entry and grabbed a light from the wall. I walked in the mine deeper and deeper looking for any evidence of what Whittington had been talking about. The mine seemed a labyrinth of sections, cuts and avenues leading into the darkness. But I continued to follow the tracks to where they ended as the ceiling became lower and lower. Then I found machinery and tools and finally a wall of coal where the men had last worked that marked the end of the mine. I turned, and began walking back out, taking note of the various sections, and thought this could take forever. On the way out I felt cool air, and noticed the eerie silence that was deep in the earth. "Few men have placed a foot on this ground" I thought.

I continued on my way back out of the mine noticing a turn and shined my light in that direction. I felt compelled to take this new direction and began to hear pumps pulling water from what appeared to be a much older section of the mine. I noticed a walled portion to my left. I kept walking deeper back into the black. I looked to my left and on a bricked wall I noticed something strange. I could make out what appeared to be a symbol on one of the bricks. As I walked closer I shined my light directly at it making out a symbol of a large upside down Y inside a circle with two dots clearly marked on each side. It was a symbol of the Sons.

I put my hand against the wall and thought about all the gold behind it. "Riches enough to last a man a hundred life times, likely," I thought. I breathed in, and patted the wall and said, "Riches enough to help the Southern States gain their independence." I walked off from that wall and eventually found the fresh air of the night. I was more drained than expected, and wondered if it was the excitement of the night or the long walk inside the mines thin air. Either way I was glad to be back outside under the stars.

I climbed back inside the vehicle and headed for town. There I called my Grandfather, and told him in message form that a couple of old friends, and I had made a mess at the old mine and it would be best if it were cleaned up before anyone stumbled across the scene. He knew what I meant, and immediately called members for help.

I ditched the car in a safe place, and went home to Shadow Wood. Grandfather wasn't there when I walked in. I waited a few moments then walked upstairs and passed out in bed. I was still covered in dust and dirt from the mine but too exhausted to care. I woke to Grandfathers voice asking me to come downstairs. On the way down I saw that Tanner and Peabody were already sitting in Grandfather's den.

"Hey, there sleeping beauty," stated Peabody.

"Ida, coffee!"

"I ain't getting your grumpy self nothing. Unless of course you ask me nicely."

"Please Ida!" I said

"That's better." She replied back from the kitchen. Tanner and Peabody of course both laughed and mocked me. Then Grandfather said, "The men have been informing me about last night."

"Sorry about the mess is that getting cleaned up?" I asked.

"Yes, we have some people handling the situation." He replied.

"Do I want to know what they do with the bodies?" I asked.

"No, best if you don't" He replied. Then he stated, "My god you're filthy. What did you do?"

"Sir, I swear when we left he was clean and fit," stated Tanner.

"Treasure hunting," I replied.

"Treasure hunting?" he asked.

"Nothing," I replied and then said as I smirked, "I like having my secrets too."

"Bad call going into that situation all on your own James. You need training," he stated.

"Maybe," I said as Ida handed me the coffee. "Tanner did you kill any Germans last night?" I asked.

"Nope," He said. "I work for the Treasury Department. We don't kill foreigners, but Peabody on the other hand laid him open."

"You didn't scalp him for god's sakes did you?" I asked looking at Peabody.

"No," he replied.

I took my first good look at him and said, "You look better, as a matter of fact, much better. Did you find an Indian gal and get married? Maybe make a couple of babies?"

"No, it's only been a few months," stated Peabody.

"I expect a lot out of you Michael. Seriously, did you find anyone you were related too?"

"One very old man, cousin of some sort, but I was treated like close family and made good friends." Peabody replied.

"And the booze?" I asked.

"Still hard sometimes, but that will pass."

"Good Michael I'm glad."

"Conner, I've got some news for you," commented Tanner. "I can't notify the Treasury Department of what I learned last night. It's too close for comfort for the Sons. I'll have to find another way to get them pointed in the right direction. But, as your Grandfather and I discussed, I have another issue. I'm going to have to lay low for awhile. I've been pulled in too many directions, and crossed some lines."

Not thinking much of what he had just told me I stated, "One man on the porch wasn't all dead."

"Which one?" he asked.

"The one that drove off in the Studebaker," I said smartly. And then I continued, "The smaller of the men that helped kill Wallace."

"You have to get a handle on that," he said. Then he asked my Grandfather, "Where am I going to lay low since I've been compromised?"

Grandfather turned to Tanner and said, "Son it's worse than just being compromised. If they connect you to any of this they could hang you for treason. You're not married is that correct?"

"No sir," Tanner stated.

"He opened the briefcase stacking half the contents on the table. How do feel about going a little further south?"

"Florida?" asked Tanner.

"Even further," stated Grandfather and he pulled out a map of South America. "We have friends in Brazil. Southerners, whose families moved there after The War for Southern Independence, Tanner, how do you feel about being a Confederado?"

"Confederado?" he asked.

"That's what they called the thousands of them living in South America. They will hide you until it's safe. Then they will give you a new a new name, a new identity, and in time we can get you back in the country. You can live life free of it all if you choose. We owe you that," said Grandfather.

"Sir, South America sounds good. Real good actually," stated Tanner.

"And you Peabody. What do you want?" asked Grandfather.

"I hate to see my friend head south all alone. He tends to get in trouble."

"Done," stated Grandfather, and he handed him the other half of the contents from the briefcase. "No one knows where this belongs anyway." My two friends stood up, and Grandfather put his arms around them and said, "Boys I'm proud of you, very proud."

Then Grandfather said, "If you boys will excuse us, I need to speak with James for just a moment."

I laid Black's journal on my Grandfather's desk. He turned the pages examining the contents and said, "The Whittington's had a play book did they."

"Yes, it seems so," I stated.

"Very good find James, I'm very proud of you also.

"Thank you. There's more though. Tucked inside the book was a list." After handing it to him I walked to the window and said, "See how the names are crossed off? Do you see my father's name?"

Grandfather sat back and said, "I know most of these men. Many were good men."

"Grandfather, the Latin phrase at the top of the page Resurrecto Per Factum. I've seen it before. When I was at Bransford I had only two things in common with Whittington. One was the knife with the scorpion emblem. The other was that they were both given to us by our fathers. His had that Latin phase inscribed on the blade."

Grandfather sat back and said, "James pour me a glass of the brandy please. Then I'll need a moment for my thoughts."

I poured the glass and asked, "Should I kill him?"

"Certainly not James," then he paused and said, "The betrayal was to me and the Sons. I shall handle this in due course."

I walked to the front door to say good bye to my friends. The realization hit me that they would be off in some foreign country, and I was left with Grandfather to handle this mess. Tanner stood at the end of the walk with Peabody nearby crouched over fiddling with his motorcycle. I walked toward them and said, "Gentlemen, I can't thank you enough."

"It's a habit. We've been keeping you out of trouble for years," stated Peabody.

"That's true." I replied.

"Watch yourself," he said pointing his finger at me, "Sounds like we're going to be on another continent, and that's a little too far to be keeping an eye on you."

"Yes, I know it sounds great. I wish I could go with you.

"Me too," stated Tanner.

"But you have it all here, and you need to stay and do some good for the Sons. It sounds like you have your work cut out for you."

"Yes, it does."

"Your grandfather is a shrewd man but he is getting on in age and will need his right hand by his side," said Tanner.

"Yes, I know. But he's not as much fun as you two."

Grandfather walked out and handed Tanner a note. You'll leave from New Orleans. We can you get out through there. On this paper is the name of your contact. Find him, and all you need will be provided."

"Thank you sir," he stated. Then he asked Peabody, "You riding with me?"

Peabody just smiled, and kicked his bike to a start, "She's going to Brazil with me."

"Can't damn ride a horse but that thing you'll drive anywhere," remarked Tanner shaking his head.

Peabody smiled as he lowered his goggles. I shook his hand and he said, "I'll see you again Conner. I'm sure I'll have to drag your ass out of some situation before too awful long."

"Take care," I replied.

"Get going!" yelled Tanner as he honked his horn. Then he pulled up and leaned out the window. "Kirby Smith," he remarked as he shook my hand.

"Don't you ever give up either. Take care." I said.

I stood in the drive watching my friends drive off as they followed each other out of town.

"Good friends," Grandfather said.

"Yeah, they seem to be in short supply." I replied

"It gets that way James," he stated then turned to walk inside Shadow Wood, leaving me standing there alone.

Mr. Conner sat there for a moment quietly. I think picturing the memory of his friends driving off. I was of course full of questions but sat respectfully watching him and the expression on his face. Finally, he broke from his trance with a crackling voice said only one word.

TWENTY

"*Revenge!*" *stated Conner.*

Somewhat stunned I hesitated for a moment and then asked, "Mr. Conner did you get your revenge?"

"My revenge was a different sort. Those men that killed Wallace were evil men. Wallace was an innocent bystander caught up in events in which he had no control over. Killing the man from Chicago would only in part satisfy me. My revenge had to be exacted on the surviving Whittington to bring justice to the situation but he was nowhere to be found." He Replied.

"Did you get your justice?" I asked.

"Are you wanting, a death bed confession?" he retorted, "It's not my death bed, just yet, but it's only fair that you know of my darker nature."

I wasn't a patient man like my Grandfather. I tended to be reckless in those days. With Whittington in hiding, I had to exact my retaliation out on those I had available. Grandfather refused to let me go out and find any of them, but I felt I had to do something; something for Virgil and myself. I dared not share my rage with Grandfather or he would put a stop to my plans. Finally, an opportunity for business in Chicago arose and I accepted it. Tanner had given me all the information on the men, I likely needed.

Once in Chicago, I rented a room and went about my business. I laid there resting and thinking about my possible solutions to the situation.

The sights and sounds of the city reminded me of another time and place not so long ago. But I fought back those melancholy thoughts, and tried to remain focused on my task at hand.

I formed my final thoughts on a plan, and went to the locations named in the file Tanner had given me. I came across the man at a pool hall where he made daily rounds. Staying far out of sight I followed him making notes and tracking his routine for a day or two. The time had come and the decision was made where this event would happen.

All that was left was to decide what weapon to use. I chose a knife for its stealth and kept my .32 caliber pistol for a backup in case of trouble. Having no proper knife, I went out that day and bought one with a six inch blade capable of doing the job.

The man rode with a new partner and I decided it would be best if I waited for them to separate because I wasn't there to start a war. I just wanted to settle a score, and only needed the blood of the Wallace's murderer.

For the confrontation I had picked a quiet alley that they frequented daily. My victim's partner went inside for about thirty minutes likely to visit a girl friend or a lady of the night. I leaned against a wall holding a bottle of whiskey. Inside my pocket, I gripped the knife and thought about the moment that the edge would slice into his body. I never questioned whether I would actually do this or not. The thought never crossed my mind. Just in the wisdom of the decision, and a nagging worry that my plan might fail. Patiently, I waited as the men fell behind on their past two day's routine. Night came and darkness covered the alley. I began to worry that they wouldn't show.

I had about given up just as the men slowly drove past me. They parked at the far end of the alley. I watched as the new partner left my victim, and walked to a side door of a large six story building. He waited inside the vehicle with his hat over his face catching a moment of rest. I sat there for a moment to make sure everything was in place, and I set my bottle on the ground in front of me. My heart began to race. I stood upright, and took in a deep breath. I stepped forward, and started to walk toward the rear of the vehicle. My foot grazed the bottle causing it to fall over. It began to roll making a sound that echoed off the walls of the alley, but I continued to walk toward the car anyway.

As I approached the car I could make out the driver in his mirror. He was sleeping soundly. I breathed a sigh of relief that the racket I caused hadn't alerted him. Gripping the knife, now just steps away I neared the open window. I leapt forward with my final step, knife in hand, preparing to drive it into him. Just then I heard the man let out a snoring sound, as he slept calmly with not a worry on his mind. Pausing I thought that there was just something that didn't seem fair or honorable about killing a sleeping man. Momentarily I just stood there considering the notion and then again prepared myself as I wrapped on the door with the butt of the knife. He woke and asked, "What do you want?" Then he looked down and moved is right hand from behind his neck again saying, "What do you want Mac? Damn I was sleeping," he snapped angrily.

The fog of sleep must have lifted from his eyes because he looked at me closely and asked, "Don't I know you?"

"Yeah, Mac ya do," I replied as I flipped the coin of the Sons on his lap. He looked down, then up, as I reached in the window grabbed his hair with my left hand and thrust the knife into the side his neck with my right. His hands lifted to mine as I pushed harder with the knife against his neck. A gurgling sound came from his throat, and warm blood gushed from the wound splattering me and the side of the car. Finally the man died. I struggled to pull the knife out of his neck.

I stepped away from the car and looked at the bloody mess. Just then the side door of the building opened and his partner stepped out tucking in his shirt. We were now standing just feet apart. Both of us surprised at the sight of each other. He made a quick glance toward the car, and reacted quicker than I did. I still had the bloody knife in my hand as he grabbed my arm with one hand, and hit me with the other. Disoriented, I fell to the ground as did the knife. He stepped over me and punched my face with the hardest punch I had ever felt. I was taking a pounding but found the clarity to reach into my pocket and find my revolver. It took only seconds before I pulled the trigger and shot the revolver through my jacket. The bullet pierced his body, and he groaned stumbling backward in the process. But he managed to still keep his grip on me. Again, I fired, and it seemed to have no effect. Finally after a third round, he let loose of me and fell to the ground. I was now covered with two men's blood plus that of my own.

The shot had attracted attention from the widows above, and I darted into the building from which the man left. Quickly, I scrambled to the stairs stepping over debris on the way up. A man yelled inside the building, "Stop him he killed Marco! Stop him." I ran into the first door that was open. As I stepped inside, I felt something strike my head and a strange sound rattled in my ears. It was all I could do to put my hands down in front of me before I hit the floor. I laid there, unable to move as the world went black.

I woke a short time later, my head pounding. I began to make out a figure standing in front of me. It was that of a scantily clad woman smoking a cigarette. At first I tried to move my hands to my throbbing head but soon realized that they were tied tightly to a corner post of her bed. "What are you doing to me?" I protested. "Shut up! I can pretty much do as I please right now." She said as she held my pistol. "Now the question is what should I do with you? I could call the cops but that would just be trouble for me. I could make it easy on myself, and just kill you. Maybe even collect a bounty on you for killing Marco and Ciro. Or if you're a good boy, I could just turn you over and let their boss handle the situation."

"Do I get a vote?" I asked.

"No," She said.

"Didn't think so." I replied.

"You hungry?" She asked.

Almost in shock by the question I wasn't sure what to answer but let out a reply of, "Yes."

In minutes she squatted down and fed me with a fork. It came to mind that she wasn't going to do any of the three options that she had in mind. I figured I could talk my way out of the situation but a knock wrapped on the door, and I heard a voice say, "Their gone." She walked back in my direction and I said, "If it's money you need, I can get you some."

"Now, you tell me." She said as another knock wrapped on the door. "Come in she yelled."

Two large men entered the room. I looked at her and said, "I thought you hadn't decided."

"Didn't you know women lie? I just fed you to keep you quiet until the cops left." I began to struggle, but no use. The two men quickly grabbed me, and carried me to a waiting car outside in the alley. They threw me in the backseat and retied my hands. We drove just a few blocks and entered the back of a large building. The men climbed out and carried me from the back seat.

The room had five men standing there waiting on my arrival. But it was the one man who stood in the center that grabbed my attention. He just stood out from the rest. He was dressed in the best of clothes and looked to be all business. I stood before the group of men hands still bound. The well dressed man asked, "Who do you think ya are killing my men?" I wasn't sure what to say, so I stood there saying nothing. He said, "I'm giving you just one chance, and if I think you're lying; you're dead. Understand?" I stood my ground beginning to resign myself to the possibility of an unwelcome outcome. Again he asked, "Why you going out and killing my men? You're too sloppy to be working for somebody of any importance."

"He killed my friend." I stated.

"So?" he replied. "He's killed lots of people."

"They weren't friends of mine though." I stated.

"Who was this friend?" he asked.

"Virgil Wallace, we had been friends since we were kids. He murdered him for no reason." I said.

"Don't know the name, and he only kills who I say. So, that would make what you say. Not possible." He said.

"I don't think he was working for you then. He was working for a fella named DeAngelo." I stated.

"Yeah, he was working for me because DeAngelo worked for me," he said. That statement gave me the opportunity to roll the dice.

"Nah," I said, "DeAngelo only worked for DeAngelo."

"What do you mean, DeAngelo was like family?" he asked.

"DeAngelo was a traitor to you." I stated boldly. I could see his expression and demeanor change, as he became angry from the comment. I had struck a chord and he wanted to find out more.

"I'll explain if you give me a chance." I said.

"It's best for you if you do," he said. Now, I had to explain the meeting at the mine without revealing information regarding the Sons. I began by saying, "A few months back, DeAngelo had a meeting down south. As a matter of fact he has had quite a few meetings down that way I would suspect."

"We do business down that direction." He said.

"DeAngelo didn't come back did he?" I asked.

"No, what do you know?"

"Everything," I stated. "And I know he was planning on double crossing someone to gain power within his organization. Which I would assume was you?" The man nodded.

"He was meeting with a man in my organization named Whittington who was also a traitor of his own people. I'll kill him too if I get the chance." I stated.

The man looked at me and asked, "What's your name?"

"James Conner,"

"I know that name too." he said. Then he paused and said, "Everyone leave the room." While the men exited the building I stood there unsure of what to expect. He walked around behind me and lifted my hand that held the ring of the Sons. He then cut the ropes that bound my hands. He stood close and raised his hand and I reluctantly put mine in his to shake it. To my surprise he gave me the secret hand shake and said, "I'm a member of your little club."

Realizing that he was what we called an affiliate and only privy to the most basic of information I knew to be sparing with my words even though I was grateful for this bit of luck. He put his arm around me and stated, "Now, tell me what has happened brother."

I sighed and carefully weighed my words. Before I could speak, he interrupted me and said, "Let me make this easy for you. We know more about the Sons of the South than you think. We like to know all we can about who we're doing business with, but none of that matters now. We have our understanding and do our business accordingly. Just tell me what you can without revealing any of your..... Well, trade secrets." So, I began telling the events of the night leaving out only particular details. He sat back and listened with great interest.

"That rat," he stated.

"We have our own rats." I replied. "So, you believe me?"

"I have little doubt that what you're telling the true. Most men wouldn't make the journey to settle a score unless it's personal." He said. "Let alone create such a story. You acted sloppy Conner, but I like your nerve."

"It was sloppy?" I questioned.

Ignoring my protest, he went on and said, "Conner, this arrangement that Whittington and DeAngelo had in mind about moving money. It is a problem for us. What do you think?"

"Even though I am indebted to you, I think the size of our organization could cause unneeded attention to be focused both of our ways. I know I acted recklessly recently, but I tend to error on the side of caution in most matters. It will be looked into though."

"I can do business with you Conner."

"I never asked your name?"

"Mancinelli," he replied.

"Mr. Mancinelli, I have to ask another favor of you."

"What is it?" He asked.

"What happened to those men, and my involvement, not be found out by my grandfather. I would just prefer....."

"Say no more, I had a grandfather too." We shook hands in the manner customary to the Sons which Mr. Mancinelli seemed to get a peculiar thrill from and he said, "Conner sounds like you did me a big favor."

Never again would I be so lucky. I left the city that day, and headed in the direction of home, and for the safety of Shadow Wood.

"Mr. Conner, you were lucky more than once that day. What was it like to kill a man? Did you feel as if you got justice for Wallace?"

"Campbell, ending a man's life is the most personal act one can do. I'd like to keep it that way. Besides, we need to move on."

"Of course. Please continue."

My Grandfather has had his share of blood on his hands. Of that, I am sure. What I wasn't sure of, was how he would handle the situation with the eldest Whittington. They were supposed to be bound by honor, blood oaths, and brotherhood to each other. But he was responsible for the murder of his only son, and I could only guess the worst. Although the politics of the Sons complicated the situation, I was certain that

Grandfather would rely on his years and wisdom instead of his emotions. I was also certain that his vengeance would be more devastating and more complete than any simple bullet would accomplish.

When he was ready he called a meeting of the ten executive council members, and they drove to the home of Grandfather Whittington. Whittington still with allies had obviously been warned and covered his tracks. The evidence that was brought forth concerned the meeting his grandson, George Whittington, had at the mine. The council was alarmed at the boldness of the plan, and the rogue group was now officially called, The Maverick Seven. Even though we all knew who pulled the strings in the family. All the evidence that was gathered implicated young George, but not his Grandfather.

The members called Grandfather Whittington to the table. Through lies and master political maneuvering, he began to counter the accusation. In truth no direct evidence could link him to the activities of his grandson. The council was hamstringed and voted to exile young George Whittington, but could only temporarily limit the authority of his Grandfather. Their hands were tied to do much else. With a membership split by the activities of the Whittington's, a Maverick Seven running about, and secret pacts of war being made, the council had plenty on their hands.

Grandfather's view on the situation was that the account with the Sons of the South was settled. He had exposed Grandfather Whittington as a threat, and to the best of their authority they handled the situation. By doing so he set the Sons back on the proper course with honor and dignity. I had asked Grandfather about the list being used to help in the implication, but he replied that the only connection could be to George's father and he was already exiled. The whole affair made Grandfather Whittington smugger, than ever and he did for now at least seem untouchable.

Grandfather, a more complex man than I had realized had his own agenda, and didn't mind taking matters into his own hands. His best attribute being patience, he knew that most things in the life are a matter of timing, and sometimes you just have to wait for the right moment. He called in his chip to settle an old debt, and the gentleman was more than willing to make his account right.

On the birthday of Grandfather Whittington, his son peeked his head out of the hole where he had been hiding. The two men celebrated over dinner together at his favorite restaurant. The city where he lived was a relatively small town with the main street being only a few blocks long. A church stood at one end and a river on the other. The city was typically a bustle of activity for a town of its size, but on this night two powerful forces blew into town. The first was a storm with heavy rain, and lightening keeping the residents safely at home. The other was a chestnut mare carrying a lone rider over the back roads into the town. The rain poured as thunder crackled in the stormy night's air, covering the sounds of the mare's hooves striking the wet brick streets.

The rider entered the main street stopping under a light pole. He adjusted his rain soaked hat, and steadied his mount after the sound of crashing thunder caused her to stir. A moment later both Whittington's, father and son, walked out of the restaurant dodging the rain as they quickly walked toward their vehicle with its driver holding the door open.

Opposite the rider, on the other end of the block, stood a parked vehicle from which a man exited and slowly walked in the direction of Whittington's vehicle. His black coat and hat quickly become drenched in the downpour. The man's vehicle flashed its headlights three times as a signal to the rider. Who in turn dug in his spurs and beckoned the horse to move forward. All figures now on course and converging to the same exact location. The rider stopped his mount a few paces from the front of the vehicle blocking its path. A small cloud of steam exhaled from the mare's nose as she shook her head from side to side. The driver looked up at the menacing sight, and saw the mounted man's Colt revolver pointed at him. He reached inside his coat for his weapon, and before it could be drawn a flash was produced from the Colt. It lit the night and splattered blood from the driver's chest as his body fell back, arms flailing outwardly just before he hit the ground.

Grandfather Whittington ducked and crawled toward the car. Lightening again flashed, unsettling the wild eyed horse as it began to stammer for footing on the slick streets below. The rider quickly regained control. His overcoat opened, and another flash from the sky briefly exposed the riders gray Confederate uniform hidden underneath. Whittington's son's reaction was slowed as he bore witness to this sight, but he still managed to draw his weapon in the rider's direction. It was no use. The quicker rider fired first. With a flash and loud crack, the colt revolver had once again found its mark. Grandfather Whittington sat in shock at the sight of his dead son's body. The man in black, now close enough to draw, pointed his small pistol at Grandfather Whittington crouching beside the car. The old man looked up knowing death was near. His eyes met his assassins. "You!" he exclaimed. Before anything else could be uttered, the hammer fell and the old man died, clinching his chest with a look of astonishment on his face. The shooter looked to the rider, who tipped his hat, and then dug in his heals letting out a cry of, "Yaaaa." His horse responded to the request, and galloped down the brick streets. The sound of hooves now echoed over all other sounds of the night. The signal car pulled out when horse and rider passed. Then it stopped to pick up the shooter standing calmly near the dead bodies. He entered the vehicle and sped off into the darkness.

The heavy rain, thunder, and lightning bought the men needed time and covered the commotion they had caused. The only witness to the event reported in the paper the following day, "That a lone mounted

Confederate Calvary man had ridden down Main Street on a horse from hell. He stopped in front of a parked vehicle, drew a revolver, and gunned down three innocent men in the street. A fourth lucky soul was spared by the apparition, and quickly sped out of town fleeing for his life."

Upon hearing of the death of Grandfather Whittington the council convened once again. The membership had no issue pointing the finger of blame toward my grandfather. He, of course, denied any involvement in the episode, and they had no proof. Interestingly enough it was Mr. Bedford that rallied to my Grandfather's aid and the matter was quickly put to rest. He was likely satisfied with just his son being alive. Of course, Mr. Bedford wouldn't have much to do with me, but he quickly put an end to the involvement between Charlie and George's sister.

Sightings of the apparition are still rumored in the city today. I questioned my grandfather only once shortly after the event. He suffering from a cold, and after a long pause stated only this. "I heard your Mr. Downey has retired from Bransford." I myself can only assume Downey felt his exile and debt had been satisfied. Nothing more was ever mentioned between us about the event.

TWENTY ONE

Backing up a step, after my near death experience with Mancinelli I was again on the road. I had time to consider all that had happened to me over those few days. I had tracked and killed two men. I was captured and tied to a bed by a woman. The realization struck me that I had been a little more than just lucky. I reached up and grabbed the medallion that hung around my neck, and thought that maybe there was someone watching out for me. My thoughts drifted to my parents, my brother, and to that little house on the dirt road. I turned the Romeo in that direction, and headed to the home of my youth.

Along the way I focused on those times, and certain events came to mind. Mostly, the care the Fenton's had shown me and my family was far more than most would ever consider. I had often set my mind to writing the Fenton's once I left Bransford to let them know I was well. I even made a promise to myself to look in on them, if I ever passed through. When you're young and the world is ahead of you, the next adventure is around the corner. And, you tend to focus on that possibility, and not what's behind. You think you have all the time in the world and the reality is that it's not standing still waiting on you. It's not the place that's frozen in your mind. It too has changed and may have moved on in its own way.

Here it was years later when I finally made it to their home near Campbell's crossroads. I had no illusion of their likely welfare. I paused outside the Fenton's home that had fallen into disrepair. It's circumstance likely due to the times. In my mind I saw it differently. I saw it as I re-membered. With the smells of Mrs. Fenton's cooking and Mr. Fenton's pipe on those warm quiet nights while sitting on the porch. I drove a little further down to my house. To my disappointment, all that was left was a foundation as the only reminder that a home had once stood there. I stopped and walked the ground remembering all that had been there. It was a home filled with love, life and a family. The barn remained intact holding its own on the property and I peered inside. I was reminded of my father's death, and how he was brought there in the company of his friends. It wasn't hard for me to imagine my parents going about their routine and young Will asking me to go with him to the creek and play.

I now stood on that land the lone survivor of a family that once was. All the family memories were locked inside my mind alone. I walked away, and then drove to the cemetery just up the road. I came upon a set of markers with a name that I recognized. It was the Fenton's. They were buried just a few rows from that of my parents. I noticed the dates and that Mrs. Fenton had passed first, and Mr. Fenton followed her less than a year behind.

I had brought flowers for my mother's grave, and took one quietly placing it on Mrs. Fenton's marker. I thanked them both for the safety and smiles that they provided for me. The quiet courage they showed and for knowing just what to say to a young boy in such a time of turmoil in his life. They had a quiet dignity and peace within the world that they lived. Thinking back, I wondered if it was their age or just their nature that cause them to be this way. Either way they seemed to know that you're not holding the reins in this life. That it's not a fiery beast you can dominate and control but one that goes where it wills and you're pretty much just going along for the ride. But still we do have choices, and I guess all one can hope is that he can point the beast in the direction he'd like it to go.

As I walked away from their graves, I thought for a few moments about why I came to these crossroads. I realized that maybe I had come because I was at one myself. There was still something unsettled in my mind, and I still wasn't sure about the direction my life had taken. It also seems, whether they are living or dead, that there is something about mothers that beckons us to return.

I stood before the stone where she rested, and those of my father, and brother in hope that I might find an answer or at least some solace for a moment. Knelling down, I spoke to them as if they could hear my words. "I see Grandfather made good on his promise and provided better markers for the family. They are nice just like he said they would be." I ran the tall grass between my fingers eventually tearing off a piece, and began to split it into small shreds as I continued. "I guess I came here to talk with you again. I wanted to thank you and tell you that I was sorry for believing that you had chosen to leave me. I guess I closed you all off for a long time now, and I wanted that to change. I want to remember it all again; the good and bad. Ma, I can still see you in Pa's arms with the red bow in your hair. You were beautiful, and Pa you were strong and a giant of a man at least to me. We had good times. I want to remember them and I want to carry them with me like a man should. I looked over to the far marker and said, "And you Will, you'll always be a kid in my mind, but it was good to have brother. I wish we could have had more time and more good memories. I don't know. I guess I just wanted you all to know that it doesn't matter whether you're gone or not. I still carry you with me. I guess I was just mad at you all for leaving me alone, and I guess I just wanted you all to know that I'm not mad anymore."

I sat there crouched down quietly thinking to myself. I seemed to have a moment of clarity and knew what path I would take. I rose up and said, "I know you were all with me the whole time, watching out for me. I love you, and I was lucky to have you. I hope you know that."

Then I walked away leaving the little grave yard at the cross roads.

Mr. Campbell once again became silent for a moment. He looked over to me and asked, "Remember me speaking of Father McIver's thoughts on a connection between the living and those already gone. I do think that they look down on us in this life. I really do. I believe it's one of the mysteries of the love that bond people together. I just don't hold much account that we're not here for some reason, something bigger than ourselves and whether we just amount to a small drop of rain in the sea or a giant splash. It doesn't matter. Its likely part of a bigger wave anyway."

"I'm not sure what to think anymore Mr. Conner. It seems to me that I haven't made the splash I wanted that's for sure." I said.

"That's why you're here son." He stated.

"I appreciate this opportunity you gave me to tell your life's story. I have to be honest, when I took your wife's call, I wasn't sure if I would even make the trip over here. I'm very glad that I did."

"This story's about over Campbell. But I didn't bring you over here to tell you a story that could be told."

"I'm not sure I understand sir." I stated.

"Campbell, life just came to a cross road for you."

I said nothing but as I looked he said with a smile, "Let me finish son and you will."

I had made my decision to stay with my grandfather and make his works and deeds my own. My happiness became just a matter of accepting the wind, and making only the slightest of adjustment. There were dangers mind you; primarily the fact that Whittington and his associates had moved underground once a cleansing of sorts was done within the organization. Against my grandfather's protests, I took my place within the Seven to regain control. This move added insult to injury for the remaining members of the Maverick Seven. Although the group was fractured it was still a threat to be taken seriously. My life was often at risk, I lived looking over my shoulder. The world around us was being threatened too. Both Germany and Japan were beating the drums of war. While the United States stood on the sidelines thinking war would never affect its shores.

Four years had passed since I last saw my friends drive off to their new home in South America. Grandfather had taken ill and was in bed recuperating. A knock wrapped at the door to the Shadow Wood mansion. Henry was out in the garage working on the latest addition to the Conner's stable of automobiles. Ida was cooking another of her splendid meals. I opened the door and there stood Little G. He took off his hat and said, "Mr. Conner good to see you again." I stood in shock for a moment and then asked him inside. We sat in the parlor and briefly caught up with one another. Finally, I came to the question that I burned to ask, "Have you heard from Sally?" He sat on the edge of the chair looking down to the hat he was holding and said, "No, sir it's been quite some time." I was saddened, but then again somewhat relieved by his answer. He then said, "Mr. Conner I had this all planned out, but I find myself stumbling for the words."

"Go on Little. It's all right really." I said.

He sighed deeply then continued, "Miss Sally has been dead for just over three years now."

I was taken back, and a deep hole of emptiness now formed in my gut. This was not the response I had expected. Little looked at me and continued by saying, "Mr. Conner she left this world giving it a gift. She died while giving birth to a son. Mr. Conner she labored hard, and after the delivery she bled so badly that they couldn't get it to stop. When her light faded she asked that I never ….." He then pulled a piece of paper from inside his jacket and said, "Maybe it's best if you read this. We found it amongst her belongs."

James,

I have no idea where you are in this world but I hope that you are safe and back where you belong; standing next to your Grandfather on the porch of Shadow Wood. Oh, how I wish I had just once seen your home. You spoke so fondly of it.

I am certain you are angry with me but I hope that you will forgive me for leaving you standing there alone. Because I just couldn't take that all from you. I wanted what was best for you and for you to be in the place that you're supposed to be, not some far off country catering to me.

I know it doesn't seem right but in the end you will be grateful. Besides inside me is a constant reminder of how much I loved you. This child will grow, and know that his father loved me and him. It's kind of silly to say this but I just know I am carrying a boy. I guess the whole letter is silly because you will never read a word of it anyway. But I do so miss you and miss talking to you. I hope that your heart will find love again and that I didn't bring too much pain your way. But if not it will be all right James because I carry enough love inside me for the both of us in this lifetime.

Love Always,
Sally

A feeling of great relief overcame me because even though I was certain of our mutual love I still had a lingering doubt and nothing was ever more certain for me than my love for Sally. But her leaving me the way she did left me with this concern that I may have alone in the feeling and if I was alone in the feeling then the love would forever be tarnished. Even after all this time I needed her validation.

My eyes began to tear up at the news. "I just knew she loved me" I said out loud. I regained my composure and asked Little what had happened to the child. He said, "My sister Lydia has taken the boy on. Even though I had promised Miss Sally that I would never tell you. I see no other way that would be right. Your son is three and half now, and she loves him very much. She wants a life of her own, and wants to get married soon. I also fear that it's going to be no life for him living between the worlds."

"Is the child here?" I asked.

"Yes, he's in my car." Little said.

"Go and bring him to me." I stated.

Little went outside while I regained my composure and made myself presentable. Little came back inside, leading the small boy whose hand was swallowed by his giant hand. The contrasts between the two made a note worthy sight. The small boy eyes were wide as he looked at his surroundings in the foyer. He seemed to notice everything. That is everything but me. Finally, they neared and his eyes turned to mine. I crouched down to the child and smiled. Standing there he placed his head on Little's massive leg. "Hello, I'm James," I said. The boy stood there not saying anything. "What's your name?" I asked. He stood tall and proudly said, "Jimmy Conner." and he stretched his small hand out for me to shake. Little looked down smiled and said, "I taught him that." I shook the boys hand as I looked at him closely. He had Sally's eyes and shape but the child reminded me very much of my brother Will. Just then Lydia appeared at the door way. "Come in Lydia." I said. "How have you been?" I walked over to hug her. "Fine," she replied.

"Are you keeping Maxine's in order for Little?"

"As much as I can," then she said, "Sally, wanted to give him your name, and felt that it wouldn't be a problem all the way up there but now I wonder. Either way this is where the child should be."

Just then Miss Ida walked in looking at us with an inquiring expression on her face. I introduced everyone but the child. She bent over looking down at the boy and said, "Now, who are you?

"I'm Jimmy Conner, Pleased to meet you." She held her position for a moment."

"I taught him that," Little said once again proudly.

"Oh, Lord," she replied. Then turned and walked out of the room looking back shaking her head.

I knelt down to the boy and said, "How would you like to stay here with me and Miss Ida for awhile." The boy looked up at Little and said, "This is what we talked about. This man will take care of you now." He ran over and said," Uncle G."

"Now, be brave and go with Mr. Conner." Lydia knelt down, hugged the child and left the room in tears. The boy said, "His name is like mine."

"Yes, it is," said Little. "Now run along."

"Miss Ida, I need you could you come here please." She peeked her head out of the kitchen door. And I said, "Could you please take the boy and find something for him to eat." She reluctantly walked out and kindly said, "Come with me child." He took her hand and followed her to the kitchen.

"Little, thank you for bringing him to me," I said.

"It's the only place that seemed right for him. He tended to stand out with my people." He said.

"You taught him well. He seems like a good boy."

"He is. I'll miss him but this is what's right," he said and he walked for the door.

"One question Little. When is his birthday?" I asked.

"March 4th," he replied.

I quickly made did the math and thought, "The beach."

I walked into the kitchen and leaned against the counter watching the boy eat his meal. Miss Ida held her head down while she cooked. I leaned over and grabbed some food off a plate near her. She tossed her spoon down and said, "Now, you've done it."

"Done what?" I asked

"What you done is sitting there at the table. What are going to do with him?"

"I'll figure it out." I said. "You never asked if I thought he was mine."

"It's written all over his face."

"What happened to his Mother? Who is she anyway?"

"She's dead and her name was Sally"

"Oh Lord, James bringing up a mixed child here..." She started to berate me, but paused then looked at me and said, "Your Sally's dead and she carried your baby." She then asked," Are you all right James?"

"Yes, I am. She gave me a couple of gifts that made it better." I handed her the letter. As she read it, she brought her hand to her chest. "Oh, James," she said then hugged me. "I am sorry." Just then grandfather walked in. He stood in the doorway, and looked to the boy and said, "Who's that child?" I smartly replied, "That child is a Jimmy Grandfather." He grumbled something then said, "Ida, I'll be eating in the study," and walked out.

"What are you going to do about him?"

"He won't mind." I said with a smirk. "I'm just glad he's up and around. Jimmy, do you mind staying here with Miss Ida while I go talk to your great grandfather?" The boy said nothing just eagerly ate his food. Miss Ida rolled her eyes and said, "I'll pray for you."

I walked in and told Grandfather all that had just happened under his roof. He just sat there, and turned toward the window not saying a word. I said, "Well it's settled then." Then I walked out of the room.

I knew his quiet approach was usually worse in the end. I could tell that he was quite upset. He walked into the kitchen to a look at the child. He looked, stared, and walked out without saying a word. I came in behind him and spoke to Ida, "See, he handled it well." Come with me Young Jimmy let's get some air." I grabbed an apple and walked out with the boy. The little fella just followed me outside not saying much. We walked over to the garage and looked at the cars. Henry was just outside working the grounds. "Who do you have there?" he asked. "My son." I replied in a matter of fact tone and then asked "Can we take the Romeo?"

"Your son?" Henry asked.

"Yes, Sally and I made him. He is likely a product of a very fun night on a New Jersey Beech."

"Take the pick-up." He said.

"The pick-up?" I asked. "They boy wants something fast."

"Take the pick-up. She has fuel. Besides, I need to clean the others this afternoon."

I thought why not, and pulled two fishing poles off the wall then said, "Jimmy, how about we try and catch a fish."

He said nothing but smiled. "You don't say much do you?" I asked. Then I opened the door, and placed him inside the truck.

Before driving away Henry commented, "Try and not have any more accidents while you're gone."

The boy and I stopped to get some bait while we were in town, and headed out into the country. We spent the day fishing and catching blue gill. I talked a lot and he listened. I took great pleasure in him concentrating on the red and white bobber as it floated over the bait. I thought it best if we spent some time together while I figured out what to do. I wish he had been older and had known his mother. If nothing else so we would have something more to say to each other. He was a fine boy, and adapted without a whimper to his new life. He only cried on occasion for Lydia, and at times asked when his Uncle G would be coming back for him. It seemed to grow less and less important to him with each passing day. Miss Ida was very happy to have new young blood in the house.

Grandfather was the only person who fought the issue. He wasn't ever mean about the situation. I think in part because I seemed so happy. Then again, Grandfather also had his moments of weakness, likely because the boy was so amiable and pleasant. I caught him talking to him as if he were another adult as he softly scolded him for getting into his office. He even patted him on the head when the discussion was over.

The one thing I was not to do was openly discuss the heritage of the young child until we could figure out an explanation of where he came from. I did my best to keep him out of town and away from any questions I might be asked. But weeks later, just before going out to the pond for our daily ritual of fishing, I stopped in the service station to fuel up the truck. On the other side of the pump a convertible pulled in, and I heard the voice of Lucy Bedford. When she noticed me, she at first turned her head away like she had done at every chance meeting before. Unfortunately this time she came to my window and started to say something, likely to my belittlement. Then her eye caught the boy and it stopped her cold in her tracks. Finding her words again she spoke up and asked, "Why who is this young fellow?" Not knowing exactly what to say I said, "My fishing partner." He smiled at her, and then she said, "Well, now whose son is this? James I thought you didn't like children? I am quite surprised anyone would trust you with their child, because of your tendency to abandon people." She remarked.

"I have no such tendency." I replied.

"I beg to differ." She said.

"And for that matter I happen to love children especially when they are mine. Most of all I like the ones that are real and not some made up concoction." Smiling I drove off leaving her standing there.

We made our way to the pond laid out a blanket on the bank and began to fish. Young Jimmy hadn't mastered the art of the cast. I had to toss the bait out on the end of the cane pole for him. He loved to fish, and I loved to watch him hook one. The expression on his face was a sight to behold. I liked being a father. I really did. Fatherhood taught me about the simple pleasures in life and gave me a sense of responsibility that I never had before.

The afternoon went on and my son started to become tired. It was time to head back home, and after a small battle I put the boy and our tackle in the truck. Once the motor began to rumble he fell on my lap, closed his eyes and went to sleep. Smiling at the sight I pulled away from the pond, and began to slowly drive on the dirt path that led to a gravel county road and our way home. A car came into view and quickly closed in. As I sat there waiting for it to pass it stopped in the middle of the road and two men jumped out. They fired bullets in my direction riddling the truck with holes, and shattered the glass in the windshield. I ducked and I noticed another car coming from the other direction. When I reached for the shifter a bullet entered my wrist. I laid their crouched over my son and heard the first car pull away. In agony, I didn't move for a moment, and then asked if he was all right. Jimmy answered, and I quickly knew he was fine. The blood from my wrist covered his shirt and the window behind him.

The man from the second car stood at my window as I leaned up he asked, "Are you all right?" I opened the door and stepped out. Glass fell from my clothes. When I reached in to grab Jimmy I felt a pain in my side. "Yes, I think so." I said. "They just got my wrist." He looked at me and said, "You're bleeding" and pointed to my side. I then looked down and noticed the blood on my shirt and could feel it's wet warmth trickle down my side. They had shot me twice. I sat back down and he said, "I better get you some help!" He half carried me to his car where a terrified wife sat waiting. Young Jimmy sat between them, and I lad on the backseat.

They drove me into town and took me to the hospital. A call was made and my Grandfather, Miss Ida and Henry all quickly showed up.

The doctor patched me up and I made a speedy recovery from the safety of my room at Shadow Wood. The experience reminded me of the life that I led and set me to thinking. A few days had passed and Grandfather came into my room. "How are you feeling Jimmy?" He asked.

"I'm fine I should be up in a few days."

"This may not be the time but ...."

"You don't have to say anything." I closed my Bransford bible, sealed an envelope then handed him the letter that I had just written and said, "I need you to send this to Tanner."

"What is it?" He asked.

"It explains the situation. Please send it out quickly." I then tried to stand up. He looked at me with an expression of concern on his face and said, "I'm sorry Jimmy he is a fine boy. But I'd........" interrupting him again I said, "I know. If he was hurt, I'm not sure I could stand it."

It was just a couple of weeks later while I was in the kitchen with Ida talking. The door bell chimed and Henry answered the door. I walked out just a moment later and there stood Tanner and a beautiful woman. He said, "Looks like your recuperating well."

"I'm fine." I replied. He turned and said, "Conner I want you to meet my wife, Anita"

"Anita I'm glad to meet you, although surprised."

"Nice to meet you too, Mr. Conner."

"Anita and I were married two years back."

"Thanks for inviting me." I said, "You could have a least let me know." They both just smiled and I continued, "Well anyway you have a beautiful wife."

"She is, isn't she." he replied.

"Where are my manners come in let's talk in the other room." I escorted them to the living room. We sat down and I began to explain the situation in detail. Tanner asked, "Do you have any idea who took the shots at you."

"Just suspicions at this point," I replied.

"Who then?" he asked.

"The Maverick Seven or whatever they call themselves now?" he asked.

"Likely, I need a favor Tanner."

"I assumed there was a good reason that you sent for me."

It was at that point that Tanner, Anita, and I decided that it would be much safer for young Jimmy to go with them for awhile. Tanner and Anita would have to reenter the country under an assumed name. They chose to live in Arizona far away from the Sons, the Treasury Department and anything else that could cause a problem for them in this new life. Tanner was ready to settle down and become a family man. Before he left I asked about Peabody. He replied, "He is fine. He's been driving that damn motorcycle all over South America. When I asked him if he was ready to return, he told me that he had a few more country's he'd like to visit, and then maybe he'd explore Africa."

"That's great to hear." I replied.

We decided to meet again just after they officially entered the country and Jimmy would go on with them from there. The date happened to be the weekend after his fourth birthday.

The time came and went quickly. The next thing I knew we were sitting at a train station waiting for my friend's arrival. I couldn't help but be devastated, and kept telling myself that this would only be for a short time. I made a game of it, and little Jimmy took it all in stride.

We sat next to them on a bench and spoke briefly. Anita had a gift for him and they began to play with it. I kissed him and told him I would see him soon. It took all I had but I stood up and walked away. I hid around the corner and watched the three leave the station.

They were to take a train to the next city and a car the rest of the way. I climbed in my car and sat there for a moment. I had a candle from his cake in my pocket and held it up thinking, "At least I had a birthday with him." Then I remembered the first train ride I took, and thought that he would likely be excited about it.

I went home to what seemed a much emptier Shadow Wood. Even Grandfather, a man with his heart kept under a raw hide cover, was much more upset about the situation than I expected. I quickly turned my attention to crushing the opposition, and was met with some resistance on the subject. In the end the process to my safety and that of my son took longer than I had ever expected.

It had been almost a year before I finally dared to visit my son. Tanner had hidden updates to his progress in letters to me. His birthday neared and I expected a very excited child when I arrived. I had driven three days just to see him and was very excited myself. I met Tanner at the park and stood some distance from my son and Tanners wife. Tanner seemed a little out of sorts, but commented that he had grown accustom to his new life here. We walked over together as Anita pushed young Jimmy on the swing. I noticed how he had grown and stepped closer as he stopped the swings motion. "Madre, I want a drink," he said.

"We're teaching him Spanish," commented Tanner.

"Hello James," said Anita as she hugged me.

"Hello Anita you look beautiful as ever. "

I knelt down to Jimmy and said, "I brought something for you." And handed him the fishing pole I had bought in Georgia. "There is water somewhere around here isn't there?" I asked.

"Yes, not far off actually," Tanner replied.

"Thank you," said Jimmy.

As he said that I noticed something about the way he looked at me. I had become a stranger in some ways to my own son. I guess I expected him to remember all that we had done in those few short weeks, because I held onto it so dearly. I think Tanner saw this and said, "He'll warm up to you." We all had dinner together that night. We sat around the table and I watched the two of them cater to the boy's every whim. Especially Anita, who was more than just fond of the boy, she had taken him as her own. I was even asked if it was all right if he attended mass at the Catholic Church. Anita was devout and Tanner had no faith that he held dear. I smiled thinking Father McIver's got one of us, gave my approval, and that was the end of it.

Not wanting to take any risks, they drove me back to the park where we parted ways. I shook my friend's hand and said, "I can't thank you enough, Tanner. You've been great to him." I stood there and watched Anita playfully push the boy as they both laughed while he once again swung.

"I think I can get used to this life Conner." He said.

"Fatherhood?" I asked.

"All of it. I'm not coming back to the Sons and as far as fatherhood." He paused and then continued. "Well, Anita and I have been trying, but the Doc says she can't have children."

"I'm sorry to hear that Tanner." I said.

"Yeah, she was very ill when she was a child. It's a tough break for sure." He said. "Tell me are you still in danger?"

"It appears as if I will be for a while." I said. Changing the subject he asked, "How's your Grandfather?"

"He's getting old and tired but not so tired that he can't be ornery."

"I suspect not," stated Tanner.

I hugged my son one last time, and thanked Tanner and Anita. On my drive home I was drained, confused, and had a mixture of feelings that I couldn't quite get a handle on. Young Jimmy seemed happy and content, but I was restless to get my son back to Shadow Wood. I had already missed so much and he is all that I had of Sally. I drove on with the intent set in my mind to resolve this issue and bring a state of peace and safety back into my life. When I arrived back at Shadow Wood I could barely carry myself inside. Miss Ida was full of questions, but could tell I was mentally and physically exhausted. She ran a bath for me, and turned down my bed.

The next day I came downstairs and Grandfather awaited the news from my trip. I told him little Jimmy was well and in the best of care. Grandfather replied, "That's good news James. Your friend Tanner is a better man than most."

"He is, and his wife is something special too." I replied. Grandfather could tell what was on my mind, but knew better than to say anything regarding the subject.

I set my mind to have my son back in the next six months, but that goal was elusive. Tanner did his best to keep me informed, but as time went on I began to wonder what was really best for my son.

On the eighth month grandfather had taken ill. Between what I had to do to keep him going, and manage our affairs I had little time for anything else. It was on that ninth month that he passed and the affair was quite a spectacle. He would have been very proud of the way he was honored. I took a moment for just the two of us and spoke these words to him. I said, "I am sorry for the anger and bitterness that we had in the past. I'm proud to call myself a Conner and your Grandson. We may not have always agreed but you always did what you thought was best for me. And, in the end, I can see that you were mostly right. Thank you"

The seat left vacant within the Sons Council was filled by none other than me. With it came a new set of responsibilities and duties. I looked out the den window of Shadow Wood and watched the snow fall for the first time in years. Miss Ida and Henry came in to wish me a good night. I realized that Ida wasn't many years behind my grandfather and Henry wouldn't be able to keep up his pace for many more years either. One day I would be alone in that castle. All that I knew would pass before me. All but one small child who was tucked in the safety of a man I called my friend. I pulled out my bible and composed Tanner a letter within a letter. The encrypted message read:

Tanner my brother,

I am sure that Jimmy is well. I know in your care he will grow to be a fine man, with good morals and a good heart. One day let him know of his mother and that she loved him so much that bringing him into this world she had traded her own life. But of me let him know nothing because I don't want the winds of my life to guide his course. I want him to venture out and find his own valley in which to soar. I think you know what I mean. Most of all I want you to know that I couldn't have picked a better Father than the one in you or a better mother than Anita. I take great solace in knowing he is in your care.

I love you all
James Conner

"That must have been an incredibly hard thing to do Mr. Conner." I said to him. "It was but it was the right thing." he replied. "On more than one occasion I went back and checked on them. Young Jimmy grew into a fine man living a fruitful life. He never knew me as anything but a friend of his fathers. I had intended that if I out lived Tanner that I might let him know different. I was never sure if that would be the right thing to do or not. Unfortunately it was Young Jimmy who died first leaving a wife and son of his own."

I sat there, hinged, waiting for the next word from this man's lips. It was then that he sat up. His eye's looking into mine as if he could see inside my head. "Campbell, we come to the end of this story with knowledge of all sorts. Much of it can do harm to certain people but there is one person that this story can open an entire new world too. It's the real reason I told this tale. It seems to me that you have come to a crossroads without ever knowing you where on the road at all. But on a road you were and all that is left is a name. It's a very important name to you because when I say it. It could change your world if you so choose. That part of the story I leave to you. When Tanner came back into the country he didn't come back as John Tanner, he came back as John Campbell. The man they called son was who you called father and before you now sits the man that is your grandfather. It is my blood that flows through your veins. That is what you're here to know and find out." I sat there stunned making no comment. "I know it's a lot to take in but my time is short and you are my only heir. You have a choice to make and little time to make it. My gift to you is this story. You can print it and tell it to the world if you like but if you choose the other turn and make this your life you must guard this secret. I'm offering you the keys to a new life and it's up to you to decide where these new winds will guide you."

Still stunned I eyed him but said nothing. I just stood up and walked away not even saying good bye. I never questioned the validity of what he had told me because I knew in my heart that his words were true. Eventually, I made my way home and looked at the life that was mine and somehow it seemed forever changed. I walked about the apartment looking at its story and it seemed of little value compared to the rich one I had heard in past days. Mine seemed to no longer matter.

With only a few words his story had consumed mine and I somehow became a continuation of it. A choice was made and with the simple act of closing the door behind me the decision was carried out. A new boldness overcame me. Perhaps because of the new winds that had entered my valley a new course was set. Armed with confidence and baptized in a new truth of who I was but more importantly who I could be. I took that first step and in that action alone I became a Son of the South.

The End